HEAD IN GREEN BRONZE

Books By

HUGH WALPOLE

HEAD IN GREEN BRONZE and other stories

The London Novels

FORTITUDE
THE DUCHESS OF WREXE
THE GREEN MIRROR · THE CAPTIVES
THE YOUNG ENCHANTED
WINTERSMOON · HANS FROST
CAPTAIN NICHOLAS
JOHN CORNELIUS

Scenes from Provincial Life

THE CATHEDRAL
THE OLD LADIES · HARMER JOHN
THE INQUISITOR

Herries

ROGUE HERRIES · JUDITH PARIS
THE FORTRESS · VANESSA

·

THE WOODEN HORSE
MR. PERRIN AND MR. TRAILL
THE DARK FOREST · THE SECRET CITY
A PRAYER FOR MY SON
*THE PRELUDE TO ADVENTURE
*MARADICK AT FORTY
*PORTRAIT OF A MAN WITH RED HAIR
*ABOVE THE DARK TUMULT

·

JEREMY · JEREMY AND HAMLET
JEREMY AT CRALE
THE GOLDEN SCARECROW
THE THIRTEEN TRAVELLERS
THE SILVER THORN
ALL SOULS' NIGHT

·

Omnibus volume

FOUR FANTASTIC TALES
(*including the novels marked with an asterisk*)

BELLES-LETTRES

JOSEPH CONRAD: A Critical Study
ANTHONY TROLLOPE (*English Men of Letters*)
THE APPLE TREES (*Golden Cockerel Press*)
THE CRYSTAL BOX
THE ENGLISH NOVEL (Rede Lecture)
READING: An Essay
THE WAVERLEY PAGEANT

·

(With J. B. Priestley)
FARTHING HALL: A Novel in Letters

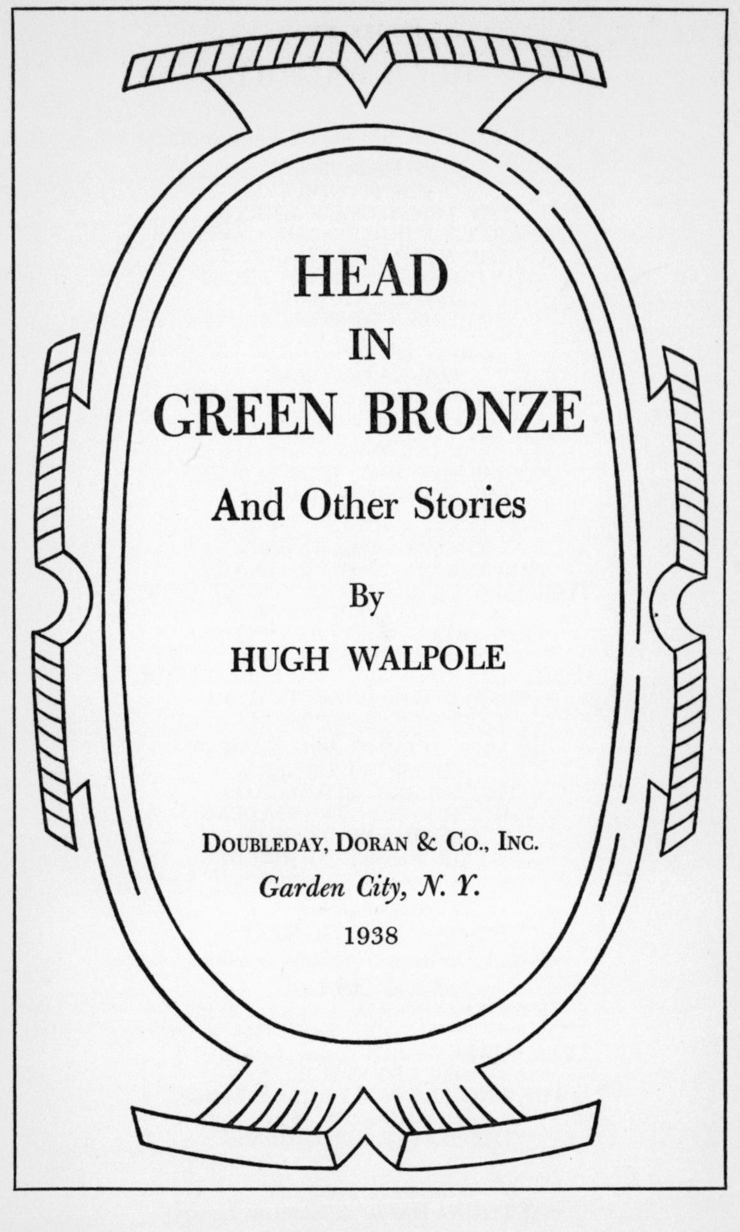

HEAD IN GREEN BRONZE

And Other Stories

By

HUGH WALPOLE

DOUBLEDAY, DORAN & CO., INC.
Garden City, N. Y.
1938

PRINTED AT THE *Country Life Press*, GARDEN CITY, N. Y., U. S. A.

FIRST EDITION

For

GEORGE CUKOR

With Love

PREFATORY LETTER

DEAR GEORGE

I am giving you this volume of short stories because I want to give you something, and I know that you will never read a whole novel of mine right through.

In these days if you write a very serious short story, probably gloomy and full of atmosphere, you are instantly compared with Tchekov and there is an end.

Personally I agree with H. G. Wells, who once said that the short story should entertain for anything between fifteen and fifty minutes and that it can be about whatever you like. Captain Kettle, The Dolly Dialogues, *H. E. Bates and A. E. Coppard—they are all grand. I don't pretend to be with those masters, but I* do *think that some of these stories are entertaining, and I don't care who says nay. Which brings me to the real reason of this note. I wrote the 'Bore' stories some fifteen years ago and never expected that they would ever be rescued from the kind hospitality of the* Windsor Magazine *and Fred Black's* Dearborn Independent.

Life is queer though, as you long ago realised, George. Some excellent novels of mine, laboured over for years, are now forgotten, alas. These 'Bore' stories, written very light-heartedly, have insisted on surviving. By that I mean that still, fifteen years after their first appearance, people say: 'By the way, there was a story of yours I read once. . . .' So here they are.—Your friend,

HUGH WALPOLE

CONTENTS

HEAD IN GREEN BRONZE

HEAD IN GREEN BRONZE

The Lord God Almighty was busy that time examining the artists. This was a tiresome and monotonous job, for He had been doing it for thousands and thousands of centuries and, with one or two exceptions a century, artists are always the same.

About Him stretched into everlasting space fields and fields of light, rather as on an early summer evening, when the harvesters have drawn away home and the sun-drenched soil is left to its own peace.

But every artist as he appeared for his examination brought with him his own personal memory and consciousness, his individual litter. . . .

It was the authors whom just now God Almighty was examining. The examinations were very brief.

Against the vast eternity of light—light upon light upon light and of a stainless purity—the impedimenta of each separate little soul seemed incredibly mean and paltry. Now, for example, there was William Newcombe with his country cottage, old oak beams, settle by the fire, flagged garden path, refrigerator and most modern bathroom. Also his twenty-three travel books and his blank-verse drama called *Armageddon.*

'They all sold very well, I hear,' said God Almighty.

'Well,' William answered modestly, 'they did. Except *Armageddon*, which didn't sell at all.'

'Why did you write that one?' asked God Almighty.

'Because I wanted to,' said William, blinking his old eyes a little at the unaccustomed light.

'Good,' said God Almighty. 'Because of that one book you may have with you, while at work, any one of your earthly goods and chattels you prefer.'

'My dog Caesar,' William said promptly. All his impedimenta, oak beams, garden path, bathroom, *all* the travel books disappeared, and only a charming fox-terrier with engaging whiskers, frisking in the light, remained. William and Caesar, in the charge of an Archangel, passed into light.

A flock of angels cut the brilliant air like a wave breaking through mist.

'Next one,' said God Almighty.

This was Peter Bentham, whose consciousness provided him with four very thin books of poetry, a life of Rimbaud, a small painting by Dali, and a cough mixture in a dirty blue bottle.

God Almighty looked at him. 'How have you allowed your body to get into such a miserable state?'

'I never *was* very strong,' Peter answered with that rather shrill staccato little cry that had before now thrown so much terrible scorn on prosperity and success.

'I'm afraid,' said God Almighty gently (for there was something very touching about Peter), 'that you have prevented yourself from enjoying too many amusing and vivifying things.'

'That,' said Peter firmly (he was not going to be put down by a God Who, all his life, he had asserted did not exist), 'is because my taste has always been perfect. I have never been able to endure any kind of athletics, popular novels and novelists, optimistic essays and sentimental plays, patriotism, or anyone, male or female, in rude health.'

'What *have* you enjoyed?' God Almighty asked.

'My own poetry,' Peter answered, 'the paintings of Dali, Miró and Léger, the music of Tschenakivitzky, free love in Russia and a cocktail called "Flowers of Parnassus."'

'I like your honesty,' God Almighty said, 'but you are a little too serious, especially about yourself. However, what you really need is fattening up. Without your earthly clothes' (for now all Peter's worldly impedimenta had vanished) 'you are frankly a miserable object—nor have you washed as frequently as you should. However, we shall soon change all that. I shall hand you over to Henry Fielding for an aeon or two.'

And then came Margaret Cunningham, a tall, fat, red-faced woman whose teeth because they had not been kept back in childhood now protruded over a receding chin. Without her clothes she was shapeless, helpless, innocent. Her impedimenta were an untidy two-roomed flat, a tortoiseshell cat, some London chimneys, her working tools and some twenty-four misshapen clay heads with long necks leaning to right or left.

'Well, Margaret,' God Almighty said kindly, 'I'm afraid you haven't made much of a living out of this work of yours.'

'Well, no, I haven't,' Margaret said frankly in her Woman's-Club how-are-you-all-girls voice. 'Of course there was the teaching twice a week.' She felt the light on her nakedness with so keen a pleasure that her brown-grey eyes shone with delight. 'It's like the Riviera, which I've never been able to afford,' she said.

'But this,' said God Almighty, 'has been always your secret longing'—and there, solid against the light, was the curving road, the sign-post 'To Watendlath,' the newspaper placard 'Mussolini Attacks Britain' and the stream, the shelving green hill, the mouse-shaped clouds watching a cat-faced moon.

'Yes,' Margaret murmured. 'That and the head in green bronze.'

'Head of whom?' God Almighty asked.

'Of no one in particular. Simply a grand head of some

hero—in dark green bronze. I've imagined myself for years and years creating such a thing. I could, I believe, if I'd gone on. I was really improving. But then I caught cold and pneumonia followed—and here I am!'

'There's plenty of time,' God Almighty said. He looked at Margaret kindly. 'Here's where you've always wanted to be. You're a true artist although not as yet a very good one. Donatello shall give you a lesson or two. . . .'

Margaret was on her bare knees looking into the stream behind Rosthwaite. Beside her was a little pile of clay.

'God Almighty thinks I can help you,' a voice said.

She looked up and saw Donatello, naked and glorious. He knelt down beside her, taking the clay in his hands.

'Now let us see,' he said. 'Head of a Hero in green bronze. . . .'

THE GERMAN

THE DATE OF THIS STORY is 1933. The date is very important because in no other year in the world's history, perhaps, could things have happened just as they did in 1933. What I mean is that if it had not been for the things that happened in 1933 the soul and body of Hans would not have been rent with such fearful storms and stresses as they were. This is Hans's story.

Hans was a dachshund. He was both the pride and property of the Conistons.

The Conistons were a very nice family who lived in Hyde Park Gate, and they still live there and are still a nice family. The family consisted of Alfred Coniston, Nellie, his wife, Rupert, aged twenty-two, and Margaret, aged twenty-one. Their cook was called Hammond and their maid's name was Fanny Sutcliffe, which everyone who knew anything about cricket thought a very odd coincidence. But the Conistons knew nothing about cricket. Alfred Coniston might have said 'What are Hobbs?' just as someone asked, in an earlier day, of Keats. The fact was that the Conistons were eaten up with Causes. Alfred Coniston had retired, and had therefore plenty of spare time for his hobby. Mrs. Coniston had time, too, because Hammond and Sutcliffe were such excellent servants and Margaret Coniston took so many things off her mother's hands. Alfred and Nellie Coniston had hearts as tender as were to be found in the whole of London.

They were too tender, in fact. They were always bleeding. They bled for things as different as Out-of-Work Musicians, Itinerant Greeks, Negroes in America, Overworked Navvies, and the Old Destitute Ladies' Society. They were not well off, but quite comfortable as people go in these difficult times. They would, however, have never had a penny for themselves, have been as destitute as any of their Causes, had it not been for their son Rupert, who was made of much sterner stuff. Rupert had a high position in the Custom House and so learnt, day by day, what rogues and rascals people could be. He, too, cared for Causes, but in a more impersonal and abstract way. His parents looked up to him very much indeed and he thought it quite right that they should do so. He cared for his parents' affairs and saw that they were not too foolish. They often appeared shamefaced in his presence.

And now about Hans. Hans had been given, when he was a puppy, to Mrs. Coniston by her husband on the occasion of her birthday. The fact was that Alfred Coniston had been, on this occasion, really puzzled as to what to give his wife. A subscription to the Cancer Hospital was what she wanted him to give her, but, for once in a way, he determined that she should have something for herself. She needed nothing. Her jewelry consisted of her wedding ring and a necklace of amber beads. She wished for no more. She had plenty of serviceable clothes, she never read a book but only pamphlets, she was not greedy, she did not wish to look beautiful. What *could* he give her? He passed the Bond Street dog-shop and there was Hans in the window. He looked dejected and unhappy; two men, staring at him from the street, were poking fun at him. He became at once therefore in the eyes of Alfred Coniston a Cause. Alfred went in and bought him.

He was at that time a very comical-looking creature indeed, with a long, thin body like a black hose-pipe, a thread of a tail, and very large black ears. But his eyes were of a melting brown and his coat of so silken and warm a sleekness that in cold weather (Mrs. Coniston's birthday was in November) he was as good as a hot-water bottle.

The whole family (including Hammond and Sutcliffe) took to him at once and he took to the family.

He was every bit as sentimental as they were. He had the softest of hearts and the most trusting of natures, which was just what the Conistons preferred. With the exception of Rupert. Rupert, from the first, thought of him as a foreigner. For Rupert any kind of frontier was a barrier. It was from behind frontiers that people wickedly brought into England cameras, clocks, silks, scents, and the rest of the list. It was on the other side of frontiers that people learnt to be wicked, deceitful and sly. Rupert profoundly distrusted all foreigners. Nor did Hans quite trust Rupert. In spite of his soft heart Hans was not altogether a fool. He was a selector of persons. There would come into his warm, brown eyes, at times, a sharp, suspicious look, and he was capable of secretly nipping the ankles of anyone he disliked.

The fact that he was a foreigner and a German did not distress the other members of the Coniston family. They strongly approved of it, for Germany had, for a long while now, been one of their Causes.

Mrs. Coniston did not sleep at night properly for thinking of the poor Germans. Someone had told her dreadful stories of the bread-line in Berlin; another friend had stayed in a small German town where the courage of the middle-class ladies was almost terrifying. So the Conistons were pro-German and very anti-French indeed. Had Hans been a poodle his lot would have been a poor one. He would have been charged with immoral literature, taxing the English for their occupation of the trenches, and mean avoidance of the American Debt.

As it was, he flourished. He was, like all dachshunds, very well able to look after himself. The dachshund, more than any dog save the Pekingese and the French bulldog, knows exactly what he wants. His needs are partly material, partly spiritual. The satisfaction of both is essential to him. He will, for instance, quite naturally droop and pine in any house where the food is insufficient, but he will also droop and pine in any house where he is misunderstood.

He has also a very strong and almost ironical sense of humour, a sense of humour that is, strangely enough, not German at all, but French rather in its lightness, gaiety, and absence of any moral prejudices. In addition to these things he is a very sporting dog and will chase anything that runs, not minding at all if he looks ridiculous (as he frequently does) in the act. The spirit is all!

Hans had all these qualities. He was as gay as a flattered baby, as ironical as Anatole France, as greedy (when he was hungry) as Pantagruel, and a perfect Jorrocks when out for a walk. And, as I have already said, he had a most sensitive and affectionate heart.

The only part of him that the Conistons did not understand was his irony. They had no irony at all in their own composition, and when a friend of theirs, Mrs. Burrows, said one day, 'How delightful it is to see people to whom everyone else's affairs are their own,' they agreed smilingly that they were a fortunate family in that respect.

There were occasions when Hans looked at them ironically —once, for instance, when Mrs. Coniston tied a blue bow round his neck at Christmas, once when Mr. Coniston went to a Fancy-Dress Ball for the Distressed Crofters of Scotland dressed as a Bavarian peasant in very tight shorts. But he soon discovered that irony was lost upon them, and he liked them so much that he forgave them. His gaiety they appreciated, for they were themselves (with the exception of Rupert) essentially gay people and laughed at almost everything. Hans liked to play with them, and every evening after supper a chewed and dissipated black ball was produced. This ball was thrown for him by Mr. Coniston, hidden under the bookcase byrs. M Coniston, and bounced on the floor by Margaret. Hans played this game (it always lasted fifteen minutes exactly by the ormolu drawing-room clock) very prettily and pretended to take it seriously because of his love for them, but his real amusements were quite other. What he truly enjoyed was to exercise his imagination and surprise people. Hammond and Sutcliffe adored him and would grossly have overfed him had they been able, but Hans realized that, hungry though he might be, true pleasure in food came from delicate choice. He was something of a gourmet, something of a sensualist. Like all sensualists he knew that one must refuse often in order to enjoy much.

Behind his gaiety, his irony and his greed was his devotion. He had never loved any other human beings because of his tender youth, and, as he grew, love became a necessity of his being. His trustfulness of all the world made him amiable to almost everyone; but the Conistons, even Rupert, commanded his entire devotion. He loved them in this order: Margaret first, Mrs. Coniston next, then Mr. Coniston, lastly Rupert—but he loved them all. When, for several weeks, Mr. Coniston lay in bed with a stomach complaint (indigestion was his weakness), Hans led a bewildered, apprehensive existence. He could not understand why Mr. Coniston lay in bed, why he groaned, why he, Hans, was prevented from the room where Mr. Coniston was. He imagined that some enemy had done this and barked at everyone who came to the house. When Mr. Coniston at last appeared downstairs, very pale, very melancholy, Hans did everything that he could to amuse him. And when Mr. Coniston, at last stirred to life by the injustices of the Moscow Trial of the English Engineers, woke to activity again and wrote a long letter to the *Daily Telegraph*, Hans was overjoyed and became a perfect Don Juan in the Park.

Such was his life, sheltered, you would say, safe, prosperous. But who is safe in these times? It is a commonplace that what happens in one country dreadfully affects all the others, so close are we to-day to all our fellow human beings.

What happened in Germany became Hans's tragedy.

I don't know when exactly it was that the Conistons became aware of the Nazis. Because Germany was a Cause, therefore everything that happened in Germany was right—until, quite suddenly, everything was wrong.

The Conistons had never considered the Jews very carefully, which was odd because the Jews have been a Cause ever since the beginning of Genesis. Alfred Coniston numbered several Jews among his friends—there were the Hotzheims, the Goetzes, the Richters. He was very cordial towards the Hotzheims, who were as warm-hearted as he himself. Mrs. Hotzheim, stout, red-faced, extremely voluble, was so very good-natured that her flat in Knightsbridge overflowed with the destitute. She was for ever wiping the noses of street children and buying sweets for them.

It was, in all probability, through the Hotzheims that the Conistons first became aware that something was wrong in Germany. Oscar Hotzheim had a brother in Berlin. Oscar Hotzheim's brother committed suicide. It made no difference that it was well known that Mr. Hotzheim's brother was nothing very much and had been in bad financial trouble long before the Nazis—the fact that he had shot himself inflamed the Coniston imagination. Hitler came to full power, Einstein and Feuchtwanger and Thomas Mann were ex-communicated, there were Concentration Camps, stories of persecution and horror. The Conistons were not of those who quiver for accuracy. Emotion takes the place of facts. Here was a new Cause—one of the finest that they had ever had.

It was one fine morning at breakfast that Alfred Coniston suddenly realised that Hans was a German. The sunlight was flooding the room, the silver gleamed and glittered, the kedgeree was perfectly seasoned—nevertheless Alfred was uncomfortable.

'Is anything the matter, dear?' Mrs. Coniston asked.

'No, I don't think so.' He drank his coffee. 'Here is a letter, darling, from Oscar, suggesting that we should sign a paper demanding the trial of Hitler by a Central European Council. What do you think of the idea?'

He looked about him, his eyes wandered from the oil-painting of his father to the Medici print of a Vermeer, thence to the floor, finally to Hans who was lying, his black stove-pipe body stretched contentedly before the fire, one large brown eye watching Margaret's plate, for there were occasions when something excellent came his way. Alfred Coniston regarded Hans: Hans regarded Alfred Coniston. Hans's eyes twinkled, his large ears flapped as though he scented a fly.

'It's that dog,' Alfred said, suddenly.

'What dog, dear?' asked Mrs. Coniston.

'Hans. I've never thought of it before. It's foolish of me—but do you realise, darling, how *very* German Hans is?'

All eyes were on Hans.

Rupert, getting up to be on his way to the Custom House, said: 'I always said so—a beastly foreigner.'

'What nonsense!' Margaret cried. 'He was born in England. He's no more German than I am.'

'It isn't where he was born,' Alfred said, very solemnly. 'It's what he looks like. I suppose there's nothing in the world looks more German than a dachshund.' Finally he said before he left the room: 'I can't help it. But the sight of that dog offends me!'

How subtle a thing is atmosphere! Within two days everyone in the house was conscious of Hans's very German appearance. Unfortunately for Hans the papers were full, just then, of Nazi atrocities. Every day brought fresh horrors. No one was safe in Germany. Someone was kicked in the stomach and died because he would not salute the Nazi flag.

Never, never before had there been a Cause so exactly suited to the Coniston temperament. Mrs. Coniston paid visits to the Hotzheims and the Goetzes. Alfred Coniston signed papers, wrote letters, Rupert cut a fellow official in the Custom House because he was of German origin.

And Hans? It did not take him very long to be aware of a difference. He noticed first that people spoke to him very little. He enjoyed nothing better than constant conversation. What he liked was that as soon as he was near a human being that human being should recognise his presence. On his side he might come to the conclusion that nothing was to be done beyond a bark or a sniff at a trouser-leg. The point was that there should be contact. In the Conistons' house contact had always been instant. He could not enter any room without someone saying: 'Oh, there's Hans!' or 'Come here, Hans!' and his reply would be what he chose to make it, jovial, ironical, sentimental, proud or humble. . . .

Now there began to be silence. At first he thought the trouble must be in himself. He had been with the Conistons so long that he was growing casual, not taking thought as once he had done. So he barked, played, ran as never he had done before. Margaret took him for a walk in the Park, and never in all his life before had he tried so hard to be entertaining.

She sat on a seat and looked at him, and for the first time real trouble entered into his soul. The sun sparkled through the trees, children ran happily about, a most attractive female fox-terrier made coy enticing gestures in the neighbourhood. Hans paid these things no attention. His eyes were on Margaret.

She motioned him on to the seat beside her. He sprang up and laid his head on her lap. She stroked his warm sleek back.

'Do you *feel* German, Hans?' she asked. 'Do your instincts go back to your forefathers? If you were in Germany now, would you be a Nazi dog or an anti-Nazi? It would depend on the politics of your master. That's a good point I will tell them at home. *Your* politics are the same as ours. Now bark when I say "Hitler"!'

She made a motion with her hand and he barked. They went home very happily, for now surely everything would be well.

At tea-time, Margaret said 'Hitler! Down with Hitler!' and Hans barked, but, unfortunately, Mr. Coniston followed it with 'Down with the Jews!' and Hans barked at that, too.

'You see,' Mr. Coniston said, gloomily. 'He has no pro-Jewish feeling.'

The alarm that had come to Hans did not now leave him. He knew that something was wrong. Even in the kitchen things were not as they had been.

'He do look German, don't he?' said Sutcliffe to Hammond. 'What *is* all this the Germans are doing? The master was raving at lunch.'

'They are massacring everybody,' Hammond said, 'who don't think like they do. They kicked a man in the stomach in Berlin.'

'Well I never!' said Sutcliffe. 'Would you believe it? It's like the War back again.'

She snapped rather sharply at Hans who had jumped on to a chair, a favour always granted him.

'Now then, come off it,' Sutcliffe said. 'Dirtying the chair . . .'

And Hans, desperately puzzled, came off it.

That night, a terrible thing happened. Hitherto he had always slept in a basket in Mr. Coniston's room. His basket was taken down to the pantry.

'I don't know why it is,' Mr. Coniston said. 'It's ridiculous, but that dog reminds me too much of what is going on. I doubt if I should sleep a wink.'

Hans did not sleep, either. The pantry, commonplace in the daytime, was terrifying at night. Things rustled and shook and trembled. He lay there, his sharp nose on the edge of the basket, wondering what crime he had committed. He knew again what loneliness was. The horror of the dog-shop in Bond Street had been that he did not belong to anyone. During these last happy years he had forgotten the dog-shop, but now in the grim loneliness of the pantry those old terrors returned. Once again he was without protection. Friendship had given him a multitude of safeguards. Even when he had done wrong, his punishment had been followed with additional love. As the night continued his terrors increased. He was, as are so many human beings, a demon of courage when the world thought well of him, but a coward under ostracism.

Dimly, too, his faith in life was shaken. The change had come so abruptly and without reason. Cause and effect were essential for him if he were not to be bewildered. He slept at last, but miserably; he dreamt that he chased a bone and the bone became a man with a whip. He woke, in the cold dawn, to see all the things in the pantry grin maliciously at him.

Then, once more like a human being, in disgrace he behaved disgracefully. Nothing would go right with him. He was afraid to bark, to lie before the fire. He was not taken for a walk by Margaret, but by Sutcliffe, who dragged him on a lead, saying 'Oh, come along, do!'

The streets were wet and he made muddy marks in the hall. He slunk into a corner. They all asked what had happened to him. It was exactly as though he knew how disgracefully his countrymen were behaving. Margaret made an outburst on his behalf, and this did him no good.

Rupert, in the sitting-room, said: 'The dog should be in the kitchen. I've always told you so.' Mrs. Coniston said: 'Well, perhaps.' Margaret told them all her opinion, that the dog had done no harm, it wasn't *his* fault if the Germans behaved badly. *He* knew nothing about Einstein. How *could* they change so abruptly? 'Mother, I wouldn't have thought you capable——'

Then Mrs. Coniston, who was tired and overwrought because Mrs. Hotzheim's flat, where there had been an anti-German meeting, had been so hot and noisy, burst into tears. Mr. Coniston said: 'It's all that damned dog.' Hans hid behind the sofa.

Two days later Mrs. Hotzheim, hot, voluble, too brightly attired, came to tea.

'I always do like that little dog,' she said.

'You may have him if you like,' said Mr. Coniston. 'You don't mind his being German.'

'I'm German myself,' said Mrs. Hotzheim, quite amiably.

This Mr. Coniston had never considered. After all, Hans *might* be a German Jew. Then why all this ill-feeling? But no. He looked at the dog again. Nazi seemed to be written all down his long back. He swallowed his disgust.

'Take him with you, Mrs. Hotzheim,' he said. 'And keep him.'

Now Hans's story passes into something timeless, eternal. It has nothing to do with contemporary politics. Its emotion is universal. He was a creature longing for someone whom he had loved and lost.

The Hotzheims, who were well-off even in these hard times, lived in a large Knightsbridge flat that looked over the Park. Besides Mr. and Mrs. Hotzheim there were four little Hotzheims. Ruth Hotzheim succeeded Rachel Hotzheim who had died, childless, of pneumonia. Because Rachel had been quiet, shy, and fond of writing poetry, so was Ruth exuberant, jolly, careless, and fond of noisy entertainment. She felt that Mr. Hotzheim liked variety. So he did. So did the little children. This was, very possibly, the noisiest, untidiest flat in all London.

So Hans found it. He suffered agonies of discomfort, apprehension, disgust. He had been always a fastidious dog. He appreciated good manners; he liked doors to be shut carefully, people to look where they walked, voices to be soft.

It is one of the chief ironies of the situation that, had he been in Germany, he would have disliked the Nazis very much indeed.

Meanwhile, how he hated the Hotzheim children! They were not, in themselves, bad; rather, badly trained. That is, they were not trained at all. Mrs. Hotzheim shouted, laughed, slapped, kissed, pushed and patted. Little Isaac, Rebecca, Ada, and Joseph shouted, laughed, slapped, and kissed in return. And they thought Hans the most comical dog they had ever seen. They laughed at everything, his shining nose, his long-barrelled body, his black tail. They held him up by his front legs, pulled his long ears, rolled him on the floor, stuck fingers in his eyes.

And Mrs. Hotzheim only called out, roared with laughter, rushed to and fro endeavouring to do all the things for which there was so little time.

Everyone rushed to and fro. The rooms were in frantic disorder. Everyone was good-natured and happy and untidy. Everyone was happy save Hans. He did not know that he was in hell because Hitler was taking the salute in Berlin from one hundred thousand passionate-hearted men.

He *was* in hell. Can dogs not suffer? Ask the myriads, brown and black and silken-coated, who move with ghostly tread in the dogs' Valhalla!

This is hell to be in a prison where there is no rest, no understanding, and always rasping sound. How he hated the Hotzheim children! At first he thought it his duty to be forbearing because for some reason those whom he loved and once had trusted had sent him here. Most of all were his ears sensitive. To have them pulled by rough hands was torture to him—so one fine morning he turned with a snarl (he had not snarled since the dog-shop) and bit little Isaac in the calf of his fat leg. Didn't little Isaac howl! But Mrs. Hotzheim was no ordinary woman. She slapped little Isaac and told him not to annoy the poor dog.

And Hans felt the deepest shame. He had never bitten

a human being in his life before. It was the first law in the Canine Tables of Stone—'Thou shalt not bite a human being!' He shrank away into the only place of security that he had found, a corner of the cloak-room where the coats and mackintoshes were kept. It was cold, it was draughty, but he could not be seen there. So he lay curled up, breaking his heart, wondering why this misery had come to him.

Another great trouble was that he was fed on irregular scraps. The cook, a little woman like a squirrel, hopped about and gave him what came to her hand. This feeding disagreed with him. His outside lost its gloss; his inside was uncomfortable. Worst of all was his loneliness and the sense of degradation that went with it. He was ashamed of himself because he had lost his friends. He must have lost them through some fault of his own. But *what* fault? What *was* it that he had done? Finally, the worst torture of all—the fear that suddenly one day he would bite another of the Hotzheims. If this dreadful thing happened a second time he would be lost for ever. Never would he hold his head up again. Then truly he would be abandoned. So, for weeks, he resisted. He suffered the children, he endured the cook, he allowed Mrs. Hotzheim to stroke him with her hot, perspiring hand—only in his eyes there developed a look of the lost, of the hopeless, of the desolate. . . .

And the doom fell. He bit Mr. Hotzheim.

One bright morning the master of the house was about to set forth for the City. Mr. Hotzheim was stout, his legs were large, his trousers close-fitting. He was happy and joyful as were all the Hotzheims at the beginning of a new, splendid, promising day.

He picked Hans up by the ears, swung him gaily, landed him on his short feet again. With a growl of pain, insulted privacy and despair, Hans bit him—bit him, knowing that this was his doom and the end of all good things. . . .

Mr. Hotzheim yelled.

'The dog's bit me!' he cried, and then, of all astonishing

things, began to laugh. He laughed and laughed and laughed. He bared his fat leg, iodine was applied, he shouted:

'Why, who'd have believed it? That black little devil!'

'You swung him by the ears,' Mrs. Hotzheim remarked, indulgently. 'Dogs don't like that.'

And little Isaac added with complacence: 'He bit me, too.'

They were simply the most good-natured family in all England.

But for Hans the final insult! Had he been whipped, starved, even shot! No—simply laughter. He slunk away, to his corner in the cloak-room. Only one thing remained to be done. He must escape. He would find his friends, take what punishment might come to him, die if necessary—anything was better than mocking laughter.

And, at this same moment, Hitler was saying to Goering: 'We will make a new world!'

This was the bravest thing that Hans had ever done—the bravest thing that in all probability he ever will do. It may indeed become a Legend in his family. I can fancy him, in future years, with his grandchildren gathered round him, saying to them, most solemnly (and the younger of them yawning because it is a story that the old boy is overfond of telling):

'I will never, never forget that morning. It is impossible for you, dear children, brought up in so happy and kindly a home, even to imagine what I suffered, what cruelties, indignity. . . .'

Yes, like all dangerous things, fine in reminiscence, dreadful in actuality. It was not that he was venturing into the world alone for the first time. It had been often enough difficult for the Conistons to keep him within doors. No, the frightfulness of this adventure was that he was going into the world, alone, as a pariah. Was he aware at all that he was bearing on his back the sins of a whole nation, nay, of all mankind—mankind that refuses to subdue jealousy and envy and cruelty? No. In all probability he was aware only of these two facts—that he had bitten Mr. Hotzheim in the leg and that he had not a friend in the world—two things quite enough of themselves to make a pariah.

When he set out he did so blindly. A butcher's boy with a basket stood in the open doorway of the flat—Hans stepped out, down the stairs, and when the liftman opened the main door for a stout lady bound tightly in purple, Hans seized his moment.

Once in the street he turned his sharp nose to the Conistons. How was he so sure? How is any dog so sure? It may have been that he sniffed the Albert Memorial, which smells, as everyone is aware, of soap, gold leaf, and the damp personality of the Prince Consort. It may have been that he was aware, at that same moment, that Alfred Coniston, attending an Anti-Nazi meeting at the Goetzes', was almost sick unto death from boredom, central heating, and marzipan cake. 'There is something to be said for Hitler after all,' Alfred Coniston was saying. 'When I get home I shall tell them so.'

Perhaps Hans was aware of this. Perhaps it was only that a lady with a Pekingese on the end of a cord was walking in the Albert Hall direction. Hans adored Pekingese—they seemed to him the cream of civilisation.

Once a lady Pekingese of the highest pedigree—but that exotic romance does not belong to this story.

He followed the Pekingese, but at a decent interval because he was a pariah. He looked neither to right nor left. In spite of his degraded state his spirits were rising. Whatever might come nothing could be worse than the Hotzheims. He would never see the Hotzheims again. His spirits would have risen even higher could he have known that at that very moment Mrs. Coniston, shopping in Harrods, was finding herself exquisitely bored by Mrs. Mances, one of the leaders of the movement for Succouring Distressed and Exiled Germans. 'I am sure,' she was thinking, 'there is something to be said for Hitler. After all, he is restoring German hope and confidence.'

Then Hans saw the posters outside the Albert Hall. He knew them well, for they had been of frequent convenience to him in his daily walks. The Pekingese stopped and the lady with him also reluctantly paused. It was then that Hans realised that he was no longer a pariah. The sun was shining, the breezes blowing, there were smells everywhere, smells of trees, flowers, warm palings, soil and pavement, petrol, Albert Memorial. Hans sniffed them all. Then he sniffed the Pekingese. They had a delightful word or two. Civilised China had recognised him. He turned down Hyde Park Gardens.

At that moment Margaret Coniston was reading the paper. Hitler said that the only thing in the world that he wanted was Peace. No government in the world was as peaceful as his government.

'I've always said that there was something to be said for Hitler,' she said.

The sun was pouring into the house through the windows, through the open door. Sutcliffe was cleaning the door-knocker.

Hans, his brown eyes shining, came up the path.

'Why, Miss!' cried Sutcliffe. 'Here's Hans!'

Margaret, who had been standing at the top of the stairs drinking in the sun, ran and threw her arms about the German nation.

'Oh, you darling! We have missed you so! It's all right! The family politics have changed!'

Hans walked into the house.

THE EXILE

In Hollywood there are many Englishmen. However long they may have resided there, they are always very easy to recognise. When I look back and trace through my memory that row of good, honest, slightly staring, faintly unhumorous faces, the one most vivid to me is certainly Hector Montgomery Cathie's. I should like to attempt here a portrait of him, because, simple though his little story is, he stands for something very generally felt by most human beings, very seldom expressed. When I think of him many nostalgias in my own life are explained to me.

I first saw him working as an extra in an historical picture entitled, I think, *Lucrezia Borgia*. Pictures come and go so quickly that I can't be sure that that was the name of it. It was, in any case, one of those pictures elaborately and expensively produced just before the invasion of colour. And I remember very vividly that when I walked on to the set searching for a friend of mine, Willie Adams, who was directing this masterpiece, after making sure that the light was not shining and the little bell not ringing, I pushed back the heavy door and nearly stumbled over a brace of large white dogs held in leash by their rough-looking protector. I was quite blinded by the brilliance of the scene I beheld and at once thought to myself, 'What a pity this can't be in colour.'

It was one of those scenes of Renaissance Feasting, where,

under brilliant lights, crowds of revellers were supposed to be eating and drinking with heady enthusiasm from gilt goblets and heaped bowls of coloured wooden fruits. On a raised dais, the aristocratic Borgias were revelling brightly, with eyes alert for possible poisonings. There were monkeys and dwarfs and parti-coloured Fools and trumpeters in a row chewing gum. There were cameras to the right of one and cameras to the left. And just as I arrived there, some perspiring gentleman in shirt-sleeves bellowed: 'Camera!' The trumpeters ceased their gum-chewing and a movement, as of sleepers suddenly awakened, rhythmically began—everyone eating and drinking, a Fool turning somersaults, the dogs moving across the vast shining floor, and Lucrezia herself holding up her goblet for more wine.

It was then that I noticed one of the handsomest old men conceivable move with tremendous dignity across the floor, mount the steps and pour wine from a goblet into Lucrezia's cup. He is, I thought to myself, seventy if he's a day. But his carriage was superb. He looked in his Renaissance clothes as though he'd been born in them. He was by far the most aristocratic person present. Afterwards, when I reached Adams, I questioned him.

'That's a grand old man,' I said, pointing.

Adams, who unlike many directors was imperturbable and nonchalant whatever the crisis, remarked, 'Oh, yes, that's Hector.'

'Hector?' I enquired.

'You should meet him. He *is* a grand old man. He ought to be King of Scotland. Maybe he is.' Adams looked up, called across the floor, 'Say, Hector, come here a minute.'

The Scottish gentleman drew himself together and then walked towards us with a serene dignity that made him seem royal indeed. When he reached us, Adams said: 'Here's an Englishman who wants to meet you. Now don't stick him with a dagger or anything. You English and Scotch are deadly enemies, aren't you?'

With a deep and rich majesty Hector replied quietly, 'I'm not a Scotchman, you know.'

'Good Lord! aren't you?' said Adams. 'The name's Scotch, anyway.'

Hector smiled charmingly and, looking at me, said: 'I was born of English parents, Penrith, Cumberland.'

Now I knew Penrith, Cumberland, extremely well and I said to him: 'Wouldn't it be fine if we had Lord Lonsdale's yellow coach rolling through the studio? That would make them sit up.'

He answered in that same rich but melancholy tone: 'It is forty years since I last saw Penrith.'

It was time for things to move on again, and once more the same little movement, like a recurring motif in an elaborate piece of music, took place. The Fool turned somersaults, the dogs crossed the floor, and Hector advanced up the steps and filled Lucrezia's cup. Afterwards, while the cameras were being shifted, I asked Adams some more.

'He's the finest-looking old man I ever saw in my life,' I remarked.

'Yes, he is, isn't he? He's been an extra ever since the earliest days.'

'I should have thought,' I said, 'that, with that magnificent carriage and that rich voice, he should be a proper star by this time.'

'Unfortunately,' Adams said, 'he can't act. He never loses his dignity. But he's quite contented, I believe.' Then Adams corrected himself. 'I don't know about contented though. His one desire is to take a holiday and see his own country again. He's always talking about England. He even gives lectures about it.'

'What prevents him taking a holiday?' I asked. 'If he's constantly in work, he ought to be able to save.'

'They don't get such a hell of a lot, extras,' Adams answered. 'For some reason or other he can't afford to go home.'

'He's certainly a good-looker though.'

'He is. The girls are crazy about him.'

So much for that. I forgot him. And then by an odd chance I talked with him. Alone in Hollywood one evening, going to a picture and wanting to eat something first, I stumbled into a small restaurant near Grauman's where my picture was to be, sat down in the first empty booth that offered itself, and found beside me Hector himself. He didn't recognise me, of course, and I was about to get up with a word of apology when he said, rather like a king welcoming a favourite subject, 'Plenty of room here, sir. I've no objection if you haven't.'

His smile was magnificent. The aristocratic head with its fine broad forehead, high cheekbones, dark colouring (he was sunburned and looked amazingly fit) reminded me of the other finest old man I'd ever seen in my life, Robert Cunninghame-Graham.

'You don't remember me,' I said.

'No,' he answered, looking me straight in the eyes, 'I don't.'

I reminded him of where we had met.

'I apologise,' he answered, 'but the fact is, when I'm working I can think of nothing else. I take my work very seriously,' he added.

I could see at once that he took everything very seriously. Humour would not, in all probability, be his most remarkable quality.

'You've been here a long time,' I said.

'Yes,' he answered, gravely. 'Every year I think I'm going home, but I never do.'

The waiter was standing there. I ordered one of those strange beers in tins, very cold and refreshing (by the way, why don't countries copy the best things from one another?), a New York cut and a large baked potato.

'Medium or rare?' asked the waiter.

'Medium,' I said. 'Why don't you go home if you want

to?' I asked Hector. Then, as he hesitated, I added, 'I hope I'm not being rude.'

'Certainly not.' I fancied a little sketch of a bow. 'I don't go home because I can't afford to.'

'It doesn't cost so much these days.'

He looked at me with a mournful kindliness. 'I might never get back into work here again.'

'Why don't you stay at home? The pictures are forging ahead in London, they say. There should be plenty to do for anyone as handsome as you are.' This time there was a real bow.

'Thank you,' he said. 'Good-looking old men who can't act are not greatly in demand. I have continuous work here because so many people know me.'

'And trust you,' I said.

'Yes, they like me. The Americans are the kindest people in the world.'

'I should have thought,' I said, looking rather mournfully at my tomato-juice cocktail, which I always drink in America although I dislike it exceedingly, 'that there is a good deal of cruelty in the picture business.'

'Not cruelty—indifference. Indifference, I mean, to anyone's personal fate. There's too much money risked to leave much time for individuals. The star here has a very anxious time; only obscure persons like myself are comparatively safe.'

You should have heard the way he said 'obscure persons.' We were becoming a little intimate. We liked one another, I knew. 'Tell me,' I asked, 'are you married? Have you children?'

He smiled. 'I could never support a wife properly on what I earn. And children—who would be selfish enough to bring them into this horrible world?'

'Oh, you feel it horrible then?'

'No, I don't personally. I enjoy each minute of it. I'm seventy-two years of age, and I hope I live to be a hundred.

I should like to spend my last twenty years in England.'

'What part of England do you think of most?' I asked.

Something crept into his eyes with that question. Something very beautiful, very tender, very romantic. That sounds sentimental, but it is a true and harsh fact that there are tender and beautiful moments, places and persons in the world. It is sentimental not to recognise that this is so.

'Oh, Cumberland, the Lake District,' he said. 'I was born in Penrith.'

'But you've not been back for forty years.'

'No, but I see Cumberland exactly as though I had lived there all my life. The hills are very small, you know, and very often the rocks run right down into the fields. The sky changes so often and so quickly that no place looks the same five minutes together. There are fifty different kinds of rain and you can climb for five minutes and see six lakes, the sea and twenty valleys.'

'Yes,' I answered, smiling. 'That's the way the novelists write. They make one suspicious.'

He looked at me reprovingly. 'Don't you like to read about places you love, then? I have quite a library of books about England and I have my lantern slides.'

'Your lantern slides?'

'Yes, it sounds old-fashioned, doesn't it? But I give lectures about England. Oh, in very small places, you know. Schools, little groups, anywhere that wants to fill in an evening for nothing. I show the slides and they're really quite charming. More restful than the film, and you can look at something for quite a long time without its moving.'

'What do you tell them in your lectures?' I enquired.

'Oh, little things. That's the whole point—tiny details. One of my lectures is a walk from Keswick to Ambleside.'

'Forgive me,' I said, 'but do they really listen? I'm sure your lectures are charming, but Wordsworth——'

'Yes, Wordsworth,' he answered very solemnly, as though he were speaking the name of God Himself. 'I read his poetry. A piece out of Dorothy's Journal. They listen most attentively.'

His voice dropped into half a whisper. 'The only thing is that I get so homesick myself when I lecture. I come back to my room sometimes and can't sleep. I think that I'll take the next train and risk it.' He shook his head. 'But I never do, never do.' Then, looking out over my head into space, he murmured, 'Oh, to go home . . . to go home only once.'

There was a little, rather embarrassing silence. I said, 'I must come and hear you lecture one day.'

And I did. I had a very agreeable evening. He asked me to dine with him before the lecture. I went to his rooms somewhere off Vine Street. Two rooms on the second floor of one of those old wooden houses, now swiftly disappearing, with a verandah, two rocking-chairs and a neat little garden at the back. His sitting-room was small and spare. On the walls was a photograph of Buttermere, the view of the little beach and the amphitheatre of hills behind it. There was a bookcase filled with books, a radio and an old lady who was introduced to me as Miss Mullins. Miss Mullins was a strange old thing, lame of one leg, one shoulder higher than the other and the suspicion of a beard. She had a vibrating nasal voice and looked discontented with everyone and everything. She reminded me strongly of Dickens' Mr. F.'s Aunt. We sat down to a very bare and simple meal and I understood Mr. F.'s Aunt had cooked the meal herself. But once again Hector Cathie was so serenely regal that I might have been dining with His Majesty the King in Buckingham Palace. He was regal with a good deal of self-abstraction, like a monarch with subjects who are giving him a little trouble on some distant problems. The old lady, Miss Mullins, sat at the table snorting every once and again, making little pellets of bread which she absent-mindedly flipped with her finger. Then suddenly, like her Dickens prototype, coming out with sentences like, 'It's just too shameful, the way the girls go naked on the beach.' Or, 'If they're going to give me curry, let them give me curry that is curry, that's what I say.' Remarks that had nothing to do whatever with the general conversation. After our meal we hurried off to the lecture, which was to be delivered to a school somewhere in Glendale. I took them in my car and we found the rather obscure little place with some difficulty. But there we were, Miss Mullins and I, sitting in the large and draughty schoolroom, with waves of icy cold blowing down our backs one moment and blasts of infernal heat in our faces another. There was a number of children gathered together and a few older persons. A thin, very dyspeptic-looking man introduced Hector, and then Hector began.

It was strange, indeed, to see magic-lantern slides once again. And my youth came back to me with such overpowering nostalgia that I felt the mountain breeze caressing my naked knees and a small paper packet of sweets sticky in my trouser pocket.

The slides moved me very deeply. Their ancient technique and rather shrill colouring seemed to belong so exactly to those early years that I'd spent in the English Lake District, climbing Great Gable by moonlight, having picnics on summer days on Stye Head, picking primroses in the lanes behind Buttermere village. But more moving than the slides was the deeply passionate emotion of Hector Cathie. He was not on the surface sentimental nor unduly patriotic. He did not pretend, as some do, that the little Lake District was the greatest landscape of lakes and mountains in the world. He did not say that there was no place so beautiful. On the contrary, he made a gospel of its smallness and his talk was all in glorification of tiny detail. It was hard indeed to believe that he had not been there for forty years, for he knew about all the gates that you must open going from Braithwaite over the fells to Crummock. He knew how enchanting were the little waterfalls in Stonethwaite. He knew of the queer ancient silences of Skiddaw Forest. He had these things, I suppose, from books, but gave them so personal and concrete a character that we heard the little becks tumbling through the room, saw with our own eyes the first fresh green of the bracken and the rain falling like twirling silver sixpenny pieces while the rainbow broke over Derwentwater.

It was this minuteness, this freshness, this constant change of colour and storm that penetrated the imaginations of those in this American classroom. I felt it all around me. They realised, those boys and girls, that there was something very small and very precious six thousand miles away. Something in which they themselves had strangely a hereditary right. It was old—very, very old. It was green—very, very green. And it was cosy, comfortable, kindly, in spite of the storms and the falling rain and the bare horizons of the fells. They felt, also, Hector's own emotion. At the end he said:

'Don't imagine, boys and girls, that I don't love America. I do. But you will understand how one longs for one's own country. How nothing else can supply the want of it. If I could go back for only a little while, I would remain satisfied, I think, for the rest of my life.'

They applauded. The clergyman made a speech of thanks, saying that what the world really wanted was that England and America should stand together. Upon which Miss Mullins shook her head and one had a dreadful feeling that she was going to rise to her feet and speak. But she didn't. She only cracked her fingers and muttered, 'Poisonous doctrine. Let America keep out of things. That's what I say.'

When, however, later on Miss Mullins had gone to bed, and Hector and I were alone for a moment, he burst out with:

'What I said isn't true! I don't love America—I hate it! It's a beastly country, with its tin cans, and its advertisements, and its celery and olives, and its showers, hot and cold, and filthy newspapers and——'

I interrupted. 'I thought you were very happy here.'

'I'm not! I'm not! I'm not! I want to go home. . . .' I

thought he was going to cry. He seemed crumpled up. A poor, desolate old man, mad with home-sickness, scarcely knowing what he was saying. There was nothing at all regal about him now. 'Forgive me,' he said. 'I always go on like this after a lecture. It isn't good for me. I oughtn't to give them. I've seen those slides hundreds and hundreds of times, yet it's always the same. I shan't sleep to-night. If I could only go back for a month——' He broke off.

'Let me,' I suggested, 'lend you something. I'll be delighted.'

He drew himself up. He was the head of all the clans that had ever figured in Scottish history. 'Excuse me,' he said. He flashed a look of almost contempt into my eyes.

'Forgive me,' I murmured. And that was all we ever said about money.

I had him after that constantly in my mind. When all is said and done, the great and eternal point about Hollywood is not the pictures, the stars, the fantastic salaries, the grand parties, the ridiculous scandals—but only this—that on no other piece of ground in the whole world, equal in size, are so many interesting, touching, admirable, unusual figures to be found. It is not, on the whole, a happy place. It is often vulgar, evil and sterilising. It is a tremendous place, easy for you to lose your soul there. But for the incongruous juxtaposition of almost incredible human beings, it is unique. And you think about them. After you've left them, you continue to think about them. They are so odd, so unexpected, are in many cases meeting such peculiar and unusual problems that you wonder constantly what their next step is going to be. So it was with Hector. On the surface it was a simple case. Here was an old man with very little money, who, because he was continually thinking of it, was eaten up with a desire for home. His problem could be solved in only two ways. Either by death or by return. I thought of means whereby I could, unknown to him, supply him with money enough for his adventure. But it was difficult. His pride was terrific. And I had a superstitious sense, too, that if he didn't go home in the right way, it was better for him not to go home at all. I was still considering the matter when Fate stepped in and provided, as she always does, her own solution.

Oddly enough, I encountered him again in a very personal manner. I found that he was to work in a picture of my own. When I say a picture of my own, I'm exaggerating, because all I had done in the matter was to write the script. And everyone in Hollywood knows how important the writer of a script is. But it happened in this case that both director and producer were great personal friends of mine and I looked forward to a happy time. This was a rather rough-and-ready adaptation of Walter Scott's *Heart of Midlothian*, an admirable subject for the cinema. I had wondered why they had not used it before. Joe Bennick, the producer, said to me, 'We got a wonderful old Scotchman running right through the story. He doesn't say anything because, unfortunately, he can't act. But he will look superb in kilts.'

'Hector Montgomery Cathie,' I said.

'Yes, how did you know? Although Hector's been in so many films and he's no stranger to anyone. A pity he can't act.'

'Let's write a little scene in for him,' I said, 'and see what he can do.'

'All right, but I warn you. You'll find him hopeless.'

And so I wrote in a little scene. Hector came to me and begged to be excused. 'I can't do it. I'm too self-conscious.'

'Nonsense, man. And you'll get $25.00 instead of $5.00.'

He shook his head, as by this time he was greatly attached to me. Looked on me rather as his son, I think. He had exactly the attitude just then of an indulgent father who doesn't want to disappoint his growing boy.

'Miss Mullins will be furious,' he said.

'Why?'

'She's always afraid I'll make a fool of myself.' Then he

added, in a kind of parenthesis, 'I hate that woman. I'd do anything in the world to be free of her.'

'But surely that's not difficult.'

'She's old,' he answered, speaking as though he himself were not a day more than thirty. 'You can't throw her out into the street.'

He did his best. His scene came quite early in the picture, where outside the old Edinburgh jail he harangued the mob and had a touching scene with his young daughter before he was killed by one of the rioters. It was quite true. He couldn't act at all. What I suffered that day watching Burrows, the director, go patiently over the scene again and again, take the old man kindly aside showing him exactly how it ought to be done, seeing Hector's whole soul nakedly agonised in the effort he was making, till I had to turn my eyes away from his self-consciousness, and at last heard Burrows saying to me: 'It's no good, he can't do it.'

Afterwards, when I was alone with Hector, I was surprised to discover him quite cheerful. 'I knew I couldn't,' he said, in a very lordly way, as though he was implying that acting was the lowest thing a human being could do. 'It was nice of you. I'm very grateful. I can lecture, but I can't act.' Then, with a sigh, he added, 'But I think I shall have to give up the lecturing.'

'Why?' I asked.

'It's making me so dreadfully homesick.'

He drew nearer to me and whispered in my ear, 'This country offends every instinct I possess. America is the——' He was interrupted by the miracle. One of the most dramatic things that have ever occurred in my presence.

An old boy, who was also an extra and lived below Hector in the same dwelling, appeared around a corner and handed Hector three letters. 'I found them in the letter-box,' he said, his eyes rolling in his head as he spoke. (He was always looking for somebody to play poker with.) 'I thought I'd bring them along.'

Hector thanked him most majestically, looked at the letters, and his whole body quivered. 'One of them is from England,' he said to me. We were seated on some boxes behind part of the papier-mâché Edinburgh jail, hidden on the whole from general view. His hand was trembling so that he could scarcely open the envelope.

'Do you mind reading it for me? I left my glasses in my clothes.'

'It may be something very secret,' I said.

'Oh, no, it couldn't be. It's the first letter I've had from England for a year and a half. And that one all that time ago was from a wine merchant in London. All the same I kept it for months.'

I was reading his letter. It was from a London firm of solicitors and quite firmly and clearly informed Mr. Cathie that his brother, Mr. James Cathie, had died in South Africa and left him a thousand pounds. I looked at the letter and considered the matter. After all, Hector was old. This would be a shock.

'Have you got a brother called James?' I asked him.

'Why, yes. I haven't heard from him for twenty years. He went to South Africa, mining.'

'He's left you a thousand pounds,' I said.

At that moment there were irate calls for Hector, who, now that he was deprived of his acting, was happily restored to the position of walking silently in front of the mob, shaking his fist at them and falling from a blow very shortly afterwards. He stood up, erect and magnificent. 'I've got to go,' he said, his voice shaking a little.

'He's left you a thousand pounds,' I repeated. Then I added—why, I don't know—'You'll be able to go to England now.'

He looked at me. He didn't know what he was saying. He took the letter mechanically. 'So I shall,' he said, and marched on to the scene to do his bit.

Well, that's that, I thought. Life is sometimes melodramatic. We modern writers translate our world into whispers. Sometimes, in spite of us, Nature insists on a shout. I felt that that was such an occasion. I dislike to make a fool of myself, but it was all that I could do to restrain myself from rushing into the middle of the scene and crying out, 'Hector Cathie's got a thousand pounds! He can go to England!' I discovered in that moment that it had become almost my own affair. I sat there waiting, determining in myself that I would see to it that Hector's thousand pounds should be spent in the best possible way. Three hundred pounds would give him all that he needed in the way of a holiday, and perhaps when he was back there he would like to settle down. I might find some little job for him. We might buy him an annuity. He could not, after all, have many more years to live. And so happy was I, sitting there seeing Hector move down the path beside the lake, sniffing at the air as he went and seating himself on the spur of rock above the Manesty woods, entering his room in the evening with the country sounds all about him—so happy was I that I was for the moment myself translated, enjoying one of those so rare selfless experiences when life seems richer and more fortunate than one had ever expected it to be.

Hector was at my side. He said, 'I understand that my brother has died and left me a thousand pounds. Is that correct?'

'Perfectly,' I answered.

His eyes filled with tears. His voice quivered. 'The poor lad. I stole his bicycle from him once for one whole afternoon, and punctured one of the tyres. He married unfortunately.' And then he walked off, his head in the air, looking, I supposed, at Cumberland. Looking at Cumberland! What must have been his strange experiences during those next weeks! For one thing he was old, and the venture of breaking away from everything that has surrounded you for so long—that kind of uprooting after you're seventy—is a shock. For one reason or another, I was not able before a fortnight or so to be free to watch the development of my picture. And when I did plunge back on to the set again, there was no Hector to be seen.

'Where has Hector gone?' I asked Burrows.

'I don't know,' he answered, and looked vaguely about him. 'He isn't in this part of the picture, you know.' He was looking rather crossly at the stumpy and untidy figure of Willie Beresford's stand-in. Willie was the great boy-actor of the moment and he'd been put into the *Heart of Midlothian* by force, to give the picture box-office value. He was not there to-day, but his stand-in was, a stupid, ugly little boy, who was now to take his place in a Scotch cap and a kilt on the top of a rock while the cameras fixed their positions.

'What you ought to do,' Burrows said crossly, 'is to watch the other actors. See how they walk and so on. That is if you want to be an actor yourself.'

'I guess I don't,' the little stand-in muttered. 'My aunt says it's a disgrace being an actor.'

I realised that this was one of Hector's protégés. Hector was always very kind to him. One of Hector's subjects.

Burrows suddenly said, 'They say Hector's going to England at last. He's been left some money.' And at that the little stand-in suddenly looked at us with the strangest expression in his eyes. A glance of bewilderment, distress, almost horror.

Then, looking in one morning at Stanley Rose's bookshop, there was Hector buying a book. It must have been a long while since he had done such a thing.

'A parting gift for a friend,' he said, staring at me in a distressed way.

You don't look well, I thought to myself. You look neither well nor happy. 'When are you going?' I asked him, in that especially cheerful way I have with those who I think need comforting. The result is often different from my intention. He frowned at me anxiously. He'd lost a lot of his regal splendour. He drew me into a corner of the bookshop.

'I haven't been sleeping,' he said. 'And that reminds me. It's a good deal to ask, but I'd take it as a great honour.'

'Take what?' I enquired.

'Come to the station to see me off with a few of my intimate friends, Tuesday week. We're having a little meal in my rooms first. Any time from eight onwards.'

'Why, of course. I'd be delighted,' I said. 'But look here,' I went on, 'you don't seem very happy about it. This ought to be the greatest thing in your life.'

'So it is. So it is,' he muttered. Then he caught my arm and drew me to the door. 'Do you see those cars?' he asked. 'Rows and rows of Fords and Chevrolets?'

'Of course.'

'And that sign hanging across the road from Grauman's —Garbo's new picture?'

'Why, yes, certainly.'

'And all the little eating-places? The shops with the cheap crockery? And do you hear them shouting the evening paper? Do you hear that siren blowing?' He was growing more and more excited. His hand trembled on my arm. 'You see the fogs creeping up from Santa Monica?'

'Yes, what about it?'

'I've hated this street for years and years now. Of course, it hasn't always been like this. It's always changing. But it has the same atmosphere of not really being anything. Something dumped down for the night—ugly and shifty. I've hated it! It's meant poverty and struggle and frustrated ambition and always trying to seem something grander than you are, and now I can't leave it.'

'What do you mean, you can't leave it?'

'Just what I say. I've thought that I hated it and everything here. The desert and the fog and the dirty sea and the studios and the lights and American voices. But perhaps I don't. Perhaps I've got fond of it.'

'Everyone feels like that,' I said, 'just before leaving a place.'

'And how does one know,' he went on, 'that that other is going to be like I imagine it is . . . the waterfalls and the clouds and the little green fields and the rocky hills? Perhaps it won't be. Perhaps I'll be longing for this.'

'Well, then you can come back,' I said comfortably. 'You can always come back.'

'Perhaps I can't. Perhaps if I go over I won't belong to either country. This has got into my blood. It means more to me than I thought.'

'Here's your book,' said the nice young shopkeeper.

'Thank you.' Hector turned a bewildering gaze about him.

'Now don't you worry,' I said. 'Once you're in the train starting for England, you'll be mad with joy. I'll see you on Tuesday week.'

And so I did. I let myself in for one of the oddest things. I arrived about eight-thirty to find at least a dozen people in the little room, but no Hector. Miss Mullins was there, of course, busy about the supper. And the little stand-in and two or three old English actors, some elderly American ladies and two girls who had that desperate air of brightness and enthusiasm, calculated, they hoped, to pick up a gentleman from somewhere in the speediest manner possible. The table in the middle of the room was laden with food. And I couldn't help thinking that that room had probably never seen so much food before. From the very beginning, the whole business was bizarre. Miss Mullins was in tears. She wept into all the dishes and went about muttering to herself, looking furiously at anyone whom she encountered. I saw, indeed, that they were all very unhappy. One of the ancient English actors explained it to me.

'You see, old boy' (I'd never met him before), 'Hector means a damn lot to all of us. Of course, we've chaffed him a bit sometimes about his talking so much of the old country. He's been a bit dotty in that direction, if you ask me, but, after all, he's a good old stick. A jolly old boy, what?'

I agreed. But I told them all that he would soon be back again.

'I don't know,' said the English actor. 'That's the devil of it.' He became very confidential, putting his hand on my shoulder. 'That's the damnedest thing about Hollywood, if it gets into your blood you're never free of it again. You may hate it like hell, but it's part of you, like a game leg or hare-lip. I don't know what it is. Either it's the sun or the people or something crazy. You know, it bewitches you. Like they used to do in the old fairy stories.'

Then Hector came in. He apologised very quietly for being late. He seemed to me considerably aged in the last few weeks. We sat down to supper and very melancholy it was. People tried to make conversation, I amongst others, but everything fell to the ground. Drink was circulated, but even that didn't cheer anyone very much. Then the little stand-in had been deputed to make a speech. He stood up, his ugly little face not very far above the tablecloth, and really did his duty very well. He said that Hector was a swell guy and that they'd sure miss him. And then he began to choke and snuffle, but he pulled himself together and said that he wished he could go to England too. On that Miss Mullins broke quite frankly into howls and sobs and rushed from the room. Everyone cried, 'Speech! Speech!'

Hector got up very quietly and in a depressed voice said this was the moment for which he had always been waiting. That it would be very wonderful to see England again and that he'd send everybody postcards. After that we all sat about waiting anxiously for the time to go to the station. An appalling kind of silence fell upon everybody. And I don't know how it was, but I myself felt as though Hector was committing some awful crime. Perhaps he was right. Perhaps the happiness of his life had for years now been built up on this picture of England—the North of England with its little stone walls and bare fells and running streams. Maybe when he saw it all in reality it would in truth be a disappointment that might almost kill him. And perhaps behind that he'd grown to love this strange untidy place where we were all living. Anyhow, that was his affair. I remember that all I wanted was for the thing to be quickly over. For all of us to hasten to the station, bid him farewell and go home.

'I say, old boy, you'd better be going,' one of the English actors suddenly remarked.

Hector nodded his head. Nobody spoke. We hurried downstairs, got into cars and dashed away to the Santa Fé Station. Those parts of Los Angeles where that station lies have no beauty at this time of the evening. They are sinister, bizarre, dangerous. They are empty of all but abandoned life. At last we were there, standing rather huddled together, some dozen of us in the middle of the tracks. There was the big, dirty train, and there was Hector laying his bag with his night things behind the shabby green curtain. He stood looking at us as we crowded the corridor.

He tried to speak.

I thought he was going to say what I always said on such occasions, 'Now go away like good children. I hate to be seen off. Leave me to myself.' But instead of that, quite suddenly he seemed to go mad. He drove through the lot of us, actually knocking Miss Mullins back on to one of the beds. He waved his arms like a crazy man and shouted as he stumbled down the steps of the train, 'I'm not going! I'm not going! Where are my bags? I can't go!' He began to run down the track. All we could do, of course, was to follow after him, and very foolish we looked. One of the English actors was desperately concerned. He caught up to Hector at last, got him by the arm, and as I came up I heard him say, 'Look here, old man, you can't do this. You really can't. You must have been drinking. What I mean is, the train will be going in a minute or two.'

'I don't care!' Hector cried. 'Don't you understand? I don't want to go to England! It won't be what I think it is. I'm safer here.'

The English actor turned to me. 'Dotty,' he said, 'he's gone dotty. All the excitement has been too much for him.'

'I don't know,' I answered, 'perhaps he's right.'

We had all gathered together by that time. The porter by the train was shouting, 'All aboard!' and Hector was laughing like a schoolboy.

'That's settled!' he cried. 'Now come on, we'll all go home and really enjoy ourselves.'

It happened that I myself returned to England a week or two later. I was not in Hollywood again for over a year. And then one afternoon, looking for some friend, I pushed back the heavy door and walked on to the set. There, seated very regally in a gondola on a piece of artificial water, dressed in a brilliant seventeenth-century silver costume and smoking a pipe, was Hector, talking to some friends. I came up intending to greet him and overheard some of his conversation:

'No place in the world like it,' he was saying. 'God, if I could only get a month off and see it again. For forty years I haven't been there. You can't imagine it. The sky changes every second and the rocks run right down into the little green fields, and there's a hill that only takes you a half-hour to climb and you can see six lakes. But it doesn't do talking about it. It makes me so homesick I could choke. You know how it is. You'd be the same way if you hadn't seen your home all those years.' He looked magnificently in front of him, seeing the mountains and the lakes and little running streams. I left him to his reverie.

THE TRAIN

Maurice blake, age a little more than ten, thought that there was nothing very strange in not having a mother. Other boys he knew (but he did not know very many) had mothers and talked about them a good deal. Because Maurice didn't have one, they were fond of telling him how marvellous their mothers were. So Maurice, who had learned by this time to think for himself because he was so much alone, had long ago decided that mothers were a hindrance rather than a benefit. His mother, in fact, had died a year after his birth, and since he was seven his home had been in a large, dark house off Gramercy Park, which consisted almost entirely of big stone staircases and rooms so high that it hurt you to look at the ceiling.

His father wrote for the newspapers, and wrote so well and so brilliantly that he was in constant demand and almost always away from the big house. His father was rich and Maurice had everything that a boy could want, including Miss Brent, the governess, Mrs. Howard, the housekeeper, and Mrs. Howard's little girl, Lucy.

He hadn't gone to school as yet, because his father moved about the world so swiftly that he had no time to be definite about the kind of school that Maurice should go to. He was a big, broad man, with a brown moustache, bright, lively eyes, a booming voice, and he smelled, as Maurice well knew, of tobacco, shaving soap, and an especial kind of heathery scent, which last, Maurice was told, came from Scotland. On his brief visits to his home Mr. Blake, Sen., rushed about the big house, shouting at the top of his voice, and everybody rushed about with him. On these occasions the house was filled with people. There were lights and flowers and beautiful cars outside the door, and extra servants, and Maurice could have anything that he wished.

He did not want very much, and his great aim in life was to be with his father alone. There was no one, of course, in the whole world as magnificent as his father. Not only was he wonderful in himself, but his picture was constantly in the newspapers, and everyone admired him tremendously, especially ladies.

But, as Maurice often heard him say, the great thing was his splendid little boy. Where, he asked the many ladies, could you find a grander little boy, a wiser, a handsomer, a more perfectly behaved? And his father would shout out all these things, his eyes sparkling, his mouth laughing, and he would pick up Maurice in his strong arms and swing him in the air, and his sharp moustache, which was almost like a knife, would brush Maurice's cheeks and eyes, and Maurice would swim delightedly in the tobacco and the shaving soap and the heather from Scotland. Oh, they were wonderful, these special moments! But the trouble was that there were always so many other people to share them.

Maurice had in his mind a daring plan of creeping one morning very early down the stairs, along the passage, down another short flight of stairs, and so into the room where he knew his father slept. He planned then to move with the utmost quietness across the floor and creep into the bed where his father was sleeping, and stay there waiting for his father to awake. This, indeed, he might one day have attempted, but most unwisely he confided his plan to Miss Brent, who was horrified at the idea.

'Oh, that would never do!' she cried in the sharp, shrill tones that were so like the striking of the big silver clock in the drawing-room. Miss Brent, who was long and thin like a beautifully rolled umbrella, had a perpetual smile that was full of brightness but no meaning. Maurice never trusted her smile. So now, when he asked why it was so horrible that he should creep into bed beside his father, Miss Brent murmured, smiling, that of course he mustn't. 'Your father wouldn't want to be awakened,' Miss Brent explained. 'He sleeps late.'

'Oh, I wouldn't wake him,' Maurice observed. 'I'd be as quiet as anything.'

'Now, that's enough of that,' said Miss Brent sharply but still smiling. 'Don't you ever dare——'

Maurice thought that he might catch his father alone in his bath—surely he would not be sharing that with anybody else. For he could often hear his father's bath-water running quite fiercely when he was in the middle of his lessons with Miss Brent. And he did, indeed, on one occasion, run for his life down the passage and push open the bathroom door. The room was filled with steam and a large, naked man was doing exercises, breathing deeply out of his nostrils and looking so completely unlike anything that Maurice believed his father to be, that he ran back to the schoolroom again with fear in his heart and a wonder as to whether he had ever seen his real father before.

There came a time then when his father was away for a very long while indeed, and Maurice found Miss Brent less than nothing of a companion. He was forbidden to go into the park around the corner from the house, and had, I'm afraid, the dullest of dull existences, and sought companionship with Mrs. Howard's Lucy.

Lucy was a thin little girl with somewhat protruding, anxious eyes. She was pretty in a way, because she had pale flaxen hair and was always very neat. Her mother adored her. Mr. Howard, Lucy's father, had vanished one morning after eating a hearty breakfast, and gone off with a lady to South Africa. Mrs. Howard, whose second name was common sense, had washed up the breakfast things and before evening found a job as housekeeper with Mr. Blake. She'd been with him ever since and, so long as Lucy was well, was perfectly happy.

As her mother worshipped Lucy, so did Lucy worship Maurice. But she was a speechless child, unable always to express her feelings. She had been taught, of course, from the very earliest age, that she must never bother Mr. Maurice. But the boy was so often alone that he liked to go up to the room at the top of the house which was Mrs. Howard's sitting-room, and he would play with Lucy in a mild, quiet fashion, Mrs. Howard sitting in a chair sewing and wondering once in a while why the two children were so quiet and 'hadn't a bit of life between them.'

Mrs. Howard was, however, immensely genteel and loved Lucy to be what she called ladylike. What she liked best was to brush Lucy's beautiful flaxen hair, which she did by the hour, her matter-of-fact, sensible eyes staring into the room, seeing, perhaps, the past with the figure of the wicked adventuress in the foreground, but much more likely soberly thinking of the present and wondering whether the new kitchen-maid was up to any mischief and what she was going to have for dinner.

There was, however, for Maurice something comfortable and friendly about Mrs. Howard's room. The rest of the house was so large and so empty. He picked up somewhere a copy of *Bleak House*, and the illustrations therein of Chesney Wold with a gloomy avenue of trees, the marble statue at the corner of the stairs, the rays of sunshine breaking in through the latticed windows, all seemed to him very like his own home.

He lived, in fact, in a state of passionate desire for his father. Love, except with the aged, flourishes best through long absences. He'd never been with his father long enough to become accustomed to him. And there was something so heroic for Maurice in the vitality and high spirits of that large, broad-shouldered figure.

And then one day, without a moment's warning, he came back from his walk with Miss Brent in the park, to find two men meeting him on the stairs. Two very large men, they seemed to him, and behind them a stir of bustle, a sense of invading light, a richness of promise all about the house. Miss Brent fell back; Maurice took a step or two up the stairs and then stopped, staring.

The two men also stopped, and then both of them began to roar with laughter. The noise filled the whole place, like the roar of lions or tigers in the very heart of the jungle. One of the big men, quite the largest Maurice had ever seen, leaned forward and picked Maurice up, held him in the air, looking at him with warm, kindly eyes that beamed out of his rosy face. Maurice stayed there, between the two great hands, patiently without moving.

'This must be Maurice!' cried the giant. 'Don't you know who we are? We are your Uncle Blair and your Uncle Stephen.'

And the other man, who was not so big as the first one, but quite big enough, cried out, 'I'm Uncle Stephen.'

Maurice was instantly reminded of Tweedledum and Tweedledee in *Through the Looking-Glass*. But he liked the warmth and pressure of Uncle Blair's hands about him, the sense of strength, the promise of companionship. So he said nothing, but laughed and kicked a little with his legs. Uncle Blair then gathered him against his chest and carried him as though he were a small Pekingese dog down into the hall; then he set him on his feet.

'You're a fine young man. Let's take a good look at you. My, you're swell! Surprised to see your old uncles? All the way from Alaska I am, and the other one is from California, where the sun never stops shining. A lot of other things happen there too—don't they, Stephen?' And he roared with laughter. 'We've come to stay with your father a bit and stir this old house up. Aren't you glad we've come? Hasn't it been dull without us? You'll see how exciting it'll be.'

All this and ever so much more poured out in a tumultuous flood. Yes, just as though it were really a river flooding the hall, sweeping into the dining-room, beating down the door that led into the servants' quarters, and with its swelling waters bringing such a force of life and energy that Maurice was almost breathless. The hall door opened, and there was his father, looking so smart and so fresh and, to Maurice, so wonderful. Maurice stood there looking at him, forgetting altogether his two uncles. It was so utterly unexpected. He was so happy.

'Hello, kid,' said his father. 'A bit of a surprise, isn't it?'

Maurice had been told by Mrs. Howard how to behave. He walked slowly forward. 'Yes, Father,' he said. 'I hope you're quite well.'

This seemed marvellously funny to his two uncles, who shouted with laughter and called out both together, 'He hopes he's well! He hopes his father's well. Can you beat it!'

But his father bent forward, as he always did, and kissed Maurice first on one cheek and then on the other, and said, smiling, 'Been a good boy? I hope so.'

'Yes, Father.'

'I must ask Miss Brent.'

Then Blake looked over his son's head to his two brothers. 'How do you like your uncles? Ever see anyone so big in your life? Blair, you're a disgrace! You've got a stomach like an elephant's.'

He walked past Maurice, put his hands on the shoulders of his brothers, and they all walked up the stairs together, all of them talking at once, while Maurice stood staring up after them, alone in the hall, the noise of the rushing waters still sounding in his ears.

Then came Miss Brent's sharp, tinkling voice: 'Maurice! Maurice! Where are you? Come and take your coat off at once!'

'Yes, Miss Brent.'

He gave a little sigh. Would he ever be alone with his father, even for a moment? Still, it was rather exciting to have two new uncles. Perhaps something was going to happen. He felt in his heart that it was.

What happened, in the first place, was the wonderful new life in the house. Always when his father came home everything seemed to spring into life and gaiety. But this time there were three of them . . . three enormous men.

Fresh servants were engaged, and Mrs. Howard was so busy that, as she said over and over again, 'If it goes on like this for long, I'll drop in my grave.' The only person who was quiet and undisturbed was Lucy. Maurice still went up to her room to play with her, but she was only a shadow to him. His whole heart was set toward his father.

It was as though with the arrival of his two uncles he saw clearly how deep his adoration of his father was. For they were big and handsome men, too, and smelt splendidly of tobacco and shaving soap, were laughing and jolly and friendly. But they were not his father. They, themselves, seemed to feel that, for he was the only one they listened to, looked up to.

But here was an ironic thing: It was more than ever difficult for Maurice to be alone with his father; but he could be alone with his uncles whenever he pleased. They made a fuss over him. They took him to the circus. Uncle Blair often seized him to take him driving in the car.

So, with this attention from his uncles, Maurice's life blossomed. It was all gay and exciting now. But the one thing in the world that he wanted he couldn't have—his companionship with his father. It seemed to be forever on the verge of happening. His father would say, 'Hello! Want to come for a drive? Be ready in half an hour.' But then when the half-hour was over and Maurice was there all dressed and eager, something would have happened. There would be a telephone call or, worst of all, a lady would arrive.

Maurice's father seemed to be forever in the company of beautiful ladies, and oh! how Maurice hated them. Sometimes they did not notice him at all. Sometimes they would treat him as a baby, crying out in hard, cooing voices, 'Oh, the darling! How old is he? . . . Not really!' Sometimes they really liked him and wanted him to go with them. But he always refused and was sulky, because they were his enemies and kept him from his father.

With the spring came Maurice's birthday. May the 2nd. It so happened that never so long as he remembered had his father been home for his birthday. It had been quite a pleasant event without him, because the cook made a cake and people gave him presents. But always he had longed for his father to be there.

Once there had come all the way from a place called South Africa a telegram wishing him many happy returns and asking Mrs. Howard to give him five dollars. What an event that had been! It had, however, happened only once. In the other years there had been silence.

But now, miracle of miracles! On a sunny morning, there appeared in the schoolroom Uncle Blair and his father. (Never his father alone. Why couldn't he come to the schoolroom just once by himself?) Miss Brent and Maurice were doing geography and were trying to come to some decision as to what the purpose of the River Amazon really was. Then there was Uncle Blair's roaring voice: 'Say, kid, I hear you're to be ninety-nine two weeks from Tuesday. We must celebrate.'

And his father, looking so beautiful in a dark blue suit, so distinguished, so greatly superior in every way to Uncle Blair, coming over to him, said, 'How old will you be in two weeks' time, Maurice?'

'Eleven, Father.'

'Eleven? Can it be possible? Why, it seems only yesterday you were sucking your thumb.' Then he turned away, looked for a moment at Miss Brent, as he always looked at every woman, to see whether by any chance she might, in a miraculous way, turn out to be attractive. He decided very quickly that that was the last thing that she would ever be and went on: 'We must have a birthday party. A grand birthday party. Would you like that?'

'Yes, Father, I would.'

'What do you want for a birthday present?'

Maurice thought. Then his eyes became full of light. His hand trembled a little against the paper. 'What I'd like better than anything else, Father, would be a train. A real electric train with tracks that would run all around the schoolroom.'

Maurice's father laid his hand on Maurice's head and said, 'A train it shall be.' . . .

From that moment an idea took possession of Maurice like a little demon.

What he saw was one of those wonderful railways running right round the room, with stations, signal-boxes, and bridges. An electric train with little red and green cars, his father on his knees beside the railway, and Maurice close up against him. The two of them alone, no one else there, watching the train pursue its perilous journey. That would be heaven.

He formed in his mind the idea of what he would say: 'Could we do it together, Father, do you think? Just the two of us? I *would* like that.' And he would lead his father up to the room, see that there were no ladies there to disturb him—he might even lock the door.

So, during this two weeks, he thought of nothing else. He even dreamed of it. . . . He and his father, kneeling side by side; they two in perfect companionship.

The birthday arrived, as everything arrives in this only too punctual world. It was a May day of absolute splendour.

Maurice, as soon as he was awake, dressed and came into the schoolroom. And there was Miss Brent, his breakfast, and a pile of delightful presents done up in paper.

Miss Brent gave him a book, *Don Quixote*. There was something from Mrs. Howard, the cook, John, the new butler, and from Lucy a little train with two cars and the engine. The cars were painted a deep red.

'How funny!' he began. 'Lucy——' and then he stopped. Because, after all, his father might not give him a train, as he promised. But there was something pathetic about this little affair. Somehow, in some curious way, it resembled Lucy. He put it on the carpet and wound it up. It fussed along toward the table, suddenly made an eccentric turn, and tumbled over on its side, where, Maurice couldn't help feeling, it looked more like Lucy than ever.

'I must go and thank her,' he said. He went round the house thanking everybody, and when he came to Lucy, who was just going off to school, all he could say was, 'Thank you so much, Lucy. That's awfully kind of you.'

Lucy stared at him as usual, speechless. She had her hat on, an ugly one. 'Mother said that she heard you wanted a train.'

'Yes, I did.'

'I went out and bought it myself with my own money.'

He felt that she wanted him to say something, just as he wanted to be alone with his father, but he couldn't say anything. He only grinned and ran off, Lucy staring after him. Then, when he came into the schoolroom again, Miss Brent informed him that there was to be a surprise.

'We're to go out and take a walk and not come back until twelve,' she said.

Maurice said not another word, and together they went off into the green park. Here they sat on a bench. Maurice stared in front of him, while Miss Brent looked about her with the air of one who expects a romance at any moment but is determined to reject it when it comes. Maurice was thinking of nothing but the wonderful event that was shortly to occur.

It would need a little courage, but he was determined on what to do. When he came into the schoolroom, saw the train there and his uncles and his father, he would, after thanking them, say to his father, 'Would you mind if we were alone for a moment? I have something I want to say to you.'

And his father would answer, 'Of course!' And then he would turn to Maurice's uncles and say, 'Leave me alone with the kid, will you?' And his uncles would leave the room.

On returning from the walk he ran up the stairs ahead of Miss Brent and then paused outside the schoolroom. Within, there was apparently much jollity. He opened the door and went in.

An amazing sight met his eyes. The schoolroom table had been removed. Around the floor from end to end, in a great glittering circle, ran a railroad track. On the track was the most glorious train, something quite beyond anything he'd ever imagined. It had about everything that a train ought to have. A superb engine—indeed, two—one at each end. The cars were brilliantly coloured, the trucks laden with coal. Along the line there were bridges, signal-boxes, railway platforms, and even, at one end, a marvellous tunnel.

Kneeling on the floor beside the railway were his two uncles, their broad backs presented to his full gaze. At the other end of the room, looking down upon the scene, was his father, quietly smoking his pipe. He heard one uncle say, 'Not that way. Look here! I'll show you!' And one huge uncle shoved the other huge uncle.

His father said, 'I don't think either of you knows anything about it. Let me try!'

Maurice moved timidly forward. The three men all looked at him. The two uncles shouted together, 'Why, here's the kid! What do you think of it?'

And his father, suddenly going down on his knees beside his uncles, looked at him and said, 'Here's your birthday present, Maurice. I hope you'll like it.'

'Oh, it's wonderful,' Maurice sighed. He advanced a little nearer. But now three broad backs seemed to present an insuperable obstacle.

'Now I've got it!' Uncle Blair cried. 'Couldn't understand it at first. Now she's off!' And, indeed, the engine gave an extraordinary, enginelike scream, moved a little forward, then stopped again.

'There you are!' the other uncle cried. 'That wasn't the way!'

Maurice thought of the little speech that had been in his mind: 'Please, Father, let us do it together alone. Can't we?' But he couldn't say it. Those broad backs defeated him. He did, however, manage to bring out very quietly, 'May I look at the engine?' Nobody heard him.

Uncle Blair, who was now lying flat on his stomach, so that he seemed to spread across the entire floor, muttered, 'It's that little wire. It's got loose.'

'No, it hasn't!' said the other uncle. 'It's nothing to do with the wire. Something is stuck in the funnel.'

'Might I see the engine?' Maurice said again, this time rather more loudly. Uncle Blair heard him and shouted, 'Why, of course, kid. It's your birthday present, you know.' However, no one moved.

Maurice stood beside them, hesitating. It didn't seem as yet like *his* railway at all. But perhaps it soon would.

'Now it's off!' Uncle Blair shouted, suddenly heaving himself up. 'There she goes!' And the train did move with a wonderful miracle of ease and naturalness. 'All aboard!' both uncles cried together.

Maurice caught his father's sleeve. 'Thank you very much, Father,' he said.

His father, also on his knees, turned round towards him. They were now almost of a height, so that their faces were close together. Maurice saw his father's face as he had never seen it before. It was kind, indulgent, wise, but somehow remote. The eyes into whose depths Maurice could so profoundly look, were distant. They seemed scarcely to be aware of Maurice at all.

Maurice had a frantic temptation. His heart hammered. The temptation was that he should bend forward and kiss his father's cheek. He had never kissed his father, only been kissed by him. And he'd long ago been told that manly little boys didn't kiss anybody. But this was a special occasion—his birthday. The moment was there; it was gone. And, instead of kissing him, he said, 'Can I look, Father? May I?'

The train was rushing along the line like a superb master of its craft. When it passed the signal-box a little red sign jerked forward and then back again. When it passed the station platform a small automaton stationmaster jumped out of his box and then back again, and it disappeared into the tunnel. Maurice squeezed in between his father and Uncle Blair.

'I say, that's good!' he heard his father murmur. 'Best I've ever seen.'

'It ought to be,' Uncle Blair roared. 'It cost a pretty penny. Now it's round the bend!' Uncle Blair shouted, beside himself with excitement. 'Didn't it take that bend grandly?' And he heaved against Maurice, who had to step back. Now the railroad track was entirely obscured from him.

But his father may have been conscious of something, for he turned, and with that kind, beneficent look in his eyes which had won for him the confidences of so many beautiful ladies, he said, 'Do you like it, Maurice? Do you really? I hope you do.'

Then was the moment for Maurice's sentence. He caught his father's arm. 'Could we do it together, Father, just you and I—nobody else?' he murmured. But the small, hesitating tones were lost entirely in the shouts of both uncles. For the train began to spurt and snort and make extraordinary chuckles. It reared itself on its hinder end and then stayed there at a full stop—half of itself in the air.

'My gosh!' one of the uncles shouted. 'What's gone wrong now?'

'Don't touch it! I'm the only one here who understands the thing.'

'No, you're not!' shouted the other uncle. 'It was I who started it just now.'

They moved, both of them, off together toward the engine, and once more Maurice said, 'Don't you think, Father, that you and I—' But he never finished his sentence. For, in moving, his sleeve had caught the track, jerked a piece crooked, and the train, suddenly coming to life again, was dashing forward.

'Look out!' Uncle Blair cried in an ecstasy of panic. 'What are you doing, Maurice? Leave the thing alone. Here, get back! Get back! Don't touch it!' And, with his uncle's vast body rushing toward him, he hurried himself out of the way.

Now he was entirely isolated. The three men were so completely occupied that they had forgotten him. He waited, his small hands clenched. They'd all forgotten him. Then he heard Miss Brent in the doorway:

'Come, Maurice. You can play with your beautiful train later.'

He suffered himself to be led away. Luncheon was an especially fine one, with roast chicken and ice cream because it was his birthday. But after lunch, when he thought that he might go and examine the railroad quietly, Miss Brent said to him, 'Your father thinks it's better, darling, that you shouldn't play with the train until to-morrow. He's got a party to-night and he thought some of the ladies would like to look at it. So, as they got it running at last just before lunch, he doesn't want it disturbed again.'

'Oh, I see,' said Maurice.

'Would you like to go to the Zoo this afternoon?' Miss Brent asked.

'Yes, if you like,' Maurice said. At ordinary times, he

adored the Zoo. But he didn't enjoy it at all that afternoon.

He had his supper and was put to bed, fell asleep, and then awoke abruptly to the fact that there was a great deal of noise going on in the schoolroom. Loud voices, screams of laughter, and once and again he fancied he heard his father's enchanting tones. He told himself that he must not listen, and he hid his head under the bed-clothes.

Then he could endure it no longer. He jumped out of bed, hesitated for a moment, standing there in his pyjamas; then timidly he opened the schoolroom door.

What a sight met him there! There was the railroad track and there was the train buzzing around, and there were ladies and gentlemen, all in the most brilliant evening clothes, his two uncles, each of them with an arm around a lady, some ladies and some gentlemen on their knees, and a perfect babble of cries:

'Oh, look! Isn't it marvellous?'

'Don't touch it, darling.'

'There—it's stopped!'

'Give it a push!'

'Look out! You'll upset it!'

And then his father suddenly dropped on to his knees and cried out, 'It's done that twice! We had a terrible time this morning with it.'

Then his father looked up. He saw his son, very small in his striped pyjamas, staring at him. He jumped to his feet. 'Why, it's Maurice! What the devil——!'

Everyone turned and looked. But Maurice saw only his father.

'Please, Father,' said Maurice.

'Here, what are you doing? You ought to be in bed. I'll go and put you there.'

Maurice's heart beat wildly. Was it, after all, to happen? But a beautiful lady, on her knees beside the engine, looked up and cried to Maurice's father, 'Look here, silly; I found out what's the matter.'

'Oh, have you?' said Maurice's father, his eyes suddenly becoming tender and translucent. He moved across to her.

Maurice closed the door and went back to his room. His eyes were filled with tears, so that he saw but indistinctly. Nevertheless, very clear to him was Lucy's little train, lying on its side on the floor. He knelt down and picked it up and turned the little wheel on its side. With a ridiculous clicking noise, like an old lady whose false teeth were not securely fastened, it started across the carpet. Maurice looked at it. . . .

Poor, sad, neglected little boy. . . . That might be the end, as it has been of so many stories. A remarkable thing, however, occurred. Maurice discovered that although his eyes were filled with tears, his heart was unexpectedly filled with rage. Why, it was *his* train, *his* birthday! *His* train—nobody else's! *His* train! And he hadn't been allowed even to touch it the whole day long!

He stood up. Suddenly he moved back to the schoolroom again. In another moment—and it was as though he were not truly himself—he was standing there. Now they were almost all on their knees, crowding the railway line, even pushing one another to get nearer to it. He cried out in a voice shaking with temper:

'It's *my* train! It's *my* train! I haven't been near it all day!'

Everyone looked up. There was a kind of spiritual gasp. Some lady said, 'Doesn't he look sweet?'

But his father had sprung to his feet and was staring at him as though he'd never seen him before. 'Why, Maurice——'

Maurice's fists were clenched, his eyes glared at his father. 'It's *my* train! You said it was! Why shouldn't *I* play with it?'

His father looked at him, went across to him, picked him up, and rested him on his shoulder. 'By George! He's right! It's right what he says. Look here—get out, all of you! Go downstairs and make merry. I'll be with you later. Meanwhile, Maurice and I are going to have this to ourselves. Go on—clear out! Clear out!'

With laughter and cries and a general kind of orgy of merriment, out of the room they all went. Maurice was put down on the floor.

'And now,' said his father, his arm around his son, holding him close to him, 'let's make this thing work properly. It's been sticking all day. What it really needed was *you* to attend to it!'

THE HAIRCUT

'WELL, THEN, that settles it,' Mr. Preston said, biting the nail of his left-hand thumb in the way which she so especially detested.

'Yes, that settles it,' Mrs. Preston answered. 'We've made a terrible mistake and had better admit it.'

'What I don't understand,' he went on bitterly, 'is why you married me in the first place. I'm no different. I'm just exactly the same man to whom you said only a year ago that you hadn't believed such perfection of character . . .'

She interrupted him angrily. 'Oh, be sensible, Hamish. When one's in love, one says the most ridiculous things and then afterwards one sees clearly. I could not have believed,' she went on meditatively, staring at him, 'that I should ever see anyone as clearly as I see you at this moment.'

'And all about a haircut,' he said sulkily.

Yes, it had been. The little, absurd episode had been a symbol. She had wanted him to go with her to the Cathedral and he had insisted that he must have his hair cut. Nothing more ridiculous. He needed it. She hated men whose hair was rough on the back of their necks, but why just then? And so she had told him that if he went and had his hair cut, she would divorce him. His refusal to please her seemed to stand for everything—his self-assertiveness, his selfishness, his egotism, his man-conceit, his deliberate lack of consideration for her. And after she had spoken that dreadful word 'divorce,' she felt sure he would give in, but he hadn't. He had had his hair cut.

It was a hot July morning and they were sitting in the untidy, sun-glaring bedroom of the Barcelona hotel, he on the unmade bed, she holding the blind, which after all did not keep away the sun, a little aside. She was looking out on the narrow street, with the church and the wine-shop and the little bazaar that sold shawls and fans and castanets to simple-minded tourists. She knew it all so well although they had been in Barcelona only a week, but she knew him—oh, she knew him—still better. She turned back and looked at him, sitting humpishly on the bed, swinging his stout, thick legs (how could she ever have thought him handsomely built?), pulling in perplexity his short black moustache, whilst his little black eyes stared angrily in front of him. He looked like a child who had been desperately hurt, and as, for a moment, that occurred to her she had an instant of tenderness which was quickly checked. He might look like a child, but he certainly wasn't one, with his meanness and bossiness and brutality. How he had hurt her last night after they had come back from the café! Bruised her wrist. She looked at it now and was surprised to find there was no mark on it.

'Well, that's final,' he said again. 'I'll arrange everything. You had better go back to your mother to-morrow. I'll stay on here, I think.'

He got up and was so stocky and square and, at the same time, so childishly disappointed in her that she burst out into violent protest. 'Don't look at me like that, as though it were all my fault. After all, I can't help it if I've stopped loving you. It's your character that's the matter. No woman in the world could endure it.' But she turned away from his steady gaze. 'Oh, it's been my fault, too, I know. I haven't been very patient sometimes, and I've got a rotten temper, but all the same, let's be sensible. The fact is that we don't love each other any more. You don't love me, and I don't love you, and so it's silly to stay together, isn't it?'

His steady gaze never left her face.

'Yes, I suppose it is. Well, I'll be going along to Cook's place and see about your getting off to-morrow.'

She did not answer. He had been sitting there in his shirt-sleeves. Now he put on his thin silk coat and went out.

He was at first so deeply preoccupied with this tragedy in his life that he noticed nothing. He really could not understand how it had all occurred. Only a year and a half ago they had been married in Edinburgh with, it seemed, every possible happiness in front of them. They were crazily in love—he was no fool, being thirty years of age, and he knew that here was the girl whom he wanted for life. And she was no fool either, being modern, wide-eyed about everything sexual, loyal by nature, but she had a devil of a temper and she had been spoiled by her old hag of a mother. That was why he had brought her away on this holiday, to see if something couldn't possibly be done.

He really didn't know how it had all come about—the change from that passionate love to this anger and recrimination and stolidity. The change had been so gradual, first her temper and his obstinacy; then her aesthetic friends; then her taste in paintings like Cézanne's and Renoir's—music like Bach's—books like that fellow, Aldous Huxley's. He just thought Huxley's novels were plain dirt and that Bach's music said the same thing over and over again, and that Cézanne's pictures (she had dragged him all the way to the Tate Gallery to see a Cézanne painting of a hill) were like nothing real. You couldn't say, not if you tried ever so hard, that nature was like that. But then he didn't complain of her taste. It was everybody's right to like what they liked, and he liked Puccini and Low's cartoons and stories by Oppenheim. He really did not see why that should make her angry, but it did. And she got a lot of Cézanne's reproductions and paid £4 apiece for them, and he said it was rotten extravagance and they had a most fearful row.

That was the beginning of it. And then the old mother, who always had a damp, furry look like a piece of blotting-paper, would come with her soft, sibylline voice and take her daughter's side, so gently and so firmly that Hamish felt a most intolerable cad, and at the same time knew that he was right. But none of these things should have led to this catastrophe. After all, everyone was aware that the first year of marriage was a difficult one. They had been married a year and a half, and the difficulties had just gone on. Every married couple had them. What he could not understand was how they had ceased to love one another. One could be angry with someone and yet love her very dearly, but now they hated to be together and everything aggravated one or the other. It had been, of course, foolish to come to Spain in the hot weather, but they were going on to the sea at Malaga.

He stopped abruptly where he was, because, to his complete astonishment, a bullet went singing past his ear. . . .

Nancy Preston stood at the window for some little while after her husband had left her. She was staring out, but not thinking of what she saw. When they had first come there she had loved this little street. It had seemed to her so Spanish. The little church with the figure of the Madonna and Child over the carved doorway had been so friendly, she had wondered whether after all the two of them might not come together again. But he had been, oh, so exasperating. The trouble with Hamish was, she reflected, that he would not talk. He had no vocabulary and his brain was so slow that long, long after she had finished a subject and was beginning on another one, he would arrive at the first one, and then when she chaffed him, not unkindly, about his slowness, he would look at her and say:

'You married me for what I was, you know, not because I was a blooming centipede.'

And she would think how odd that was, for she had loved him at first for the very qualities which now she disliked in him so much. 'Oh! it's a shame,' she thought, twitching the blind angrily. 'Why should I have stopped loving him? I don't want to stop.' And at that moment, to her surprise, she saw running down the street a little company of men with guns in their hands. They gathered almost exactly opposite her window on the steps of the church and consulted together; otherwise everything was very quiet. In Spain, during the morning hours, everybody is sleeping. It was strange to see this group of men with guns, discussing so earnestly opposite her window. It was the stranger because there was no sound anywhere. Suddenly, as though they had decided something, they turned and ran up the steps into the church. A moment later there was a knock on the door, and that idiotic woman, Mrs. Furness, was standing there.

Mrs. Furness was like a great ripe plum, purple of face, very often wearing purple-coloured clothes, stout and hot and untidy and terribly muddle-minded. She had haunted them most obstinately from the very beginning of their journey. She had appeared on the train from Calais, and then at their hotel in Paris, and then at the Spanish border, where, of course, she had lost her passport, and then to their horror and disgust turned up at this very hotel where they were. She was looking, she explained to them again and again, for Mr. Furness, who had started with her on their holiday, but had been lost at Dover and was now apparently determined to go on being lost. She told them, with tears and desperate heavings of her enormous bosom, that she knew that he was not unfaithful, that she was certain that it was just absent-mindedness, he was such a careless man—a perfect darling, but terribly careless.

'But I don't see how you can lose a wife,' Nancy Preston kept saying out of sheer exasperation, implying that to lose

Mrs. Furness was surely something beyond anybody's power.

'Oh! you don't know Edward,' Mrs. Furness kept saying. 'He's been the same all his life long. Why, when he was quite small, he lost his father and mother for weeks.'

'He is obviously very independent,' Nancy Preston answered.

But now Mrs. Furness was not thinking of her husband. She was in a state of alarm.

'Oh! do forgive me, Mrs. Preston, the last thing I wanted to do was to interfere, and I know you are always so busy, but there's something dreadful going on.'

'Dreadful?' interrupted Nancy sharply. 'What do you mean?' For some strange reason her thoughts instantly ran to Hamish.

'Oh! I don't know, I'm sure. It's just a feeling I have, and that nice Mr. Bannister I met yesterday says that they are working up for terrible things here—the Communists and the Fascists, you know. And the Government, he says, is really Communist although it doesn't pretend to be, and the army is Fascist, and so there you are,' she ended.

'I wish you would tell me what you do mean,' Nancy answered crossly. She had turned back to the window and was surprised to see that one of the young men, who had run into the church, had come outside again and was standing on guard at the top of the steps, his rifle in his hand.

'Can I have a word with Mr. Preston?' Mrs. Furness said. 'I wouldn't bother him for more than a moment, but I do want to get away and to get back to Paris if I can. I'm sure that's where my husband is.'

'Mr. Preston has gone out,' Nancy said shortly.

'Oh! gone out,' said Mrs. Furness agitatedly, pressing her hand to her bosom. 'I'm sure that isn't wise this morning. I do hope he's all right.'

'Of course he's all right. He can look after himself perfectly.'

And then there appeared at the doorway a big, tall, thin

man, with a high, very spiky white collar, pince-nez with a cord attached, and a melancholy, rather severe, expression. This was Mr. Browne, the schoolmaster from the Midlands who, Mrs. Furness thought, admired her very much. It was Nancy's opinion that he admired nobody but himself. She disliked him extremely and she turned on him a rather haughty stare.

He regarded her gloomily. 'It's no use your looking at me like that, Mrs. Preston,' he said. 'I know you don't like me and would rather I were anywhere but here. All the same, I have come for your good. The sooner the lot of us get to the station, the better.'

'The station?' said Nancy. 'Why, what's the trouble?'

'It's every kind of trouble,' Mr. Browne said. 'They are fighting down on the quays now.'

'Fighting?' Nancy cried.

And Mrs. Furness said, 'Oh dear, oh dear! It's the first time I have been abroad for five years, and everything's gone wrong from the very start.'

'Now it's no use making a fuss,' Mr. Browne said sharply. 'Facts are facts. What we've got to do is to find the hotel 'bus and get away as soon as possible. One thing leads to another,' he added. 'We may all be shot by the evening.'

'My husband went out,' Nancy Preston said slowly, 'to see about some tickets.'

'Went out?' said Mr. Browne in his most melancholy voice. 'Tchut! tchut!' He had a most maddening fashion of clicking his false teeth together. 'That was a great mistake. He may be arrested, and you'll never see him any more.'

'Arrested?' said Nancy angrily. 'What nonsense! He's an Englishman, with his passport and everything.'

'You may be as rude as you like, Mrs. Preston,' Mr. Browne replied. 'I won't take any offence at all, but to be an Englishman may be in twenty-four hours from now as useless as being a Hottentot.'

Then they stopped and stared at one another in silence

because, just outside the window and almost as clear as though it were in the room, there was a sound of two rifle shots.

'Well, I'm damned!' said Nancy, turning back to the window.

She had then a very odd experience, for the little street that she had known and loved was gone. Of course, in the physical sense it was still there. There was the window with the gaily-coloured shawls (a bright purple shawl, with dark red flowers, could be seen, a magnificent splash of colour, as clearly as anything from the hotel window), the small café, with four little chairs and two tiny tables outside, the church with the worn steps, the patient, pathetic Madonna and Child. All these were still there, but spiritually, in every way that really mattered, the street of ten minutes before was gone. The queer thing was that there was nobody to be seen, except the young soldier who had taken guard on the church steps with his rifle, and he now, instead of standing sturdily there, his dark, rather sallow face looking sternly in front of him, was lying flat on the step, one leg bent under him in a very unreal fashion. It was this figure that had in one moment changed the street. He was dead, and even as she looked the door of the church very cautiously opened. Two young soldiers came out, looked swiftly about them, and then dragged the fallen body into the church with them.

Then people *did* die! They were shot right in front of you in a perfectly ordinary street, in the middle of an ordinary shopping morning. She turned back, looked at the room, and saw that Mr. Browne and Mrs. Furness were gone—she was alone.

What about Hamish? She hated him. She was divorcing him. She would, in all probability, never see him again after to-morrow, save for one or two horrid little meetings at the lawyers'. And yet most certainly she did not wish him to be shot. For a moment the thought came to her that he had deserted her, seeing how difficult things were going to be, and then almost as swiftly as the thought was the certain knowledge that whatever she did, even though they were going to be divorced within a week or two, he would never leave her in a hole, or indeed anyone for whom he had the slightest responsibility. And at that she would have begun to feel proud of him again as she had used to do were it not that there he was, standing in the doorway, carrying a small paper parcel.

'Oh! you've come back, have you?' she said angrily. It was the strangest thing, that the sight of him, thick and stubborn and obstinate, roused all her animosity again. The sight of the pale, hair-cropped back of his neck exasperated her still more. If he had not insisted on that haircut they might, by this time, be out of this horrible town.

'Of course I've come back,' he said quickly. 'We've got to get out of this. They are fighting near the post office and there are several churches on fire. The thing for us to do is to get to the Consulate as quickly as possible.'

'Aren't you being rather melodramatic?' she said haughtily.

'No, I'm not. I'm exaggerating nothing. It's a revolution, my dear, and not only here, but all over Spain.'

She looked at him as though she detested him. He irritated her so intensely, behaving as though he still owned her after all that had happened.

'Well,' she said slowly, 'if you are frightened, that's no reason why I should be. You can go to your Consulate.'

He made a movement as though he would. When he was very angry all colour left his brown cheeks and his black eyes turned darker. She had thought, in the old days when she loved him, that this was really some kind of proof of personal immortality, because it was exactly like a lamp going out, the lamp of his personality. His soul had withdrawn because it was so deeply hurt that it was indecent to look at it. He made a half-movement as if to go, but he did not.

'You can say what you like,' he answered; 'there's real danger and I've got to look after you.'

Then she lost her temper altogether. 'You haven't got to look after me. You haven't, you haven't! That's why the trouble always came, you're so damned bossy. You think that I'm an infant still. I can look after myself perfectly.'

But she stopped because he was gone.

The room seemed most remarkably empty, and while she looked about it in a kind of bewildered fashion, she heard very clearly the pit-pat, pit-pat of a machine-gun. She looked out of the window again and saw that now, at one end of the street, a number of men were building up a kind of barricade. They had an upturned taxi there and some big pieces of wood, which looked as though they had been torn out of the streets. Their eyes seemed to be fastened on the little church. She went to the door of her room, opened it, and stepped out into the passage. There was not a sound anywhere and the deathlike stillness of the hotel frightened her more than anything else had done.

She looked down the long passage, which had so often resounded to the merry bustle and traffic of waiters and tourists and friends. There was no one there at all. A blind somewhere was tapping against the window. She had never felt so hopeless in her life. 'What ought I to do?' she thought, and then, in spite of her resolve to remain calm, she moved back a few steps hurriedly into her room, and instinctively shut the door because the pit-pat of the firing was suddenly much louder, right in the street below her window.

She stood there thinking, and, oddly, what she was thinking was not about herself, but about Hamish. What she wanted, she discovered, more clearly than anything else, was to prove that he had not deserted her, and her desire to prove that irritated her, because, after all, her life with him was finished, and whether he deserted her or not was of no matter. And yet it was of terrible importance to her that he did not desert her. It looked like it. There was the hotel, so silent, fighting in the street beyond the window, and herself quite alone in the world. Had she irritated him so profoundly that he had really decided never to think of her again? And at that thought there was an uneasy sensation of loss, and the silence of the hotel irritated her. There must be people about somewhere. She could not be the only person alive in the whole hotel. She would go and find someone. So down the passage she went, down the stairs, into the hall. Still there was no one within sight. She opened the side door beyond the dining-room and looked into the little street.

At the end, on her right, she saw the barricade, a lifeless, ugly thing, the upturned taxi, piles of wood, no human being. Nobody was in the street, and then, quite suddenly, as though someone had given a command, the church door opened, a man carrying a rifle ran out. He dashed down the steps, turned, and started down the street in the direction opposite the barricade. Instantly there was a sound of a machine-gun, although nobody was in sight. The man, who was a stout, thick fellow, gave a jump in the air and turned round. For a second of time Nancy saw his face quite close to her, staring at her, and it had on it an expression of extreme astonishment. She was surprised that she was able to photograph it on her brain so clearly. She would never forget it again, a broad, rather plump face, with black eyebrows. There was one stare of astonishment and then the whole body crumpled as though some inside support, an iron pole or something of the kind, had been taken away from it.

The body lay in the middle of the street, both arms spread out as though in crucifixion. She stared, horrified. She had an amazing revelation, because she saw that she loved Hamish with every part of her being and that if it had been he who was lying in that crumpled heap, her life would be over and ended. That was no sentimental exaggeration. She was not posing. She was not wishing for something she had not got. It was exactly as though she had been looking at a parcel and thinking that the paper wrapper was the important thing, as though she had said: 'I don't like the wrapper. It's a nasty, dirty colour. I won't have anything to do with it.' And then someone had torn the wrapper away and she had found inside a marvellous treasure. Something far better than anything she had ever hoped to possess. And that was Hamish. Their quarrel had been completely unreal, a host of little things, like flies, had obscured the window through which she looked into reality. Their life had been so easy, so conventionally pleasant, that trivialities had punished them by seeming important. She knew that she had been living a completely unreal life, and in this instant of revelation (because it was only an instant) she saw why it was that some men, after the war, although maimed and wounded, had told her that they had found something of value there. She understood now what they meant.

She looked at the dead man in the road in a kind of stupor, but her anxiety for Hamish was far greater than her consciousness of anything else. Her own death seemed nothing. That the whole of Barcelona should be blown up, that Spain should be reduced to a red ruin—none of that seemed to matter.

She ran back into the hotel, and inside the hall, close by the table where the porter ought to be, was Mrs. Furness, who at once gripped her arm.

'Oh, thank God, thank God!' she said over and over again. She was shaking from head to foot. She reminded Nancy of a cow she had once seen in a pen at a country market. The cow's eyes had been so bitterly terrified that Nancy had gone up to it and stroked it. She did not want to stroke Mrs. Furness. She did not mind how frightened she was. She wanted only one thing in the world—to know where Hamish might be. Mrs. Furness burst into tears. Her sobbing was almost a howl.

'They're shooting, everywhere, all round us. They'll be burning the hotel down. Where are we to go? What are we to do?'

'You had better come up to my room again.'

She dragged Mrs. Furness up the stairs. She felt that in

her room she might think more sanely, and also that it would be there that Hamish would come if he returned.

They had hardly reached her room, and closed the door, when there was an explosion so terrible that a looking-glass fell forward and crashed, a jug on the wash-stand lopsided over, and the horrible picture of a sacred bleeding heart, that had hung above the bed, slithered down the wall as though it were alive. Mrs. Furness fell on her knees and at an ordinary time would have been a figure for laughter as she waved her arms in the air as though she were swimming.

Nancy drew the blind aside again and looked through the window. She saw that some kind of a bomb had been thrown at the church, that the roof was beginning to blaze. A great fountain of smoke burst into the air as though it had been captured for years and was frantically happy at its release, and flames began to blaze about, raising their heads here and there, and then, emboldened by their success, growing larger and larger. The fierce light of the fire fought the fierce light of the day and filled Nancy's bedroom with an angry glare. There was a noise like huge sheets of paper being torn up by an angry man.

Mrs. Furness shrieked, 'There are men inside the church. Men, men, they'll be burnt.'

Nancy thought, 'Hamish is in the town somewhere. Perhaps he is dead.'

She turned back to Mrs. Furness, speaking very quietly. 'Get up and sit on the bed. Nobody's going to touch you. If I were you, I'd go quietly out of the hotel, walk down the main street, and find your way to the British Consulate. Nobody's going to harm you. Anyway, you'd better not stay in the hotel. If they throw another of those things, it won't be pleasant. As it is, the fire's only the other side of the street. I've got to find my husband.'

Two thoughts ran concurrently in her mind. Someone inside herself said to her: 'Whatever happens, whether you find him or not, you must never forget this moment of experience. If you do find him, and everything goes well again, and you pass once more into ordinary life, say to yourself often, "It's very easy to live a life of entire unreality. It's very easy for all your values to be wrong. Let no small things in your relationship with him ever disturb you again. Remember the burning church and the man lying in the road. And if you do not find him, if you never see him again, remember you lost him because you were so foolish as to let little things matter—a haircut, for instance." '

With that voice, there was also her own voice, saying: 'Now you must be practical, quite definite. I must quietly think out what is the best way to find him.'

The best way obviously was to go to the British Consulate. He might very possibly be there, trying for some way of helping her, or he might even have been there and they could tell her something about him. She was so calm that she patted Mrs. Furness on the shoulder and said to her:

'Now come with me. We're quite all right. Nobody's going to touch us.'

They went through the hotel and still there was nobody to be seen. They could hear a dog howling somewhere, and all the time there was that constant, angry whispering sound as of someone tearing paper, and the smell of burning, which seemed now to penetrate everything. They reached the street and saw a number of people running towards them—women screaming and waving their arms. They stood quite quietly on the pavement, watching the people run by. No one paid them the least attention.

'I don't know exactly where the Consulate is,' Nancy said. 'I haven't even got its address.'

Mrs. Furness said nothing, but stood breathing quickly, her mouth a little open, and in her eyes that idiotic stare, as though she were seeing nothing. All she said was, with a little shiver, 'How horrid everything smells.'

Nancy herself was bewildered. The world was on fire and she turned round a corner of the hotel, into the little street which now was wildly illuminated with the burning church. The flames were roaring to heaven, but there was no other sound, no rifle fire, no sign of anybody. Yes, there was someone. She moved forward into the middle of the street, regardless of any possible risk, because there, lying flat on his face, his legs spread out, quite obviously dead, was Hamish. She stood transfixed where she was, a roaring in her ears beyond the shout of the flames. It was Hamish, his thick, broad body, his strong legs, his jet-black hair, his thin silk coat. She had seen him lie exactly like that when, waking early, she had turned and found him with his head in the pillow, his arms bent under his face—and as she looked, she knew that she was on the edge of absolute madness. It would take something as slight as the blowing of a straw to make her go dancing and singing up the street, waving her arms and shrieking, not caring for anything in the world. She drew a little nearer. She bent down, and with that movement was already swinging over into insanity, because she planned to pick him up in her arms and sit there in the street, with the church burning above her, crooning to him, wiping the dust off his face, just sitting there with him in her arms until eternity.

She stared at him, at his broad shoulders, his stiff legs, the neat brown shoes, and then she saw that the back of his neck was covered with black hair, thick, low down, curling a little over his blue soft collar. The man lying there had not had a haircut for weeks.

She got up and walked slowly back to Mrs. Furness. Standing beside Mrs. Furness, supporting her with a stout hand, was Hamish.

'You didn't really think I'd left you, did you?' he said sarcastically. 'I've been waiting in the hall at the hotel. I knew you would come down, and then when you went out, I followed you.'

She kept her dignity. All she said was: 'I'm sorry. I've been a perfect fool.'

'That's all right,' he said quickly. 'As a matter of fact, I was going to tell you that I was the fool, in our room just now, but you wouldn't let me. I've got a car at the back of the hotel.'

They got into it with surprising ease. Nobody was there. There was shouting in the distance, the sky was lit up in places as though by an unsteady searchlight, the reflection of fires. Otherwise they might be in a sleeping world. They drove off.

Mrs. Furness began to sob hysterically. 'You must excuse me,' she said, her big bosom heaving, 'but I don't know quite what I'm saying.' She looked at Hamish. 'You've had a haircut,' she said idiotically.

He took one hand from the wheel and patted Nancy's cheek with it. 'Yes,' he said, smiling; 'but it was yesterday, a long time ago.'

LET THE BORES TREMBLE

I The Adventure of Mrs. Farbman

II The Garrulous Diplomatist

III The Adventure of the Imaginative Child

IV The Happy Optimist

V The Adventure of the Beautiful Things

VI The Man Who Lost His Identity

VII The Dyspeptic Critic

I

THE ADVENTURE OF MRS. FARBMAN

IT WOULD BE quite impossible at this later date to say with any accuracy whose idea it really was. I suspect that the credit is Chippet's, he being the romantic one of the three and the man of ideas. *I* (the professional writer) ought to have been the man of ideas, but I was suffering just at that time, I remember, from a surfeit of realism; romance seemed to me something dead and gone and long abandoned. Chippet, of course, maintained exactly the opposite of this. I can see him now with his blue eyes, his fair hair, his trustful, pleading expression, urging upon us that the London of these up-and-down after-the-war years was the most romantic place in the world. 'Stevenson's London,' he said, 'was nothing to it, and you remember how, when he brought out the *New Arabian Nights*, everyone was amazed that he could find so much colour and excitement in this drab, dull, smoke-haunted underground-driven town.'

'I don't remember,' I answered rather stiffly. 'I don't know what age you take me for, Bubbles, but I may remark that I was in my cradle when the *New Arabian Nights* was published.'

'Well, anyway,' said Chippet, 'never mind that. The point is that London has never been so romantic, so absurd, and so full of excitement as it is at this particular moment.'

It was, I believe, this very conversation that gave Chippet his idea.

We were having lunch in Borden's rooms, and we were all rather alarmed—alarmed because we were running very low in funds and saw no means of increasing them. Chippet had just retired from the diplomatic service, Borden was supposed to be a sporting journalist, but the sporting paper which had been his principal ally had just died from want of encouragement; I was a serious realistic novelist—I need, therefore, say no more as to the reasons of my penury.

Something must be done and that soon. Chippet thought it would be very jolly if we could only all go into something together. We were great friends, understood one another thoroughly, and the gifts that we enjoyed were opposite enough to make us very useful allies. It was just then, I believe, that Chippet had his great idea.

'Why shouldn't we . . .'

We all laughed.

'Oh, but that . . .' we cried.

'No, but really . . .' he answered. 'I don't see . . .'

'Come now,' we answered, 'they won't . . .'

'I believe that they will . . .' he replied.

The idea seemed certainly less fantastic when we examined it more closely. It was also a New Idea. It had most decidedly never been tried before.

'The first thing to do,' said Chippet, now immensely excited, 'is to circularise the right people. Very careful we have to be. Let's draw up a list of names.'

In this matter of circularising we were certainly fortunate, because between us we covered a lot of ground. Chippet was aristocratic, being a cousin of the Beaminsters. Borden's uncle had one of the best stables in Great Britain, and had won the Grand National. Borden's younger brother was stand-off half for Cambridge, and had every chance of gaining his International cap next season, now that Kershaw and Davies were confessing themselves too old for the game. And I? Well, I was a friend of Hallard's, and had contributed on two occasions to his high-brow 'monthly.' I was a member of the Garrick and Beefsteak Clubs, and Peter Westcott was quite a friend of mine. I stood, in fact, for Upper Bohemia. There were, indeed, very few sides of London life that the one or other of us did not touch. Our circular letter had every chance of making a true sensation. This letter was our joint effort. To this very day I pride myself on its admirable strategy and aplomb.

It ran as follows:

PRIVATE AND PERSONAL

DEAR SIR (OR MADAM),

We must apologise for disturbing you and for taking up your valuable time in this very unwarranted manner. You may be assured that we would not do so were it not for the fact that we believe that we have a suggestion of real interest to make to you. It is admittedly difficult, in these times of progress and over-sophistication, to discover some need of human beings hitherto unsatisfied. From coconuts to boot-trees everything can to-day, when transit is so rapid and trade so often dishonest, be supplied. We flatter ourselves, however, that we have discovered one almost universal need that has hitherto most curiously escaped the attention of the benefactors of the human race. Sir (or Madam), have you not in your immediate household or in your surrounding circle of friends and acquaintances a Bore? . . . We admit that the question is abrupt and startling, and that is why we have placed after it in the most modern and realistic manner those suspensive dots. It is, however, meant to startle; it is intended to shake you abruptly from the lethargy of habit and the indifference of custom. We will not define to you more nearly what precisely is intended by the term 'bore.' We do not do so because in the first place time is precious, and in these days paper expensive, and for the second more excellent reason that what is a Bore to One is not a Bore to Another. We are in this case addressing you personally and individually. We ask you to look round and, considering your household, decide whether there is not one person, man, woman, or child, whom you would like to see removed from your immediate vicinity. Perhaps there is no one; in which case we offer you our most hearty congratulations, and beg you to read no further in this letter, which is not for you. If, on the other hand, and human nature being what it is, in the more likely case there is such a one, we do beg you to apply to us and to see whether we cannot do something for you whether in improvement or modification or even in the total disappearance of your personal and individual Bore.

We need not say that all transactions with our firm will be dealt with in the most private and confidential manner, that in our manner of procedure we work by tact, kindness, and diplomacy, and, of course, in no case whatever offer personal violence, and that we are in every instance on the side of the law of our country. Will you not give us a trial? All that is needed on your side is a visit to our office between the hours of ten and five. All consultations are free of charge. May not this suggestion be the very thing for which through many months you have wearily been searching? Why not give us a trial? At least pay us a visit and see whether you like us.

We are,

Yours obediently,

BONIFACE AND CO.

I need not say that we were none of us busy men, and that we had never before written a letter of this kind. That, I think, was all to the good; the letter had undoubtedly a freshness and originality that business letters for the most part lack.

There was much discussion among us before the documents were finally dispatched. For one thing, it needed much argument and some sharp raising of voices before we finally decided on the name of our firm. 'Boniface' was my suggestion, and I flatter myself that it was a good one.

Borden, although a thoroughly fine fellow, was always a trouble in argument; he had all the Englishman's total lack of imagination, and was inclined to repeat any idea that he had over and over again, refusing obstinately to see any point of view but his own.

We had, too, a very warm time over the question of the 'suspensive dots.' Borden contended that that was a ridiculous sentence to insert in a business letter, that such a thing had never been in a business letter before, and that it would put any reasonable fellow 'right off us.' I on my side maintained that it was precisely because it had never been in a business letter before that I had inserted it, that what we wanted was to be unusual and original, and to make people realise that we *were* different.

'They'll realise that soon enough,' said Borden, grinning.

Very painful are those first weeks after your business is started, when you sit in your office waiting, waiting, waiting, and nobody comes.

We had two rooms in Conduit Street for our offices, and very effective they were, with grey wallpapers and a dark red carpet, but a grey paper and a Japanese print are small consolations for an overdrawn banking account and two shabby suits of clothes.

It was, I think, on the fourth or fifth day, when Chippet and I were sitting opposite one another in a very gloomy state of mind indeed, that the bell rang and the diminutive boy, by name Thomas, whom we had engaged at a high salary, introduced into our room a lady.

Trained as I was in human psychology, I saw at once that she was foolish, helpless and pretty. Here she was well over thirty, and there she was considerably under it, but she was dressed charmingly, and had an appealing, nervous smile that went, as I could see, straight to Chippet's uncritical heart. We begged her to sit down, both smiled at her, and then asked her if we could do anything for her. She hesitated a little, and then said: 'I received two days ago your letter, and I have come here to see whether you could possibly help me in my great trouble.'

Chippet was so deeply excited at the actual occurrence of a real live client that I could see he was ready to promise anything, so I, being older and more experienced, looking at her gravely and before Chippet could speak, made her a little speech.

'Madam,' I said, 'if you will let us know the nature of your trouble, we will do our best to serve you. Experience has taught us that it is wiser to make no promises until we know exactly what we are asked to perform. You can be sure of two things—first, that we will do our best for you, and, secondly, that anything you say to us will be treated in the very strictest confidence.'

I was myself considerably impressed by this speech. I was disappointed to observe that she looked, nevertheless, at Chippet, and it was to him that she made her appeal.

'I've never had,' she said, 'a letter like yours before. There were certain things in it I didn't quite understand. I am, perhaps, taking a very wrong step in coming to you without my husband's knowledge, but what am I to do? I am desperate—really desperate. Eighteen months of torture have brought me to this, or, rather, I should say "to you." '

Chippet leaned toward her, smiling. 'Perhaps, madam,' he said, 'if you could explain to us a little . . .'

'I will explain,' she said, nervously rubbing her hands together. 'What I am going to tell you I have never uttered to any human being before, and I do hope, gentlemen, that you will understand that I love my husband, and am only acting for his benefit, and am, indeed, thinking only of him.'

I could see, of course, that this was untrue, but it apparently impressed Chippet very deeply. The lady had the face of a pretty little pig, a very tiny nose, plump cheeks, large blue eyes, and an indeterminate chin. 'My name,' she said, 'is Mrs. Fleming—Mrs. Lestock Fleming. Perhaps you have heard of my husband?'

I saw that Chippet was about to say that he had, but, as

our policy was to be from the first an honest and open one, I interrupted him again and said: 'I'm afraid we haven't heard of your husband. Would you kindly tell us anything you can that will help us to understand your position?'

She opened her large blue eyes with an air of pretty surprise, and said: 'Why, I thought everybody had heard of my husband. He is one of the greatest living authorities on pond life, and has written several books which have been very much praised. He gives lectures on pond life up and down the country, and it is really because of the lectures that my troubles began.'

'Because you mean,' said Chippet, 'that you were not always able to accompany him on his lecture tours?'

'Why, no,' said Mrs. Fleming. 'We have children, and my place, of course, is in my home. Devoted though we are, we have spent a considerable amount of time away from one another, and that I am sorry to say has afforded an opportunity for someone else to gain a control over my husband that he deplores just as deeply as I do myself.'

'Please explain,' said Chippet. 'If he deplores it, I should have thought it the easiest thing in the world——'

'Oh, you don't know my husband!' Mrs. Fleming broke in. 'He is one of the kindest men in the whole world, as *she* very well knows.' She uttered the pronoun 'she' with such vehemence that I jumped in my chair; her eyes flashed, her little hands were clenched together, and I could not help wondering how it was that, with such an energy of detestation ruling her breast, she had needed to come to us for any assistance.

'Tell us,' said Chippet gently, 'who "she" is.'

'Oh, how kind you are!' said Mrs. Fleming, tears filling her eyes. 'I feel better already—I feel that I can say anything to you.'

'You can,' said Chippet, 'you can indeed.'

'About two years ago,' continued Mrs. Fleming, 'in Newcastle, after a lecture that my husband had given on "Newts and their Home Life," a lady came up and spoke to him and showed such evident interest in all that he said that he could not but be pleased and flattered. He wrote to me about her, and I, too, was delighted that he should have found some real appreciation. I assure you, gentlemen, that I have not a spark of jealousy in my nature, and when he returned home, and showed me her photograph, I saw indeed that I had no reason for jealousy. At first I was immensely pleased at this new friendship. My husband showed me all the letters from this lady—whose name was Mrs. Farbman—and they were letters entirely concerned with natural history and kindred subjects. The trouble really began just a year and a half ago, when Mrs. Farbman came to live in London. We were living then at Golders Green, and very soon she also came to live there. I won't disguise from you that the first time I met her I disliked her intensely, and I could not help feeling that even at that time my husband was beginning to find her rather tiresome; but he is so gentle a man, so kindly and considerate, that she soon exercised over him a most terrible control. To cut a long story short, for the last year it is almost literally true that, except for the night-time, she has not been out of our house. He has been engaged during the last eight months on a very important work on tadpoles and their development, and unfortunately my occupation in my household affairs and the children, and Mrs. Farbman's knowledge of shorthand, have given her an opportunity for being continually in his company.'

'Is she in love with him?' Chippet interrupted. 'Would you mind describing her to us?'

'She is a tall woman,' said Mrs. Fleming, 'rather like a man in woman's clothes. She must be well over forty, although she told us the other day that she had just celebrated her thirty-first birthday, and looked as though she expected us to give her a present, which I believe my husband would have done if I had not been there to stop it. She is a very dominating person, and, to speak quite frankly, our whole house is in terror of her. She comes to almost all our meals, and, of course, we are not very wealthy, and she eats with a very good appetite. She has driven many of our best friends out of the house because she talks a great deal, and generally on subjects that are not interesting to our friends. She professes to adore my husband, and think him the most marvellous of human beings, but she never allows him to have an opinion of his own, and he is now so terrified of her that last week he took to his bed for three days to escape her; but that was of no use, because she sat in the little dressing-room adjoining with the door open, and shouted to him the whole of the morning.'

Tears filled Mrs. Fleming's eyes as she got deeper into her story; one tear even rolled down her cheek, and I could see Chippet was very deeply touched.

'Well, Mrs. Fleming,' I said, 'you surely don't mean to tell us that you and your husband together are unable to get rid of this woman?'

'I do indeed,' she answered, 'and not only I, but my sister and a cousin of my husband's who lives close to us, and two or three of our best friends have done all that we can, and have had no effect at all. The trouble is, you see, that my husband has not himself the courage to get rid of her. She has a temper, and at the same time has made him feel as though he hadn't now an opinion of his own. He thinks that if she left him, all his work would stop, and that he gets a great deal of his inspiration from her. That is, of course, quite untrue. He wrote and worked much better before he knew her. He is simply hypnotised, gentlemen, and it is this hypnotism which I have come to you to beg you to remove.'

'Hypnotism!' said Chippet. 'Do you mean literally? Does she really hypnotise him?'

'No, I don't mean,' she said, 'literally that she hypnotises him, although I am sure that she does a lot of queer things that I don't understand, but he is a man very easily impressed. He is so modest, and he always believes that everybody knows better than himself, and Mrs. Farbman is clever. However much one detests her, one can't deny that.'

'In short,' said Chippet, wearing a look of grave importance, 'what you want us to do is to remove Mrs. Farbman with the greatest kindness, but in such a way that she will never return again.'

'I don't mind about the kindness,' said Mrs. Fleming, looking at us very innocently. 'I won't hide from you that a little suffering, physical or otherwise, would do her no sort of harm, but of course,' she hurriedly added, 'there must be no question of our involving ourselves with the law in any way.'

I saw very clearly that now that Mrs. Fleming had surmounted the initial difficulty of speaking to complete strangers on this rather piratical subject, she was enjoying herself immensely, and was looking forward to seeing Mrs. Farbman tortured with red pincers by several long-tailed devils in a miniature Hades. Of such are even the mildest and most gentle women when another woman has interfered with their personal liberty.

'Of course,' she went on, 'I would hate to be cruel to anyone—I even step over a beetle if I see one on the floor—but I have suffered from Mrs. Farbman for a very long time now, and if you gentlemen can really succeed in helping her to new interests in life, I shall be grateful to you all my days.'

Inexperienced though we were in business, we were both of us already aware that when a client begins to talk fluently of gratitude, it means that there will be less fluency when the hour for the commercial side of the bargain arrives, so I said very gravely: 'We will do our very best for you, Mrs. Fleming, but you must understand that we cannot absolutely pledge ourselves to success. Our terms are that you pay us one hundred pounds if our endeavours succeed, and fifty pounds in any case, succeed or fail. We cannot, naturally, pledge our word that Mrs. Farbman will never return to you again. We can only promise you that we will not claim success until she has been removed from you for three months. An occasional visit during those three months does not count against us. The way we would put it would be that, after watching the case for three months, we must all be definitely of the opinion that Mrs. Farbman's attentions have been removed elsewhere, and we shall settle this question by asking Mrs. Farbman herself whether this is so. Are these terms satisfactory to you?'

'One hundred pounds is a great deal of money,' said Mrs. Fleming, her beautiful eyes filling with tears.

I saw that Chippet would probably be touched if I left them alone. It is both fortunate and unfortunate to have in such a firm as ours a prominent official dangerously susceptible to feminine charm, so I said very sternly indeed: 'Those are our terms, Mrs. Fleming. Take them or leave them, as you please.' But, as I had foreseen, once the picture of Mrs. Farbman, unhappy and isolated, had penetrated Mrs. Fleming's imagination, she was caught and held.

'I agree,' she said. 'But please, gentlemen, be as quick as you can in helping us. I feel that if I have to suffer as I have done during these last months, I shall poison Mrs. Farbman with powdered glass or hyoscin or strangle her in her sleep.'

'What!' interrupted Chippet, greatly interested. 'Does she actually sleep in your house?'

'On several occasions,' said Mrs. Fleming, her little cheeks flushed with anger, 'she has insisted on sleeping in our spare room, in case she should have some ideas for my husband's book in the middle of the night.'

'I don't see,' said Chippet, 'why she shouldn't have those ideas in her own house as well as yours.'

'She says,' said Mrs. Fleming, 'that it's all a matter of atmosphere. Everything is atmosphere, according to her. There is, for instance, all the difference in the world between the thoughts that you have in a hot bath and in a cold one, and what you feel like after breakfast and what you feel like before tea.'

'There's nothing very original about that,' said Chippet.

'In my opinion,' said Mrs. Fleming, 'there's nothing very original about Mrs. Farbman anywhere, but you shall see for yourself.'

On the very next evening Chippet and I had our first meal in the house of the Flemings. Because I am a realistic novelist, there is nothing, I suppose, in this modern world of ours that can possibly surprise me. The Flemings' house, Mr. Fleming, the numerous little Flemings, and the great Mrs. Farbman herself, were all exactly as I had expected them. Golders Green is not itself depressing, but the Flemings' house was terrible. It was one of those houses in which the kitchen is in the middle of the drawing-room, and dusty palms in large glazed pots stand cheek by jowl with onions frying in the pan and water sizzling in the copper for the children's weekly bath. It was one of those houses in which every sound made by anybody within a five-mile radius is heard ten times intensified wherever you may happen to be. It is also one of those houses in which the boards creak, the windows rattle, soot falls down the chimney, the cat fights the dog, the babies fight one another, and the cook gives notice, all in your immediate proximity. I was very sorry indeed for Mr. Fleming, who was a very, very long, thin man with a forehead so high and a chin so receding that you felt that the only way to give his face any real help was to push it all down a little and then to hold it in position with iron bands for a year or two; but he had nice, mild eyes, a straggling and desolate moustache, and an anxious, deprecating air that so often goes with absent-minded genius.

Mrs. Farbman, of course, was exactly what I expected her to be—one of those men in women's clothing, as flat as a board, with that contemptuous curl of the lip that belongs almost invariably to masculine women when they are in the presence of the inferior sex.

She took up a great deal of room in that small house. The masculine jacket that she wore had its pockets full of papers. She was always producing a fountain pen from the centre of her masculine bosom and taking innumerable little notes in little pocket-books, writing them down with an air of finality as though it were the day of the last judgment and she was settling the destinies of all the poor human beings who were waiting in frightened, huddled masses at her large, uncomely feet. It was quite natural that Chippet and I disliked her at sight. It was equally natural that she disliked and despised us. Mrs. Fleming introduced us as two young men who had been immensely attracted by what they knew of her husband's genius and had come thirsting for more information. Mr. Fleming was as touched as a child by my eager enquiries about newts and their habits, and one or two remarks that Chippet made about snails and their different geographical varieties brought tears of pleasure into his eyes; but I realised that Mrs. Farbman detected us at once for the humbugs that we were. I realised also, during that first meal, which consisted very strangely of scrambled eggs, cheese-cakes and meringues, both that Mrs. Fleming was not a good housekeeper, and that this business of ours, into which we had entered with so light a heart, was going to be no easy one. Halfway through dinner, supper, or breakfast, whichever you like to call it, there was a sharp little contest between Chippet and Mrs. Farbman. Mrs. Farbman had a terrible habit of leaning her bare and bony elbows on the table, supporting a face which exactly resembled that of an intelligent and over-educated horse upon them, and staring at the speaker of the moment with a penetrating glance of contemptuous scorn. She was so staring at Chippet, who was trying to explain to Mr. Fleming that when he was a small boy he had kept snails in a cigar-box and harnessed them to match-boxes, and made them run races with one another, which, he went on, he would never have done had he only known, as he knew now, what interesting creatures they were.

'Humbug!' said Mrs. Farbman suddenly.

'I beg your pardon?' said Chippet nervously.

'What you're saying about snails,' said Mrs. Farbman, 'is humbug. You never cared in the least about snails, and you don't care about them now.'

'Excuse me,' said Chippet, flushing angrily. 'Allow me to have my own opinion about the things I care for and the things I don't.'

'Oh, you can have your own opinion,' said Mrs. Farbman, 'but I wasn't born yesterday, you know,' which, indeed, was the truest thing she ever said.

I saw at once that these were the worst possible tactics for us to adopt. I tried to kick Chippet under the table, but most unfortunately kicked Mrs. Farbman instead. She turned her attention to me, and I did my best to be as charming as I knew how, but really the woman was intolerable. She assumed complete command of the house, and when one of the children was heard crying in the next room, and Mrs. Fleming rose to go to her, Mrs. Farbman said: 'Sit down, Flora, sit down; don't make a fool of yourself.' When a very untidy maidservant brought in the meringues, Mrs. Farbman, glaring at her, said: 'What was that noise that I heard in the kitchen just now?'

'Nothing,' said the maid, tossing her head.

'It was the loudest nothing I've ever heard,' said Mrs. Farbman. 'That china shall be deducted from your wages.'

She ruled, in fact, the house with a rod of iron.

Now, this is the really interesting feature of this our first adventure. You will certainly say that Mrs. Farbman, as I have described her to you, is a good deal of a caricature, and to that I would reply that more people are caricatures than you probably know, and that many people are caricatures at first sight and cease to be so when we know them a little better. Now, this, I repeat, is the curious and interesting thing—that before the end of our meal I was beginning to be quite fond of Mrs. Farbman. I cannot explain this except by saying that, as I am a modern novelist, the most extravagant types have an interest for me, but, apart from this professional tenderness, there was something about Mrs. Farbman that was lonely, touching, and pathetic. With that swift perception of human nature that is one of the finest gifts I possess, I saw that she was a lonely, unloved woman, whose rudeness and masculinity were largely a covering for a longing for affection and some sort of commendation of her talents and erudition.

Mr. Fleming was, in all probability, the only human being in all her life who had appreciated her brain and industry, and it was for that appreciation that she clung to him more than for anything else.

After dinner we sat in the small, stuffy sitting-room that smelled of mixed biscuits and stale Eau-de-Cologne, and Mrs. Farbman held forth at interminable length on the connection between psycho-analysis and the suffragette movement. She had a great deal to say, and she said it vigorously, and I saw at once that she was longing for our appreciation, as eager for it, indeed, as a small girl who is reciting for the first time her school piece before a crowd of indifferent relations. That was a picture that I shall never forget—the close, ill-smelling room, overcrowded with marine pictures, china ornaments, bamboo bookcases, albums of family photographs, ferns and human beings, with Mr. Fleming's long body stretching right across the floor, his eyes closed and sunk deep into his forehead, his bony hands clasped together on his lap, Mrs. Fleming angry, watching Mrs. Farbman with indignant eyes, Chippet distressed already by the certainty that we were going to fail in this our very first case, and Mrs. Farbman, seated like a man, leaning forward, her elbows on her knees, staring into space, her voice rolling on and on, and words like 'Freud,' 'Jung,' 'Inhibition,' 'Mrs. Pankhurst,' and 'Bolshevism' spattering the floor with such vigour and energy that it seemed as though they must leave permanent marks on the faded carpet.

Yes, I liked her better and better as the evening proceeded.

I remember once, at the zoo, seeing a large monkey in the corner of its cage, chattering, making fantastic gestures, scratching itself in impossible places, doing everything it could to attract the attention of a group of bored and superior monkeys who were half asleep in another corner, and in the eyes of that large monkey there was a look of the most desperate loneliness I have ever witnessed in animal or man. Such loneliness was there in the eyes of Mrs. Farbman. More touching still was it that she herself was unaware of this, and would have been certainly most indignant had you told her of it. As she talked I saw in her all those long desolate years, that eagerness for wisdom, and longing for the possession of some human being who would care for her and her alone, that consciousness that must have come to her in spite of herself of her ugliness and oddness, that desperate sense that even this man Fleming, whom she had succeeded in attaching for a brief period, might at any moment slip from her. All these things I saw, and you may believe me or no, as you please, but before that first evening was over I felt, as I considered the project that had brought Chippet and myself to that house, something very little short of a murderer.

A murderer! Yes, that's all very well, but we had our business to consider, and at the end of the first fortnight we were bound to confess that we were dangerously near to defeat. Other things were happening at this time, other clients were coming to us—of whom I may speak on another occasion—and Borden was conducting one of these with every prospect of success, but this affair of the Flemings was for Chippet and me, our ewe lamb, our first-born, our precious pet. Chippet was nearly in tears whenever he thought of it. Mrs. Fleming was becoming frankly impatient, and I could see that if we failed there would be great trouble in extracting from her the promised fifty pounds. She had begun by thinking us perfectly delightful; there was every prospect of her ending by thinking us contemptible fools. We spent a great deal of our time under the Fleming roof. Those rooms had already overflowed before our arrival, and it was not, in very truth, vastly diverting to spend hours of the day and the best part of many an evening in a small, stuffy villa in Golders Green, stepping, so to speak, from infant to infant, and eating meals of so horrible and unnatural a kind that Chippet's hitherto admirable digestion was in danger of being permanently ruined, and I myself turned quite green at the thought of scrambled eggs, a dish in which I had hitherto delighted. But the main trouble was this increasing affection of mine for Mrs. Farbman. It baffled Chippet completely. At first he supposed that I was being diplomatic and seeking to gain an influence over her. Then when he discovered that I was winning no influence at all, and that I really seemed to like to be in her society, and when he caught me on one occasion looking into her dim and grey-green eyes as I might have looked at the face of my favourite dog, he was puzzled and finally indignant.

'Good Heavens, Seymour,' he said, 'you don't mean to tell me that you like the woman!'

'I do like her.'

'But she hates you. She hates you even worse than she hates me. She's a terrible woman!' And his voice rose into a shrill scream, as it often did when he was excited.

'I don't know that she hates me,' I answered, curiously hurt at his accusation. 'I think she's rather beginning to like me.'

'Oh, no, she isn't,' said Chippet. 'I overheard her saying last night to Mrs. Fleming that she would be very glad to know how much longer those two imbecile friends of hers were coming to the house; and Mrs. Fleming said that she thought that she would like to have a clever novelist to talk to, and I won't tell you,' continued Chippet, smiling maliciously, 'what exactly it was that Mrs. Farbman then said about you as a novelist.'

'Oh, don't mind me!' I said hurriedly, pretending not to care.

'Oh, no, I don't,' said Chippet, 'only I will tell you this—that time's passing, and if you're going to waste these precious hours by attempting to win Mrs. Farbman's bony heart, you are not playing the game, and we may as well dissolve partnership.'

I could not deny that Chippet was right. Business was business, and however attractive I found Mrs. Farbman, something must be done to further our plans. And yet how strange and even, in an obscure way, romantic those hours in her company were! I have never known so truly stupid a woman as Mrs. Farbman was, nor have I ever known any woman capable of such a flood of apparently clever conversation that was finally quite meaningless. It was with this meaningless flood that she surrounded and overwhelmed poor Mr. Fleming. He may have been once, in the days before the arrival of Mrs. Farbman, aware of the ultimate purpose and purport of his book, but she had by now so fluently confused him, she so persistently led him off the straight track the moment that she perceived him to be upon it, she flung at his enormous, but, I cannot help thinking, rather empty forehead such incessant little pellets of disconnected information, that the poor man just crumpled up and moved in a kind of stupor from phrase to phrase, seeing his newts, his tadpoles, his snails, and whatever, all scuttling away from him—I am quite aware that newts and tadpoles cannot scuttle—into a vast misty distance whence he desperately began to realise that he would never recover them.

It was for this reason, I think, more than any other, that he would really have given his immortal soul to be rid of Mrs. Farbman; but you had only to look at him, to listen to his mild, amiable voice, to watch the timid way in which he scratched his fast thinning hair, to know that he would never of himself be able to escape this bondage.

At the end of the third week the crisis arrived. We came,

Chippet and I, one day to tea and found Mrs. Fleming alone. We could see plainly enough that she was in the very worst of tempers. 'Well,' she asked us, her blue eyes flashing, her little snub nose trembling with indignation, 'do you mind telling me how long this farce is to continue? I hope you will forgive me if I say exactly what I think.'

'That,' interrupted Chippet, smiling nervously, 'is what we want to hear. I know that so far we have not been a great success, but——'

'Thank you,' broke in Mrs. Fleming, 'I am grateful to you for admitting that much. No, you have not been a great success, and I hope your feelings won't be hurt if I tell you that I am not at all sure that you are not a pair of humbugs against whom one might very reasonably bring an action. Here have we been three weeks, and Mrs. Farbman is more securely in the house than ever before. You have done nothing,' she cried, 'to persuade her to leave us! You have had innumerable meals in my house, and although I am not one to begrudge my friends any hospitality we can afford, yet my husband and I are not wealthy or we would not be living in Golders Green. You have done nothing, nothing, nothing!' She then burst into tears.

'Give us another week, Mrs. Fleming,' said I, 'and if at the end of that time we are still unsuccessful, we will call the case off, and we will not ask you to pay us a penny.'

This mollified her somewhat.

'You must consider, Mrs. Fleming,' continued Chippet eagerly, 'that we have suggested a number of plans that you have refused to consider, such as Seymour here travelling with Mrs. Farbman in an airplane to Paris and leaving her there, or hiring a motor-car and going with Mrs. Farbman to the Lake District and losing her on one of the mountains, and there have been many other schemes of that kind which you have absolutely forbidden us to consider.'

'There,' she cried, in the middle of her tears, 'doesn't that show how incompetent you are? Haven't you seen already enough of Mrs. Farbman to know that no mountains and no Paris nor anywhere else would prevent her from returning? She will follow us wherever we go. I see myself within another six months a murderess in the dock at the Old Bailey, my husband dying of a broken heart, my children thrown upon the streets!'

A very trying scene, in sooth. Mrs. Fleming's tears were as bad as Mrs. Farbman's psycho-analysis, and, quite frankly, of the two women I infinitely preferred Mrs. Farbman.

That night Chippet and I were in despair. We suspected that we had, after all, no real talent for this particular business, and it intensely chagrined us both that our partner Borden—whom we had always rather despised as an over-muscled and brainless sportsman—should be bringing his first case, that remarkable one of the Twickenham footballer, to a really successful issue while we were failing.

Upon what little chance do the wheels of life turn! Had it not been for a curried egg I might at this moment be begging my bread in the streets of London, Chippet might never have become Sir Gordon Chippet, C.B.E.—our lives, in fact, might have ended in dismal and untimely failure.

On the following evening we were once more dining at the Flemings'. It was a melancholy meal; even Mrs. Farbman was rather silent, my heart was like lead. Sardines had been our first course—those especially greasy and enormous sardines that are like miniature whales, with huge spine-bones warranted to defeat the strongest teeth. Our second course was a dish of curried eggs, better cooked, I must honestly confess, than anything that we had yet eaten under the Fleming roof. I was sitting opposite Mrs. Farbman. The dish went its round, went round a second time. It was enough for me to have caught one glance, one gesture, one spark of a grey-green eye. That night, as we found our places in the Hampstead Tube, I clutched Chippet by the arm and murmured excitedly in his ear: 'I believe we are saved; I believe I have found a way out at last.'

'What do you mean?' he replied so loudly that a row of *Evening Standards* descended and a succession of astonished faces stared in our direction.

'Wait,' I answered. 'I must think this out to-night, but I believe the key is discovered.'

On the following afternoon I went to the Flemings' house and found Mrs. Farbman there alone. I came in without her hearing me, and caught her seated low down in a crazy rocking-chair, staring in front of her, the inevitable note-book on her lap, and in her eyes that same monkey-like absorption of loneliness that I had noticed before. I stood there for a moment watching her. I knew so well what she wanted, and yet I was taking away from her the closest semblance to that need that she had ever found. In all this, as you will have by now perceived, the Flemings themselves were very shadowy creatures to me. I have a scorn of human beings who are unable themselves to remove burdens for which they themselves are responsible, and that scorn was going to make my work difficult for me in many ways. What would happen, I could not but ask myself, if it was in these cases to be always the bore who roused my sympathy instead of the sufferers from the bore? Well, if that were so, I should learn something more about my fellow-beings than I had known before, and that same learning is, I imagine, the chief aid to knowing something more about oneself, which, in its own turn, is the first purpose of life.

Well, to get on with my story. The first words that sprang from my lips—and they literally did spring, to my own intense surprise—were: 'Oh, Mrs. Farbman, I wish you liked me better—I do like you so much!'

This remark, when she had supposed that there was no one in the room besides herself, naturally made her jump. She turned round to me, notebook slipping on to the floor; then, when she saw who it was, she gave a kind of grunt of dissatisfaction and turned her back on me again. Then she said, speaking as it were to no one in particular: 'I don't like many people in this world, and young men like yourself and your friend are abhorrent to me.'

'Why?' I asked, coming forward.

'You are useless, conceited, and ignorant!'—finishing her words with a snap, as though they were final.

'You can't expect me to agree with that,' I answered. 'Chippet and I have a very decent opinion of ourselves.'

'What are you doing here?' she asked, suddenly turning round and looking at me. 'What are you here for at all? You don't like Mrs. Fleming, you laugh at her husband, and yet you come here every day. Why?'

'Maybe to see you, Mrs. Farbman.'

'Stuff!' she replied. 'You are neither of you intelligent enough to interest me, and unless I am interested I am not attractive. I am quite aware of that. Besides, it's been perfectly obvious that you have both disliked me intensely from the very beginning. Are you trying, for some purpose of your own, to get me out of this house?'

'Suppose I am,' I answered, 'is there any chance of my succeeding?'

'Yes,' she replied quickly, 'if you can offer me anything better. If you want to know the truth, I have been for many months now so bored here that I could scream. I'd leave Mr. Fleming to-morrow if I could fill my life some other way; but I simply can't face the loneliness and emptiness that would come after all my occupation here. Of course I've been cheating myself. I've been pretending to myself that Mr. Fleming's work is important—which it isn't in the least—and I've liked the sense of authority that I've found here. I like ordering about, but I know quite well that even Mr. Fleming will be delighted to see the last of me, and Mrs. Fleming, of course, will light such a bonfire of ecstasy when I'm gone that it will illumine the whole of Golders Green for miles around. But where am I to go? What am I to do? I've been calling myself for years a modern woman, and there's another side, you know, to the modern woman question that many people don't consider. We go in for men's work, men's lives, men's ways of thought, and then we have to cling on like drowning men to a raft, cling on to a boat that's overcrowded already, the occupants of which are always digging at us with boathooks to push us back into the sea again, and shouting with joy when we drop off and drown. There's room for a few of us, but not for many. Besides, as you have probably already observed, I am not really clever enough. I have got a muddled, feminine brain. I cover my ignorance of facts with lots of talk, and hope that people will be taken in. I can't expect at my time of life, and with my appearance, to take anyone in as thoroughly as I've taken Mr. Fleming, and even he isn't taken in any longer, as you see. If I lose my hold on this little boat, I drown altogether. At my time of life I must think no longer of love and marriage. Well, then, where am I?'

'I'll tell you where you are,' I answered. 'You're going to dine with me to-night at the Vin Blanc in Soho.'

At the word 'dine' she sat up and looked at me eagerly. 'The food here is awful, isn't it?'

'Yes,' I answered slowly, 'except for the curried eggs last night. But there are better things than curried eggs at the Vin Blanc. There is, for instance, *sole meunière* that is quite excellent, and they are better at whitebait than anyone in London.'

'Do they have nothing but fish?' she asked.

'Oh, yes,' I replied. 'Come and see!'

We looked at one another steadily for quite a long time.

'You're a clever young man,' she said. 'You're observant. You will get on. I will dine with you to-night.'

The next scene of this history was played out in the little white, low-ceilinged upstairs room of the Vin Blanc. A new actor was added to an already competent company. This was little Monsieur Pierre Duhamel (no relation, by the way, to the author of *Vie des Martyrs*), the proprietor of the

Vin Blanc. I have known Monsieur Duhamel through a considerable number of years. He was a cheery little soul, round and chubby, wearing always an immaculate white apron, a little black tufted beard on his chin. He had come from Paris ten years ago, had made his little Soho restaurant pay, but had never extended it, as he might have done, to something of a large and extravagant order that would have given him very quickly enough money on which to retire for the remainder of his days. He did not wish to retire. He made enough for his living; he was unmarried and preferred, as he explained to me, 'to enjoy his leisure hours.'

Now, he had always burning in his soul a curious passion, and that was to marry a truly intellectual woman. He was an immense admirer of the other sex, but always from the standpoint of brain rather than of body. Physical beauty meant nothing to him, or so little as not to matter, but a clever woman, or even a stupid woman who seemed to him clever, excited him to a frenzy of admiration and desire. What he liked best was to have as a habitual customer some member of the opposite sex who, while she discussed his *sole meunière* and his Chateaubriand steak with real human appreciation, was also able to give him a little philosophy, a few words about the advancement of women, and a hint or two as to Bergson. The unfortunate thing was, as he had so often confided to me, that intellectual women were so seldom interested in cooking, 'and, after all,' he explained to me, 'I have nothing to offer such a woman except a good meal, a kind heart, and an attentive manner.' On one occasion, I remember, I had brought into his restaurant the lady principal of a famous women's college. He had given her such a meal as I have seldom enjoyed anywhere. It was pathetic to see the way in which he hovered round her table, hoping that everything was perfectly delightful, and then venturing a word on Bergson's book on laughter, being crushed by her quite natural gasp of astonishment and air of nervousness and look at me for reassurance. 'What a droll little man!' she whispered to me. That was the fashion, alas, in which all learned women considered Monsieur Duhamel.

I will confess to you that on this evening I was immensely excited. What would come of my plan? It might so easily fail. If it failed, my last card was played. It did not fail. Monsieur Duhamel's first glance at Mrs. Farbman told him that here was an intellectual woman indeed. Mrs. Farbman's first glance at the *sole meunière* told her that this was a restaurant *sans peur et sans reproche*. I would not like to say that she was a greedy woman. I have never been able to understand why a really aesthetic appreciation of food should be held to count against anyone. I fancy that good food beautifully cooked was Mrs. Farbman's approach to the spirit of beauty, and it was an approach that had been throughout her hard and rather dreary life consistently denied to her. You could see from the way in which she ate her sole that she was not considering so much the perfection of the sole itself, but that it placed her in relation to all the beautiful things in life from which Mrs. Fleming's scrambled eggs had so long isolated her. As for Monsieur Duhamel, before the sole was finished, his face beaming with smiles, he had enquired as to whether Mrs. Farbman had yet mastered Einstein's 'Relativity.'

Of course Mrs. Farbman had not mastered it, being in that at least entirely at one with all her fellow human beings, but she had a great deal to say about it. A flood of words poured from her, words to myself quite meaningless and to herself nearly so, but sentences long and involved, containing capital letters and quite a number of proper names. Monsieur Duhamel's ecstasy was a thing to envy. 'But I see, madam,' he cried, 'that what you say is a profound truth. You have enlightened my mind. I cannot thank you sufficiently. If you knew what it was for one who is so persistently denied food for his mind by his inevitable pursuit of food for the body to meet someone as wise and brilliant as yourself. . . .'

I was soon forgotten by both of them, and when at last I pleaded an engagement, Monsieur Duhamel suggested to

Mrs. Farbman that she should drink a cup of coffee in his own little room just above the room where we were sitting. I left them together.

What more need I say? Simply this, that long before the three months were out Mrs. Fleming had delivered to us the cheque for one hundred pounds; that the Fleming household was a paradise such as I never could have imagined; and Mr. Fleming in spite of—or shall I say because of?—the departure of Mrs. Farbman, progressed with his book at double the speed of the earlier days; and that, finally, I was asked, on one beautiful summer day, to a wedding breakfast in the private room of the Vin Blanc, a breakfast that excelled both in the superb excellence of its cooking and in the vigour of intellectual conversation any meal that I had ever attended.

II

THE GARRULOUS DIPLOMATIST

On a beautiful afternoon in May, as I was walking down Piccadilly, just in the arcade of the Ritz Hotel I was touched on the arm, and, turning round, saw the highly polished countenance of Pom Banting uplifted toward me. 'Hullo, Pom,' I said, 'how goes it?'

'It goes very badly,' he answered. 'The Bankruptcy Court sees me next week and a pauper's grave the week after. Meanwhile, young Johnson, you're just the man I want to see. Are you out walking, or is your nurse waiting somewhere round the corner with the pram?'

'I'm allowed to take a little gentle exercise on condition I don't go too far and wear myself out. Meanwhile, that famous club, the Saucepan, is all agog with excitement because I'm about to lunch there, and the windows are hung with flags.'

'That being so,' said Pom, 'we will walk along together. I've something to tell you.'

'Tell on,' I said.

'Well,' Pom continued, 'is it truth or not that some months ago you and one or two other innocents scattered broadcast a letter, the import of which was that you would remove bores from the heart of Society at a moment's notice, demanding but a modest fee in return?'

'I don't know about the modest fee,' I answered. 'We've been such a success during the few months we have been at work that our fees have gone up.'

'The devil they have!' said Pom. 'What are they, anyway?'

'Seventy-five quid in any case,' I answered, 'and a hundred and fifty if we succeed.'

'Well, it might be worse,' said Pom. 'Several of us would be willing to give more than a hundred and fifty if you helped us in our present trouble.'

'Who's "us"?' I asked.

' "Us," ' said Pom, 'are me——'

'Good Heavens!' I interrupted. 'In what language do you imagine you're speaking at the present?'

'Oh, hang English!' said Pom. 'Well, anyway, there are Millie Drake, Huxter, Crawshay, and a lot of others in this, and we'll raise the coin all right if you'll do the job.'

'Well, what is the job?' I asked.

Pom dropped his voice into a mysterious and secretive whisper. 'Do you know old Marcus Pendyce?' he asked.

'What, Pendyce who was Minister at Constantinople and all sorts of other places years ago, who published his reminiscences last year, *People Who Have Seemed to Me Worth While?*'

'The very same,' said Pom.

'Yes. What about him?' I asked.

'Have you ever seen him?' Pom asked.

'No,' I answered.

'Then the Lambs must entertain you very seldom,' he replied.

The Lambs, I need scarcely mention, was that most famous and most exclusive of clubs, entering which was far harder than camels piercing the eye of the needle, whose wine is a miracle, whose history goes back almost to the days of Adam, Eve and the Serpent.

'I've been to lunch there a lot of times,' I answered, 'but I don't know old Pendyce by sight. Describe him to me.'

'Five chins, two stomachs, and a face like a beetroot,' said Pom. 'But the strangest thing about him is his voice, which is now deep like the rumbling of a gun, and suddenly shrill as a peahen in anger. He is the greatest bore that the world has ever seen.'

'Tell me more,' I asked. 'How old is he? Is he married?'

'He's well over seventy,' said Pom, 'and ought to be silently contemplating his latter end. He's a widower with no children. He's the greatest bore——'

'Yes,' I interrupted, 'you've said that already. What is it you want us to do?'

'Why, to remove him, of course!' cried Pom. 'Didn't your old letter say that you'd remove anybody so that they'd never come back again?'

'Do you mean to tell me,' I replied, 'that there are all you strong and healthy men, and you're unable to deal with one poor old one over seventy and a widower? Ought to be ashamed of yourselves.'

'One poor old one?' ejaculated Pom. 'You wait until you see him. He's got the strength of five hundred horsemen and then some. He's absolutely unbeatable. He's eternal, inevitable, everlasting. Why, do you mean to say in your clubs you haven't got bores whom no one can get rid of?'

'Try being rude to him,' I said. 'I've known rudeness work wonders before now.'

'Rude!' cried Pom. 'You can't be rude to him. He says he's deaf, which, of course, he isn't, and when you say anything to him especially nasty, he pretends to think you've paid him a compliment, thanks you for it, and clings closer than ever. The fact is, Johnson, that he's ruining our club. Like everyone else, we're in need of money. At the same time we try to keep our membership as decent as we can; but half the fellers we'd like to have now have got wind of old Mark-My-Words, as we call him, and half the other decent fellows don't come into the club simply because they're terrified of finding him there.'

'But what does he actually do?' I asked.

'In the first place he sits on all the papers. Then, when he's read them, he wanders around seeking whom he may devour. Then he begins. "I remember in '72," he says, and then you're done. Of course you can get up and leave him, but before you know where you are, he's at your elbow again, and it's a silly thing to see members wandering through the club like lost spirits, with that old thing pottering after them. It's ludicrous.'

'It's very difficult,' I said, shaking my head, 'to cause to disappear one of our most prominent men.'

'Well, there you are,' said Pom. 'Take it or leave it. You might, in any case, come and have a look at him. Come and take lunch with me there to-morrow.'

That the Lambs is a very agreeable club, everybody knows. Its old rooms, its aroma of Russian leather and the best cigars, the spirit of peace that broods over it, make it one of the best escapes from this new democratic world conceivable. Pom is an excellent companion. I enjoyed my luncheon enormously. It was when we went into the smoking-room afterward that Pom suddenly whispered into my ear: 'Look! That's him over there, talking to those two unhappy youths.'

I looked across the room and saw a stout, red-faced man with white hair slightly on end—this gave him a cockatoo appearance—holding forth to two young men, who were staring at him with the fascinated absorption of rabbits in front of a snake. He was leaning forward a little, and every once and again I caught the boom of his voice and then a reassuring murmur as though his audience were trying to placate him.

'We will join them,' said Pom firmly.

We went across, and Pom, in his sweetest voice, said: 'Pendyce, I want to introduce you to a clever young friend of mine, Mr. Seymour Johnson, the future leader of the English novel. I hope we're not interrupting.'

'Oh, no, no, no, indeed,' said one of the pale young men,

rising with exceeding eagerness. 'I must be going, I'm afraid. Appointment——' And the rest of his sentence took place in his boots.

'No interruption, no interruption,' said Sir Marcus heartily, fixing his eye upon the other pale young man as though defying him to move a finger. 'I was just telling our young friends here about the eruption in '78.'

'The eruption?' said Pom, rather puzzled.

'Yes, of Mount Paphanotis in the Fijis.'

'Oh,' said Pom, 'I beg your pardon. I thought you meant that something was the matter with somebody's face. Very silly of me indeed.'

The remaining pale young man feebly giggled and made an attempt to move, but Sir Marcus's red gout-thickened fingers were on his arm in half a second. 'Just a moment, my dear fellow,' he said; 'allow me to finish my story. It was a perfect miracle of luck that I was there at all at the moment. If it hadn't been for old Casey, of the *Bellerophon*, turning up just in the nick of time——'

'I beg your pardon,' said the pale young man, rising now firmly, 'I really have an appointment. I'm a quarter of an hour late as it is. You must excuse me.'

Sir Marcus's red-veined eyes nearly started out of his head. 'Very well, very well,' he said huffily, 'good day, good day!' And when the young man had gone, he turned around to us, saying: 'What's happened to these young fellows nowadays? Haven't got any manners and haven't got any interest in things, either. Why, that was a most remarkable affair, that eruption. I remember it as though it was yesterday. I can see now just the shape of the island, with the bay running from east to west——'

'Yes,' interrupted Pom, 'there's nothing I'd like better than to have your account of it, Pendyce, but I see Blackstone over there waiting for me, so I'll just leave you with my young friend for five minutes and come back.'

Pom rose and started across the room with what, I afterward found, was known as the Pendyce shuffle—that is, the walk that was common to all those escaping from the embraces of Sir Marcus.

Left now only with myself, he was forced to consider me, and he turned round, moving with some difficulty, and his face slowly realised mine. I was, as it were, dragged gradually into his comprehension, first a nose, then a chin, then an eye or two, and finally all of me caught, fixed, nailed down.

'Well, well,' he said, 'everyone seems very busy to-day. And so you're a painter, young man?'

'No, no,' I hurriedly retorted, 'I'm a writer.'

'What do you write?' he asked. 'Blue Books? I wrote a Blue Book once on the condition of the potato disease in Eastern Manchuria. I remember at the time——'

'No,' I said, very loudly and distinctly, 'I couldn't write Blue Books. I have a very inaccurate mind. I write novels.'

'Oh, novels,' he exclaimed, 'novels, novels, novels! Now, that's a funny thing. What do you write novels for? Aren't there enough in the world already?'

'Oh, yes, there are,' I agreed with him fervently. 'Unfortunately, it's the only thing I can write. One has to earn one's living, you know.'

'Has one, has one, has one?' he replied.

I may remark, in parenthesis, that I was already discovering two of Sir Marcus's most irritating peculiarities, one being that he said everything three times over, the other that he was curiously absent-minded except when he was talking about himself, so that when you were at the most thrilling point of your own narrative you would see his eye, like a greedy pirate, wondering upon what new victims it could seize.

'Talking of novelists,' he went booming on, 'I used to know a feller called Trollope who wrote novels. Big, heavy, stupid man. Went out hunting a lot, and had the worst seat on a horse I've ever seen on anybody.'

Here he began to chuckle over some joke which was slowly

coming up to the surface of his mind, which he already perceived in the dim, blue waters far below.

'It must have been in the late 'eighties,' he sputtered, 'that I said a good thing to that same feller Trollope. I was in the Garrick one day, lunching with old Bony Hackett. Bony couldn't stand writing men, and when Trollope came up and joined us, he was as rude as he could be. When I was introduced to him, Trollope snorted, and that put my back up. I wasn't going to be snorted at by one of those writing fellers, so I said something about novels, you know, hadn't any time to read 'em, better things to do, and all that sort of thing, and Trollope got as red as a turkey-cock, and said to me some cheek about thinking that diplomatists had plenty of time for everything, and I said'—here he began to chuckle again, and chuckled such a long time that all the clocks in the club were able to take breath, strike the hour, and recover their breath again before he'd finished—'I said—Heavens, what did I say? Well, I don't know. It was something clever about writing and all that sort of thing; and I remember old Bony Hackett was devilish amused, and told me afterward he hadn't heard anything so funny for ever so long. The writing feller didn't half like it, I can tell you. Wish I could remember what it was I said. I'll remember in a minute. It was something about writing, and I know it must have been funny because Bony told two or three fellers afterward, and they all thought it was jolly good. I'll remember what it was in a minute. Oh, yes, I know—no, that wasn't it. Anyway, I could see Trollope didn't half like it.'

Here I felt compelled to interrupt.

'Must have been very interesting,' I murmured, 'knowing Anthony Trollope and all the men of his time.'

'Well, yes, it was interesting,' said Sir Marcus. 'Not that I think much of writing fellers as a whole, you know. They're a lousy lot. When I was Minister in Constantinople, there was a chap there who said he was going to write his memoirs. Furnival his name was, or Fernbanks, or Turnbull, perhaps.

I can't remember exactly, but I know he had an awfully pretty wife. She was pretty, by Jove! We were very good friends, she and I. I remember one evening dancing with her at old Crawford Romanes's, and she had a rope of pearls on as big as pigeons' eggs. Finest pearls I ever saw in my life. She asked me whether I liked her pearls, and I said: "I like the neck they're on better." Ha, ha, ha! That was good, wasn't it? Ah, one was young in those days! The things one could do then! Swim, hunt, shoot, ride.

'Swim? Why, I swam five miles one night with the water so hot it fairly blistered you. That swim was talked of afterward, I can tell you. I remember a young cousin of mine there, Bertie Pendyce. Poor feller, got eaten by a shark afterward, lower half of him bitten right off. Left a wife and four children. Pretty little woman, she was, and they hadn't a penny. She married afterward young Sparkes, who ran off with that opera singer in Paris. What was her name? Large, fat, red-faced woman. She was always unlucky—Mrs. Sparkes, I mean. Devilish pretty, too, but never seemed to hit on the right man. She married a third time.'

Here I was compelled to interrupt. I saw Pom making signs to me from the other end of the room. 'Very sorry,' I said, feeling weak as water, but determined to prove my courage, 'but I must be off. I've enjoyed very much what you've been telling me, and hope we'll have another talk one day.'

'We must, indeed,' said Sir Marcus, rising, too, and putting his arm through mine. 'I haven't had such an interesting conversation for a long time. Come along and have a meal with me one day: 5 Half Moon Street. Always glad to see you, and you shall tell me more of your doings. Hullo, Banting! Just been hearing all your young friend's adventures. Very interesting. Very indeed. I was just telling him about poor Milly Sparkes. Did you ever know her? Married a young cousin of mine. Eaten by a shark, poor feller. All the lower half of him bitten right off. She married again afterward.

Some woman in the opera at Paris—can't remember her name—large, fat woman——'

'No, no,' said Pom hurriedly, 'I never knew her! Well, so long, Pendyce. Glad to have seen you.'

We left the diplomatist staring after us in indignant surprise. When we reached the hall I gripped Banting by the arm. 'I'll do what I can,' I said. 'I don't know that we can bring it off, but it's a public duty. We'll do our best.'

'By Jove, you'll be a public benefactor,' said Pom, 'if you do. What are you thinking of? Leaving him on a Scotch moor, or something?'

'It will need considering,' I answered, 'but I have an idea. We'll see.'

The week that followed was one of the most miserable of my young life. I saw that to carry this through successfully it was absolutely essential that I should make a thorough study of my subject. It was not difficult to climb into the affections of Sir Marcus. I telephoned on the morning following my first meeting with him and asked him whether I might see him again. He cordially invited me to dine with him that night. His rooms in Half Moon Street must have been among the smallest and the untidiest in London. He was in his bath when I arrived, and the table in the little sitting-room was laid for two. I will honestly confess that my heart sank when I saw that I was to spend the evening alone in his company. He shouted to me from his bath, and I saw through the open door a large red face, a large mottled red arm, and an enormous sponge. He talked then for the next ten minutes through the sponge, into which he seemed to bury his face in successive frenzies of excitement. Then, as he dressed, he continued to shout at me, and arrived at last in the little sitting-room, his white hair all on end, struggling with his collar and shouting for the valet. 'Where's Crundle? Crundle, Crundle, Crundle! Sorry I'm so late. Met an interesting feller as I was coming along from the club. He was just back from India. What he said reminded me of a thing that happened in Bombay once. What the——! This collar's too small. Where's that man got to? Would you mind helping me a moment? Just slip your finger in there. Give the stud a push, will you? That time in Bombay—oh, look out, the thing'll go if you don't take care! Got it! Take care, don't pinch my neck. Oh, Heavens, it's gone! Wait a minute.'

I then enjoyed one of the strangest sights I've seen for a long time, namely, Sir Marcus standing in his shirt and trousers and shaking himself up and down like a dancer learning the latest and most erratic developments of the shimmy, his eyes, as usual, bursting from his head, both of us watching in agony for the appearance of the stud. There was a little tinkle as something struck the floor, and we were then both on our knees searching the carpet. But I will not continue through the varied eccentricities of that amazing evening.

Some bores are bores because they remember so much. Some are bores because they remember nothing at all. Some are bores because they say the same things over and over again. Some are bores because their views of life are so simple that they reduce everything to nothing, and then reduce it all over again. Some are bores because they love you so much. Others because they hate you so much. Others, again, because they are not thinking of you at all, but only of themselves. Others, yet again, because they think of you so much that your natural modesty is disgusted. Some are bores because of a trick of the voice or a movement of the body. Some because they're industrious, some because they're lazy, some because they're ugly, and certainly some because they're handsome. All these bores, except the very last, was Sir Marcus Pendyce. When, after our not very appetising meal, we were seated in front of the fire, I began to suffer with that strange desire to scream, hit somebody with a mallet, or burn the house down, which is supposed to arise only from the condition of overwrought nerves. My nerves were excellent, but there was an inevitability, a monotony about Pendyce's voice that was like the howling of a dog in the night-time, or the screaming of a peacock upon the walls of the ancestral home. Pendyce's exultation as he discovered that he had here at last a victim apparently willing, helpless, and invertebrate, a victim for whom he had been searching through so many years, was an awful thing to witness. He led me from Constantinople to Berlin, from Berlin to the Caucasus, flung me from the Caucasus into the National Sporting Club, and thence back again to the waters of the Bosphorus; then, seizing me by the hairs of my head, breathless and exhausted, took me to the highest peaks of Mount Everest, hurled me thence into the purlieus of Whitechapel, then dragged me, broken and beaten, into St. Peter's at Rome, gave a final stamp across my prostrate form, then boomed away like the sea on a rocky coast.

'Well, well, it's pleasant to have a chat and find out what a man really thinks. You've opened my eyes to a lot of things to-night. One day I'll tell you a few things, too. After all, there's something in age and experience. We old 'uns know a thing or two. What says Horace?'

There began then the most dreadful pursuit of the Latin language, which, ending in a kind of apoplectic convulsion, produced only the words 'Eton, education, classics, fine thing for a boy.'

The result of this evening was that I was determined to put the plan that I had conceived into execution as soon as possible. 'Look here, Chippet,' I said, 'have you seen Charlie Black lately?'

'No, I haven't for a long time,' said Chippet. 'Why?'

'He's got to help me,' I said. 'I suppose he's in the same old place.'

He was. I paid him a visit that very afternoon.

Mr. Charles Black was a remarkable man of enterprise, who started in a haberdasher's, had been most things from a stoker to a dancing instructor, and was now safely landed in quite a successful business as a lecture agent. It is well known that in the United States of America there is a passion for lecturers on every conceivable subject, and very often on no subject at all. Here, in the less intellectual British Isles, lecturers are less in demand, and it is generally considered that a lecturer is sufficiently rewarded by being allowed to speak for an hour or so in a hall or drawing-room on the subject nearest his heart without the addition of financial profit.

Mr. Black was changing all that. He had now a leash of excited lecturers at his heels, who went yapping and barking about the country, and he had roused enough interest in many of the larger provincial towns to make a small profit possible for his lecturers and quite a large one for himself. He was an honest, agreeable, faithless haberdasher, who considered his lecturers exactly as he had in an earlier period of his career considered collars and handkerchiefs.

'This is a very good little thing that we're doing,' he would announce to Newcastle or Liverpool, 'in *The Haunted Homes of England* style, or we have a line in *The Poets of Scotland* we can thoroughly recommend. These *Princesses I Have Known* articles are wearing very well indeed, and these *Denizens of the Deep* are meeting a long-felt demand.'

Some of his lecturers, I understood, objected to the atmosphere with which he surrounded them. He was quite frank with these superior persons.

'If you don't like it, modam,' he said, 'you can jolly well lump it. Here am I creating a new style of business, and you will kindly allow me to do it my own way. Good afternoon, modam. I expect your *'Igh Life in the Cities of Europe* will be most successful without my aid. No one will be more glad than I shall be if it is so.'

As he explained to me, he sounded a sarcastic fellow; he was not nearly so sarcastic as he sounded.

He was very glad to see me again.

'Why, Mr. Johnson,' he said, 'this is a sight for sore eyes! Are you thinking of lecturing yourself?'

'Do you think I'd be any good at it?' I asked him.

'Well, you never can tell,' he assured me. 'We 'ad a woman in 'ere last week who looked as if she wouldn't say boo to a goose, she was that frightened. She told me she'd got a series on the cathedrals of England, and I was going to turn her off, but suddenly the man I'd got going down to Brighton fell through, and I sent her down instead. Lord luv a duck, but she 'ad them paralysed! The Royal Pavilion, too, where the old Prince Regent used to carry on any'ow. She made them cathedrals as thrilling as a circus. She 'ad them laughing all over the place. The best lecture they'd ever 'ad, they said.'

'Well, I've got a lecturer for you,' I said, 'who's the very thing. He's a retired diplomat, who's known everybody in his time and been everywhere.'

'Why, that sounds good,' said Mr. Black. 'Has he done any lecturing?'

'Not in public,' I said. 'Plenty in private.'

'Is he shy or nervous?' said Mr. Black.

'Not a bit,' I answered. 'Nothing can stop him once he's off. He can give you anecdotes about all the crowned heads of Europe; he's a most amusing fellow.'

'Why, that's the very thing I want,' said Mr. Black. 'It's a funny thing, but in these democratic days, the more democratic people get, the more they want to 'ear about 'igh life. Mention a duchess to 'em ten years ago and they wouldn't look at it. Give 'em a countess to-day, and they'll eat you. What's 'e look like?'

'He looks a proper old aristocrat,' I answered. 'Three chins, an eyeglass, and what's called a "portly presence." He's also got the Oxford manner. He's genial, friendly, and loves a yarn.'

''E's the very man,' said Mr. Black, in an awe-struck whisper. 'Send him along.'

Next day I lunched with Sir Marcus at the Lambs. There

is something strange and uncomfortable, not altogether unconnected, I suppose, with a bad sort of snobbishness, about being entertained in a club by a man who is immensely unpopular there. If there is some fine and righteous reason for his unpopularity, then the guest may feel all the virtuous happiness of supporting, against odds, a magnificent cause. But if his unpopularity has no greater basis than intrinsic unagreeableness, it is difficult indeed not oneself to feel unagreeable and justly uncomfortable. It helped me a little to realise that Sir Marcus was completely unaware of the general attitude to him. In the few minutes before luncheon he approached five different members of the club with an eager smile and an explanatory finger, and all those five men faded away from before him and were not. It was as though he realised that it was an essential condition of his state of life that he should only catch his company after many fruitless throws of the line and hook, and he turned this, in some wonderful way, to a deep compliment to himself, on the ground, I suppose, that the best of God's creatures are only appreciated by the few, and that nothing that is good comes easily.

We were halfway through luncheon when I made my proposal.

'Lecture?' he cried, sniffing the air like a horse out for its first morning run. 'Lecture, lecture, lecture? Well, now, why not?'

'Why not, indeed?' I said. 'I wonder that you haven't thought of it before.'

'My dear young friend,' he said impressively, leaning toward me, 'I have thought of it on several occasions. To tell you the truth, advances have been made to me, but they didn't seem to me quite worth it, nor, indeed, to tell you a little more, quite remunerative enough. Who wants me to lecture?'

I told him about Mr. Black, Mr. Black's enthusiasm, and Mr. Black's marvellous powers of organisation.

'He sounds a worthy fellow,' said Sir Marcus, in his best diplomatic manner, 'but, of course, you know, it's a ticklish business, my lecturing. Discretion needed and tact. I remember in '64, when I was attaché in Berlin, a feller in the Embassy giving a lecture, and he made just the smallest allusion to the wife of young Bonny Cooper, who was First Secretary just then. Said she had the prettiest feet in Europe, or something, and, by Jove, there *was* a row! There was to be a ball the next night, I remember, and old Blenkinsop-Smith—you know his sister probably, Mrs. Crawshay Fitzgerald; she's dead now, poor thing, died of eating too much, if you ask me; she was a wonderful woman for her meals—"I'll have some more of that," she used to cry, and would go on hours after everybody else, quite regardless——'

I called the worthy gentleman back to the business in hand. 'I am sure we can trust your discretion, Sir Marcus,' I said. 'The thing to do is to tell them just enough, you know, and not too much.'

Sir Marcus roared at this. 'That's the thing!' he cried. 'I don't suppose,' he said solemnly, looking toward me, 'that there is anyone in Europe at this moment who knows as much as I do about what goes on behind the scenes. Why, the war alone——'

'No,' I interrupted firmly, 'there must be nothing about the war. It is your earlier experiences, Sir Marcus, that will be so interesting to everybody.'

He was, I could see, excited like a child by the idea. I didn't know then, but discovered later, that his finances were in a very bad way, and perhaps he felt more lonely and isolated than I had given him credit for. This was what he wanted—unlimited opportunity for speech, audiences impressed and enthusiastic, and money at the end of it.

His introduction to Charlie Black was a very magnificent affair. It had about it that curious theatrical unreality that so often occurs in real life. Sir Marcus was unreal, I saw now for the first time, because he was so desperately a survival. His kind had been killed by the war, and if they ever came up again, it would be with some new tradition, some fresh exterior, some more modern phrase. He was very magnificent to Charlie Black, treating him with a condescension and patronage that was wonderful to behold. He was magnificently dressed, with a high black stock and pearl pin, and his eyeglass superbly balanced, and his attitude was that he had come down from the Olympus of all the aristocracy to greet some trembling mortal who had begged for his presence and was ready to pay large sums for the enjoyment of five minutes of his company.

For Charlie Black I had always had respect, but my admiration of him was immensely increased by his attitude on this occasion. He did not resent in the least Sir Marcus's patronage, although it must have seemed very absurd to him. He found out very quickly just what the old gentleman was capable of doing, he flattered his snobbery, listened to his stories, and interrupted them, when they were too lengthy, with wonderful dexterity.

Finally the arrangement was made. Sir Marcus was to attempt a tour of three months, his lecture being entitled *The Great World as I Knew It.* The plan was that Sir Marcus should talk to young Smithers, Charlie Black's most able assistant, for several mornings, pouring out to him all the treasures of his experience, and that from these Smithers should make a collective narrative which the lecturer should read. Sir Marcus rebelled a little against this, telling anybody who would listen to him that he would infinitely prefer that he should talk straight from the heart.

'Spontaneity is my greatest gift,' said Sir Marcus, 'a gift denied to many. I am my natural self when I am unfettered by notes or pieces of paper. I do beg you, Mr. Black, that you will allow me to talk freely, easily, as though the audience consisted of a few friends of mine gathered together round the club fire.'

'Later on, later on,' said Mr. Black. 'You'll forgive me for saying so, Sir Marcus, but however natural an orator may be, and I know from your diplomatic experience that you must 'ave 'ad many occasions for public speaking——'

'Indeed I have,' interrupted Sir Marcus eagerly. 'Once in Berlin——'

'Quite so, quite so,' said Charlie Black gently. 'All the same, these are my terms, Sir Marcus. Take them or leave them.'

It amazed and even touched me to see what a child the man instantly became in the hands of someone who knew how to deal with him. He was pitiably anxious about his success. The whole world stopped while he considered every detail of his approaching appearance. He bored me so desperately in the weeks that followed that on several occasions I nearly abandoned the whole affair. He was perhaps a finer artist on the telephone than anyone I've ever known. He would ring you up on the most inconvenient occasions, when you were in your bath or at breakfast, or engaged upon a serious piece of work. It was of no avail whatever to say that you were out, or ill, or busy. Against such an excuse he had the simple retort of ringing up steadily every successive few minutes until you were found to be in.

Then, once he had you, words came tumbling through the air like flakes of a snowstorm, and if you said goodbye or put down the receiver too quickly, he would be at you again in another five minutes with the remark that he hadn't quite finished what he was saying, and somebody must have cut us off.

The real cure, however, was already working. During a whole week he only once entered the club, and Pom almost fell upon my neck and embraced me in the middle of Piccadilly, and was anxious to pay me my money there and then. 'No, you wait,' I said. 'He may be back on you in another week or two. Nobody knows how this lecture tour will develop.'

Never, never, never shall I forget that first lecture. It took place in a hall in the wilds of Wimbledon. It had been well billed beforehand. There were posters up and down the streets of Wimbledon, announcing that Sir Marcus Pendyce, C.B., M.V.O., would give a lecture on 'The Great World as I Have Known It,' that nobody now alive had had quite the experiences that Sir Marcus had had, that he was a noted raconteur, and that although efforts had been made for many years to force him on to the lecture platform, it was only now that, bowing at last to the insistent public demand, he had consented to appear. The hall was packed, the walls were lined with standing people, the gallery almost shed perspiration upon the heads below it, so hot and pressed and excited was it. The chairman of the evening was Sir Muttlebury Hatt, J.P. for the district, a gentleman so curiously like Sir Marcus on a smaller and more insignificant scale that I once again admired Charlie Black's resource in that he had secured a chairman who should, as it were, prepare the way for the speaker by being just half as grand, half as large, half as impressive. Then Sir Marcus appeared. There was a storm of cheers. The two gentlemen sat on the platform smiling a little nervously, nodding to one another and looking at their watches. The chairman was not a man intended by the Deity for public speaking, and after he had muttered a few remarks about being amongst friends, everybody knowing everybody, and the great world, and how nice it was to see everybody, and how certain he was that everybody was going to be very happy, he sat down.

Sir Marcus rose, and for a passing moment I felt for him all the tenderness and pity that a mother may feel for her only son dispatched for the first time into the brutal world of school life. For once the poor man was terribly nervous, lost, bewildered, and confused. He took out his eyeglass, wiped it, put it back again. He smiled, laughed a little, and then remembered his paper, which he picked up, held upside down, and then began to murmur to himself.

Then all at once, I suppose, the blood of the Pendyces came to his rescue. He made a sudden plunge, caught and held that fine booming voice that was so familiar to all his friends, and was off. I must confess that he read very well indeed, with the only exception that he laughed a little too much before he arrived at one of the jokes that came swimming up toward him from the bottom of the page. In fact, on one occasion he broke off parenthetically to remark: 'Now, this is a good one,—you all listen to this.' But otherwise he went steadily forward to the end. Then, to my horror, I saw him lay the paper down, take a step forward with his hands in his pockets, his head tilted back, begin to discourse on his own. 'You have had, my dear friends,' he said, 'what I think without exaggeration I may describe to you as a really interesting paper, but perhaps I flatter myself——' Here he paused and waited, and as there were no remarks from the audience, he continued. 'Nevertheless, there are some other things that occur to me as I stand before you that may, I think, amuse you. Let us consider ourselves all friends gathered together round the club fire.' A group of school girls from the Wimbledon High School in the second row, who had been growing a little sleepy, all sat up and began to look interested.

'I remember in Berlin, it must have been, I think, in the spring of '71 or the late autumn of '70, perhaps——'

My heart sank. I looked round me in despair, but on this occasion it was our chairman who saved us. Sir Marcus was barely launched into his first international episode when a loud, most unmistakable snore from behind him caused him to stop, start, and turn round. Sir Muttlebury Hatt, his legs stretched in front of him, his arms crossing his stomach, was fast asleep. This disconcerted the speaker most surprisingly. There must have been many other occasions when his hearers had slept in his presence and he had continued undismayed, but this time he was beaten. He stopped, stammered, and finally broke off with: 'Well, dear friends, good night, good night, good night! I hope you've enjoyed the evening as much as I have. Perhaps one day you will allow me to come and see you again.'

There was a storm of applause. Sir Muttlebury Hatt awoke, got upon his feet, and said that Sir Marcus Pendyce had given us all a great deal to think about, that we had felt during his delightful speech as though we were all part of the great world ourselves, that we had learned, at any rate, that the great world was very little different from the small one, and so on and so on. The evening was over.

There began then one of the most curious episodes of my life. There was no reason whatever why I should accompany Sir Marcus on his tour, but there was something simple and childish about the poor gentleman that touched my sympathies. I would never have believed that a few weeks could so completely change a man of his age. It was not, of course, that he became in any way less of a bore. He was rather more of one, if possible, but the rough and tumble of that lecture showed him to be what at heart he must always have been—a nervous, frightened, rather pitiful child, flinching before the great world he was now discovering for the first time in his long life, finding it, indeed, so utterly different from anything that he had supposed. What a sheltered, safe, ordered existence those before-the-war diplomatists must have had! Will anyone ever be so safe again? To Sir Marcus the risk of the lectures, the possibility that the audiences might be slender, the further possibility that they might not like what he said, and might tell him so, the discomfort and ugliness of the English provincial hotel, the jostling and jolting of incessant train journeys, the colds and indigestions and neuralgias and headaches that hang exultingly around the path of every lecturer—of all these things he had had before no slightest hint.

In the third week of our tour, when we arrived at Edinburgh, it was wet, cold, and windy, and that night of our arrival at the Caledonian Hotel, sitting on his bed in his pyjamas, he burst into tears and then clung to me as though

I were indeed his wife, mother, grandfather rolled into one. He could give me no coherent explanation of his breakdown —he had earache, the fish hadn't agreed with him at dinner, the last lecture in Carlisle had been but thinly attended, his little jokes about queens and kings, prime ministers and beautiful ladies, had seemed, even to himself, curiously out of date and dusty. In short, he was a poor, bewildered human being in a bewildering, foggy, dangerous world.

I suggested, although I knew that I was, perhaps, losing all my chances of success, that he should abandon the tour. Not for a moment! He sprang on to the floor, began to gesticulate, searched for his eyeglass, and proved to me unmistakably that the success of his enterprise was the only thing that he now considered. I saw, in fact, a disaster approaching us. The lectures had been less and less successful, and this always for the same reason—that he would not stick to his book, but would burst, at the most unlikely places, into incoherent anecdotage that had no beginning, no middle, and no end. At Liverpool, before a very thin audience indeed, he had talked for a solid two hours, and finally had to be dragged from the platform. This loquacious habit had immensely thrived on lecturing. It seemed, indeed, as though now it was physically impossible for him to stop talking. Even in his sleep, from my room, that was next to his, I could hear him continuing: 'I remember in '71——,' and so on.

There were twenty more lectures for him to deliver. We descended from Edinburgh to Durham, and there in the small concert-room in the town hall, some twenty or thirty people were all his audience. I really could have put my arms around Sir Marcus and patted his white head when, in the little room behind the platform, the man in charge of the hall said: 'Mighty few here to-night. I should put 'em all in the first two rows and have 'em close together. Looks a bit warmer.' He made then, I saw, a truly magnificent struggle to pull himself together, threw back his head, adjusted his eyeglass and went forward, my warmest admiration bearing him full company. From the open door of the little room I could see the hall, with all its cruel exposure of empty seats, its glaziness, emptiness, and coldness, and once again—as I had felt on so many other of the cases connected with this business of mine—I wondered whether I were not too cruel to be really true. Then I noticed, sitting in the front row, two dear old, rosy-cheeked, white-haired ladies, and with them a nice-looking young man. Their eyes were fixed on Sir Marcus from the beginning of the lecture to the end. They gazed on him adoringly. The smile never left their faces, and although they did not seem to take his especial points with much more active appreciation than they took the whole of the discourse, they were quite plainly in ecstasies about the whole affair. It was quite delightful to see the way in which they nodded their old heads at one another, and one of them, at the end, actually waved her hand. I saw that Sir Marcus also had noticed them, and at the end of the lecture he went down on to the floor and spoke to them and the young man. He was with them a long time, and I waited and waited, and at last went off to the hotel, not wishing to interfere or cut short any happiness he might be securing.

Next morning, to my surprise, he told me that he intended to stay in Durham for a day or two, and that he would cut the lecture at Newcastle out of his schedule. He seemed in amazing spirits. I asked him who were his new friends. 'The Misses Piggott and a nephew. Two adorable old ladies.' He was going to lunch with them that day.

The lecture following the Newcastle one was near London, so I went down back to my old haunts, leaving Sir Marcus with his new friends.

Charlie Black, when I saw him the next day, told me quite frankly that our diplomatist was a complete failure, and that he must call off the other lectures. I begged and pleaded, but all to no avail. 'Just give him another chance,' I said. 'The whole happiness of his life depends upon it.'

Charlie Black was not to be moved. 'Silly old fool!' he said.

'I warned him not to get talking all that stuff on his own. If he'd stuck to what we wrote out for him, he would have been quite all right, but not 'e, conceited old puppet.' No, business was business, and Sir Marcus Pendyce's career as a lecturer was at an end.

I met Pom, and was about to confess to him that our plan had failed, and that the Lambs would see Sir Marcus once more in their company at a very early date. Luckily I refrained. Once more, as on so many other occasions, Fate had stepped in and saved me. I had a note next morning from Sir Marcus, headed 'Mulberry Cottage, Fetters Moor, Durham,' saying that he intended to stay for a week or two with the Misses Piggott, and he was enjoying himself very much, and that the rest of the lectures could go to Hades. I saw that my sympathy had been wasted, and I was glad that it was so.

Week after week passed. Sir Marcus did not return. Then it happened quite by chance that I met, at some dinner-party in London, a Canon of Durham Cathedral, who was having a week of theatres in the Metropolis and enjoying himself very much indeed. 'By the way,' I said, 'do you happen to have seen anything up there of an old feller Pendyce, who was once a diplomat?'

The Canon laughed. 'Why, yes,' he said. 'Old man with white hair and an eyeglass, never stops talking?'

'That's the man,' I said.

'Yes, of course; he's living out at Fetters Moor, five miles out of Durham, with two old ladies.'

'That's it,' I answered. 'Do you happen to know how long he's going to stay there?'

'Oh, he's there for the rest of his natural days! He's taken up his abode with them for ever. He's just what they've been searching for all their lives. They're dear old things, but they're the greatest snobs in Europe. They'd go miles just to see anybody with a title, and to have a real ambassador living with them gives them a happiness that is delightful to behold.'

'Yes, but,' I said, 'how can they endure it? He talks the whole time, and he's the greatest bore in Christendom.'

'That doesn't matter,' said the amiable Canon, laughing. 'Didn't you know? They're both stone deaf——'

I was paid my cheque by Pom on the following morning.

III
THE ADVENTURE OF THE IMAGINATIVE CHILD

YOUNG CHIPPET and I had many funny times together. Out of many adventures that we had I have chosen this affair that I have called 'The Adventure of the Imaginative Child' because of the strange figure who is its centre. I cannot hope to give any satisfactory explanation of John Borstal Clay. I am only stating the case as I saw it. There is, perhaps, no explanation of anybody in this strange and casual world. I sometimes think that the Potter simply throws odd pieces of material together and then lets come out of it what will. It takes more than Dr. Freud to explain John Borstal Clay.

One day in the middle of spring, when the trees were budding and the very streets humming their pleasure under the April sun, a Mr. Henry Fortescue Bumpus paid me a call. I had had so many strange visitors within the last few weeks that it was rather comforting to see anybody so completely normal as Mr. Bumpus. He was one of those little men who wear their clothes like armour, who are so cleanly shaven, save for a neat moustache, that their cheeks gleam like billiard balls, who are right and tight in their person, upon whose bodies there is no speck of dust, and upon whose souls there is no sign of any abnormal curiosities.

Mr. Bumpus, it was plain to see, was a man entirely without imagination, fifty-odd years or so, kind in the English fashion, making, one must suppose, a satisfactory income, having ten minutes' Müller exercises in his bedroom of a morning before the open window, abusing gently each day at breakfast the socialistic tendencies of the Labour Party, calling, in all probability, his wife 'mother,' and arranging what he was going to do with himself and his family on Bank Holiday months and months before the event. Mr. Bumpus, in fact, is what is known as the backbone of England. It was all the more deplorable, therefore, to see that he was in a state of very considerable distress. When something distresses a man of Mr. Bumpus' type, he is like a lost dog with a tin can tied to his tail. He has no idea where to go, to whom to speak—above all, he has no one in the world with whom he can be intimate. With his wife he has lived so long and so complacently that possible intimacy between them lies buried deep 'neath layers of domestic dust. The friends of his own sex are only on billiard, golf, or drinking terms, and his children he probably approaches in alternate gusts of anger and sentimentality, boxing their ears one day and giving them too many chocolates the other. He knows, deep, deep down, that the world is a rum place, but it is his natural tradition to set up around himself a kind of Crystal Palace hung with dark green blinds, and to sit inside it, and although he may feel the warmth of the sun beating upon the glass and sometimes hear torrents of rain like thunder on the roof, he cheats himself into believing that there is no world outside, or that, if there is, like Noah in his Ark, he has been forbidden to encounter it.

All this long explanation is necessary for my story.

Chippet was just then away, engaged upon some affair of his own. My friend Borden and I consoled Mr. Bumpus to the best of our abilities. He sat down, pulling his trousers a little above his knees, laying his plump hands upon them, and looking forward at us with a pathetic eagerness, rather as an infant bird in the nest opens its beak for an expected worm.

'You're very young, gentlemen,' was the first thing he said.

'We are not so young as we look,' I replied, smiling at him encouragingly. 'At any rate, tell us what we can do for you, Mr. Bumpus, and if it's beyond our youth, you can be sure of our discretion, and we will not, of course, charge you a penny.'

'Oh, that's all right, that's all right,' he answered nervously, 'that's really quite all right. Lovely weather to-day, isn't it?'

'Spring,' said Borden very solemnly, 'is upon us. It is the period of the year when youth is at its best. We take your coming to us on such a spring-like day as the best of omens.'

'Yes, yes, quite so,' said Mr. Bumpus, gazing desperately around the room, suffering all the agonising terror of one who must speak of intimate matters to a couple of strangers to whom he has really never been properly introduced.

'It was a Mrs. Fleming,' he began at last, 'who recommended me to ask your advice. She told me that a few months ago you helped her in a serious domestic difficulty. It is a domestic difficulty of my own about which I have come to speak to you, but really you are so young——' He broke off and ended with a rather foolish smile. 'I might be your father, you see.'

I saw that this was the moment to exert our authority. 'Excuse me for speaking plainly, Mr. Bumpus,' I replied, 'physical age has nothing to do with this matter at all. We may be able to help you or we may not. Tell us your trouble, and we will see what we can do.'

'Well, it seems so foolish,' said Mr. Bumpus, 'to come to anybody about such a matter as this, but Mother is nearly distracted. She loves her children, gentlemen, with a devotion I have never seen equalled elsewhere. Mrs. Bumpus is one in a million.'

'Is it about your children that you wish us to help you?' I asked.

'In a way, yes,' he answered nervously, and then, taking courage apparently from Borden's muscular and thoroughly British appearance, he plunged straight in.

'Some three years ago a brother of mine, who lived in South Africa, was killed with his wife in a railway accident. He was my favourite brother, and left an only child. This was a boy, then nine years of age and now twelve. My brother, in his will, as though he had a premonition that something might happen to him, left the boy to us in case of any disaster, with a very handsome sum of money for his upbringing. Mrs. Bumpus and I were proud and delighted to assume solemn charge. The boy arrived just three years ago this very month, and became, of course, as one of our own. It is about this boy that I wish to consult you.'

He coughed, looked at us piteously as though he were begging us to tell him that no further information was needed. That, of course, we were unable to do, and we could only look at him with an intelligent and kindly interest.

'The boy's name,' he continued, 'is John Borstal Clay.' He repeated these words over again as a sort of solemn incantation. 'He was a bright little fellow, nice-looking, intelligent, and amusing. We sent him to Dulwich School.' He paused, then, leaning forward toward us, repeated with the greatest solemnity: 'That boy, gentlemen, is wrecking our beautiful home life.'

'Dear me,' Borden remarked, 'so young a boy and so wicked?'

'Not wicked,' said Mr. Bumpus hurriedly. 'I don't want to say a word against the child.'

'You must tell us the truth, Mr. Bumpus,' I said. 'We cannot possibly help you unless you tell us everything.'

'But it is just that,' said Mr. Bumpus, 'that is so difficult to tell. The boy's not a wicked boy—at least, not in the accepted form of wickedness—he doesn't steal nor tell lies.' Then again, with the utmost solemnity: 'He is not a real boy, gentlemen, at all. Not like any other boy in the whole world. We are afraid of him—all of us—and when you've seen him you will know why.'

This was very interesting, and I saw Borden, who likes boys and thoroughly understands them, lean forward and watch Mr. Bumpus with renewed interest. 'Would you mind telling us,' he asked, 'about the rest of the family? How many children have you?'

'Three,' said Mr. Bumpus, 'Emmeline, Gertrude, and little Percival.'

'What ages are they?' asked Borden.

'Emmeline is thirteen and a half, Gertrude is twelve, and Percival eight.'

'And are they also in terror of your nephew?'

'They are indeed,' said Mr. Bumpus. 'And yet it is hard to say why they are. If it were simply a case of John's being unkind to them or ill-treating them, it would be comparatively simple. You see, gentlemen, I loved my brother dearly, and what Mrs. Bumpus and I wish, above all things, is to be just.'

'If the boy is upsetting your family,' said Borden, 'why don't you send him to a boarding-school?'

'We did, sir,' said Mr. Bumpus. 'He went away to school for a term, but we were almost more uncomfortable when he was away from us than we were when he was with us. What we want,' he cried, 'is for John's attention to be directed toward somebody else. We shall have no peace until he loses interest in us. That is where I want your help.'

'Loses interest in you?' asked Borden. 'That's a strange phrase to use about a small boy of twelve.'

'I know it is,' repeated Mr. Bumpus, almost in agony, 'but when you see the boy, you will understand what I mean. He is extraordinarily old for his age, and he knows much more about all of us than any boy has a right to know. He is not a wholesome boy.'

'Do you mean that he is a nasty-minded boy?' asked Borden. 'Does he tell your children nasty stories and put wrong ideas into their heads?'

'No, not in the accepted way,' said Mr. Bumpus, 'and yet he does tell them stories, too. But no, I can't explain what I mean. You must come and see him for yourself.'

'Then what you want us to do,' I summed up, 'is to turn this boy's attention from yourselves into some other channel?'

'That's it,' said Mr. Bumpus. 'Oh, if you only would, how happy and grateful we'd all be!'

The conversation ended in our making an agreement with Mr. Bumpus on our usual terms, namely, that if we were successful he should pay us a certain sum, and if we failed, only half of that sum.

The very next day I took tea with the Bumpus family. They lived in West Kensington, and their house was as right and tight as little Mr. Bumpus himself. Mrs. Bumpus was a charming, stout, friendly woman, considerably older, I should imagine, than her husband, with hair turning grey, rosy cheeks, and a voice like a kettle on the hob.

John was not present when I arrived, but the three Bumpus children were all there. They were the quietest, demurest children you ever saw. Emmeline and Gertrude would be stout and rosy-faced like their mother. Little Percival was in a velvet Fauntleroy suit, and was doing something with a set of bricks in a corner of the drawing-room. They presented a very happy, domestic picture, all of them talking in low tones, Emmeline stitching away at a small piece of cambric, Gertrude, who wore spectacles, reading a book, the clock ticking, the windows open to let in the beautiful evening sun, Mrs. Bumpus being kind and smiling at Borden and myself as though she had known us for years.

We had been there, I suppose, some half hour when John came in. He came in very quietly, closing the door behind him, shook hands with us, took his place near the tea-table in the properest manner possible. He was a short, thick-set boy with a strangely foreign appearance. This arose, I think, partly from his jet-black hair, his deep black eyes, fringed with heavy dark eyelashes, and a rather sallow complexion, in which there was, nevertheless, the colour of excellent health. I noticed at once his hands, which were remarkably clean for a boy of his age, with well-kept nails and thin, beautiful fingers. He moved with admirable grace, not at all with the clumsy awkwardness of a boy of his age, and yet he was a quite natural boy, not effeminate, nor mannered, nor artificial. He said very little. Borden, after a time, began to talk to him, asked him questions about his school, whether he liked football, and so on, and to all this he replied politely, completely at his ease. I soon noticed, however, that the family were all strangely disturbed at his appearance. Percival seemed to be no longer happy with his bricks, and Emmeline and Gertrude glanced nervously toward the tea-table, and an air of constraint crept into the comfort and homeliness of the scene. After a while John got up and walked very quietly over to Percival, knelt down on the carpet, and began to help him to arrange his bricks. Once or twice Mr. Bumpus glanced at us to see whether we noticed anything peculiar. Conversation halted. We ourselves felt awkward and uncomfortable. We were about to get up and go, but suddenly a wail from Percival drew all our attention.

'I don't want them that way!' he cried. 'That's a nasty way. I was building a cathedral.'

'All right,' said John quietly. 'Let's build a cathedral, then.'

'But I want to build my own cathedral,' Percival wailed. 'I don't like your cathedrals.'

'Now, now, Percy darling,' said Mrs. Bumpus, getting up and going toward him, 'it's very kind of John to help you.'

'I don't want John to help me,' said Percival, getting up and suddenly bursting into a flood of tears.

'Well, then, I won't help you,' said John, smiling.

Then, seated as he was on the floor, he looked up at Mrs. Bumpus, and that glance was the first revelation I had of what might be disturbing the tranquillity of the Bumpus family. It was the oldest glance I have ever seen a child bestow upon another human being—a strange glance to see in that young and innocent face. It seemed to say: 'Well, and what are you going to do about it? I know you better than you know yourself, and I want to see, just for my own amusement, to what lengths of folly you are likely to go.'

There may have been, of course, some imagination on my part; after events, however, were to prove to me that I was not far wrong. Percival was led from the room. John got up and came across to us. Mr. Bumpus tried to cover the uneasy effect of this little incident by saying in an unnatural, jocular tone: 'Well, my boy, and how's the work been to-day?'

'All right, Uncle Henry, thank you,' said John quietly. He looked at him as though he were going to say something more, then gave Borden and myself the strangest glance of amused curiosity, and left the room. No further allusion to him was made during the rest of our visit.

We have in these days the habit of discussing in learned terms and all the latest German technique the psychology of children. By this parents are influenced, and become morbidly anxious about the ethical state of their little ones; friends are perpetually bored by discoveries made by anxious mothers of the new tendencies in their darlings' little souls; the only beings entirely uninfluenced by this modern movement are the children themselves. Children form the only portion of the earth's population entirely untouched by the development of so-called civilisation. Children, like their elders, are cruel, malicious, mean, treacherous, tyrannous, greedy, remorseless, selfish, but, unlike their elders, they make no sort of pretence of pretending that these unpleasant emotions are anything but what they are. Ask a cherub of twelve and a half what during last term he did to another cherub aged nine and a half, and if he discovers that you are to be trusted, he will show you that the head-hunters of

Borneo are not in it with him for the frank indulgence of cheerful cruelty. But, more than that, small boys live so entirely in a world of their own that we cannot begin to realise what they are really doing and thinking unless we become small boys ourselves, and we do not become small boys by sitting neatly dressed in amiable drawing-rooms and talking in dulcet tones to charming old aunts, but rather by going out boldly into the boy world, stealing all we can see, eating everything we can lay hands upon, being as cruel as possible to everybody weaker than ourselves, and allowing ourselves to be torn into very small pieces rather than betray a fragment of the truth about some friend whose possessions we would instantly lay hold upon had we a moment's opportunity. There are some men and a few women who are often praised for 'never growing up'; these remain among the nastiest and most dangerous of their kind. On the other hand, there are some boys who grow up at once and are a great deal older than their elders. It was at first this that I supposed had happened to John Borstal Clay. 'He's simply,' I told myself, 'been living with grown-up people and is old before his time. The Bumpuses, on the other hand, are younger than they've any right to be, because they've allowed their imagination to die a natural death, and have developed such a strain of English prudery that they are quite incapable of seeing what's in front of their noses.'

For a week or two this explanation sufficed me. Borden and I, in the arrogance of our young hearts, agreed that it would be very easy to detach the youthful John's mind from the Bumpus family and to fix it upon something or someone else, even, if need be, upon ourselves. I suppose that there's no one in the world who dislikes boys of John's age more thoroughly than I do myself, but John was an exception. He had none of the noisy, greedy, unattractive habits of his kind. He did not interrupt his elders when they had just reached what they considered the earth-compelling portion of their narrative. He did not beg for food that would, he knew, be denied him unless he made a terrible noise. He was not uncleanly in ways that I need not more minutely define, and he watched life with a curiosity that was quite astonishing. It was this last quality in him that gradually absorbed my attention. Nothing seemed to escape him. I soon saw that there was no foolishness or weakness in the Bumpus family that he had not observed, and from that I began to see why it was they were so anxious to be rid of him. We can support with comparative ease those friends of ours who realise only the weaknesses that we have not got, but so soon as anyone puts his finger upon even the tiniest of our real faults, we begin to dislike him and think that we had better have somebody kinder in his place.

John knew perfectly well that Emmeline was cultivating, as fast as she could, all the domestic virtues because she was lazy, and found that those same virtues brought in the quickest and most tangible rewards. She lived, so to speak, for aunts, uncles, cousins, and elderly friends. She ran messages, spoke in sweet tones, and loved to group herself at the feet of some short-sighted relative and lay her head against that relative's knee and look ecstatically comfortable. John knew that she was not comfortable, and if that particular relation did not speedily produce something in the way of a gift or an invitation, Emmeline grouped herself elsewhere.

Gertrude, on the other hand, was all for aestheticism. What she wanted to be was strange and peculiar, so that people coming to tea said to Mrs. Bumpus: 'That's an original child you've got there; she should do something when she grows up.' So Gertrude was learning the piano in a quite excruciating fashion, was ready to recite *We are Seven* and *The Wreck of the Hesperus* on the slightest invitation, and very often on no invitation at all, and loved to sit on a small stool in the very middle of the drawing-room floor, staring in front of her, gazing into nothing. Little Percival was the only one of the family who pursued his gentle way without artificiality, but in his case you could not but wish for a little affectation, his natural habits, manners, and customs being of the noisiest, most provocative kind. Mrs. Bumpus was a sweet woman, with the intelligence of a very kind sheep. She just managed to get through the duties of the day without any actual disaster. These duties left her but little time for the development of her brain; she liked novels and read, on an average, one new one a day. She had never the slightest idea of the names of the authors of these novels, and had been known to read the same book three days after an earlier perusal without the slightest notion that she had ever met it before. She was, however, a very good woman, being far too stupid to be anything else. Mr. Bumpus adored her, not so much because she was good or sweet or kind, but because she was so stupid that he had no fear of anyone thinking her cleverer than himself.

Now, all these things John perfectly knew, and I soon perceived that he played with these qualities and defects, not apparently with any malicious intent, but only because he was so anxious to see what, in the circumstances, they would do. He would, for instance, ask Mrs. Bumpus very quietly where she thought Uruguay was. She would probably say hurriedly: 'Why, in Africa, dear.' He would say, 'Thank you,' very quietly, and then, days later, when relations and friends were gathered together, he would remark, still more quietly: 'Uruguay isn't in Africa, auntie—I looked it up in my atlas.' Mrs. Bumpus was always terribly upset at any exposure of non-intelligence, it being her theory, studiously developed through many years, that she knew just as much about anything as a good woman had any right to know. Mr. Bumpus also was distressed, and would look at her with surprise, saying: 'Why, surely, mother, you didn't say that Uruguay was in Africa, did you?' She would then be all in a flutter, and her eyes would fill with those large, warm tears that seemed to contain some composition of grease in them, so heavy and thick and slow were they.

With Emmeline, John had a glorious time, taking pleasure,

but not a malicious pleasure, in betraying her to aunts and uncles and any others likely to be too easily captivated.

When Emmeline was nicely seated upon a cushion on the floor, her flaxen head resting against a bony knee, uttering in a soft dreamy voice, 'And now, auntie, please tell me what you were like as a little girl,' John would look at her with such a curious, inquisitive smile that the aunt, too, would wonder whether all were well, and instead of the natural impulse to burst into sentimental reminiscence there would come forth a rather snappy: 'Not now, child. After all, there can be very little about my youth that anyone would want to know.' Also, when John was alone with Emmeline, he would say softly: 'Emmy, Uncle George is coming to-morrow; he is good for a box of chocolates, but not more than that. I shouldn't bother about him.' And Emmeline, who cheated herself, as we all do, into believing that she invariably acted from the purest and most beautiful motives, would get one of those nasty little glimpses into reality which kind friends in a temper sometimes give us, which are, indeed, almost the only link with reality that we have.

I need not emphasise this further. It will now be seen by anybody who is interested in the Bumpuses why they wanted to get rid of John.

At the end of the first fortnight I decided that I must get to know John better, and I asked Mr. Bumpus if he would have any objection to John's coming to spend a night with me in my little house in Westminster. Mr. Bumpus was delighted. 'I do hope,' he explained, 'that you don't think that we wish to be unkind to the child; it's simply that—that—well, to put it frankly, that he upsets the tempers of my wife and the children.'

'Yes, I understand that,' I answered, 'but what is still a puzzle to me is that you tell me that he upsets you as much when he's away from you as when he's with you. That, I confess, is a mystery to me.'

'It's a mystery to me, too,' said Mr. Bumpus. 'I think it's

a little this way—that we feel as though he always had us in his mind and was thinking the worst of us. Not exactly that he dislikes us, you know, but if I may put it personally, suppose I'm dressing in the morning, and lose my collar-stud and go down on my knees after it, and am, just for the moment, in the condition that—well, you know what a man's like when he loses a collar-stud.'

'I do,' I assured him.

'Well, I feel as though John had watched me, even though he's as far away as Bilton, and ten to one I get a letter from him the next day with something in it that seems to me to hint ever so slightly at that very incident. Now, you'll say that's absurd. I dare say I'm over-sensitive about John—I think we all are—but it would have astonished you to have seen the numbers of letters that John liked to write while he was at Bilton. Boys of his age don't like writing letters, you know, but he seemed to enjoy it, and every letter made one a little uncomfortable some way. Now, all we want is for him to fix his attention upon somebody else. It really is most uncomfortable, feeling that a boy of his age is watching you all the time, and regards you rather like animals in the Zoo. Mrs. Bumpus doesn't like it, and although she wouldn't say an unkind word about the boy, and, indeed, never says an unkind word about anybody, still, she isn't comfortable when he's in the house, nor, for that matter, when he's out of it, and it's for her sake, more than my own, that I have asked your assistance.'

That was a strange night when John came to stay. I shall never forget it. I lived in an old house in Westminster, just off Barton Street, under the very shadow of the Abbey—one of those old houses with crooked staircases, low-ceilinged rooms, and boards that creak at every step.

John arrived in time for an early dinner, and we went off to the pantomime at the Hippodrome, which that year had lasted from Christmas almost until Easter. I need have had no fear as to the reality of John's youth. It did one's heart good to see that little figure rocking about in his seat, laughing and shouting and crowing with that peculiar cockerel noise made by small boys when they're very happy. Nellie Wallace had only to appear for him to go into ecstasies, and when Lupino Lane vanished in and out of his numerous trapdoors, John was doubled and twisted with delight. Walking home afterward, as he said he preferred to do, he remained pure boy. 'Do you think,' he asked me, in that funny, hoarse voice of his, 'that Miss Wallace is really like that at home? Is she as ugly, do you think?'

'No,' I said, 'she's probably very beautiful. She is one of the few women in the world whom it pays to pretend to be as ugly as possible.'

'If she was more ugly still,' asked John, 'would she get more money?'

'Probably,' I answered.

'And if she was more ugly than that?' asked John.

I saw that there was no end to the heights and involutions of this enquiry, so I changed it to another one.

'Did you like the princess?' I asked him.

'Oh, yes,' he answered. 'She's the one I've seen the advertisements about, with all her teeth in a row. Don't you think it's a pity,' he continued, 'that when anybody is going to be a princess in the evening, she should be an advertisement in the daytime?'

'I really haven't thought about it,' I answered. 'It's very difficult for anybody to be a princess all the time.'

'Why?' asked John.

'Oh, I don't know,' I said; 'it's very exhausting.'

'Why?' asked John.

'Because you have to sit still, and be very proper, and dressed in your best.'

'Why?' asked John.

I am glad to say that at that moment we arrived at my Westminster home.

Now, as soon as we entered my old house and found our way up the dark staircase, John became another person. I cannot describe it better than by saying he was like a dog who sniffs a good smell somewhere close at hand. He did literally go round my sitting-room sniffing at the walls. He poked his small nose into every possible corner, and suddenly, to my amazement, flopped down on the floor and laid his ear to one of the boards.

'Good Heavens!' I said. 'What are you doing?'

'It's funny,' he answered, getting up slowly, not in the least disturbed. 'It's old. It's been here hundreds of years. Lots of things have happened in this room.'

'Yes,' I said, 'they have.'

'Nothing's ever happened in Uncle Henry's house,' he said. 'Not to Aunt Mary, nor Emmy, nor Gertrude, nor Percival. I hate Percival,' he added reminiscently.

He stood in a funny little way against the hearth, as though he were trying to balance himself on a rocking floor. 'I like you,' he said, smiling. 'Do you think it's wrong not to like Uncle Henry and the others? Because I don't like any of them.'

'No, I don't know that it's wrong,' I answered. 'If you don't like them, you had better go away and live with somebody else. With me, for instance.'

'Oh, no,' he answered. 'It's fun living with them. I can make them ratty in no time.'

'Well, it isn't right,' I said, 'to like making people uncomfortable who've been good to you.'

'They've only been good to me,' he said, 'because they'd be uncomfortable if they weren't.'

'Good Heavens!' I exclaimed. 'How old are you?'

'I'm twelve and a half,' he said, 'by years, but do you ever have that funny feeling, Mr. Johnson, as though you'd been a lot older really, and seen everything before, and knew just what was coming next?'

'I have known that,' I answered, speaking to him, in spite

of myself, exactly as though he were my age, 'once or twice at moments, but only for a moment.'

'Well, I know it often,' he said. 'At school there's a master who's got a bad leg and he goes limping around. Well, I know I've seen him limping somewhere else a long while ago, and he was all in red and green.'

'Red and green?' I said.

'Yes,' said John, laughing just as he had laughed at Nellie Wallace, 'and it was so funny. He was a man everybody laughed at, and that's what he was there for, and he hit people on the head with a balloon.'

I was beginning to feel uncomfortable.

'Well, we won't talk about that now,' I said. 'Only look here, you mustn't do things that make your aunt and uncle unhappy. They've been kind to you, after all.'

'I don't want to make them unhappy,' he said, 'but they're so silly, and if you know that if you do something somebody else'll do something, and then you'll do something again, it's awfully jolly to make them do something.' After which explanation I took him down to the little dining-room and gave him something to eat. In the middle of supper I said:

'You know, John, I oughtn't to be giving you supper. Little boys oughtn't to have supper just before they go to bed.'

'Why?' he asked.

'Because it makes them dream and talk in their sleep.'

'Oh, I always dream,' he said, 'every night. Last night I dreamt that Aunt Mary was a cow, a large, white cow with flowers on her head. It was a funny thing, but I was sorry for her last night. I'm never sorry for her in the daytime. But the one I really hate,' he added, becoming confidential, 'is Emmeline. Isn't it a silly name—Emmeline?'

'Yes,' I said, 'it is rather.'

'I sometimes feel,' he said, 'that I'd like to get Emmy into a corner and twist her hair round and round and round. She's a sucker-up.'

'Most girls are,' I answered.

'Why?' said John.

'Well, because they're not so strong and they can't hit back.'

'No, but they can pinch and bite,' said John. 'Emmy does when you're not looking.'

'And why,' I asked, 'do you write them so many letters when you're away? Most boys don't like writing letters.'

'It's such fun sometimes,' he answered, 'to write something that you know they won't expect. It's just as though I were at home with them and saw everything that they were doing.'

'If you didn't think of them any more,' I said, 'and thought of someone else, wouldn't it be a bit of a change for you!'

'You see,' he answered very seriously, as though he were sixty years old, 'I like to have somebody to think about and to do things with—like playing draughts, you know.'

I took him up to bed and put him into a small dressing-room next to mine. He asked questions through the open door all the time he was undressing. 'I say, isn't this fun?' he called out. 'Is Miss Wallace married?' And then, 'Are you married? Have you got any children? Do you go to the theatre every night? I saw *Charley's Aunt* once. I like Nellie Wallace better. Don't you think it's a shame when you don't like cricket that you have to play? Have you got a boiler in your bath? We have at Uncle Henry's. Do you wear a nightshirt or pyjamas? Is this the first time you've ever had a boy in your house? Do you know all Aunt Mary's hair isn't real, and she can take some of it out when she likes?' To all of which questions I attempted suitable answers. I had just put on my pyjamas, and was going to see him safely into bed, when he appeared in the doorway quite naked, and, with the most enchanting smile on his face, cried, 'Mr. Johnson, can you do this?' and was suddenly down on his hands, and started walking, feet in air, across my room. Midway he paused and, with a most amazing little chuckle, began to turn somersaults round and round and round.

I've always done my best to curb my too tempting imagination, and I intend, in this case, strictly to tell the truth, but something extraordinary occurred in that room as that little naked figure went tumbling from side to side. It was as though a light flashed through the air, the kind of reflection that a piece of glass, turned in the hand, throws upon the wall. He was not distinguishable as a human body. He was rather a piece of colour transmuting the whole place, as though, had I turned off the electric light, the beam would have passed glittering, now here, now there, objects in the room starting from the shadows as he touched them—strangest and most incommunicable of sensations, bringing me back, it seemed, to something that I had once known, promising me some future confirmation of something for which I had always hoped. I sat staring, scarcely venturing to breathe, lest the enchantment should break.

He stopped; with a kind of jerk he was on his feet in the middle of the floor, an ordinary naked smiling little boy. 'You can't do that, I bet, Mr. Johnson,' he said.

'No,' I replied, 'I'm much too old.'

'I'll never be too old,' he answered. He came across to me, held out his small and now very grubby hand, and with an air of infinite age and generations-past courtesy, said: 'Now I think I'll go to bed. I've enjoyed my evening very much.' And to his room he went. . . .

One of the most tiresome of Chippet's many tiresome relations was the old Dowager Countess of Pruxe. She was tiresome in all sorts of ways, one of them being that she had lived beyond her time, having had an elder sister who had been danced on Byron's knee (the only drawback to this story was the doubt, natural to any literary mind, as to whether Byron had ever dandled anyone under twenty on his knee). She was more inquisitive by nature than anyone else of her own sex in the British Isles. She was uglier than any human being had any right to be, and she was a bully. No one knew what her age was. She was a very distant cousin indeed of Chippet, but whether it was that she had nothing else to do, or that she really had taken a kind of liking to him, whatever her mysterious reasons might have been, she continued to come of a morning into our little office, sit upright on one of our smallest chairs, looking like an angry, overpainted cockatoo with an enormous Roman nose, and ask us all sorts of questions about our business and private affairs that she had, of course, no right to ask at all. The trouble with her, Chippet said, was that she had too much imagination. We would have rid ourselves of her cantankerous company in no time at all had it not been that we dared not challenge her ever. Old though she was, she could be still a terrible enemy, and having no affection for the truth, and all the romantic anecdotage of very old age, she could ruin somebody's reputation in less time than it takes to poach an egg. She was marvellously vigorous, and always brought with her a miserable-looking, impoverished, pale-faced companion, who snored through her nose so disconcertingly that my only explanation of Lady Pruxe's engaging her was that she added to the general terror of the atmosphere and the old lady's dignity.

She came to the office the morning following John's visit to me, and, while she sat there, in her ugly, husky voice asked questions that Chippet did his best to avoid answering. She vaguely reminded me of someone. I looked at her again and again, but the connection would not come. Where had I seen somebody like her, or, at least, where had I heard that voice before, and who was it who took that curious, almost malicious interest in their fellow-beings' weaknesses? There was something, somebody. . . .

However, the increasing difficulty of the Bumpus case soon absorbed my attention again. I could see that the Bumpuses were beginning to regard us with suspicion, even as Mrs.

Fleming had once done. Further than that, I could see that Bumpus himself disapproved of my liking for Johnny. I could not disguise that John was a million times more interesting to me than all the Bumpus children put together, and in the eyes of the Bumpus parents it became apparent that I was encouraging John in all his natural wickedness. Then with dramatic swiftness the crisis arrived. One night I was going to bed, and was standing at my bedroom window listening to the wind and the rain that came beating and howling up the little Westminster street and whirling away round the great walls of the Abbey, when my telephone bell rang. A moment later the trembling, agitated tones of Mr. Bumpus came through to me. 'Is that you, Mr. Johnson?'

'Yes,' I answered. 'What is it?'

'Is John with you?'

'John?' I said. 'No, why?'

'Oh, dear! I thought he might be, and Emmeline, too.'

'Emmeline?' I cried. 'What's she doing out at this time of night?'

'Oh, we don't know! We don't know!' wailed the voice at the other end. 'Would you mind coming round at once and helping us? We are in the greatest trouble.'

I detected in his voice the implication that I was considered largely responsible for the catastrophe. Of course I hurried through the rain and arrived to find the Bumpus parents walking up and down their drawing-room literally wringing their hands and making unhappy little exclamations.

'Well, now, what is it?' I asked.

It was difficult at first to discover what it really was, but from the agitation that fell during the next quarter of an hour like a shower about my head, I discovered that John and Emmeline had slipped out of the house about half-past seven that evening, Mr. and Mrs. Bumpus being out at a dinner-party and the governess asleep over a novel. No one had discovered their absence until Mr. and Mrs. Bumpus, returning, went up to see whether they were quietly sleeping.

They were not there. A maid in the house next door had seen them come out of the gate. After that there was no news.

During the whole of this, the look in the eyes of the poor little Bumpuses and the plaintive whine in their voices showed me that I was held entirely responsible for this horrible occurrence. What a night followed! All the policemen of London were out in the wind and rain. All the telephones were ringing in agitated convulsions, and by three in the morning I was held to be very little less than a murderer. By that time I was myself so agitated, so wet in body and so exhausted in soul, that I had determined to give up the whole of our business, although now it was making such hopeful progress, and I was wishing that I had never thought so confidently to plunge into that most confused of all foreign countries, the psychology of one's fellow beings. Then as the clock struck four, and the tenth policeman was being offered a drink by the now tearful Mr. Bumpus, John quietly walked in, dragging with him a bedraggled, hysterical, dripping, but triumphant Emmeline.

Mrs. Bumpus, with a shriek of joy, threw her arms round the neck of her dripping daughter. An odd thing then occurred. Emmeline pushed her mother away, saying peevishly: 'Don't fuss me, mother. Can't you see I'm tired?'

John was not, of course, in the least perturbed. He seemed to be scarcely wet, his little overcoat, with its upturned collar, giving him a strangely grown-up appearance, his eyes watching us all with the same critical, amused, slightly scornful glance that by now I knew so well.

'Where have you been? Where have you been? Where have you been?' cried Mr. Bumpus, exactly like an excited clock striking the hour.

'We've been on Primrose Hill,' said John quietly.

'Glad to see it's all right, sir,' said the constable, finishing his whisky and preparing to depart.

'All right! All right!' cried little Bumpus, obviously now

in a state of hysterics quite beyond his control. 'It's not all right—it's terrible!'

The constable looked a little confused. 'Well, if you want me in the morning, sir—' he said, and departed.

'Don't be so silly, father,' said Emmeline. 'John and I had a wonderful time. We would have been back before, only we lost the way. There was a lovely old woman——'

But her father could do nothing but turn upon John. 'You're responsible for this!' he cried. 'Leading my daughter . . .'

'Not now, not now, dear,' interrupted Mrs. Bumpus. 'We're all so tired. I'm sure that we shall discuss it better in the morning.'

Next morning, at ten o'clock, I was summoned to a family conference. When I arrived I found that I was, in the eyes of both Mr. and Mrs. Bumpus, the villain of the piece. It was still very uncertain what exactly Emmeline and John had done the night before. It appeared that John had tempted her with some story of meeting an old man on Primrose Hill who had bags of gold that he distributed for the asking. It seemed to me that it was very unlikely that Emmeline, a matter-of-fact child if ever there was one, would believe such a story as this, but more than anyone I've ever known, she was one who loved, beyond all else, the consciousness that she was getting something for nothing. John had had for a long time past a certain power over her, and I imagine that she was flattered by his so definitely pleading for her company. However, she went. The interesting fact now about her was the fashion in which she returned. Already, so few hours after her adventure, it was plain she was entirely changed, or, rather, not changed, because no human being ever changes—simply this accident had brought to the surface qualities that no one had seen before. She was independent, scornful, and imaginative. She talked about a little man in a green cap, about three stars that had hit a tree, about the rain dancing in circles around a heap of stones, and about an old woman with a basket of apples who had offered her a silver bodkin.

'Bodkin?' cried her father, now terribly afraid his favourite daughter was completely out of her mind. 'There isn't such a thing.'

'That's what John said it was, father,' said Emmeline. 'He said he'd had one once just like it.'

'Well, where is it?' asked her father.

'The rain blew the old woman away,' said Emmeline. 'If I go out there another night, John says she's sure to give me one.'

After this, can it be doubted that the little Bumpus was in a frenzy of despair? He took me into his stuffy little study and there told me quite plainly what he thought of me.

'You come into this house,' he cried, 'with some cock-and-bull story about helping us in our trouble. You deliberately encourage the boy in all his worst faults, you help him to abduct my daughter and to turn her head crazy with mad fancies, and now I suppose you expect us to pay you seventy-five pounds and say "Good-bye, and thank you very much."'

'Not at all, Mr. Bumpus,' I answered. I will admit that I was feeling frightfully tired and dishevelled after my stormy night's experiences. 'If you want me to tell you what I think, it is that John has woken your daughter up to some semblance of real life, and if he is given time, he will wake the rest of your children. Give me another twenty-four hours, and I may yet succeed in my task.'

Poor little Bumpus could do nothing else. He was in despair. John might be removed, but how would that help matters? His influence over the family would be as strong as ever. Poor little Percival would be the next to be corrupted. Wake up all their imaginations, and Heaven knew what might happen. Why, even Mrs. Bumpus . . . And at this thought he burst suddenly into tears and sobbed like a child.

'I don't know what's happening!' he cried. 'The world used to be such a straightforward place.' You knew where you were, and things were either right or they weren't. The people, too. Now everything was upside down, and nobody was shocked any longer. If he lost his children, he didn't know what he'd do, and if they weren't going to respect him, then he had lost them, and so on and so on. He ended by turning upon me.

'I dare say to you, Mr. Johnson,' he said, 'this all seems very funny. You're one of this new generation who don't believe in God, and think the only thing to do is just what you want to do; but you're corrupting the young, and I tell you the next generation will have to pay for the sins of this one.'

'Excuse me, Mr. Bumpus,' I answered, with all the dignity I could, 'you didn't engage me to come here and talk morals and modern sociology. I dare say you're perfectly right in what you say. My business is to remove John's attention from your family, and if I don't succeed within the next twenty-four hours, I will admit myself beaten, and make no further demands upon either your time or your purse.'

I left him with all the dignity I could command, but it was all very well—I had not at that moment the slightest idea of how I was going to win my case. I felt a beaten man, and I tell you that I was pretty miserable and conscience-stricken over the whole affair. When I had gone a little way down the street, I heard someone running after me, and was caught up by John. He informed me that they were all so foolish that morning, and that it was too late to go to school, and that therefore he would accompany me to my office for an hour or two. I tried to get from him the explanation of last night's adventure.

'Well, you see,' he said, 'I've been wondering for a long time whether I couldn't do something with Emmeline, and suddenly it occurred to me that if I took her out in all the rain and lost her, it would be funny to see what she'd be like afterward.'

'That was very wrong, John,' I said.

'Why?' he asked.

'It's always very wrong,' I went on, 'to make people unhappy just for your own pleasure.'

'Why?' he asked.

'Well, of course it is,' I continued. 'What we're here for is to make people happy, not unhappy.'

'Who said so?' he asked.

'You want people to make you happy, don't you?' I asked.

'I don't care what they do,' he answered. 'I can be happy or unhappy all by myself.'

'But don't you mind what other people do or say?' I asked him.

'Why should I?' he asked.

'Other people can make you feel all sorts of things.'

'Why?' he asked.

'Well, because they're so close to you, and we're all mixed up together.'

'I'm not mixed up with anybody,' he answered. 'I just wanted to see what Emmeline would do, and what Uncle Henry would do, and what the policeman would do, and what you'd do. I haven't finished,' he ended, with a chuckle, 'seeing what Uncle Henry will do. I'm sure he'll do something silly. Emmeline's not so bad,' he added reflectively. 'If you tell her stories, she believes them.'

I will frankly admit that I was in despair when we entered the office. I was beginning, ever so slightly, to understand, in my own experience, why the Bumpuses were so anxious to be rid of John. I was beginning to wonder how long it would be before I myself would yearn to escape from that curious, inquisitive, sarcastic glance.

We entered the office and therein found Chippet, very bored indeed, and his distant cousin, Lady Pruxe.

'Good morning, Mr. Johnson,' she said, and as soon as she spoke I realised where it was that I had already heard that odd, husky voice. Other realisations were achieved at that same moment.

John gave a little gasp, and stood in the middle of the floor, staring. The old woman looked down from her chair and stared in return.

'Who's that strange boy?' she asked.

'A little friend of mine,' I answered, 'come in to pay us a visit.'

From that moment, you may believe it or no, as you please, the two never removed their eyes from each other's face.

'Come here, boy,' the old woman commanded.

John came over to her.

'What's your name?' she asked.

'John Borstal Clay,' he told her.

'Where have I seen you before?' she asked.

He shook his head.

'What do you wear all that jewellery for in the daytime?' he asked.

'Because I like to,' she replied.

'Why?' asked John.

'Because they're pretty,' she answered. He looked at her with that funny sarcastic glance of his, but this time there was something in his smile that I had never seen before, something of recognition, of acclaiming that at last he had found someone worthy of his companionship.

'Feel as though I'd seen you somewhere before,' she said slowly. But he was looking at the rings on her fingers.

'I know that green one,' he said, pointing, 'only I don't know where . . .' He shook his head. 'Somewhere, a long time ago.'

She looked at him queerly. 'That was given me by my husband,' she said slowly, 'sixty-three years ago, and it was in his family——' She broke off.

'You're a queer little boy,' she said. 'Will you come back to my house and have lunch with me?'

'Yes,' he answered. 'Have you got peacocks in your house?'

'No.'

'Why not?'

'We have peacocks in the country, not in London.'

'Why?'

'Oh, because they like to move about, and they make such a noise.'

'I like you,' he said, nodding his head confidently. 'You're more clever than the others.' Then he turned and saw the pale companion. I watched creep into his eyes just the expression, the malicious, inquisitive, humorous, sporting expression that I had once seen as he watched Emmeline, Gertrude, and little Percival, and I knew that he had found a new occupation. . . .

John Borstal Clay has taken up his permanent residence in the enormous gloomy house in Portland Place owned by the Dowager Countess of Pruxe. The old lady has already had four different companions during the three months of his stay there. She herself declares that she has a new joy in life. Many weeks ago Mr. Bumpus paid the firm of Boniface and Company a cheque for one hundred and fifty pounds and wrote a little note expressing in the warmest terms his appreciation of our efforts on his behalf.

IV

THE HAPPY OPTIMIST

DURING thirty-seven troubled years I have learnt something about life. One of the most romantic incidents in that life—one from which I learnt a very wholesome lesson—I am now going to relate.

I have a certain reputation for helping people out of their difficulties, and sometimes complete strangers, by my advice.

There came to my office one day a thin, harassed-looking woman, with grey hair and pince-nez, soft, kindly eyes, and clothes not of the smartest. She introduced herself as Mrs. Lane, and asked whether I could give her ten minutes of my time. 'I have heard of you from a friend of mine,' she said, 'a Mrs. Bumpus, whom you helped at a rather difficult moment in her family history. I was telling her my little trouble the other night, and she said that you were just the person to help me out of it.'

'I will certainly do what I can,' I said. 'What's the matter?'

'I do hope it won't seem to you too foolish,' she went on rather nervously. 'In a way, nothing's the matter, and in a way everything is. In any case, I must have some advice. I'm a woman of thirty-eight, and I've been married for fifteen years. I am married to one of the kindest, most amiable, most faithful of human beings, and that is saying a good deal nowadays, men being what they are. You will think it very curious, therefore, that, after saying this, it is nevertheless about my husband that I have come to speak to you.'

'Perhaps he's too kind and tender,' I said. 'I know that that can be monotonous. You want me to help him to a little ill-temper?'

'How wonderful you are!' she cried. 'You're nearly right and at once, and I'm so glad, because now I needn't explain all sorts of things which would take a long time and serve no purpose. It isn't that I want any ill-temper, but it's nearly that. The fact of the matter is that my husband has grown through all these years into the most terrible optimist. He is so persistently cheerful, looks so deliberately upon the bright side of things, refuses so entirely to be upset by anything, even toothache, that the children and I and an aunt who lives with us, to our horror, are discovering that although we all love Charlie very much, we are beginning to avoid his company, to go out of the house when he comes into it, and to stay away with friends whenever a chance offers itself. What becomes of marriage, Mr. Johnson,' she asked me solemnly, 'when the wife avoids her husband and the children shrink from their father?'

'Yes,' I answered, with becoming gravity, 'that is certainly the beginning of the end.'

'But it's not only that,' went on Mrs. Lane. 'His men friends and my friends, everyone who comes to the house, in fact, is beginning to feel it just as we do. He doesn't notice anything himself, and just gets happier and happier. I don't know if you're a married man, Mr. Johnson.'

'No, I'm not,' I answered, and added, 'unhappily.'

'If you were,' said Mrs. Lane, 'you would understand how terrible it is to know that, however irritating things are, your husband will always feel that they're for the best; that however gloomy you yourself may be when you wake up in the morning, you will inevitably hear your husband singing in his bath; however bad the weather may be, you will certainly be told that it's going to be fine to-morrow, or was beautifully sunny yesterday; however many mistakes our wretched Government makes, you will be assured that any other Government would make errors far worse. I'm sure this seems ludicrous to you, but this simple thing is breaking up our home life and making me almost hate my husband, and yet I love him, how deeply no one can know.'

Mrs. Lane appeared to be greatly distressed.

'And what do you want me to do?' I asked.

'I thought—I don't know—of course it seems silly, but I wondered whether perhaps, as you're so clever, you could think of some way to make him a little less cheerful, not so invariably optimistic. I've tried one or two ways myself, but they've all failed. I asked his Aunt Bessie to come and stay with us—all his side of the family are agreed that she is one of the most tiresome old women ever known—but the more tiresome she is, the more cheerful he becomes. Then I developed nervous headaches, because I was told that there was nothing more irritating to a man; but all he said was that I'd be better soon, and then I'd be so glad that I was better that it would really be worth while having had the headaches. Then I happened to overhear him say to a friend that the one article of diet he couldn't bear was lobster, and I gave him lobster four nights running, and all he said on the fourth night was that it showed what habit could do, because he'd always fancied that he didn't like lobster, but now that he'd had it once or twice he was becoming really very fond of it. This must all seem, Mr. Johnson, perfectly fantastic to any ordinary person, but I assure you that I just long for an outburst of temper, some expression of discontent. I've seen that his bath is lukewarm, that his collars come back frayed from the wash, that his studs are never where he expects to find them, that his bootlaces burst just when he's in a hurry; I've asked for twice as much housekeeping money as I ought to have; I've put the children in his way just when he wants to take a nap; I even had one of those little Pomeranian dogs in the house because I knew he didn't like them, and, indeed, I hate them myself—all to no effect. Unless something can be done, I shall have to leave him. It's becoming a perfect obsession with me, and I don't know what foolish or mad thing I may do if you won't help me. He'll be round here in a moment to fetch me. I told him to call for me here because I thought you ought to see him.'

'This is a very difficult case, Mrs. Lane,' I said, shaking my head. 'After all, if I were to succeed in spoiling his temper, you mightn't thank me afterwards, you know. You might look back with longing to these earlier happy days.'

'Never, never, never!' said Mrs. Lane, with the utmost determination. 'Anything would be better than this. And he never can be very bad-tempered. He hasn't got the build or anything. Just a little temper about once a month would make all the difference to me.'

At that moment a small boy announced 'Mr. Charles Lane to see you, sir,' and there came into the room a large, jolly-looking man with a red face, a slight tendency to corpulence, pince-nez set a little crookedly on his nose, and a cheery smile on his face that instantly, in the words of one of our favourite novelists, 'lit up the dingy office as with rays of sunshine.'

'This is my husband, Mr. Johnson,' said Mrs. Lane rather nervously. 'Charlie, this is Mr. Seymour Johnson, a friend of Mrs. Bumpus, with whom we were dining the other night.'

'Why, I'm delighted to meet you, Mr. Johnson,' said Mr. Lane, coming forward, a large hand outstretched. 'What a charming place you have here! I've just looked in to fetch my wife for a little shopping that we're going to do together. Well, little woman, how are you? Ready to come along?'

'Yes, Charles,' said Mrs. Lane, getting up with a weary air.

'That's right. Splendid morning for shopping. Bit overcast outside. Very thing to make you like to be under cover. Wonderful weather we've been having, Mr. Johnson.'

'Well, I don't know,' I said. 'It's rained pretty steadily the last few days.'

'Oh, we must have some rain sometimes,' said Lane. 'Nothing so bad as a drought, you know. Let's have rain now, and we'll have fine holiday weather later on. What do you think of the general situation?'

'Seems to me,' I said, 'about as bad as anything could well be. Strikes every week, all our trade going to foreign countries, income tax going up every minute—no, I must say things are pretty serious.'

'Do you think so?' said Lane. 'I wonder at that. After all, what can you expect after a war like this last one? Everything's improving, it seems to me. I think it's marvellous that we've come through these years since the Armistice with as little trouble as we have. You wait another six months and you see how our trade will run ahead. Things couldn't be better, in my opinion, and I'm not generally an optimist by any means, am I, old woman?' he asked, turning round to his wife.

'Well, Charlie,' she said nervously, 'I couldn't exactly call you a pessimist.'

At that he roared with laughter, slapping his chest and making the maps on the wall shake the dust off their glaze as though they also agreed with him.

'I suppose I'm not exactly a pessimist. Why should I be? I've enjoyed splendid health, Mr. Johnson, all my days. I've been a lucky man, too, with the best wife in the world and three of the most ripping little nippers you ever saw in your life. I attribute my health,' he said, coming close to me and looking at me with intense seriousness, 'to having a cold bath every day of the year, winter and summer, quarter of an hour's Müller exercises before the open window, and eating a good hearty breakfast. Now, breakfast is the meal to build the day on. You have a good breakfast, and nothing can go much wrong.'

To myself, who find a small cup of tea and a thin piece of bread-and-butter as much as I can manage in the early morning, there was something truly cannibalistic about

Lane's morning diet. It is quite true that I felt more deeply depressed during his five-minutes' conversation than for many days past, and that I wished him earnestly to go.

I did see Mrs. Lane now as a real victim, and I said to her as she turned about to go: 'In that matter about which you were speaking to me just now, Mrs. Lane, I will see what can be done. I'll communicate with you further.'

'Thank you,' she said, and went out with her husband.

The Lanes have a jolly house in Maida Vale, and one beautiful afternoon I found myself sitting in their garden watching Lane, in his shirt-sleeves, bend over the little beds that ran beneath the old red brick walls, pulling out weeds and doing mysterious things with a trowel. He was certainly a fine figure of a man, I thought, as I watched his broad back and stout, strong legs, the absolute negation of ill-health, indecision, and any sort of nervous trouble. I'm never going to turn that back and those legs into the working apparatus of a pessimist, I said to myself. I am beaten at this game before I've begun it. He straightened himself and turned round, his broad, red face flushed with his exertions. 'By Jove, it is jolly,' he cried, 'this weeding! There's nothing like it for sheer fun. Why everybody doesn't spend all his time weeding, I can't think.'

'It's a good thing they don't,' I said rather irritably, 'or there'd be nothing ever planted.'

'Oh, do you think so?' he said, laughing. 'Planting's very jolly, too. Anything to do with the garden is splendid.'

I discovered that my earlier determination to force Lane into loss of temper as soon as possible would not be an ungrateful task on my part.

'I simply don't agree with you,' I said crossly. 'If you will forgive my saying so, I think you're talking nonsense.'

'I dare say I am,' he answered cheerfully. 'I do talk a great deal of nonsense. Don't you like gardens, then?'

'Oh, the gardens are all right,' I said.

'You mean the people in them are so tiresome?' he said. 'Well, I can't agree with you. I love my fellow humans. People are fascinating, I think. Nobody's dull if you really get to know him. Everyone's so much jollier than you would expect.'

'Oh, really, Lane,' I said, 'I haven't known you very long, and perhaps I've got no right to speak, but whom do you know? I could introduce you to one or two whose jolliness would be difficult even for you to find.'

'I dare say you're right,' he answered, 'but in my opinion the great thing is to see the best side of people. We all have a good side, you know, as well as a bad side, and if you only look at the good side—well, naturally you like people better. Then I'm not a clever fellow like you. I do admire men who write and that sort of thing. Now, tell me,' he said, looking at me cheerfully, his hands on his broad hips, 'how do you write? I mean, how do you begin, for instance? How do you ever think of all those things that they say to one another? How does a book start in your head?'

I groaned. This case was going to be very difficult.

'Look here, if you don't mind,' I said, 'we'll talk about all that another time.'

'Oh, I say,' he asked, with great anxiety, 'you're not feeling ill, are you? Is the sun too much for you? Let me move that chair into a shady corner.'

'For Heaven's sake, leave me alone!' I burst out. 'Forgive me if I seem a little irritable.'

'Why, of course,' he said. 'I know what it is to feel irritable. I quite understand. You won't feel irritable long on a day like this. I tell you what,' he went on very seriously, 'when I'm feeling a bit off colour, I just go up to my bedroom, strip and do a few Müller exercises. Puts me in condition in no time. If you'd like to wave your arms a bit, you're quite welcome to the room upstairs.'

'Good Heavens, on a day like this!' I murmured.

'Oh, well, perhaps it is a bit warm, but there's nothing like a good sweat for making you see things cheerfully. Are you musical, by any chance?' he added, after a moment's thought.

'I am a little,' I said weakly.

'Because I don't know if you like the flute. It's rather jolly sometimes to sit in a garden and to listen to somebody on the flute. Of course, I'm not very good. I'm really only learning, but there are two or three tunes I have pretty nearly got now, and if you like to sit under that tree——'

'No, thanks,' I said, very crossly indeed. 'If you don't mind, I think I'll go to sleep for a bit.'

'Certainly,' he replied. 'You go to sleep for a half an hour and you'll wake up as jolly as anything. Do let me move that chair of yours into the shade. You won't mind my going on with my gardening, will you?'

It was a strange thing that somehow the thought of that broad back and those stout legs exposed in earnest endeavour once again before me was more than I could endure. I was wondering what excuse I could make to escape, when Mrs. Lane appeared.

'Hullo, darling!' cried Lane. 'That's splendid! Come out and join us. We've been having a most delightful talk. Mr. Johnson's been telling me all about his writing. Most interesting. Now he thought he'd have a nap for a little.'

'Oh, no,' I said hastily. 'It was only a moment's suggestion on my part. I didn't really mean it. One gets a bit sleepy sitting in this garden.'

'An awful thing's just happened,' said Mrs. Lane hurriedly. 'If Mr. Johnson will forgive me, the housemaid has just——' She whispered in Lane's ear.

'Oh, has she?' he said laughing. 'What a funny thing to do!'

'It isn't funny,' said Mrs. Lane indignantly. 'She's broken about a pound's worth of china—all that pretty breakfast set!'

'Never mind, dear,' he said, patting her shoulder; 'we'll get another one in no time. In my opinion,' he said, turning cheerfully round to me, 'maids don't smash things half often enough. One gets so tired of always seeing the same china at every meal. We haven't had a new breakfast set for ever so long.'

'Oh, of course, if you're a millionaire——,' said Mrs. Lane, tossing her head.

'That's all right, darling,' he answered, wiping his forehead with the back of his hand; 'don't you worry. We'll be in to tea soon. Or shall we have it out here? By Jove, it would be jolly to have tea in the garden!'—speaking as though no one had ever had the idea before. 'Just think, having tea in the garden! What a jolly thing to do!'

I suddenly felt that the last thing in the world I could ever do would be to have tea in the garden.

'I'm awfully sorry,' I said, getting up, 'but I must be getting back, I'm afraid. I'll come and have tea another day.'

As I went down the Edgware Road on the top of a bus, I was conscious of a deep and all-pervading melancholy. The world, although the sun was shining, was suddenly grey. I could believe in no one's goodness of heart. All my friends, as their names occurred to me one after the other, seemed to me treacherous and false, all my little ambitions vain and absurd. I realised, with a sudden mental jerk, that Lane had done this for me, and did I spend many weeks in his company I would become a misanthrope, a true hater of my kind. In the succeeding days I considered every possible medium through which I might work upon Lane's mind. The case became an obsession with me as none of the others had ever been. I realised, as I said just now, that most of the other problems had been solved by the readjustment of surroundings. How was I to readjust Lane? Into what company could I throw him that would depress him and lower his vitality? What was there latent in him which, if exaggerated, would turn sweet to sour, amiability to bitterness, love to hatred? There was golf, for instance. He did not, so far as I knew, play golf. That would undoubtedly be good for both his figure and his temperament. Or there was bridge, or I might interest him in some freak religion, or drive him into stamp collecting. No, as I thought of all these things, their futility froze my inventiveness.

At breakfast one morning I was especially bothered by my problem. The thing was beginning to disturb my sleep. I was neglecting the rest of my work for it. I idly turned over the pages of *The Times*, then, looking down the agony column, my attention was suddenly caught by this: 'Society for the Promotion of Happiness. All those who are interested in the happiness and well-being of their fellow creatures are cordially invited to pay a visit to the offices of the above Society (hours 10 to 10), where they will realise that gloom and depression are not natural to the spirit of man, and may be avoided by the simplest methods. Offices: Cumberland House, Victoria Street, S.W.2.'

I scarcely know what it was that suddenly determined me to pay these people a visit. It was not that I could hope for any real help from them with regard to Lane's case, but here were obviously some more optimists of Lane's own kind. I was, perhaps, curious to see whether they beat him at his own game.

The next afternoon I climbed the stone staircase and knocked on a door. I entered a quite ordinary-looking office, where, behind the usual wooden barrier, a girl was seated typing, and an elderly lady at a table was biting the end of her pen. 'Is there anything I can do for you?' she asked, looking at me rather sternly.

'I was interested,' I said, 'in your advertisement in *The Times* yesterday. I came round to see something of your work.'

'You must talk to Miss Allan,' said the lady. 'I'll enquire whether she's free.'

She returned a moment later, saying that Miss Allan would see me, and I went through into a farther room that had a bright red carpet and was hung with framed supplements from the illustrated papers.

Miss Allan was a strong, rather stern-featured woman, dressed in a bright orange that clashed somewhat painfully with the carpet, having every sign about her that she knew her own mind, and was not going to stand any nonsense from anybody.

'You've come to enquire about our work?' she asked, pushing her spectacles a little farther back on her nose.

'Yes, I have,' I answered. 'I was interested by your advertisement.'

'Our work,' she began in a high singsong voice, as though she were reciting an oft-repeated lecture, 'is an effort to bring into this grey-tinged world the spirit of life, happiness, and gaiety, to make men and women realise that it is in themselves to command their destinies, and that by taking a little thought, practising certain simple exercises, and refusing to allow their minds to be invaded by ill-disciplined thoughts and desires, they may attain a high standard of cheerfulness and sociability hitherto unimagined by them, and that by laughter, and the happy employment of music, and the sturdy practice of vegetarianism, they may bring gaiety into the lives of their fellow human beings and light up the world with sunshine.'

She paused to take a little breath. She went on again: 'To look on the bright side of things is, after all, easy enough for all of us, if we do but obey certain simple rules. Selfishness is the curse of the modern age, and we have found that by a steady reiteration of some of the more obvious rules of a well-ordered life, by such simple things as early rising, cold baths, a few exercises, and the steady practice of healthy laughter, the world may be turned into a garden, and we may go dancing through life, our heads up, our voices lifted in song, our mood an inspiration to all those around us. Our charges are,' she added rapidly, 'three guineas for a course of six lessons, five pound ten for twelve. Families of more than three can be dealt with at a cheaper rate.'

'Thanks very much,' I said. 'Can you show me any of your work in progress?'

'Certainly,' she said, looking at me with some suspicion. 'Are you from a newspaper, by any chance?'

'No,' I answered. 'I'm simply a private individual.'

'Have you got sickness in your family?' she asked quickly. 'Has your wife left you, or are you in any way financially embarrassed?'

'Really,' I told her, 'that seems to be my own affair, or, at any rate, should remain so till I've agreed to take some of your lessons.'

'Oh, certainly, certainly,' she answered with indifference. 'I should say that a dozen lessons would do you all the good in the world. However, you shall see first exactly what we're doing.'

I was taken into another room where five or six persons, male and female, were sitting in a row on chairs, watching a stout young woman who was saying: 'Now, when I get to six, laugh. You will find it easier if you begin to smile at two, let the smile become broad at four, a faint ripple of laughter at five, and a broad outburst on the word six. Now, one, two, three— No, no, Mrs. Browning, that won't do at all; that's not a natural smile. Let it come to the lips straight from the heart.'

Mrs. Browning was a rather elderly woman, and looked much nearer tears than laughter. She gave a little gasp of protest.

'I'm very sorry, Miss Jones,' she said. 'I think, perhaps, I could laugh when you say two, and then smile later, after the laugh. It seems to come to me more naturally that way.'

'Nonsense!' said the young woman. 'Now you watch me.'

There followed then the birth, progress, explosion and

death of the most extraordinary laugh that I had ever been privileged to see on any human countenance. It was too much for me altogether. I burst into a loud guffaw, at the sound of which all the six students, who seemed to be sunk into a like depth of depression, turned to me with hopeful eyes. The young woman was delighted. 'That's the way, that's the way,' she said. 'Listen to that gentleman. Now you must try to get something as natural as that. Don't be disheartened. Now begin again with me. One, two, three——'

We went into a further room. Here there were some half-dozen men, all middle-aged or over, all with their coats off, engaged in bending down, trying to touch their toes. A thin little man, the instructor, was dancing about in a perfect tempest of rage. 'No, no, no, that won't do at all!' he cried. 'You've got to touch your toes as though you like it. Don't look so gloomy, Mr. Green. As I told you before, you'll find it much easier if you think of something pleasant while you're doing it—green fields and mountain-tops, or a good run in the park before breakfast—something really healthy and fine. Now, then, straight up with one, arms out with two, three half bend to the hips——'

'These,' explained Miss Allan to me, 'are all City men who are either in danger of, or have actually suffered from, severe financial losses.'

'It must be rather melancholy,' I said in the same stage whisper, 'all together like that. Wouldn't it be better to mix them with a few men whose affairs are rather brighter?'

'That's not been our experience,' said Miss Allan. 'We've found that the thought of one another's losses cheers them up. They like to feel that there are some others in the same position as themselves.'

It was at this moment that the great thought struck me. Here, if anywhere in the world, was the true place for the solution of my obstinate problem.

I was taken into a third room, where half a dozen rather elderly men and women were seated in couples, trying apparently to develop friendly conversations with one another. 'This,' said Miss Allan, looking at her pupils with great severity, as though they were most certainly not doing what they were supposed to be doing, 'this we call the Friends in Council Room. We introduce here to one another lonely folk who have not friends or any great interest in life. They come here for an hour in the afternoon and talk together.'

The lonely folk did not look at all as though they were enjoying themselves, except one fat little man, who was pouring out a flood of words into the ears of a rather grim-looking lady, who kept trying to interrupt him with little desperate ejaculations of 'I don't think— But why?' and so on, without his paying the very least attention to her. When we had been there two or three minutes, this lady jumped up and came towards us. 'Miss Allan,' she cried, in a voice not far from tears, 'I have not paid my twelve guineas to come here and be insulted. I don't like this gentleman. I don't want to talk to him any more. I'm going straight home, and you can whistle for your other five guineas.'

I saw then a sample of Miss Allan's remarkable firmness. 'Now, now,' she said, 'Miss Sturgis, hysteria, hysteria! You know that when the clock strikes the half-hour you can all change partners. Why, I wonder at you! How are you ever going to be happy and make nice friends if you don't give them a fair test?' Meanwhile it was amusing to observe the blank look on the face of the little fat man, who obviously thought that he had been a great success. It was when I saw Miss Allan's wonderful firmness, and the sudden submission of poor Miss Sturgis, that I was more than ever confirmed in my belief that this was the place for Lane.

When we returned to the office, I said to her: 'Miss Allan, I have been immensely interested in all that I have seen. I have a friend who could, I think, very much help you in your work. At any rate, he would, I know, be himself greatly assisted by seeing this.'

'Is he melancholy, overstrung, unhappily married, or

suffering from any incurable disease?' she asked with eager curiosity.

'Not at all,' I said. 'He's a very happy man, and it's just there that I think he can help you. I can't quite explain what I mean just now, but do let him come and see you. I believe it will be worth your while.'

'Certainly,' she answered. 'I'm delighted for anyone to come and see us. Now, confess, Mr. ——'

'Johnson,' I said.

'—Mr. Johnson, that you have been struck by the radiant spirit that lights up these rooms—the happy faces, cheerful carolling voices.'

'I have been struck,' I answered. 'I've never seen anything like this before, and if anyone had told me about it, I shouldn't have believed him. We live and learn.' With which sentiment Miss Allan entirely agreeing, we shook hands and parted.

I lost no time in conducting my friend Lane to Miss Allan's offices. 'I want you to come,' I explained to him, 'because I think you'll do real good there. The object of the place, as I told you, is to put cheerfulness into people's lives, and, to tell you the truth, from the little visit I made I gathered that the one thing that was absent was that same cheerfulness. Now, you're one of the most cheery fellows I know.'

'Am I?' he asked, his face flushing with pleasure.

'You are indeed,' I answered. 'I never knew anybody who looked so persistently on the bright side of everything, and here you'll find people optimists by determination just as you're one by nature.'

When I introduced Lane to Miss Allan, I saw that at first sight she was disappointed. 'You don't look sick or anything,' she said to him, which indeed he did not.

He burst into a roar of laughter. 'Oh, I'm not sick,' he said. 'Never was better in my life. Isn't this jolly? Isn't it charming? I do like the colour of those walls. I think this is one of the nicest places I've ever been in in my life.'

Miss Allan was a little mollified. 'I'll just show you what we do,' she said. We went once again into the rooms where I had been on an earlier occasion. In the first room to-day a little group was seated, while the stout girl read aloud a piece of Dickens, having given instructions beforehand that at such and such a place they were all to laugh. It was the account of Sarah Gamp and Betsey Prig having tea in Mrs. Gamp's bedroom. All the pupils were waiting so anxiously for the words that they'd been told to expect, that they missed them when they came, and a severe scene of correction would certainly have followed had not Lane burst into such a roar of laughter that he did duty for all of them. 'By Jove, that's good!' he cried. 'That's jolly old Dickens, I know. That's awfully good.' All the pupils then faintly tittered, and Miss Allan, I saw, began to be aware of some of the uses to which Lane might be put. I left him there, and did not see anything of the family for three or four days. Then I had a letter from Mrs. Lane.

DEAR MR. JOHNSON [she said],

I know you're trying to help me, and I'm sure you have some clever plan, but I really would be glad to know what purpose you hope to serve by introducing my husband to that place in Victoria Street. He is very interested in it, and has been there every afternoon, and he has come back each evening in most boisterous spirits. He says that it is quite wonderful work that they're doing, and he is thinking of introducing some of their methods into our family. He frightened Johnnie and Dulcie, our two eldest children, last night, out of their very lives by making them laugh according to numbers, with the result that they both burst into tears, and were sent to bed without their supper. I'm sure this kind of thing isn't what you intended, and I think you ought to know what's happening.

Yours sincerely,

VIOLA LANE.

I wrote back—

DEAR MRS. LANE,

Have a little patience and you will see that I am right. I don't want to explain more just now. Give me a week.

Yours sincerely,

SEYMOUR JOHNSON.

Two days after this Lane appeared in the office. He was looking his jolly self, but for the first time it seemed to me that I noticed in him a rather puzzled, hesitating air.

'Well, Johnson,' he said, 'how are you getting on? Isn't it a splendid day?'

'If it weren't for there being no sun and its drizzling hard, I should agree with you,' I answered.

'Well, of course it's not exactly a day for being out-of-doors,' he added, 'but this is the kind of weather when one loves to be under a roof with a book and a pipe. It makes you feel good. Are you doing anything this afternoon?'

'Yes, several things,' I said. 'Why?'

'Well, I'm going to pay a call on Miss Allan. I'm helping her with one of her pupils. I had a little argument with her yesterday. It seemed to me that she was forcing her pupils into a mood a little too obstinately. What do you think?'

'Perhaps there is something in that,' I said.

'As a matter of fact,' he said, looking at me very solemnly, 'it's a pretty awful thing really when somebody's cheerful the whole time. Those people at Miss Allan's never drop it for a moment. You've always got to be laughing, smiling, singing and dancing. Of course they're delightful people, and I do admire the work they're doing, but I think they make it a little too monotonous.'

'Did you say this to her yesterday?' I asked.

'Yes,' he answered, looking at me doubtfully, 'and she didn't seem to like it very much. I wish you'd come along with me this afternoon.'

'I will,' I said.

When I had spent five minutes with the two of them, I discovered two things. First, that Miss Allan felt that she had now in her hands somebody who was going to be of the greatest use to her, an ideal instructor, and, secondly, that she had her firm grip upon him, and he was held a great deal more securely than he knew. She made him her model before the class. 'Now, ladies and gentlemen,' she said, 'you just watch Mr. Lane. You watch him laugh, and I beg you to notice how all the muscles of the face are involved at precisely the same instant. Even the body has its share in the general convulsive movement. Please notice the hands, the gesture of the right arm. Now, Miss Beaumont, would you mind reading a little?'

Miss Beaumont was to-day reading from Jerome's *Three Men in a Boat*. 'Now,' said Miss Allan, 'at the words "and in he fell" you will see Mr. Lane convulsed with laughter. Watch him very carefully, please.'

For the first time, I suppose, in the whole of his life Lane did not laugh. Miss Beaumont read the words, paused, all the class turned as one man, their mouths open, their eyes wide, staring, and nothing happened.

'I'm awfully sorry,' said Lane nervously. 'Somehow, when you all expect it like that— Besides,' he added, dropping his eyes before Miss Allan's stern ones, 'I don't think that's very funny.'

'Oh, indeed,' said Miss Allan very severely. 'Miss Beaumont, will you please pick out a piece a few pages on? Let me see—yes, page two hundred and twenty-nine, "then the dog barked." Now, ladies and gentlemen, at the word "barked" it is hoped that Mr. Lane will laugh.'

I was really beginning to be very sorry for my poor friend —he looked so incredibly foolish and at a loss. At the word 'barked' he did bring to the surface a feeble kind of titter. 'It's awfully hard to laugh to order,' he said to Miss Allan. 'Perhaps another day I'll be better.'

We went out finally to have tea in a tea-shop close at hand. He was quite distressed. 'I really do like Miss Allan so much,' he said, 'and I admire so much the work that she's doing, but I do think that she's not spontaneous enough. What do you think?'

'Yes, I agree with you,' I said. 'But why go there if it bores you?'

'Oh, no, I don't want to let her down,' he answered. 'I'll help her as much as I can.'

Three days later Mrs. Lane came to see me, and reported that her husband had actually sworn at one of the children. Her face was wreathed with smiles. 'You really are clever, Mr. Johnson,' she said. 'He's always perfectly sweet in the morning, but when he comes back to dinner, after seeing those people in Victoria Street, his temper is quite uncertain, and he told me this morning that he thought it a great mistake for people always to be cheerful. I'm going to give him a bad egg for breakfast to-morrow morning, and have the greatest hopes of the result.'

Miss Allan now had her clutch skilfully fastened upon poor Lane. She introduced him to an offspring of the Victoria Street work, 'The Merry Musical Evenings.' This was a gathering that met in a studio in Kensington with the avowed purpose of all being lively, cheerful, and convivial without the aid of any intoxicating liquor, simply with the assistance of a piano and a Mr. Giles Merryweather, who was famous for his funny stories. Lane, of course, was summoned to these evenings, which occurred every Friday night from 8.30 to 12. He took me with him to one of them, and I have never spent a more horrible time. The cheeriness was overpowering. Everybody was wreathed in smiles, elderly ladies kissed one another repeatedly and said over and over again: 'But you're looking too sweet to-night, dear—that frock exactly suits you.' It is needless to say there were no young persons present. They all told their best stories, songs were sung, and at last there was a little jolly dance. At the conclusion of the whole affair a rather tired-looking clergyman got up, made a final address in which he said that they were indeed carrying on a good work by raising the voice in merriment and song, that they were showing to the world how happy one might be without anything stronger than lemonade, that laughter and joy were beautiful things to carry through life; and then there was something about David dancing before the Ark, the full purport of which I missed, as I was trying to find my coat, that had been hidden in a corner with a number of others. I may say that it did not add to my personal merriment to discover that my coat had been stolen earlier in the evening. When I acquainted Miss Allan with this, she said it had obviously been taken by mistake, begged me to say nothing about it just then, lest it should disturb the merriment of the party, but she was sure it would be found in the morning. I may remark that it never was.

Lane's progress was, after this, extraordinarily rapid. He arrived in my room a week later, about tea-time, looking quite upset.

'I say, Johnson,' he cried, 'I'm hanged if I'm going to their Merry Evenings!'

'Well, I shouldn't,' I remarked. 'You're your own master.'

'No, but Miss Allan's so persistent. She'll come round to the house and fetch me. She's been round several times already. She orders me about as though I'm ten years old. She scolded me like anything yesterday because I couldn't laugh at one of old Merryweather's stories. I tell you what,' he went on, 'it's an awful thing the way they're all determined to be cheerful. It makes one quite blue.'

'I'm sorry for that,' I answered. 'I should have thought nothing would ever make you depressed.'

'Well, so should I,' he said, looking extremely gloomy, 'but you do get tired of that sort of perpetual optimism. Look here, can I spend the evening with you? I'm really afraid to go home. You don't know what a Tartar Miss Allan can be. She never loses her temper or anything. It would be splendid if she'd only swear a bit.'

We had quite a lively evening together, and I found him much better company than he had ever been before, and as we were coming out of the Oxford Theatre, when a man lurched against him and dug him in the ribs, he turned round and swore most heartily.

'I thought for a moment,' he said to me as we walked away, 'that was one of Miss Allan's staff—that man Bright who does the funny conjuring tricks. If it had been, I believe I'd have hit him.'

'Oh, you're getting on,' I said.

'Getting on?' he asked me. 'What do you mean?'

'Nothing,' I answered.

A few days later Mrs. Lane invited me to tea. 'I really must thank you,' she said, 'before he comes in. It's wonderful how he's improving. That Miss Allan rang up on the telephone this morning, and he wouldn't go near it, and told me to tell her something really dreadful. And when Dulcie woke him up last night by accident from his after-dinner sleep, he snapped at her just like a real man. I am so grateful.'

While we were seated at tea, the door-bell rang, and before we knew what was happening Miss Allan was in the room. I could see that Mrs. Lane was thoroughly frightened of her. 'I'm so glad you've come to tea, Miss Allan,' she said nervously. 'I'll have some fresh made in a minute.'

'I haven't come to tea,' Miss Allan said sternly, fixing her eye upon Lane. 'Your husband has broken his word to me, Mrs. Lane. He promised that he would be with us this afternoon at our Funny Story Circle, and I've come to know why he was not present.'

'Why, look here, Miss Allan,' said Lane, getting up slowly on to his feet, 'I'm not to be ordered about this way, you know. I was busy over other things.'

'Now, Mr. Lane,' said Miss Allan very calmly, 'you know that's not right. You gave us your solemn promise to help us, and now you're drawing back. When a gentleman's given his word, he keeps it.'

'I hadn't given my word,' said Lane. 'I simply said I might come. Well, I thought better of it, that's all.'

'Mr. Lane,' said Miss Allan, shaking her head, 'is this right, is this good, is this the way to make others happy?'

'I don't care a hang,' he burst out, 'whether others are happy or not! I'm sick of seeing people happy. I tell you what, Miss Allan, your place would be a lot better if there was a little more ill-temper in it. All that cheerfulness has got on my nerves, and it's not real cheerfulness, either. I'm not coming any more.'

'You are coming, Mr. Lane,' said Miss Allan, 'and you know you are.'

I was then present at the very first occasion in all history when my friend Lane thoroughly lost his temper. He was crimson in the face. 'You dare to say that before my wife!' he burst out. 'Do you know where you are? Why, you've only known me three weeks, and you speak to me as though I'm a schoolboy! I tell you I'm not coming to your beastly place. I'm not going to laugh to order, and I am going to lose my temper when I want to. It's a poor sort of man who doesn't get angry sometimes. You're trying to force all those wretched people into false happiness. There's nothing in the world more tiresome than somebody who's always cheerful. I'm sure my wife will agree with me.'

'I do,' said Mrs. Lane, looking at Miss Allan with awe. 'I do, indeed.'

I beheld Miss Allan with deep admiration. She was imperturbable. 'You may criticise my work, Mr. Lane,' she said with dignity. 'I know what I'm doing. You have turned your hand from the plough, you have set your face from the light. Upon your own head be it!' She went.

'Well, I'm hanged!' cried Lane. 'Of all the infernal, meddlesome old women—by Jove, I'd like to break something! Why do you sit staring at me like that, Viola? Don't you think it's irritating enough to a man to be scolded in his own house without having his wife stare at him as though he were an animal out of the Zoo? By Jove, it's enough to make any man lose his temper!'

'That's right, dear,' she said soothingly. 'We'll have some fresh tea up, and you'll feel quite a different man.'

She flung me a glance of triumphant satisfaction. The glance said: 'You have made me a happy woman. I can now act in my natural role of man-consoler and man-tranquilliser. I shall also from day to day be able to act in my other natural role of man-irritator and man-exasperator. At last my life is fulfilled, and I have you to thank for it.' All this her glance said. She went across and patted her husband's head. 'There, there, dear,' she said, 'you needn't go and see those tiresome people any more. I'm sure we've got a lot to thank Miss Allan for.'

'To thank her for?' he burst out. 'Tiresome, meddling old——'

'Mary, some more tea, please. You'll spend the evening with us, Mr. Johnson, won't you?'

'I shall be delighted,' I answered.

V

THE ADVENTURE OF THE BEAUTIFUL THINGS

AMONG THE MANY EPISODES with which during this year I was concerned, this is, perhaps, the only shameful one. When I say shameful, I mean that I have still, looking back, scruples of conscience about it. From the aesthetic point of view these scruples are unjustified; from the moral—well, I don't know. You shall judge for yourself. The case centres round Mrs. Hartington, who was a very remarkable woman. Her real name, of course, was not Hartington, but it is only her death, some six months ago, that enables me to tell this story. Even now her friends may perhaps recognise this account of her, and if they don't recognise her, they will possibly recognise her still more remarkable husband.

Charles Hartington died in the autumn of 1923. He had some business of some sort—what it was does not matter. He was never, I should fancy, very wealthy, but he had a passion for collecting beautiful things, and, with his exquisite taste, his very great knowledge, and the freedom that his business allowed him for travel, he managed to gather things around him as every man can manage if he really cares enough and has sufficient leisure. Cares! Charles Hartington did not, I suppose, care for anything else except his beautiful things. I saw him only once, when he was showing an aunt of mine over his house in Evelyn Gardens. I was with her. The things that he showed us were so lovely that I paid very little attention, I am afraid, to himself; but that is as he would have had it. He was like the voice of his possessions, and you felt that if they were not there he would not be there either. This question of the living and breathing vitality of concrete objects is acknowledged by some people and entirely denied by others; you either feel it or you don't. It is one of the really great divisions between people, and the exact essence of this division has never been better put, I imagine, than by Henry James in his exquisite *Spoils of Poynton*. I must ever apologise to that great man for this little ghost of his magnificent art.

Hartington was not a collector of any especial kind or period; if a thing was beautiful enough, and he could afford it, he got it. And yet the house in Evelyn Gardens in no way resembled a museum. The true drawback, I take it, to any museum is that the things therein do not really belong to anybody. They feel themselves that lack, and I am entirely in sympathy with De Goncourt when he said that he would leave his wonderful collection to the auctioneer's hammer to be broken up and scattered once again among private individuals rather than to the cold indifferent chastity of a vast impersonal building. On that day when I visited Hartington with my aunt I remember that he picked up a Tang horse with a deep blue saddle and held it, stroking its gleaming patina very much as my aunt herself would cherish her trembling Pekingese. He was, I think, a long, thin man with a raddled grey moustache and a stammer. I had the impression, I remember, that he wanted us to be gone; my aunt, of course, said all the wrong things.

Mrs. Hartington I came to know rather well because I was a friend of her son David. David was, at the time of his father's death, about thirty years of age, a long, thin, shy man, very inarticulate, hiding deeply his feelings.

I had not become his friend until, one day a few weeks

after his father's death, meeting me somewhere, he took me aside and begged to speak to me. 'I want your advice,' he began shyly, but with great earnestness.

'Rather,' I answered, 'if there is anything I can do.'

'It's like this,' he went on. 'You know my father died some weeks ago. He left everything to my mother.'

'Yes,' I said. It seemed such an unlikely thing for him to have done.

'He made a will on the day he married her, and never another afterwards.'

He hesitated and then came out with it. I found to my surprise that he loved his father's things passionately, had always loved them since he was a child. He wasn't, he explained to me, in any sense a collector, didn't want to acquire more things. He didn't care for these things for their monetary value, nor for their rarity, simply for themselves. He had had them round him since he was a baby; he had come, he explained to me, to feel about them personally, so personally that he didn't want any other friends—he didn't think that he would ever find any other friends half so good. He told me this nervously, obviously expecting that I would think him an awful fool; but when he saw that I did not, he sighed with relief; he perceived that I had something of the same sort of feeling myself. He then went on to explain his mother to me. This was difficult for him, because he wanted to be loyal to her, had a deep affection for her, and understood her point of view much better probably than she did herself. The point was that she had never cared for her husband's possessions, not only not cared, but had been continually exasperated and irritated by them. I understood that this question had been, from the very beginning of their married life, the one great division between them. Mrs. Hartington must, when she was a girl, have been very beautiful, and I imagine that Hartington had added her to his collection with a great deal of aesthetic enjoyment; but Mrs. Hartington had, of course, been broadened and thickened and hardened by daily living, and as her spirit had never been aesthetic—far from it, indeed—there was soon nothing left in her to respond to Hartington's kind of beauty. That is, of course, the great advantage that beautiful things have over beautiful people. I don't imagine that Hartington ever cared greatly for moral qualities or splendid principles.

The point now was that Mrs. Hartington intended to sell everything. She was going to move into a flat, and would retain only the quite essential furniture. The discovery of this intention had come to David with a shock of the completest surprise. He had never dreamt for a moment that there would ever be a time when these things would not be with him and he with them. He told me that the morning, after breakfast, when his mother had told him quite casually that everything would be sold, had been the most frightful morning of his life. He had made, he was afraid, an awful scene. He had taken his mother, of course, by complete surprise, she never having known him make a scene before; they had always been the best of friends. I suppose that all through her married life subconsciously she had been looking forward to the time when she would be able to sell everything. She was not a cruel woman nor a revengeful—she had cared for her husband in a pitying, maternal sort of fashion—but she had looked on his purchases as desperate extravagances, justified only by their becoming one day excellent investments. It must have seemed to her a kind of insanity that a grown man should go all the way to Pekin, neglecting his business, to buy a blue plate, and now, to her amazement, here was her only child giving an exhibition of the same sort of insanity. I imagine that even though she had not before been determined to sell everything, now, after this hysterical exhibition of her son's, she was absolutely resolved.

What it came to, after further talk, was that I should take luncheon with Mrs. Hartington and see whether I could make any impression upon her. It was rather pathetic, this idea of David's that I should be able to make an impression.

His belief was, poor dear, that anyone would be able to make a better impression than he. He had great confidence in me. I had on this occasion very little in myself. However, the matter was arranged. Mrs. Hartington would be very glad to see any friend of David's and show him her husband's things. Part of her message to me was that I had better hurry up, because they wouldn't be there to show very much longer.

As I stood rather nervously waiting in the drawing-room of the house in Evelyn Gardens, I realised that everything was the same as it ever had been, everything had a permanent look about it, and you needed, I reflected, a great deal of ruthless determination and a complete absence of sensitive imagination to dare to uproot this perfectly adjusted beauty. But when Mrs. Hartington came in I saw that she was exactly the woman to effect these changes. She was an exceedingly English type. America produces determined women, but they are determined for certain very definite purposes; they have their work to do in the world and know it. But Mrs. Hartington was determined and resolute simply because she was Mrs. Hartington; it had never occurred to her that she should not have her way about everything, nor that her way would be anything but the absolutely right one. In physical appearance she was square, ruddy-faced, with eyes that were good-natured, but that never questioned anything. I suspect that she had never shown surprise nor remorse nor apprehension nor desire; it was impossible to conceive her in love. She was not so much a woman as a fact. She would be honest and honourable, and would be one of those persons who would tell you just what they thought of you, and then be sure that they had done you a service. She would be excellent on committees, and would have clear views about everything. If she knew aches and pains, she would never say so. If you were in trouble, she would be an excellent person to go to for advice, but you would never dream of going to her.

She greeted me with kindly patronage. I was David's young friend, she was David's mother, and so she would be kind to me, but without considering me at all. I was to her, I fancy, something like a very easy problem in algebra. I found it difficult at first to think about her at all because of the things in the room. I have, as I have already said, been terribly susceptible to beauty; I say terribly because if you care very much you will be for ever wanting more than you can get, not possessively wanting, of course, but imaginatively. There were so many lovely things in the room that I was bewildered. The Tang horse with the blue saddle on the mantelpiece, the small Constable study for his picture 'A Summer Afternoon After a Shower,' an exquisite, jewelled crucifix, two Rembrandt etchings, 'De Jonghe' and 'The Artist Sitting at a Window Drawing'—these were some of the things that I especially noticed. The room must sound to you something of a jumble, but the extraordinary thing was that there was no confusion at all. Hartington had obviously studied deeply the exact position of everything in the room, and in some way had transmuted them all into a general pattern of colour and symmetry. When we went into the dining-room to luncheon, I began to feel, against my will, a hostility to the good lady. I have always felt envious of those lucky people who are so insensitive to personality that they can pursue their purpose without prejudice. I suppose it was my conceit that irritated me with Mrs. Hartington. I was so inconsiderable to her that if the pretty servant-maid had brushed me aside with the crumbs she would have scarcely realised that I was gone. She asked me questions about myself in that kindly and indifferent manner that charitable ladies use when they are visiting the neglected poor —where had I been to school and had I been to Cambridge or Oxford. She supposed I played games, like most English young men. It was such a pity that David didn't play games better; she believed in young men playing games. Had I a father, mother, brothers, sisters, cousins, aunts? Where did

I live, and didn't I find the English winter absurdly long? I answered all these things as well as I could, and then, towards the end of the meal, most foolishly burst into an ecstasy about the lovely things on every side of us. It was the worst move I could have made, but I expect that that was one of Mrs. Hartington's attributes; she was for ever forcing people into absurd situat ons because she was herself so calm and so indifferent. From the moment of my enthusiasm I was lost as far as she was concerned.

'I am glad you like them,' she said; 'they have been, of course, very greatly admired. For myself, I don't understand this passion for collecting. It gave my husband pleasure, and so I acquiesced in it, but what I say is that there are plenty of museums, there are better things, you know, to spend one's money on.' She was so sure of this that I was bound to contradict her.

'I don't agree,' I burst out, cursing myself at the same time subconsciously. 'There is nothing I envy anybody so much as being able to have such things near them. A museum is such a cold place. Why, that Forain would be nothing in a museum; there would be fifty others as good, and thousands of other wonderful etchings as well, but here, all by itself, it knows that you care for it, and it responds and is grateful.'

At least after this I had forced her to consider me. She looked at me with the gravest suspicion. 'I do hope you haven't been telling my son these things,' she said. 'I am going to sell everything.'

'You're going to sell everything!' I exclaimed. 'Oh, Mrs. Hartington, how can you? Of course I agree that it's better to sell them than to send them to a museum; but they belong here—you'll miss them yourself terribly after they're gone.'

I had cooked my goose with a vengeance. She took me over the house with a speed that showed that she wanted to get rid of me as soon as possible. There was a room upstairs, with some Corots, a Daubigny, and a Sisley, that seemed to me the most perfect place of rest that I had ever seen. The walls were a very faint primrose, the curtains some soft silver grey, there was a little cabinet holding some pale blue porcelain, and the Daubigny had in it a wood and a stream of such perfect peace and contentment that I could have gazed at it for ever. I was allowed the merest glimpse; it seemed to me that the room sighed behind me as I left it.

In the hall, as she said goodbye to me, these were her parting words: 'Please don't encourage David in his extravagant ideas; now that his father is gone, he must realise facts.' She said 'facts' as though she were slamming the door on all the exquisite things that life contains. She was wearing, I remember, a dress of dark green that encased her square hard figure like a sheet of armour.

I am sorry to say that I had a strong mad impulse to pinch Mrs. Hartington and see whether she would scream. How relieved I was when I found myself in the street without having created a scandal! I had been a complete failure, but now I was resolved, as I had never been resolved about anything before, that the matter should not end here.

My next conversation with David was distressing; he had had such great confidence in my success. 'But why should I have succeeded?' I asked him. 'I had never seen your mother before. There was no reason why I should influence her; she had the greatest contempt for me from the first moment she saw me.'

'Not contempt,' said David quietly; 'she isn't contemptuous—she's indifferent.'

'Those are the hardest people to influence,' I said. 'You may as well make up your mind to it. So far as I am concerned, I shall only influence her the wrong way.'

We sat staring at one another blankly; then, in his gentle, hesitating voice, he came out with his awful proposal. 'We shall have to steal the things,' he said.

You can imagine my surprise and almost consternation. There are some people from whom one expects desperate suggestions, and there are others who we know have no moral principle at all, and for these people, let us deny it as we may, if we like them we often shift our own moral code. If anyone had ever told me that David Hartington would one day calmly suggest that he should rob his own mother, I would, of course, have given him the lie.

'I know it sounds bad,' David went on, not at all apologetically, 'but I can't help that. Mother's got heaps of money. If she loses some of these things, she won't financially feel the difference—in fact,' he continued excitedly, 'I don't think she will even realise that they're gone, and that's the test. If we take them away, and she looks round and doesn't know they're not there, it will mean that they've meant so little to her that she's got absolutely no right to dispose of them. That's an immoral theory, but aesthetically it's just. If someone has a beautiful thing, and doesn't even know he has it, then he's got no right to it whatever.'

'Don't be so foolish,' I answered him. 'You mean to tell me that if you took that Tang horse away from the mantelpiece she wouldn't miss it? Of course she would.'

'That's my belief,' he answered. 'I know my mother better than you do. She's astoundingly blind about some things. She never would listen to my father when, in the old days, he tried to tell her about his acquisitions—she made a point of not listening. The Tang horse doesn't mean more to her than a soup tureen, and not so much; she's never looked at the thing individually at all. She never looks at anything unless it's so bright in colour that she simply can't escape it. That's the test—that's the test. Of course we won't take everything—we couldn't if we wanted to—only a few of the most beautiful things.'

I stared at him in amazement, he said it so calmly. 'You,' I cried, 'you to talk like this! And why we? You can commit your own burglaries.'

'All right,' he answered. 'It is my affair; you shan't be dragged into it if you don't want to be.'

And then, most perversely, I did want to be, simply, I

think, because I had had luncheon with Mrs. Hartington. I wanted to pay her back a little of her indifferent patronage. 'Well, I'll see,' I answered cautiously. 'Tell me your plan.'

'I shan't tell you my plan,' he said, 'unless you agree to come in with me. It's much better you should know nothing about it unless you're going to share in it.'

'I'll help you,' I agreed. 'I am ready to go to prison for those things.'

He was greatly relieved. 'That's fine,' he answered. 'The thing's quite simple. We will go one day when she's away in the country, have a car outside, put the things into it, and go off with them. More than that, I shall put the things up in my flat, ask her to tea, let her look round and take it all in, and if then she doesn't say anything, I am justified completely.'

'It's impossible she shouldn't notice,' I answered.

'You don't know my mother,' he told me.

I was, after this, strangely haunted by some of these possessions—the Tang horse, the blue plate, the jewelled crucifix, the Daubigny, were present to me as though I had them in my own room. You may say that these things had no life. I say that they had, and am convinced that the Tang horse was fully aware that its future was at stake. You know how a dog, when his master is going away, will be conscious of this for days beforehand; so was the Tang horse conscious, and I am sure that he hated Mrs. Hartington with a deadly hatred. On the day of our adventure—a Saturday—there was a fog, one of those especial London fogs that are never still, but creep up and down the town like an invading army. It collects all its forces in one especial spot, has great fun there, choking everything and everybody, bewildering the unimaginative, exciting the romantic, aggravating the practical, delaying the amorous, throttling the avaricious, and then, when it has had its fun, moving on, with a throaty chuckle, somewhere else and beginning its games all over again.

It was not very thick when we arrived outside Evelyn Gardens. The houses there stood out of it as though they were surrounded by water; spirals and whorls of yellow mist played about the walls. Here there was a shining knocker, there a pair of nice clean steps; here three peering windows, there a crooked chimney. Only a little way there was blackness, with shouts and lighted flares and discordant hootings. The nice little maid, Elsie, opened the door for us, and of course showed no surprise at David's presence. Mrs. Hartington had gone for the week-end. At first she had thought she would not go, the fog was so bad, but at last she had made up her mind. She would be back on Monday for luncheon.

'That's right, Elsie,' David said kindly. 'We shan't want you any more. I have got something to do for my mother.'

We went into the drawing-room, dim with a sort of grey mist, turned on the electric light, and considered things. There was no hurry—we had two days if we pleased. David had been quite clear as to what he wanted, but now, when he faced the room, he was not so sure. Everything pleaded to be taken—of that there could be no possible doubt; it was as though they had all crowded around us and besought us. Only the Tang horse was quiet and composed, because he knew that he would not be left.

'Well, then,' said David, looking about him, 'there's the horse and those plates, the Constable, the two Rembrandts, the Forain upstairs, the amber box, the Georgian sugar-castor, the porphyry bowl——'

'The Daubigny,' I interrupted.

'Yes, the Daubigny, the crucifix——' And he went on enumerating one thing after another until I called on him to stop.

'This is absurd,' I said. 'We can't take more than a dozen things at the most. Your mother may be blind, but if the whole house was stripped she must notice something.'

'Well, then,' he began again, 'there's the Tang horse, the Daubigny, the two Rembrandt etchings, those two plates——' And so he went on with a list as large as the first one.

'We shall not take more than eight things,' I said firmly. 'If you won't agree, I'll leave the house instantly, and will have nothing more to do with it.'

He saw reluctantly the justice of this, and we spent then a most pathetic half-hour, taking things up, putting them down, stroking them, holding them under the light from every possible angle, sighing and exulting and sighing again. At last, however, we got to work. We chose the Tang horse, the two Rembrandts, the two plates, the Daubigny, the Constable and the jewelled crucifix. Fortunately these things left no very striking spaces. The pictures hung from a cornice, and a very little shifting of other pictures filled the empty squares. We put a Chinese camel in the place of the horse, and a lovely dark-red bowl where the plates had been. The real trouble then began. About the Forain—he must take it, he loved it better than anything there. It was the exquisite 'Return of the Prodigal Son,' and if anything was ever vocal in its appeal to be considered, that was. But I was firm. No more than eight, I said. I knew that if this was admitted, there would be trouble about something else—we should be there all day. 'I'll leave the crucifix and take the Forain,' he said. And then he looked at the beautiful ivory Christ, so pale and gentle and appealing. He shook his head. 'No, I must have the crucifix. It's been there ever since I was a kid; it belongs to me more than anything else in the house.'

Meanwhile I had wrapped up the pictures and etchings and put them in the car. I was holding the Tang horse in my arms, and just about to wrap it up, when the door opened and we heard a voice: 'David, you here! I have been at that station a whole hour. There's no hope of the train. It's too provoking! How do you do?'—rather stiffly to me. My heart hammered. I had mechanically put the horse back on the mantelpiece, where it stood rather indignantly beside the camel, and then gazed like a fool, with my mouth open.

David, however, was marvellous; he rose to the situation as though he had never known any other. 'So sorry about the train, mother,' he said; 'it is bad luck. But you'll have a nice quiet Sunday, with no engagements with tiresome people whom you don't really want to see.'

'That's all very well,' she answered impatiently, looking about her. 'How foggy this room is! It seems to get in everywhere. Where's Elsie? I must have something to eat. You've had your lunch, I suppose?'

'Yes, mother,' said David calmly, 'we have. We're just off.'

She looked about her, and, as it seemed to me, most penetratingly; it was the fog that disturbed her. She walked up and down, indignant that anything should dare to interfere with her well-arranged plans. My heart seemed to stop beating; she actually went up to the mantelpiece and in an absent-minded way laid her hand on the camel. Then she walked off again, and, to my horror, stared straight at the place where the two Rembrandts ought to be. 'This fog makes everything so filthy,' she said. 'I can't imagine why they haven't discovered something to stop it. How stupid people are!'

There was worse to follow. She turned towards us with that determined jerk of her head that I was already beginning to know so well. 'I know what I'll do,' she said. 'I suppose that's your car I saw standing outside. If you're going off now, you shall take me as far as the Women's Constitutional; I'll have something to eat there.'

Even now David didn't lose his head. 'All right, mother,' he said. 'You'd better speak to Elsie about your being here over the week-end, then come along with us.'

'Yes, I will,' she answered, and moved out of the room.

He turned to me. 'We haven't a moment to lose. You take the horse; I've got the plates.' In another moment we had everything in the back of the car, had covered up the parcels with a rug, and I sat firmly beside them. 'She'll have to sit in front with me,' he said grimly, 'otherwise I'll strangle her!'

—a most regrettable thing for a son to say about his mother. So we sat in the car waiting, the fog whirling about us, driven by a cold and biting wind, and behaving exactly as though it knew what we were doing, and was malignantly delighted with our wickedness. Mrs. Hartington came out. She made as though she were going to get into the back of the car.

'No, mother,' said David, 'you sit in front with me; it'll be warmer for you.'

Here I think her dislike of me assisted us; she would rather not sit with me if she could help it, and she planted herself in her solid, determined, ruthless fashion beside her son.

Once she looked back, 'Have you been shopping?' she asked. 'What are all those things under the rug?'

'Yes, I've been shopping,' David answered. 'Please don't talk, mother, if you don't mind; this fog makes driving so difficult.'

We did indeed have a most helter-skelter journey, and took a long time to reach the Women's Constitutional. When she had at last disappeared behind those gloomy portals, I could have cried with relief.

'You see, I was right,' he said excitedly, as we drove towards his flat. 'She didn't notice a thing.'

'You didn't give her much chance,' I replied. 'The test will be when you've got them up in your flat.'

As we approached the final climax, my excitement became terrific. There seemed to me to be very much more in this than Mrs. Hartington's anger or David's disappointment. It was a test for the whole of humanity. Could it really be that there were people in the world, healthy, normal, intelligent people, who cared so little for beautiful things that they simply did not see them when they were right in front of their noses? I had myself known something of this. I was in my own way a small collector—some etchings and prints, a few rare books, some bronzes—and I had realised what every collector realises, the disappointment when some friend who appears to regard life very much as you do sees nothing at all in something that stirs the very depths of your being. 'Well, I do think that's pretty,' a lady had once said of my Méryon 'Morgue,' a rather poor impression, because, of course, I couldn't afford a good one. The Méryon 'Morgue' pretty! It certainly takes all sorts to make a world.

But here would be the supreme unquestionable test. Here were some of the most beautiful things in the world, things she had known all her life; we surely could not escape.

As you may imagine, we had an exciting time arranging them in David's flat. The flat was small, but the sitting-room was a nice, square chamber with a high ceiling. What he had in it was good, but not so good, of course, as these new possessions.

'If you put the Tang horse on the mantelpiece,' I said, 'you're simply asking for it; it's impossible that she should not notice it.'

But he was determined; his conscience would not be appeased unless he set himself the uttermost test. The Daubigny was in his bedroom, the jewelled crucifix on his writing-table, the blue plates in his dining-room. Then he asked his mother to lunch, and asked me, too.

'Oh, I'm not coming,' I answered. 'For one thing, I couldn't bear the suspense; for another, if there is a row, it would be so awkward, my being there.'

'Of course you've got to come,' he answered irritably; the strain was getting on his nerves. 'The very fact that she doesn't like you will take her attention off the room. You can't desert me now.' And I couldn't; my curiosity was too strong.

The fatal day was beautiful, spring-like, warm and full of sun; everything showed up as clearly as could be. I couldn't believe but that in the first minute she would exclaim at the Tang horse. She stood there looking about her; she obviously had something on her mind. She gazed around, her eyes lighting first here, then there. She went up to the mantelpiece, stared straight at the horse, gazed and gazed at it.

Well, now of course we were done. I know that David thought so; I could see it in his eyes. Well, what of it? He was, after all, her own son. She could not put him into gaol; she could only indignantly have the things sent back again, and sell them immediately. It would mean ignominy for me and bitter disappointment for him—indeed, I saw that it could in a way ruin his whole life. He would always be longing for these things; they would persistently destroy, by their absence, his pleasure in any other of his possessions. He would never be able to afford to buy them back; he was, in a way, a ruined man.

She turned round; we waited for our doom. Her eyes rested on the two Rembrandts. 'David,' she said, her voice passionately determined, 'I want another word of five letters for mantelpiece; you must help me.'

'You want what?' David gasped.

'Another word of five letters for mantelpiece. I have nearly done the thing. I have been at it all the morning. Now, just think.' She produced a cross-word puzzle, cut from an evening paper, out of her little bag. 'You see,' she explained, 'table's all right, and it must be "Sahara," but forty-one down beats me altogether.'

He threw at me a look of triumph. 'All right, mother, we'll see what we can do.' His man murmured something at the door; we all went in to luncheon.

VI

THE MAN WHO LOST HIS IDENTITY

THE ESSENTIAL POINT about this story is to prove how eagerly and readily one's friends will join in a game or a plot if the object thereof is to make some other human being miserable and uncomfortable. In saying this I am by no means the cynic that I appear. I have tremendous belief in human nature, and am perpetually surprised at the heroisms, unselfishness, and touching gratitude shown so often against desperate odds by my fellow mortals. But it is not surprising that we should all enjoy a game, and if that game involves the lowering in the general estimation of some unfortunate—why, then, the higher go ourselves.

Do not think that Pritchard, the hero of this story, could really be called unfortunate. Before this adventure he was a fairly happy man, the self-satisfied bachelor, and after it—well, you shall see, if you read far enough, how happy he was after it.

My attention was first drawn to Pritchard by the visit of a little man, Meening, to our office. He was a fellow member of the Rococo Club, and there I had met him on various occasions. He was one of those little men who can attract attention only by being constantly at your side. For months and months you hear them speak, see them move, watch them eat, listen to their sighs, their laughter, and perhaps their tears, but are nevertheless unaware that they exist. Then one day, after their persistent company, you exclaim, 'Why, who's that?' and in a leisurely kind of way you take steps to discover. So when Meening came to our office (I was alone there at the time), I could only vaguely remember his name, and, I am afraid, called him Menzies throughout the whole of our first interview, although he quite often in his weak, supplicating voice corrected me. The point was that Meening had become engaged to Pritchard's sister, that she was a dear little woman (according to Meening, devoted to him), and that he was the happiest man in the world except for one thing, and that thing was Pritchard.

Miss Pritchard was apparently dominated by her brother, and not only was she so dominated, but all the Pritchard family, mother and father, other sisters, brothers, aunts and cousins, were in the same case. What was the matter, I enquired, with this domination? Was Henry Pritchard a bully? No, indeed, he was not. He was a kindly, good-natured, amiable man of forty or so; he had apparently been clever in his own way, had made a lot of money during the war, with ships or something of the kind, and had had the good sense to save it, and now did no work at all, went about the world, discursive, amiable, and desperately complacent. I gathered from Meening—who, a gentle little man by nature, nevertheless spoke with some bitterness about his future brother-in-law—that Henry Pritchard was the most complete and devastating egoist yet known to history—Napoleon, Frederick the Great, and Catherine of Russia were nothing to him in this respect. The fact was that poor little Meening simply did not think that he would be able to marry Miss Pritchard unless some change were made in Henry Pritchard's character, and yet marry Miss Pritchard of course he must.

It appeared that Henry Pritchard was very fond of his sister, and intended to see a great deal of her after her marriage, and neither Miss Pritchard nor Meening had character enough to keep him out of the way. 'You see,' said Meening in his mild little voice, 'it has really come to this. If I hear very much more from Henry of how fine he is, how clever, how rich, how handsome, or how well he played Rugby football fifteen years ago, or why it is that he likes eggs scrambled rather than boiled, of the fun that he gets from using a certain sort of brown polish on his shoes that nobody else has yet discovered, of the extraordinary morning in his life in which he discovered that his hair looked much better without a parting than with one, there will be one day a very nice murder somewhere in the direction of Chelsea, and Daisy will be a widow almost before she's realised that she's a bride!' Little Meening has quite a sense of humour in his own particular way, and real pain and suffering lent vigour to his remarks. 'You see,' he went on, 'I understand that you and your two friends have undertaken a number of cases of just this kind—removing people who are tiresome, changing their characters, and making them see life differently. Of course, I don't want any harm to happen to Henry —Daisy would never forgive me—but you're so clever that I thought you might think of something. Tell me your terms; I am sure money will be no trouble.'

'This is our general custom,' I explained to him. 'I must meet your future brother-in-law, consider the case for a week, and then, if I have a plan that promises success, I will tell you. Then you pay me seventy-five pounds down and then another seventy-five if I succeed within a reasonable period.'

He sighed with relief. 'You've already taken a weight off my mind,' he said. 'I am sure you will think of something, and then not only will I be grateful to you for the rest of my life, but the whole Pritchard family, and perhaps Henry himself.' He spoke more truly than he knew.

Shortly after this I made Henry Pritchard's acquaintance. He was a bullock of a man, one of those Englishmen who, having worshipped athletics in their youth, have in middle age allowed their muscles to run to fat. He must have been six feet three or four in height, and he was as broad as he was tall. He had one of those big round bullet heads with snub nose, large smiling mouth, and eyes looking for ever Narcissus-wise at their own likeness. He was something of a dandy in his dress, and wore bright ties that represented on different days of the week various athletic clubs which had the honour of his genial membership. Genial he was: he not only slapped you on the back in the first five minutes of your meeting him, but roared with laughter at nothing at all, and then, drawing your arm through his, became instantly loudly confidential about some exciting matter connected with himself. I had luncheon with him and Meening at the Rococo Club. In the first five minutes he explained to every-one within a hundred miles' radius that he liked his steak not exactly underdone, but very nearly so, and that he found that, in his experience, sauces always spoiled a fine piece of meat, that of course other people might disagree with him, but that that really didn't matter, because that was the sort of man he was—he had always been like that since quite a kid. 'The fact is,' he said, putting his hand on my shoulder and shaking his heavy sides at me, 'that I am not quite like other fellows here. I know exactly what I want and why I want it. I attribute my success in life,' he went on quite frankly, 'to that very thing. You may not believe it about me, but many people have noticed that in my whole make-up, if I may say so, I never hesitate, but go straight for a thing and take it. And when I have got it I keep it,' he ended with a roaring laugh, gripping my shoulder with so tight a hold that he almost lifted me from the ground. Our lunch was all like that; neither Meening nor I said very much, but we listened and admired and remembered. By the end of the meal I had conceived a plan.

What attracted me quite frankly in this case was neither Meening nor Pritchard nor the addition of a hundred and fifty pounds to our income. We were doing very well now, and might pick and choose among our clients; the point was that

I saw here an opportunity of settling an interesting question that had for a long time past intrigued me. The point was just this: Can a human being, if sufficient persuasion be brought to bear upon him, be led to believe that he is not himself, but somebody else? And I mean, of course, a quite normal human being, not in ill-health in any way, and in full possession of such faculties as God has given him.

Within a week after my first meeting with Henry Pritchard I had evolved my plan. This case was different from any other we had had, because it needed for its successful issue the collaboration of several of our friends. We had always considered it rather a point of honour that our office should, so to speak, do its own dirty work, and Chippet and Borden and I had generally found ourselves equal to our task. But in this affair outside help was inevitable. I had better, perhaps, describe events just as they occurred. One afternoon, about teatime, Pritchard was relaxing his enormous body in an enormous chair in the Rococo Club, reading a newspaper, when a man whom I will call Brown came up to him and said: 'Hullo, Forrester! I am glad to see you. Where have you been? I haven't seen you for ages.'

Now, Pritchard had never seen this man before. He was a nice-looking ordinary Englishman, just the sort of man whom Pritchard would naturally like. Pritchard, as I already have said, was the most genial of men, so he looked up smiling from his paper and remarked amiably: 'Sorry, you've got the wrong man.'

Brown laughed. 'My dear Guy,' he said, 'what's the matter with you? It's true that we haven't met for eighteen months, but don't be silly. I want to talk to you.'

Pritchard said rather more brusquely: 'I am very sorry, sir, you've made some mistake; I have never seen you in my life before.'

Brown also stiffened. 'Look here, Guy, are you tight or something? Don't be a silly ass. I want to thank you for all you did for Everett; you're really wonderful, the way you take trouble——'

Pritchard's sense of his own dignity began to suffer. He rose slowly from his chair and, looking Brown full in the face, said quite sternly: 'You are wrong, sir; you are mistaking me for somebody else,' and walked, with great pomposity, away.

He was, I think, made a little uncomfortable by this episode, because, as it appeared, there was somebody else about the place very like himself, and he had always fancied that there was no one like himself anywhere. Next morning, passing the derelict ruins of Devonshire House just where the buses stop, he felt himself tapped on the shoulder. He turned round and found himself confronted by a little dapper man with an eyeglass, a complete stranger. 'Hullo, Forrester!' said this little man in a shrill piping voice. 'I am glad to see you. Where on earth have you been all this time?'

Pritchard looked at him very haughtily. 'I beg your pardon,' he said. 'You've made some mistake.'

But the little man clutched his arm.

'Don't be an ass, Forrester,' he piped. 'You haven't forgotten Monte Carlo. I am Bennett.'

'I don't care the devil who you are,' answered Pritchard. 'I have never seen you before in my life, and I——'

But Bennett did not relax his hold. 'Look here,' he cried—and his voice was one that in its shrillness would always attract attention in a public place—'I have got to speak to you. I have been wanting to see you for weeks. That business of Emily Clay is all settled.'

Pritchard roughly shook him off. 'I tell you, sir, I don't know you!' he almost shouted, and turned fiercely down Piccadilly. He was angry, he was furious. There must be somebody in London exactly like him. Twice in two days! What an extraordinary thing, and why had it never happened before? And how could there be anybody exactly like him? He had never seen anybody in the least like him anywhere. He brooded about it all day. That night he was dining with the Pritchard family. He gave them a full account of the affair; they couldn't, of course, understand it.

'You know, it's awful!' he cried to his mother. 'If there's a fellow going about London just like me, he may be buying things at shops, leading a disgraceful life, or anything. No one's ever heard of such a thing, and it isn't as though I was just like anybody else.'

'No, dear, it isn't,' his mother assured him. All the family assured him of the same thing.

Two nights later, finding himself unexpectedly free, he dined at his club and went to that amusing musical comedy, 'The Girl With Bobbed Hair.' During the first interval he went out to have a drink. There was rather a crowd at the bar, and a man, pushing past him to order something, turned round and cried: 'Hullo! Why, if it isn't old Guy!'

This was serious. Pritchard looked at the man. He looked a very nice fellow indeed, thick-set, clear-eyed, jolly, with no nonsense about him. The thing was past a joke. Pritchard took his drink and led this stranger gently aside. 'May I have a word with you, sir?' he said.

The man stared at him in amazement. 'A word with me? My dear Guy, don't touch that drink—you've had enough already.'

Pritchard stood over him, gazing into his face with intense seriousness. 'Will you listen to me a moment?' he said. 'My name is Pritchard—Henry Pritchard. I have chambers in Half Moon Street. I have never seen you in my life before. Within the last week three men, complete strangers to me, have addressed me as Guy Forrester; they apparently know me well. There is obviously someone in London who is exactly like me. I am sure you will do me the courtesy to believe that I am telling you the precise truth.'

The other man stared back at him, his face absolutely bewildered. 'Look here, Guy,' he said, 'don't be an ass. I know you were annoyed with me at Wimbledon the other day, and

I suppose you've got some game on now to pay me off. I am sorry about the other day, but it was a crazy thing to double on that hand of yours when you knew that I hadn't any hearts.'

Pritchard, holding himself in control with great difficulty, replied: 'I assure you, sir, that I have never seen you in my life before to-night. Would you mind telling me who you think I am?'

'Who I think you are?' the other man answered. 'Well, if you want to go on with this silly game, I'll inform you. You're Guy Forrester, and I am Anthony Bellows, with whom, three winters ago, you went out to St. Moritz, who gave you some good shooting last autumn, who wrote to you ten days ago asking where you were, whose letter you never answered, and who, weakling though he is, will give you the rottenest hiding in your life if you don't drop this silly nonsense and come to your senses!' He was laughing—obviously a charming fellow—and he meant every word that he said.

Pritchard, in an agony, began: 'I assure you——' when another man came up and touched Bellows on the arm, saying:

'The bell's gone, old man. We've got to trample on millions of people to get back to our places so we'd better go.'

'You'll hear from me in the morning, Guy,' Bellows said. 'It's a poor joke—not a bit funny,' and he went off.

Pritchard went back to his chambers. This was the most awful thing that had ever happened to him. There were several letters for him on his dining-room table. He felt a great sense of relief when he picked them up; they were all addressed to Henry Pritchard, Esq. He walked up and down the room, thinking the whole thing out. First, there was somebody in London exactly resembling him; this somebody was plainly a very agreeable fellow whom people were delighted to see. Pritchard was no fool, and he realised that these three men who had spoken to him had addressed him with an eagerness and a cordiality that was not the manner with which his own friends greeted him. We go on from year to year so thoroughly accustomed to our own habits and ways of life that it is very difficult to realise that they could ever be otherwise. Pritchard was at heart, like most Englishmen, a sentimentalist. He adored to be liked, and at one time, in earlier days, he had been extremely popular; but he had known, although he had never confessed it to himself, that of late years the increased geniality and heartiness of his own manner had covered up a little the absence of heartiness in the manner of others. All great egoists are subjectively suspicious of themselves; they have built up a great wall of defence around their personality and conditions, and at all costs this wall has to be kept absolutely intact. Let the tiniest hole appear and the whole edifice crumbles instantly, and then has at once feverishly to be built up again. Every post, every little implied criticism, every chance encounter, is a desperate danger. Pritchard, although he would never admit it for a moment, had during the last few years been feeling the loneliness of the middle-aged man whose value to the outside world is diminishing. It was, in fact, quite a long time since anybody, whether in the club or the street or the theatre, had addressed him eagerly with excited anticipation. Alone in the silence of his room that night he faced several facts about himself. He had liked extremely the look of that man Bellows at the theatre—just the sort of man he did approve; it seemed a shame that here was the opportunity of a friendship exactly of the right kind offered to him in London, and yet at the same time forbidden to him. Why did not men of the Bellows type come up to him, Pritchard, in that sort of way? Could it be possible that there was something wrong with him? Let the true egoist once start on the broad road of self-suspicion, and there's no end to his horrible discoveries. Could it be that his own dear family were sometimes bored with him and wanted him elsewhere? Could it be—worst suspicion of all—that he sometimes talked too much about himself? He had, he told me afterwards, very little sleep that night. For a man of Pritchard's habit that means a great deal.

There next occurred a piece of marvellous luck for our firm. I had, as I think you will agree, laid my plans very carefully, but my final crowning success does not lie to my credit. Towards seven o'clock one evening, soon after these events, I was walking down the Haymarket, when I encountered a great friend of mine, Miss Helen Freed, one of the prettiest and nicest girls in London. She was a girl who led one of those modern independent lives at which our most up-to-date novelists are always hinting terrible things, whereas there is nothing terrible about them at all, but only a pleasant freedom and an honest disregard of Victorian silliness. I asked Helen where she was going. She told me that she was intending to have a bite of something somewhere, and afterwards would join a girl friend at the theatre. At that very moment—and surely these things are arranged by an all-watching and often benevolent Providence—Pritchard passed us, stopped one instant to look at the posters outside His Majesty's Theatre, and then vanished down the steps into the Carlton Grill. It was then that I had my inspiration. 'Do you want to have a little fun,' I asked Helen, 'and to do some good at the same time?'

Of course she did. Without being at all priggish about it, these were her two objects in life. Then I quickly explained things to her, told her about Bellows and Brown, informed her of the imagined Guy Forrester's supposed position and attributes, assured her that Pritchard was, behind his absurdities, a thorough gentleman, that no harm could possibly come to her, and that much good might be the result. Of course she hesitated, and I think that if the evening had not been lovely, the Haymarket crammed with that spirit of romance and adventure that London, in spite of its grime and the County Council, continually provides, she would not have taken the risk. In the light of after events there was, I fancy, one other inducement—she had looked at Pritchard as he stood for a moment near the theatre. You know how quick women are to make up their minds. I think there was something about him that she liked from that very first glance. She went into the Carlton Grill—she had often been there before—and was ushered with much friendliness to a table. She looked at Pritchard for a quarter of an hour; that decided her. She told me afterwards that, in spite of his health and ruddiness, he looked helpless and desolate. She was touched by him, in a way, of course, that no man ever would have been; it was her maternal instinct. Just as Pritchard had finished his sole and was wondering gloomily why it was that in these days he was so often alone, he heard a charming voice: 'Guy, my dear, how lovely to see you, and alone, too, you, the most popular man in London! What a piece of luck!'

So it had happened again! A shiver ran down Pritchard's spine, but he was not now unprepared, as on the other occasions he had been. Moreover, looking up, he saw one of the prettiest girls ever constructed by Nature (in the main), but also with a little assistance from art. He had the wildest temptation to succumb to the whole thing, to allow himself just for half an hour to be this charming Forrester, the most popular man in London, and to ask this girl to sit down beside him and to continue to smile at him in that perfectly charming way. He did stammer, 'Oh, won't you sit down?' and then, when she did so, because he was a very honest man, he tried half-heartedly to explain. 'You've made a mistake,' he began, his heart thumping as he spoke, 'but never mind—at least, never mind for a moment. I think you'd be interested to hear about the mistake. It's a most extraordinary thing,' he went on, stammering a bit. 'I don't want you to bother about that—at least, what I mean is that if you do bother about it you won't talk to me any longer.' And then he broke off because a waiter approached, and Miss Freed gave the waiter to understand that she would have the rest of her meal at this table; she had met an old friend.

'My dear Guy,' she said, 'I don't know what you're talking

about; you look quite upset. But it is the luckiest thing in the world that I should get you alone like this, with a chance of telling you that I think you were simply splendid about poor Lance. That you should have taken all that trouble about a man whom you scarcely know, simply because—well, because you've got a certain liking for me, I suppose—is flattering, to say the least.' And then, as Pritchard tried to interrupt: 'No, don't say anything about it. I know—I've heard from lots of people—it's the hardest thing in the world to get a job for anybody these days, and the trouble you must have taken about Lance is simply marvellous, and I'll never forget it.'

This was indeed awful for an honest man. Oh, how he wished—how fervently he wished—that he had taken trouble about Lance, whoever Lance might be! But, indeed, it was a long time, as he now too clearly perceived, since he had taken any trouble about anybody. 'Look here,' he said urgently, staring at her beauty and dreading the moment when that light of pleasure and gratitude must fade from her beautiful eyes, 'do believe me, do listen to me. I can't let you praise me for things I haven't done. You've made a mistake. It's happened to me several times lately. There's some man going about London who's exactly like me—he must be my very image. I'd like to be him if I could, but I can't if I'm not, can I?'

Helen Freed laughed, so that several people at tables near by looked up and smiled; she was extremely charming when she laughed. 'Guy,' she said, when she'd recovered a little, 'are you doing this for a bet, or are you trying to tell me that you want to be by yourself this evening, or what is it? We've always been honest with one another, and we may as well go on being honest now.'

'Oh, I am being honest—I am indeed!' he cried. 'I tell you what I say is true. My name is Henry Pritchard, and I live in Half Moon Street. I have never seen you before, although I wish to Heaven I had. I don't know your name nor anything about you, but—but I'll be Forrester or anyone else you like, I'll take credit for any good deed in the world, if only you'll stay for a little and talk to me!'

She looked very serious then, and answered in a voice full of tender kindliness: 'I don't know what your game is, Guy, but whatever it is, I'm with you. You've got some reason for this, I suppose, and if you like to be a mysterious man in Half Moon Street for the rest of our meal—why, go ahead. As a matter of fact,' she went on confidentially, 'I have often thought what fun it would be to take on somebody else's character for a little. I have imagined myself all sorts of people at different times, so while I eat my chicken you shall pretend to be somebody else, and if I like the person you pretend to be, I'll pretend to be somebody else, too; it will be most refreshing for both of us.'

How delighted he was! How eagerly he began to tell her all about himself—what a famous footballer he had once been, how cleverly he had made his money and kept it instead of losing it, as most people did, of how nice his family was, but of how strangely, during the last few years, things had seemed in some odd way to go wrong with him, of how he was very often alone now, and of how he was beginning to wonder whether, after all, in some mysterious way it might be his own fault, and then of this extraordinary thing that had happened to him—of how four people had spoken to him in the last ten days as though he were somebody else, and of how pleased these people had been to meet him, more pleased, he was beginning to think, than anyone had been for a long time to meet the real him that was Henry Pritchard.

They sat there for an hour at least, Helen Freed treating him with a wonderful mixture of attention and kindliness, with just a hint in her smiling eyes that of course this was only a game, quite an amusing one and entirely novel. Then she had to go. She was late as it was; she must meet her friend. 'You'll see me again?' he said. 'You will, won't you?'

'See you again!' she cried. 'You're really extraordinary to-night, Guy. Is there ever a time when I'm not delighted to see you? Come and lunch with me to-morrow—you know, the same old rooms, 18A Walpole Street, Chelsea, one o'clock.'

'But I don't know your name,' he said in an agony, 'I don't really. It isn't a game. I have told you nothing but the truth. I have never seen you in my life before, but, Heaven helping me, it isn't the last time I do!'

She turned to him as she was about to go up the stairs. 'Well, you shall have your way,' she said, laughing. 'We'll play the game to the end. My name is Helen Freed—with two "ee's," not with an "a," as you once spelled it; spelling was never your strong point, Guy.' And she was gone.

Poor Pritchard had no sleep at all that night. He walked his room trying to invent pieces of poetry, and when he could see through the thick intoxicating haze that surrounded him, puzzled again and again as to how he could keep her, as to whether he couldn't in reality continue to be this strange Guy Forrester. Impossible things seem so possible at three o'clock in the morning.

He arrived at Walpole Street half an hour too early, walked down as far as the Town Hall and back again, turned off towards the river and then back once more, and then at last, trembling with a deep and really humble excitement, he climbed a flight of stairs and rang a bell. Her room was very pretty. He knew nothing about pictures, but here, in love as he was, the water-colour drawings and the orange sofa, the amber bowl with its roses, enchanted him; he was in a land of magic. She came in happier to see him than anyone had ever hitherto been. A moment later he was kissing her. He did not know how it had happened; he did not think that he had never seen her before yesterday, and she did not know it, and she did not think it either. 'And now,' he said, standing away from her, 'it's Henry Pritchard who is asking you to marry him, it's Henry Pritchard, it's

Henry Pritchard, it's Henry Pritchard. I don't know anything about you except that I love you, and that I believe that you love me, and surely whether my name is Pritchard or Forrester doesn't matter. If it's Forrester's character you care for, then I'll have Forrester's character; I'll be just what he was, and then I'll be better than that because he isn't married to you and I shall be.'

'Wait a moment!' she cried. 'We can't go as fast as that. I don't know you at all, and you don't know me.'

'You don't know me?' he returned fiercely. 'Why, you told me yesterday that you'd known me for years, that I was the best friend you had, that you were terribly grateful. If you don't know me, what about Lance, for whom I got a job the other day? Why were you so glad to see me if you don't know me?'

'I was glad to see you,' she answered, 'because I had never seen you in my life before, and you'll never want to me see again because I behaved disgracefully, and am ashamed of myself, and glad, too, because if I hadn't behaved disgracefully I never would have spoken to you and never would have had the happiest hour of my life. And now you'd better go, and I shan't be surprised if you cut me the next time we meet.'

He asked her then to explain, and she did. She didn't know, of course, the whole of the affair; all she knew was what I'd told her in the Haymarket. At her mention of my name he was more than ever bewildered. He knew me scarcely at all, and he could not conceive what I had to do with his affairs, but dimly saw that there was a plot. He realised at least that there was no Guy Forrester, and mixed with the relief at that, there was, as he tried clumsily to explain to me afterwards, an odd sort of regret; he was beginning to like Forrester—at least, he was beginning to like the attitude to Forrester that other people had.

But it says, I think, a great deal for his amiable character that he bore no malice against anybody. How could he?

He was so terribly in love that he could think only well of all the world. If somebody had played a practical joke upon him, perhaps, after all he had deserved it. He explained to her that he had been too much alone lately, and that perhaps that had forced him to think too much about himself. With the *naïveté* of a child he declared: 'It isn't about myself that other people want to hear; they want to talk about themselves.'

'I want to hear you talk about yourself,' she told him, 'for weeks and weeks.'

'Yes,' he answered with, for him, amazing perspicacity, 'but when we've been married a year you won't want to.'

'Well, let's get married and see,' she said.

It is scarcely necessary to add that little Meening paid our firm the second seventy-five pounds without a murmur.

On Pritchard's mantelpiece there is a photograph of a man; a pleasant, smiling face he has. When people ask him who this is, he says: 'Oh, that's Guy Forrester—my best friend.' But he doesn't know who it is. He found it one day in a photographer's shop. But it has just that kindly, good-natured, jolly expression that Guy Forrester is certain to have had.

VII
THE DYSPEPTIC CRITIC

I HAVE BEEN occasionally asked what was the most romantic thing that ever happened to me. The adventure I am about to describe would nearly win the prize, I think. It began in this way.

Two friends and myself, bound with the Universal Unemployment ties, spent some of our idle time by endeavouring to help our companions out of difficulties into which their temperament led them.

The hero of this little adventure was one Everard Tallboys.

Tallboys at this time must have been about thirty years of age, was reviewer on the *Athanasian*, the *Blue Review*, the *Protestant Weekly* and the *Quidnunc*. He was also responsible for two published dramas, *The Queen at Bay* and *The Scarlet Fool;* a volume of verse, *The Lute at Dawn;* three novels, and a critical book, *William Morris and His Times*. I had seen him on one or two occasions at literary parties and we had once exchanged a word or two of rather heated discussion about a plate of sandwiches which I wanted for a lady and he wanted for himself. He was long, thin, black-haired, with a piercing, bitter nose, eyes grey and cold, and teeth slightly discoloured. His clothes were shabby and his hands not over clean. I am aware that this is not a pleasant description, and indeed I have seldom, in all my literary experience, seen anyone whose appearance was more thoroughly unwholesome and musty than that of Everard Tallboys. His favourite attitude at a party was to stand in a corner, balancing himself on one leg like a stork, look superciliously at the people around him, and say as little as possible to anybody. He had made that important discovery that if you want to be taken for a clever man, the less you say the better. It is the garrulous who are the fools, and Tallboys very quickly obtained a real reputation for wisdom and sagacity by dealing entirely in monosyllables and by saying, 'Do you think so?' in a high, shrill voice to anybody who was courageous enough to offer an opinion.

It will be seen quite clearly that I did not like Tallboys, but I did like him afterwards, as the story will show. It proves perhaps that I wronged him in the first place through ignorance. But, after all, if you never say anything and never come into close quarters with anybody, you stand a risk of being misunderstood; Tallboys was misunderstood by a great many people. He first appeared as critic anonymously and committed, in my opinion, the unpardonable crime of reviewing the same book in various different papers without signing his name, and as he invariably disliked the books that he reviewed, it may be said with truth that somewhere about 1915 almost all the more critical press began to be abusive to current works of fiction, and in many cases to poetry and belles lettres. Then he was forced out of his anonymity, was taken up by Hallard, the editor of the principal literary weekly, who thought that there was a great deal too much general praise of inferior work going about, and in the years that followed the Armistice, Tallboys could be discovered in all sorts of papers, sneering and carping and damning, with a languid superiority that enraged all sorts of suffering authors but did himself great credit. At the same time, such was the impulse of his genius that he was, for himself rather unfortunately, driven into creating works that went to other people for review. These works were of a universal mediocrity. The plays were in the good old pre-Raphaelite tradition admirably illustrated in Max Beerbohm's *Savonarola Brown*, the novels were in the weaker realistic manner, giving excellent descriptions of tables, chairs and stair-carpets, but leaving something to be desired in the analysis of the human beings who used these pieces of furniture. As to the volume of verse, by general consent the less said the better.

Our writers in general have many very obvious faults; they are weak, vain, credulous, sensitive creatures, but they have good points too, and taking criticism in general, a rather touching faith in the authority and honesty of their critics. It is, however, difficult for them to be patient when a critic comes bearing in one hand abuse of their work and in the other examples of how it ought to be done, examples thoroughly mediocre and incompetent.

By the end of 1920, Tallboys had nearly as many enemies as Lloyd George. Just at this time, for some reason or another, his photograph began persistently to appear in some of the illustrated papers: 'Mr. Everard Tallboys, the eminent critic,' 'Everard Tallboys, one of the brightest of our younger critics,' and so on. There was something about Tallboys' face in these photographs which caused simple men to long to set to work upon it, to do something to the superior nose, to stretch yet a little farther the protruding ears, and to snatch a tuft or two from the already thinning hair. I am sure that Tallboys himself was quite unaware of the indignation that he was exciting; the small fragments that came to him probably stirred his vanity and made him feel himself to be a real force.

One evening, I sat next at dinner to A. E. P. Braun, that well-known and justly popular young writer of romantic fiction. Braun was almost laughably like his name, thickset, bull-necked, his nose crooked, from his contest at the National Sporting Club with young Minards of Plymouth, his mouth too large for his face, but a smiling, genial person, pleasant to meet and talk to. Now most writers of romantic fiction in these days care nothing for the critics, but Braun had in his manly bosom a real ambition to be considered by the superior papers an elegant writer. It was true, as he said to me, that his favourite subjects, Spanish Treasure, Pirate Ships, and the '45 Rebellion, were not entirely suited to modern realistic methods, but he did write, he maintained, a great deal better than these literary fellows pretended.

Tallboys had especially got upon his young nerves. That night at dinner he unburdened himself to me. Tallboys had published in the *Quidnunc* only the week before an article purporting to examine the reasons for the popularity of certain novels; Braun had been one of his victims. He had decided that Braun was popular because of his *naïveté*, love of platitudes, and execrable English. 'Damn the fellow,' said Braun. 'Who does he think he is? If he could write a novel himself, there might be something in it, but I never read such stuff as that last book of his.' He paused, looked at his plate very solemnly, then leant closer to me and whispered, 'Look here, Johnson, somebody was telling me the other day that you and young Borden have a scheme for getting rid of tiresome people. Why shouldn't you turn your attention to young Everard? Think how many people would be grateful.'

'Murder him, do you mean?' I asked.

'Well, of course, that would be much the best, but it might lead to unpleasant consequences for all of us. No, the thing would be to turn his attention to something else. I tell you what. Improve his stomach.'

'What?' I asked.

'Yes, all his mangerly criticism comes from indigestion. I'm sure of it. Look at all the superior critics—Burroughs, Wontner, Hallard himself. Have you ever seen such a miserable lot of men? You can see their bones through their clothes, and their dirty white faces look as though they haven't sniffed fresh air for months. They're all the same. I tell you that dyspeptic criticism comes from dyspeptic insides. Cure those insides and you cure the criticism.'

'By Jove,' I said, 'there is something in that. I'll think it over.'

I should, nevertheless, have in all probability taken no steps in the matter had it not been that three days later I met Tallboys at the house of a mutual friend. He was that day at his most unpleasant.

I am at my worst with anyone whom I dislike, uneasy, unnatural, and over-garrulous, but on this occasion I was squeezed into a corner with Tallboys and we were forced to talk together. Of course I talked too much, said one or two things which were platitudinous and another two or three things that I did not really mean, and, equally of course, Tallboys said 'Do you think so?' and looked at me with that sarcastic patronage that is the hardest thing in the world to bear from a fellow human being. I was stung to the weakest kind of retaliation, saying something about my regret that his last novel had not sold more copies, and then felt exceedingly ashamed of myself for my meanness and cheapness. There followed then one of those silences that are so unagreeable between people who do not wish to be together but cannot escape. When I at last left the party, I asked myself indignantly why Tallboys should consider himself so superior. People will forgive you murder, rape, robbery, cheating at cards, and adultery, a great deal sooner than they will forgive you patronage. The one thing that every human being needs is outside confirmation in the stability of his own position. I have, unwittingly perhaps, patronised in my own time, and it is those to whom I have on some occasion, however slight and fleeting, been arrogant that will bear me a grudge to my dying day. The real reason why everyone hated Tallboys was not that he was a bitter critic, sickly in appearance, unhumorous, narrow-minded, but that he was arrogant.

Those few minutes in the corner of that overcrowded room determined me. It would, I thought, be most delightful to bring Mr. Tallboys down a peg or two. I discussed the matter with Borden, who, being the exact antithesis of Tallboys in every possible way, was just the man for this crisis. We discussed it for a long time. He thoroughly agreed with me that it would be very amusing to 'make the feller jump,' but how? 'If we can only remove him,' I said, 'or change the course of his criticism, or turn his interests to sausages or growing cucumbers, we shall not only please our own natural feelings, we shall earn our £150 as well. What about a lonely farm-house somewhere?'

'By Jove,' cried Borden, smacking his thigh, 'why not the Island?'

If I may be allowed for a moment to reveal to the gentle reader the intimate privacies of the Tallboys' home, the critic and poet may be seen in a very loose dressing-gown, sitting over his morning egg and reading the following letter.

The letter is headed—

BIRDS' ISLAND,
TRELISS,
CORNWALL.

DEAR MR. TALLBOYS,

You must, I am sure, be overwhelmed with correspondence from all parts of the country; I am therefore extremely reluctant to take up even a moment of your most valuable time, but it would seem to me ungrateful were I to let no expression of gratitude escape from me when you have given me, during these last weeks, such exquisite pleasure by your two books The Lute at Dawn *and* Rosemary at Play. *Your novel seems to me without any exaggeration the greatest masterpiece that the 20th century has yet given us. The nobility and generosity of your hero, Hugo Tremayne, the self-sacrifice with which he gives up one whom he loves so truly as he does Dora to his best friend and companion, the drama of the silent struggle between the two men as they stand one on each side of the fireplace saying nothing but feeling so much, the poetry of your descriptions of dawn and sunset and moonrise, the walk on the moor, the bathe in the sea, all the lovely sights and sounds of nature, these things are revealed by a master hand.*

As to your book of poetry, what shall I say? To one who has found during many years of trial and hardship, constant, sweet companionship in the genius of Shelley and Keats, it is perhaps no mean thing that he should feel that that marvellous company has now a third added to its number.

Forgive me these halting words. I feel too deeply to say all that I would wish.

Yours humbly,

HORATIO BICKERSTAFFE.

Three days later another letter was received in the Tallboys' home. It ran as follows:

DEAR MR. TALLBOYS,

Your kind reception of my little letter has made me a proud man. I live on this beautiful island a sheltered and retired existence. Books and birds, with an occasional rabbit, are my principal companions. Do believe me when I say that I meant and shall always mean every word that I wrote to you in my last.

You say that you know Cornwall but very slightly. Would it not be possible for you to snatch yourself away just for a day or two from your London labours and to seek the quiet and refreshment which this country scene affords? I cannot indeed offer you much in the way of excitement and adventure but at least your brain will be rested as you listen to the lisp of the waves upon the shore, the singing of the birds in the little wood behind my house, the ripple of the stream that chatters at the bottom of my garden.

I am a bachelor and quite alone here. If you cared we could discuss many things, or if you preferred it, I would leave you entirely alone.

The journey is an easy one. You go from Paddington to Truxe without a change and from thence a side line quickly takes you to Treliss. There a boat will await you and row you across to my island, a mile out to sea.

I throw this out as a suggestion, tempted by the extraordinary pleasure that your visit would give me.

Four days later a further letter was received.

DEAR MR. TALLBOYS,

This is indeed delightful and beyond my wildest dreams. I shall expect you then next Tuesday and can only hope that the weather during your stay will continue to remain as fine as it now is.

What were the motives that impelled Tallboys to take a little holiday? They were not, I imagine, very difficult to discover. It is possible that a good deal of Tallboys' arrogance arose from the fact that he had had during his writing career so little praise and was a hungry man. He was also, I have no doubt, a tired man, working a great deal too hard, sitting up late at night over his reviews and criticisms.

Cornwall in the month of May is no light temptation, and Mr. Bickerstaffe, although his praise was certainly a little foolish and extravagant, could probably be endured for a night or two without difficulty. In any case, on a beautiful May evening Tallboys might have been seen, a rather grimy bag in one hand and a waterproof in the other, standing on the little Treliss pier and looking about him. That it was a most beautiful evening I can bear witness, because I myself was present, not close to Tallboys but waiting discreetly in the background under the rocks where some of the smaller boats are drawn up at high tide.

Treliss, a magic circle of gold and topaz, hung over us veiled in thin purple mist, and the sea, very faintly blue, drew up to the shore and faded away again with a gentle hiss of cosy peace and satisfaction.

Tallboys was a very noticeable figure standing there on the little pier. Presently a fisherman came up to him, touched his cap and said, 'Be you the gentleman for Mr. Bickerstaffe?' 'I am,' said Tallboys. 'There's a boat here, sir, to take you across to the island. Mr. Bickerstaffe asked me to say, sir, that he was partikler sorry he couldn't come across hisself. He's just finishing some letters for the post. If you'll come with me, sir, we'll be over in no time.'

Tallboys climbed into the rowing-boat, with that rather clumsy movement peculiar to landsmen, seating himself very carefully and clutching his bag, and soon was rowed away. When they had rounded the corner of Trust Point, the little island came into view. Very tiny it looked with the wood a dark tuft against the sky, a white building and a thin strip of golden sand. Tallboys didn't attempt any conversation; it was not easy for him to talk to men not of his own kind. I have no doubt and I like to think that he enjoyed the beauty of the evening, the fresh sea breeze, the colour of the sea and sky, and that for those few minutes, at any rate, he was a happy man. He was not, alas, to remain happy very long.

I have travelled in many parts of the globe but I say definitely that I know nothing more beautiful than that gate into Birds' Island, where a little path leads up from the beach over rocky boulders, breaks on to a stretch of coarse-grained down, and finally, skirting a wood where all the trees, blown sideways by the wind, look as though they were listening for some important news coming across the sea, leads into the rough, ill-paved courtyard that stands in front of the farm. It was in this same courtyard that Tallboys met Borden, and it was from Borden that I received the next portion of this story.

Tallboys stopped in the yard and looked about him and then saw Borden advancing towards him, but that young man's stocky figure, bull-dog countenance, and general air of being just sent down from Oxford for conduct 'unbefitting a gentleman,' was not at all what our friend had expected Mr. Bickerstaffe to be. However, he held out his hand, which Borden gripped and shook vigorously, and said, 'Mr. Bickerstaffe?'

'No,' said Borden, very cheerfully, 'my name is Borden. Let me carry your bag. Come inside out of the sun.'

Even then Tallboys had apparently no suspicion of the truth; he sat down opposite Borden in the low-ceilinged sitting-room, across whose floor streaks of sunlight like yellow gauze were filtering; then smiling a little nervously, he said to Borden, 'Mr. Bickerstaffe is finishing some letters, I understand.'

'Oh no, he isn't,' said Borden. 'Any letters he had to write he finished long ago. What I mean is that there isn't any Mr. Bickerstaffe.'

What a pang must then have struck the tender, trusting heart of Everard Tallboys! Borden tells me that he turned a pale green, that his long thin legs began to tremble.

'I don't understand,' he said.

'It's very simple. I and a friend of mine wrote those letters and signed them Bickerstaffe. We were so glad you were able to come.'

'Signed them Bickerstaffe!' cried Tallboys, getting up from his chair. 'What do you mean? I still don't understand.'

'It's just this,' said Borden, in the friendliest manner. 'There are half a dozen fellows in London who think you've been working too hard and haven't been sleeping well of nights. They'd hate you to have a breakdown or anything of that kind, and they knew that you were so conscientious that you'd never take a holiday of your own self, so they thought they'd give you a holiday, get you down here, and then when you saw how much you liked it, why, of course you'd stay.'

That must have been a terrible moment for Tallboys, whose sense of humour was limited, whose dignity was very easily affronted, whose physical strength was nothing very much to boast about.

'Do you mean to say,' he burst out, 'that those letters weren't genuine?'

'Of course they weren't,' said Borden. 'I've never read a line you've written. Johnson had read a bit, and we made it up from that.'

'Johnson!' cried Tallboys. 'Do you mean Seymour Johnson?'

'The very same,' said Borden. 'He'll be here in a few minutes, and very glad to see you.'

'This is a plot,' cried Tallboys. 'Exactly,' said Borden, 'a good old-fashioned melodramatic plot like they have at the Lyceum, only instead of a very beautiful heroine, we have—well, Mr. Tallboys.'

'My God, you shall pay for this,' cried Tallboys, in the most approved melodramatic manner, striding up and down the room. 'I'll have you in jail for this before I'm a day older.'

'You can't do very much to-day,' said Borden, 'there's no boat going to the mainland; Mr. Perry and his two splendid sons run this little farm and are devoted friends of ours; except for one boy who is next door to an idiot and an old woman who is next door to heaven, there's nobody on the island at all. There isn't a telephone and there isn't a post office. Of course, you can stand on the seashore and wave your handkerchief, or you can build a fire in the good old *Treasure Island* fashion and watch its smoke ascend to heaven, or you can climb a tree with a spyglass, or you can swim to the shore. After all, it's only a mile, and most beautiful weather. If all these things fail you, unless you have an airplane in your pocket, you'll be almost compelled, I am afraid, to spend a day or two with us.'

'But this is infamous,' cried Tallboys. 'I'll have you in jail before the week's out.'

'Yes, and it'll be a lovely story for the papers,' said Borden. 'We'll be in jail, but you'll look terribly foolish. I can see the headlines. "Kidnapped Poet on Deserted Island"—"Lured to Captivity"—"Poet and His Tormentors"—and you know what everyone in London will say, that you were off on some nasty little adventure of your own and got in further than you meant. And then there are Mr. Bickerstaffe's letters. They'll look splendid in print: "Young poet gratified at praise from stranger hurries to deserted island," and so on.'

'By God, I'll have the law on you,' screamed Tallboys, now in a hysterical state and really not far from tears.

'Now look here,' said Borden, 'it's very foolish to make such a fuss. This is a perfectly charming place; the weather looks as though it will hold for a week at least; the water really isn't too cold for bathing; old Mrs. Bolitho is a simple cook, but you get so hungry here that you really don't want Carlton fare; the bed is very comfortable; there are no mosquitoes yet; we've a very nice library, you can compose poetry to your heart's content. I think a fortnight here would do you all the good in the world.'

'A fortnight!' screamed Tallboys. 'What about my work? My articles, and the rest of it?'

'Well, I'm afraid,' said Borden, 'we can't allow you to send anything by post for the first week or two. Not until we see the bloom of health beginning to steal into your cheeks. You can write as much as you like, only there's no post. Of course the world will be simply all in pieces at having nothing from you for a whole fortnight, and if articles begin to appear in the London Press about the missing poet, we're in for it, I suppose. But won't it be interesting? You'll really be able to test your public importance. I admit that it might hurt your feelings if you were down here for three whole weeks and nobody in London realised it, but on the other hand it will make you feel very free and independent.'

It was at this moment that I, who had followed in another boat, came in. When Tallboys saw me, he made a sort of spring in my direction, as though he would like to tear me limb from limb, but men who have like Tallboys developed their brains at the expense of every other part of them never meet these situations very effectively, and all he could do was to repeat his parrot-like cry, 'By God, I'll have the law on you.'

'Now we must be sensible,' said Borden. 'The real truth of the matter is that two or three of us want to test a theory that we have, a theory that, if it's tested thoroughly, will really make a difference to human conditions, and when something is for the good of the race, we are all, I'm sure, ready to make a little sacrifice of our personal interests and comforts. The theory is that artistic criticism, in the direction it takes and the spirit behind it, is based largely upon Stomach. Now you won't deny that you have for a number of years been the gloomiest critic in Europe, and that, we maintain, is because your inside is all wrong, because you don't take enough exercise, because you live too much with men of your own kind, and because your sense of humour is so lamentably undeveloped. Now you've really never had a holiday of this sort in lovely surroundings, lots of light and air, plenty of time to sleep, good food, and company who don't in the least respect your opinions. Of course we may fail. It's quite possible that you will hate both us and the place more and more every minute that you stay here, but even then, we flatter ourselves that the after-effects will be excellent and that in days to come you will look back to these hours with longing and even think of us with kindness, and if it should happen that you take life a little more cheerfully and see it a little more thoroughly in the round, how well worth our trouble will have been. You will be happier, we will be happier, and countless thousands of young novelists, poets, and critics will be happier. We really will belong to that small group of earnest men and women known as benefactors of the human race.'

Tallboys turned to me. 'You shall suffer for this, Johnson,' he said. 'I won't rest till I've made you regret this hour.'

'That's all right, Tallboys,' I answered. 'I quite expected you to be upset at first a bit. I quite understand that you shouldn't have at this moment the friendliest feelings towards Borden and myself, so we're going to leave you in better hands than ours.'

I went to the door and shouted 'Jim.' There quickly appeared the large body and rubicund smiling countenance of

Jim Perry, the young farmer, some twenty-five years of age, six feet three in height, almost as broad as he was tall, one of the best fellows in the world, with an intelligence active enough as regarded birds of the air, the fish in the sea, and nature generally, but his reading limited to the *News of the Globe* which he spelt out slowly word by word on Sunday afternoon. It had been explained to Jim that we were to have as guest a gentleman from London who was tired and worn out with overwork, whose friends had determined on his taking this holiday, who would certainly protest and try to escape in a boat, whom Jim was to look after as he would his own child, that he was to be kind, tender, and cheerful, and not to let him out of his sight.

This had seemed to Jim a capital game, and he looked at Tallboys with exactly the expression that I had seen him use once to a damaged owl whose wing was broken; the bird had been nursed by Jim week after week with the care and kindness of a mother to her only ailing child.

'Oh, yes,' I added, 'there's one other thing. We know you like reading, and so we've selected a library for you.' I waved my hand towards the bookshelves. 'Here you'll find a number of books that I'm sure you've never read. Here are all the works of Sir Arthur Conan Doyle, Rider Haggard, A. E. W. Mason, Stanley Weyman, Henry Seton Merriman, Phillips Oppenheim, and a gentleman called Mr. Rice Burroughs, who has written several books about a jungle man called "Tarzan," and a lot of others, too, that will be new to you. We have also the poetry of Walt Whitman, and the *Ingoldsby Legends*. Now we'll leave you and Jim together. You needn't see more of us than you want to, and I do hope you'll have a happy time.' Then Borden and I left the room.

Those were indeed strange days for all of us. I will confess that during them I had many misgivings. It will have been noticed by anyone who has glanced at any other of these adventures that most of my cases have been solved simply by a little reshuffle of individuality; I proved to myself in the course of them a great lesson, namely, that no one is a bore to everybody and that the art of getting rid of a bore is simply to find someone to whom he isn't a bore. Old Sir Marcus Pendyce, for instance, was a terrible bore to the Lambs, but a sheer delight to the old ladies in Durham, and Mrs. Farbman drove the Flemings crazy, but was exactly what the host of the Vin Blanc needed.

It is also a fact about human nature that the people you dislike are on the whole the people with whom you do not come into close contact, that it is very hard to know anybody very well without discovering their good points. Now Borden and I agreed, after two days in Tallboys' company, that he was indeed a dreary dog but that his enthusiasm for literature was something extremely fine, finer than anything we ourselves possessed.

On the second morning after his arrival, I came into the sitting-room and found him, quite unconscious of my presence, looking at the bookshelves. Suddenly he gave a little cry of delight, a very touching little cry, the sort of cry that Penelope must have uttered when she saw Ulysses coming up the garden path. I heard him murmur, 'Oh, how fortunate!' and I saw him take from the shelves a thin red-covered book, most obviously not a novel, and from where I was standing realised that it was the Oxford edition of the Collected Poems of Robert Bridges that had slipped somewhere by mistake in amongst his coarser, more bovine brethren. A smile illumined Tallboys' plain features as he went to the window, clutching the book in his hands; I crept out of the room noiselessly, feeling that although it might wreck our plan, I couldn't but be glad that Bridges had broken in. Tallboys' attitude to us during those first two days was one of silent loathing. I suggested that he should have his meals in his own room if he preferred it, and he gave us to understand through Jim that he did.

The afternoon of the second day was most glorious weather,

and I overheard on the upstairs landing some fragments of a funny little conversation. First there was Jim. 'Do 'ee come down, Mr. Torboys, and 'ave a swim. It's warm as summer. It'll make 'ee less homesick.'

'Thank you, Perry.' Tallboys' voice was making a struggle for dignity and failing. 'I can't swim.'

'That makes no matter, Mr. Torboys,' came Jim's voice. 'I'll look after 'ee.'

'I haven't got any bathing things,' said Tallboys.

'Oh, that's nothin',' said Jim. 'We don't wear no cloes in this place. There's only old Mrs. Bolitho and she'm over eighty and 'alf blind anyway. Do 'ee come down and try.'

'I suppose I may as well do that as anything else,' came Tallboys' answer.

Later I watched from a knoll in the little wood the two on the seashore. Jim, a magnificent figure, poised on a rock at the farther end of the beach, standing for an instant with hands above his head, then cleaving the air like a flash. Tallboys, strangely grey in the sunlight, stepping timidly into the water, walking out like Agag delicately, soon surrendering himself, and five minutes later, supported by Jim, making absurd splashes and futile strokes with his arms in the course of his first swimming lesson.

That same night Borden and I, seated with our pipes and playing chess in the sitting-room, suddenly saw Tallboys enter. 'May I have a word with you?' he asked, stiffly, standing in the doorway.

'Certainly, as many as you like,' said Borden, smiling. 'Have a smoke.'

'No, thank you. You know that you've done a most dastardly thing. You are stronger than I at this particular moment and I am in your hands. I do beg of you to let me go home to-morrow, and, if you do, I promise you I'll not say a word about this affair.'

Borden answered him seriously. 'Look here, Tallboys, it's quite natural for you to hate us, in fact, if you don't mind my saying so, I think you ought to hate us a little more than you do. We've taken considerable risks in this affair and now we must play it through to the end. In three weeks from now, we will know whether we've succeeded or not. Of course, we don't pretend that we're going to change you altogether, but we do hope and believe that you're going to be a bit different after your three weeks' rest here away from your own rotten set and getting to know a first-class feller like Jim Perry. We must see our experiment through. Here you are for three weeks. I know that yesterday you tried to get a letter through and that you offered Bill Perry ten quid if he'd row you across, but you see, those three men happen to be the very best friends Johnson and I possess. They're loyal as you make 'em, and you may as well know right away that it's perfectly useless trying to bribe them or to get them to act against us in any fashion whatever. Now you may as well make up your mind to these three weeks. If you'll forgive me for saying so, you look better already. I don't want you to admit it, but you enjoyed that bathe this afternoon and you know you did. Johnson and myself are not, I am aware, the companions you'd have chosen if you'd had a free hand, but really we're not so bad. You don't like Johnson's writing, but he's just as enthusiastic as you are about good things in his own way, and upon my word, I can't understand why you writing fellers who all care about good stuff in distinction to the rest of us who don't know good stuff from bad, why you should spend your time in quarrelling and getting into little sets, hating one another. I know nothing about literature, but I am not a bad companion and I could show you one or two things on this island that would astonish you. Why not make the best of a bad job and be friendly while you're here? You can have us up in the courts when you get back, but enjoy yourself while you may.'

'Thank you,' said Tallboys, looking at us both with unutterable loathing. 'I'd rather die than spend five minutes with either of you,' and he departed to his room.

I've often wondered since what went on in Jim's mind during these curious weeks. Tallboys was something quite novel to him; it was rather as though the Archbishop of Canterbury had to stay with him, a native from Central Africa, for a week or two. It was just because of this strangeness that he developed towards Tallboys a kind of protective affection that did resemble exactly his attitude to the wounded owl of which I spoke before. Tallboys to him was a sick, melancholy, broken-backed, ignorant creature. All Tallboys' knowledge of the *vers librists*, the modern novelists, and the rest, was to him less than nothing, and he was soon talking to him in the indulgent, kindly voice that a nurse uses to a small, miserable, unhappy child. 'Now don't 'ee, Mr. Torboys,' we used to hear him say, 'don't 'ee take on so. You'll be better in no time. You're getting some colour in your cheeks now. You won't know yourself in another week's time.'

I saw that in spite of himself Tallboys' appetite was magnificent. He was sleeping superbly. On the fourth night of his stay he took up to bed with him that admirable romance of Mr. Mason's, *The Watchers*. I perceived then that book after book disappeared from the shelves. On the fifth day I was sitting alone, sunning myself in the little wood, when Tallboys turned the corner and came upon me by mistake. He made as though he would retreat again, then thinking better, he came towards me.

'Look here, Johnson,' he said, 'hasn't this gone on long enough? Let me go to-morrow. I don't bear you any malice, I don't indeed. Of course, I think it was a rotten thing to do, but I won't deny that I do feel better for these three or four days. I hadn't, as a matter of fact, been sleeping very well in town, and I had been overworking. Perhaps there is something in what Borden said about my getting a bit narrow. I used to feel it myself sometimes, although I'd never admit it to anybody. Let me go to-morrow.'

'We must stick to our three weeks,' I answered. 'You're through the first week very nearly. You'll find the rest of the time passes ever so much more quickly if you talk to Borden and me a bit. Borden's a very decent fellow, really, and his views on life in general quite worth knowing.'

Tallboys stood there, looking out to sea. 'It is lovely,' I heard him say under his breath, 'more beautiful than I'd ever imagined.'

'Stay here a bit,' I went on. 'I'll admit that this thing began partly as a joke and partly because a lot of us thought you were too damned arrogant for anything.'

'Arrogant?' cried Tallboys. 'I?'

'Why, yes. You thought your own opinion so mighty important, and that you and your little crowd were the only people that mattered. All sorts of things go to make up literature. It isn't only a perfect style and supercilious taste that count. But I don't want to get preaching to you. I shall be as bad at my end as you are at yours, but if you like, I'll confess something to you. I couldn't stand the sight of you before you came down, and now I'm getting quite keen on your company.'

Tallboys suddenly laughed. 'Of all the infernal cheek!' he said. 'How you ever dared do it!'

'If you hadn't been so conceited,' I told him, 'you never would have come. I never believed that such absurd letters as those of ours could have brought you.'

Tallboys flushed. 'It's all very well,' he said, 'but you'd have gone yourself if you discovered a whole-hearted admirer somewhere. Why shouldn't we care about somebody liking our stuff? We spend all our days and nights thinking about it and trying to do the best we can, and if there's somebody who likes it, well, it's awfully comforting. I think the thing I felt sorest about is that there wasn't anybody after all. Do you suppose I don't realise,' he went on fiercely, 'that I'm not first-class, that it wouldn't matter to anybody if I stopped writing for ever to-morrow? But because I'm not first-class myself, it's no reason that I shouldn't want other people to do first-class things.'

'No, I suppose it isn't,' I answered, 'but it's the way that you deliver your opinions that people mind. We're all in the same box, we are most of us second-rate, and we might feel a little more kindly towards one another.'

The result of that conversation was that Tallboys held himself no longer aloof. He was still shy with us, there were many moments when he broke out into abuse of us, many moments when we abused him in return. But there was always Jim in the background, proving to all of us that our little corner of the world was a mighty small one and that while we quarrelled about literary values, Jim was looking upon us as the merest children in arms who knew nothing, had seen nothing, and could do nothing, with the possible exception of Borden who fished and swam and walked more like a possible human being.

After that the days flew on wings. The middle of the following week, Jim had a birthday, and a number of fishermen and their wives came over from the mainland to celebrate it. That afternoon, before they arrived, I said to Tallboys, 'Look here, there's going to be a party to-night and some men are coming over from Treliss. If you like you can give us the slip. Don't say anything to anybody but go back with one of them after the party is over if you want to.'

Tallboys said nothing.

That was a wonderful night. June had set the calendar at defiance and slipped into May. It was so warm that we had supper outside the farm on a ridge overlooking the sea. The sky was thick with stars, soft and milky with a kind of white spray of silver. The fishermen and their wives shouted and sang, and when the meal was over, an old man and a boy produced two fiddles and the dance went on up and down the turf while the sea murmured below a humming accompaniment of approval and benediction.

Jim looked after Tallboys as though he were his especial property. The drink that was provided was nothing very strong, but the night, the stars, sea, and the mild air went to our heads, and resting suddenly breathless from one of the wildest of the country dances I looked up and saw Tallboys being whirled round, a thin fantastic figure against the night sky, while the old fiddler, seated on a tree-trunk, played for his life, and Mrs. Bolitho, who should have been in bed long since, tears of pleasure running down her furrowed cheeks, clapped her hands and beat time with her feet. I stole away up into the little wood and heard, as it were behind a curtain of trees, the screaming of a violin, the laughter and the shouting, and, strangely, more penetrating than any of these, the swaying whisper of the trees above my head.

I went off to bed.

Next morning Tallboys was at breakfast. I said nothing to him until quite casually in the afternoon I remarked, 'Look here, write any letters you like, I'll see that they go.' He nodded his head. I saw him sitting on the beach half an hour later when I came down to bathe, deep in a novel of Stanley Weyman's.

Six weeks afterwards, there appeared in the columns of that superior paper, the *Athanasian*, an article headed 'Romance and the Joy of Living.' Its opening sentences were: 'In these days of realism some of us are perhaps inclined to over-emphasise the virtues of technique and to lay too strong a stress upon the perfection of form, forgetting that there are other things more important in life than the petty disputes of the schools, and that there are many gates into the temple of literature. . . .' This article was signed 'E. Tallboys.'

A few nights later I tumbled on to Hallard, the editor of that superior weekly. 'I hear,' he said, 'that you've been having Tallboys down in Cornwall with you. It's done his health a lot of good, but can't say that it's done so much for his brains. He was actually advising me to read some rotten story by that fellow Mason.'

'Yes,' I answered, 'I think he enjoyed himself very much.

You'd better come and stay with us, Hallard, down in Cornwall.'

'I think I will one day,' said Hallard.

But after all, it would scarcely be fair to Jim Perry, would it?

THE HONEY-BOX

I SUPPOSE that no one who reaches the age of sixty in this bizarre life but comes to the conclusion that it is stupidity and not wickedness that prevents the world from going round as it should. Stupidity of oneself as well as of others. This little story is an instance of one very good man's stupidity and of why it was a pity that he was so stupid.

I have changed, of course, the names of all the people concerned. Humphrey Smith will not recognise himself, nor will Lucy Brown, nor most certainly the present Mrs. Smith.

I went one early September to spend a month in the valley of Borrowdale in Cumberland. I went to work. I engaged a bedroom and a sitting-room in that charming little hotel which I will call the Rosthwaite. This was not its name, but it was near that most charming village.

I see that I have already used the adjective 'charming' twice. Bad writing, but true to my story. Let me say at once that the month I spent there was one of the most beautiful, one of the happiest of my not altogether unhappy life. I am a Cornishman by birth, and in Cornwall I spent most of my youth. I am not a traitor to the South—I could not make my home in the North—but it so happened that the comfort of that little hotel, the loveliness (as it chanced) of the weather during that month, and the pleasant acquaintances that I found (and incidentally the way that my work happened just then to be going) make that holiday in retrospect unique. I know all that you and anyone else can say. Only this very week a highly-coloured and excitable young woman novelist has published a volume of reminiscences (there is to be a second, I believe, and she not yet thirty!) the burden of which is, the papers tell me, the superiority of everything foreign to everything English, and especially the superiority of foreign hotels, foreign food, foreign travel. It is a familiar cry and it is easy to pillory the tepid fish with the cold blue eye of the railway restaurant, the hard beds of the country inn, the chilly rooms, the Victorian pictures on the walls and the rest. Nevertheless, in Italy and France, Spain and Germany, I have found trains unpunctual, fleas in the beds, spaghetti, omelettes monotonous. But then I am an old gentleman over sixty, and the young lady—well, she could be, I believe (although both she and I are glad that she is not), my grand-daughter!

About Cumberland weather there is also, I understand, a great deal to be said. It is always raining, I am told. Well, it also rains in Cornwall and Kent, in Wiltshire and Norfolk, although no one would suppose it. It happens that I had a month of glorious weather in Cumberland. I have never risked a repetition of my experiment. It was altogether too successful to be repeated.

But it was not only the comforts of the inn, the weather, the beauties of the country, the fact that I ate well, slept well and (if I may be pardoned for saying so) wrote well, nor that I read there for the first time Turgenev's *Torrents of Spring* and the beautiful and mad plays of Beddoes, that makes that month so memorable for me. It was also and chiefly that I met and made, I think, a friend of Miss Lucy Brown (whose true name was, of course, something quite different).

On the first morning after my arrival I was standing at the door of the inn, looking at the little garden and the soft green hill that rose gently beyond it when someone spoke to me.

'Lovely day, sir,' he said, not with great originality.

I turned and saw standing beside me one of the most amiable-looking of human beings. Humphrey Smith was, is, and always will be of all men the most amiable. He was at that time in danger of stoutness (I understand that since then Mrs. Smith has checked that danger) but his stoutness was neither unpleasant nor unhealthy. He was squarely built, with brown hair, a ruddy-brown complexion, of a good height, and his eyes were as merry and friendly as any in the world. He looked as fresh and clean and healthy as any Englishman could ever be accused by a neurotic young novelist of being. Nor did he appear stupid. (That he *was* stupid at least once in his life, will be apparent, I think, before the end of this little story.) He was wearing stout boots and a heather-coloured tweed and was smoking a pipe. His eyes, his mouth, his round comfortable chin beamed friendliness and simplicity. He was Quixote and Pickwick and Colonel Dobbin and Colonel Newcome all rolled into one. I like kindly people. I liked him at once.

It seemed that he liked me. It seemed that he had read some of my novels and enjoyed them. Every novelist, whatever he may pretend, is pleased by the honest flattery of an honest reader. Why should he not be? Why does he write books if he does not wish them to be enjoyed? So, very quickly, we made friends and before the day was out I had learned a good deal about him.

He was a bachelor, had means, had two sisters, had a house in Wiltshire and, as I very quickly discovered, was afraid of approaching loneliness. He asked me, on the very first day, whether I did not fear a lonely old age and I said not in the least.

'I suppose,' he went on wistfully, 'that you've been a bachelor so long——'

'I'm not a bachelor,' I told him. 'I'm a widower. My wife

died ten years ago. No man was ever more happily married than I.'

'I should have thought you'd be all the more lonely now.'

'You don't always lose someone you've loved when they die. I don't feel lonely.'

'You're lucky,' he sighed.

'Well, why don't you marry?' I asked him, laughing.

'I expect I shall,' he said.

He was exactly the man for a woman who wanted someone to protect. He was absent-minded, not very practical, often, I should imagine, foolishly kind and impetuous. His heart was better than his head. Not that he was a fool. He was a good listener and not a bad judge of character, although he liked to find happy traits in a man and then hold on to him. He was an enthusiast, which a cynical woman would have found tiresome, but then no cynical woman of mature years likes men of Humphrey Smith's type. They prefer bitter men of the world with whom they can exchange chagrins.

That evening after dinner he came up to me and said:

'Westcott, a friend of mine would like to meet you. She has read your novels.'

This was annoying. The kind of friend of Humphrey's who had read my novels would be most certainly tiresome.

He led me across the room and introduced me to Lucy Brown.

Do you remember the delightful summer day that you spent in Mrs. Dalloway's company? Are you not a friend of Elizabeth Bennet's? Have you not walked behind the grim walls of the Brussels *pension* with Lucy Snowe? Has Jane Welsh never handed you a cup of tea nor Dorothy Osborne waved her hand to you? If none of these things have ever been your luck, then imagine for yourself the most enchanting English lady ever seen by you—but she must be over thirty-five, not at all modern, and quite clearly, oh, very clearly indeed, not married!

Did not the unmarried ladies of England formerly produce once and again in their great array a specimen of perfection to be found nowhere else in the world? Can they do so any longer? Is there in fact to-day any difference between the unmarried ladies and the married? But once there was a difference. Lucy Brown was just young enough, just old enough to be both of the other time and this. She was lovely to look upon, that is, if you do not demand dyed hair, carmined lips, crimson finger-nails. She was slim, tall, and carried herself like a flower—a flower of silver-grey, shell-like delicacy. That night she was wearing a dress of silver-grey with three deep red carnations at her waist. But what words are these? What shall I, who have all my life through been trying to describe people and failing, say of the beauty of her eyes so clear and so noble, of her cheek so gently coloured, of her hair with its faint shadow of silver, of the gaiety and yet shyness of her smile, of her dignity and yet her friendliness, her apartness and yet her companionship, her purity and yet her understanding of and sympathy for the sins and weaknesses of mankind?

Instead of describing her I will quote Wordsworth:

The stars of midnight shall be dear
To her: and she shall lean her ear
In many a secret place
Where rivulets dance their wayward round,
And beauty born of murmuring sound
Shall pass into her face.

You see I liked Miss Lucy Brown from the first and I think, indeed I know, that she liked me. For one thing she at once praised (and had obviously remembered) a novel of mine that had been unpopular. Unpopular? Nay, scarcely read. If a reader will find quickly his place to a writer's heart, let him praise that book that everyone else scorns and ignores. So she praised mine.

'I don't like all your books, Mr. Westcott,' she said gently.

Then, further than that, I discovered that her taste in letters was excellent. She preferred Hazlitt to Lamb as essayist, FitzGerald to Walpole as letter-writer, and she liked the novels of Henry Kingsley. She thought Vernon Lee the best living writer of prose and Mr. Wodehouse one of the half-dozen best humourists in the English language, following, with his head up, the succession of Chaucer, Fielding, Dickens, Lewis Carroll and Calverley. She could quote Mr. A. P. Herbert's verse, and yet again, was intimate with the poetry of Crabbe, Cowper and D. H. Lawrence. . . .

And the third bond before the evening was over was her sensible enthusiasm about the district in which we then were. She did not say: 'It always rains in the Lakes,' she never mentioned Wordsworth, she was not a rock-climber. But she did say: 'The lovely thing here, you will find, Mr. Westcott, is the sky. A very exciting sky. It never lets you down,' and: 'The hills are kindly—sometimes in a bad temper though, so that you may not forget how powerful they are. Boasting a little.' She had a book on her lap and read to me a line or two from it. It was Dorothy Wordsworth's Journal:

'I went to lie down in the orchard. I was roused by a shout that Anthony Harrison was come. We sate in the orchard till tea-time. Drank tea early, and rowed down the lake, which was stirred by breezes. We looked at Rydale, which was soft, cheerful and beautiful. We then went to peep into Langdale. The Pikes were very grand. We walked back to the view of Rydale, which was now a dark mirror. We rowed home over a lake still as glass, and then went to George Mackareth's to hire a horse for John. A fine moonlight night. The beauty of the moon was startling, as it rose to us over Loughrigg Fell. We returned to supper at ten o'clock.

'Yes,' she repeated. 'To George Mackareth's to hire a horse for John. A fine moonlight night. I come to the Lakes every year,' she said.

In the next day or two she told me a little about herself,

but there was not very much to tell. She was the daughter of a Canon of Winchester Cathedral. She had some means of her own.

'I am a perfectly useless person,' she said. 'I cannot type. I know no shorthand. I cannot speak French so that anyone can understand me. I have never earned a penny in my life.'

I discovered, however, that she had a perfect network of friends and that most of them depended on her for something. But she liked to be alone at times. She confessed that she was afraid that this was growing upon her.

'Like Alice,' she said, 'I shall wake up one day and find myself in the next Square—the Square of the complete old maid. I'm not there yet, but very near it.'

She was interested in everything and professed that never before in history had there been such a wonderful time in which to be alive as the present. I enquired whether any aspects of modern life shocked her.

'Shock me? Oh, no. Some things, I think, are a pity, but they are always understandable. I don't like people who are unkind to animals, nor women who play bridge on a fine afternoon, nor the Nudists. But they are all understandable, I think.'

She thought it a pity that so few people to-day were interested in religion. 'Much the most interesting thing in life so long as you don't force it down other people's throats.'

I said that I thought that to-day many people *were* interested.

'Yes, so long as they don't have to do anything about it. It's like backgammon. You've no idea how good it is until you've practised a bit!'

Once I was passing her room and she called me in. It was an ordinary hotel bedroom, but in a moment I saw that its ordinary character had been transmuted by her.

'I carry a few things round with me,' she said. 'It makes things homely.'

She had a square silver clock, a piece of Persian embroidery, a small Chinese figure on a horse, a little water-colour sketch of some grey hills and a little white house, and a jade paperknife.

She showed me a box. It was made of blue and white enamel and on its lid was printed: 'Unto the End I Love my Friend.'

'Smell it,' she said, opening it.

I sniffed. There was a delicious smell, the scent of honeysuckle.

'I don't know why it smells like that. It did when I bought it. It is eighteenth-century. I call it the Honey-Box. When I give it away I shall have crossed the Square. I shall be an old maid.'

I discovered soon that she and Humphrey had met in the preceding year and were very good friends indeed. She called him Humphrey and he called her Lucy. She chaffed him gently and he liked it. He told me that he thought her a most remarkable woman.

'The trouble with Humphrey,' she said to me, 'is that he has far too much money and always has had. It's not for me, who have been completely idle all my life, to reproach him with laziness, but that's really what's the matter with him. And it's all wrong in these days for anyone to be rich. He should sell all that he has and give to the poor.'

'I should think he's generous,' I said.

'Oh, of course. He's got too much heart. He'd give anything to anybody. He's no system. But then neither have I. That's why I see so clearly that he hasn't any.'

But, of course, she had a system. With her slender means she did innumerable wise things. She was a sharp judge of character, and knew a humbug when she saw one. She was as wise as she was kind—a rare combination.

So I spent a delightful week with my two new friends. We walked and we hired a car. The Lake District is, in extent, as small as a big pocket-handkerchief, and it is packed with beauty. With more than beauty, for it has that queer quality, I think, that belongs to only a few places. In my experience I have found it in the hills around Assisi, in Cordoba and Seville, in Arizona, but not, oddly, in Sicily, in Southern France, anywhere in Scandinavia—the quality of *inexhaustible* interest so that going back again and again you make always new discoveries in one small square of ground. I cannot say wherein this quality lies; possibly it is simply personal and every man makes his own adventures. I found it here—in Watendlath, in the little beach of Buttermere ringed round with the watching hills, in the high ground above Ullswater, in Borrowdale (and especially in Stonethwaite), in the ground between Newlands Church and Robinson, in the John Peel country behind Blencathra. I could return to these quiet and untroubled places again and again and always find them new, as one returns to the plays of Shakespeare, the poems of Donne, the novels of Jane Austen and Hardy. So we had, the three of us, a most beautiful time.

After sixty one does not, I suppose, make new friends easily, and I have never been a man to make friends: one great friend, a Cornish fisherman in my youth, an elderly lady who, at that same time, helped and mothered me, my wife, one or two more. The list of *real* friends is with me, as it is with all of us, a short one. But now, in the course of one evening, I added two to the list. What memories of that week! Walking over Buttermere Hause with the sun stroking the green slope, the clouds piled above Seatoller like a tangle of grapes in a cup of snow, Rydal dark under a sheet of stars and the Watendlath Tarn blown to a froth of spray by the wind. Yes, we were all contented. . . .

And then, quite suddenly, for no reason that I could define, I began to wonder whether, in this case as in so many others, two were company and three were not. Not that they made me feel anything—far from it. They seemed to be glad to have my company. I am, perhaps, a foolishly sensitive man. I have lived, in these last years, a good deal to myself, and there is nothing in life, I fancy, more tiresome than some old fellow determined to keep abreast of the times and show the younger generation that he is doing so. Not that either Humphrey or Miss Brown were young, but they were younger than I.

Thinking over it in bed I started up almost with a cry. Why, of course! They were in love!

How could I have been so blind, and how charming, how right, how absolutely right this was! Humphrey was rich and lonely. He was kind and faithful, but he needed caring for. Lucy Brown was made, built, conceived to do that caring. She would give him just that extra bit of sense and wisdom that he needed, and he would give her something to love, protect and guard. Yes, how right, how very right! One of those rare things in life designed for perfection. I was so happy in my discovery that I found it difficult to sleep. What a beautiful thing and how lucky I was to be permitted to witness it!

And then she told me.

We went up the path above Rosthwaite towards Watendlath, and sat among the rocks looking down over Borrowdale. It was a glorious evening, and the setting sun, its reflected glories falling in rosy misty ladders of light upon Scawfell and Gable, drew out the September colours of the waves of bracken that swept the lower slopes.

We had been talking of Humphrey.

'He is a great dear,' Lucy Brown said, 'but he needs looking after.'

'And you are the woman to look after him,' I said.

Her face lit up at that. She could not help herself. She smiled and seemed transfigured.

'Nonsense!' she said.

'Of course. You are the woman for *him* and he is the man for *you!*'

'Oh, do you think so!'

She was like a girl of twenty. She hesitated and then very

shyly told me that she had fallen in love with him at first sight the preceding year. No one knew it but I. ('You are so sharp, Mr. Westcott. You see everything.') Above all things, Humphrey was never to know.

'Well, if he doesn't know that,' I said, 'he knows that *he's* in love with *you*. He'll tell you so very soon.'

'Oh, do you think so? An old woman like me?'

'He's no chicken himself.'

'No. I'm so glad. I don't care for young men.'

Then, very delicately, with great shyness, she confessed to me that she had been thinking of him during the last year without ceasing. They had written to one another. She had tried *not* to think of him. Impossible.

'You know, Mr. Westcott, this is my last chance. Oh, not of marriage! Until I met Humphrey, I'd given up all idea of marrying. But now—if he cares for me—I shall be, I think, young always. I shall keep my youth. If he does not, why, then—I cross the Square, I gather together my knitting and buy a dog. A Pekingese, I suppose. You novelists would call it the crisis of my life, wouldn't you?'

'Some of us would,' I answered.

We walked back to the hotel in a very close and friendly companionship.

'Thank you,' she said, giving me her hand. 'I'll never forget your kindness.' As we went in she caught my arm. 'Oh, what a beautiful girl!' she said.

Standing in the doorway, looking out at the hills, now wrapped in crimson dusk, was a girl. She was certainly beautiful, very slender, with dark, shingled hair, wearing a blue frock and that air of assurance and indifference about her that belongs to the contemporary young.

She stood aside as we passed, but did not even turn to look.

That night, just as I was getting into bed, there was a knock on my door and Humphrey came in. He had been having a bath and was in a dark woolly dressing-gown; his hair tousled and on end, he looked like a large blundering sheep-dog.

He wandered about my room, picking things up and putting them down while I lay in bed finishing my pipe.

He examined my wife's photograph.

'What was her name?' he asked.

'Mildred Trenchard.'

'I asked because I knew some Trenchards once.'

'These came from Glebeshire—Garth-in-Roselands. Her brother has made a bit of a name as a writer. Henry Trenchard. Wrote a good comedy called *Knife and Fork*. You probably saw it.'

'Oh, Henry Trenchard? Yes, I know the name—never remember the names of plays though. . . . I say, she looks jolly. I'm awfully sorry, old man.'

'Oh, that's all right.'

He sat down on the bed.

'I say, we've made friends in these days. I hope we don't drop it.'

'Oh, *I* shan't.'

'You bet *I* won't. I've never known an author before—not to *like* him. Frightened of authors. They generally have their chins in the air.'

'Oh, no, they haven't——'

'They can always put you in a book, you know . . .' He went on, looking at me affectionately. 'Friendship's a grand thing—nothing like it. I like men in general better than women. All the same—all the same—I want to get married.'

'Yes?' I said encouragingly.

'Lucy . . . she's a splendid woman, isn't she?'

'Simply grand,' I answered.

'Do you think she'd have me if I asked her?'

'How can I tell?' I answered.

'She's independent in a way, isn't she? I mean—I doubt if she's a marrying woman.'

'You try her and see,' I said.

'Do you really think so?' He smiled like a baby. 'I believe

I will.' He beamed at me. 'I'm getting on, you know. Of course I like a pretty girl like anyone else. But that's different. Girls don't make good companions for men of my age. It's all right at first, but later on——'

'You never spoke a truer word,' I said.

'And you think Lucy would have me?'

'Try her and see.'

He ambled away and at the door smiled back at me. Yes, Humphrey's *heart* was all right. . . .

And next morning, I met the beautiful girl. A lady, elderly but elegant, with a face that had certainly been lifted but not too indiscreetly, one eyebrow a fraction higher than the other, with clothes beautifully made but ten years too young for her, caught me as I sat in the garden reading the newspaper.

'Mr. Westcott?' she said.

I admitted it.

'Will you think me very rude if I speak to you for a moment?'

It seemed that she *adored* my books, that she had read them all and, as I soon discovered, could remember the names of none of them. But she just *had* to speak to me. Would I forgive her. . . ? She introduced me to her daughter.

'Mr. Westcott, this is my little girl, Rose,' said Mrs. Potter.

I am greatly struck when I read a very modern novel written by a very modern young man or young woman by the glee with which they malign their own generation. The young men in their books are always anæmic and perverted, the young women hard and not so much immoral as entirely amoral. From my distant perch I perceive them quite otherwise. The girls of this generation are, I think, kind, courteous and excellent company. If they seem hard it is because they have learnt some things too early and other things not at all. That puts them on the defensive. If they seem selfish it is because they will stand no humbug. But with all their faults and virtues they have grand qualities. Rose Potter was a modern young woman. She had no use either for humbug or elderly novelists. She was even more beautiful than I had first thought her. . . .

That afternoon I insisted that Humphrey and Miss Brown should go off by themselves. I was suffering, I said, from a headache. I waited all that afternoon in a state of quite absurd agitation. When you live by yourself and feel that the course of your own life is finally settled, you take sometimes a very active interest in the lives of other people.

These were my two friends. I discovered that afternoon that I quite passionately wanted these two to marry. I felt now just as I had done when the possibility had first come to me that here was a perfect thing. Indeed, I saw then, as I see even more plainly now, that here were two lives really quite seriously in the balance. Not only would Lucy Brown cross her Square if she missed him, but he would also cross a yet more serious Square. He would never find anyone so perfect again. One is given in life many second-rate chances, but first-rate ones—well, one is lucky if they recur! I have a belief, too, that somewhere in the world the right person is waiting for everyone, but there is only one right person, absolutely right, I mean. Plenty of adventure, many brilliant encounters, and friendships, but only one perfect thing. So I waited for them to return. Did I, on that afternoon, have my first breath of danger or am I now, in retrospect, imagining it? I don't know. I am only aware that I sat all that afternoon in the garden with Lowes' *Xanadu* on my knee and waited for them to return. I was sure that he would propose to her.

They did return. He had not proposed.

As he came in, laughing, half-way across the hall he paused. Then he saw me. He came up to me and told me that it had been glorious; they had walked to the bottom of Stye Head. Then he touched my arm.

'By Jove, Westcott—what a *lovely* girl!'

Do you know what it is to be caught for a time into the experience and feelings of someone else? Not only to guess pretty shrewdly at their emotion, but also to become, for a brief while, a very part of them, to share their crisis so vividly that it becomes your crisis? I became, during the next few days, part of Lucy Brown. Never, since the death of my wife, had I liked any woman so much as I did Miss Brown, but it was more than that. I understood her pride, her reticence, yes, and that tide of passion that had overwhelmed her, a passion she must have felt so ludicrous for a woman of her age, a passion absurd—looked at from the outside—for a man of Humphrey's age and physique. And yet during these days I myself loved Humphrey—that is, I understood why *she* must love him, how he seemed to her, and how, although to no one would she ever show it, this was life and death to her.

And yet there she was as gay and independent and sensible as ever, not giving a sign to anyone that she needed anything or anybody. And there was Humphrey with the chance of his whole lifetime waiting for him.

Mrs. Potter was an adventuress of the good old-fashioned sort. She was living, I soon discovered, on her wits. Mr. Potter, I found, had basely left her and was, it was supposed, in South America.

She became very quickly confidential.

'You are a novelist, Mr. Westcott, and a *great* novelist. You understand everything. I've been treated abominably, but what's the use of complaining? I live now only for my girl. She's lovely, isn't she? But she will have to marry money —a nice man with money. That's my ideal for her.'

Humphrey played bridge with them. He took them out in the car. He stared at Miss Potter when he thought no one was looking. She was very gracious to him indeed.

This time I went to *his* room.

'Look here, Humphrey, don't make an ass of yourself over this girl.'

'What do you mean?'

'Oh, you know what I mean. She's not for you. You can't seduce her and you certainly mustn't marry her. You'd be miserable in a week.'

He confessed to me at once that I was right. He wasn't dreaming of marrying her. He hated her mother. But *wasn't* she beautiful? Had I ever seen such eyes, such hair, such a figure. . . ?

'She sort of bewilders me,' he said.

'Bewilders you!' I repeated contemptuously. '*That* girl! And with the most splendid woman in the world here at your side.'

'Lucy! Lucy!' he repeated, as though her name were a kind of salvation. 'If she'll have me I'll be the luckiest man. . . .'

Your natural reflection at this point will be, if you have had the patience to listen, that Humphrey Smith was the kind of fool about whose fate there could be no kind of interest. But he wasn't, and as to his fate it was, I want to insist, the fate of all of us that hung in the balance, of Lucy Brown, of Humphrey Smith, of Mrs. Potter and of Rose Violet . . . yes, and, possibly, of myself. Nor was Humphrey a fool. I could see many a wise man enchanted by that lovely creature. Enchanted. An enchantment that depended, I am sure, on the evidence of its physical beauty to hold you. I myself noticed that when Rose Violet was not present she seemed, in retrospect, a little vulgar, a little unreal. But as you approached her the intoxication grew. In her presence I found myself saying absurd things of the lights in her hair, the delicate bloom of her cheeks, above all her figure, which was more naked with clothes on than without them . . . Well, Humphrey was only human.

I saw very clearly that the mother and daughter had marked down Humphrey for their prize. He was designed exactly for them. They had been cruising around, I don't doubt, for a long time. Rose Violet was young, but not so young as she looked. Yes, here was their safe and certain refuge.

How soon did Lucy Brown perceive what was happening? I never knew, but in little hotels, on a fine summer holiday, everything moves very quickly and everything is very open. Everyone in the hotel knew as fast as an eye twinkles that the Potter girl was setting her cap at Mr. Smith. And, of course, Lucy Brown knew. She gave no sign. She said the girl was lovely. She behaved to her most charmingly. I am sure that the girl had no idea at all that this middle-aged, quiet and amusing woman cared for any man in the world. So high is my opinion of the modern girl that I fancy, had she known, she might even have retired in Miss Brown's favour. Yes, and *dared* her old mother, who could, I've no doubt, be a considerable tartar in private. . . .

But Rose Violet did not know. She simply saw that here was a good chance and it was good business to take it. She was not in love with Humphrey in the very least, of course.

Yes, things move quickly in these little hotels and before we knew where we were the crisis was upon us.

In Rose Violet's presence Humphrey was simply not himself. He behaved like a gentleman. It is here that perhaps our delicate code of morals is to blame. Had Humphrey been permitted by law to snatch up Miss Potter and in exchange for a decent sum down (with Mrs. Potter in the background, it would have been *quite* a decent sum!) to take her into the fastnesses of Eskdale for a full week-end, all parties would, I think, have been satisfied. But no. We must all be moral human beings. Humphrey must be a gentleman, myself another gentleman, Lucy Brown and the Potter family decent English ladies. Decency is all right in its way, but when a tiresome human little animal passion needs settling. . . .

Of course Humphrey should have seen where all his good fortune lay, *of course* he was a fool not to, and *of course* we are all angels and wise men and pure as the mountain water—and *of course*, I may venture as a rider to these axioms, we are all fools together.

The moon was up, a full orange moon sailing in lazy majesty through a web of sparkling stardust. I knew that within the following day or so Humphrey would propose marriage to one of the two. He must propose or burst. I knew it. Lucy Brown knew it. Rose Violet knew it—at any rate, so far as she herself was concerned.

One fine moonlit evening when there was no sound abroad but the water running from the rock, Humphrey sat with Lucy in the garden and was so silent, so intense in expression, so happy that it was as good as a proposal. But alas! It was not one in actuality. Yet I am resolved that next day the proposal would have come. It hovered, it trembled, it was already in the air. . . . But next day. . . .

In the morning Miss Brown came to me with a letter in her hand.

'Mr. Westcott, I must go to Bradford. I am leaving in half an hour.'

'Bradford!' I was aghast.

'Oh, only for a night.'

'Oh, no!' I cried. 'Not even for a night!'

But it seemed that a friend of hers, a silly, worthless girl, was in dreadful trouble. She was going to have a baby. The man responsible had deserted her. She might at any moment destroy herself. . . .

'Wait!' I said. 'Wait until to-morrow. They exaggerate these things. . . . Girls exaggerate things. . . .'

'No,' said Lucy Brown. 'Waiting may be fatal.'

She knew and I knew. We looked at one another. It was a test, quite in the *Old Mortality* manner, of her fineness. A little less fine and she would be happy for life. Humphrey had suggested that they should go alone that afternoon in his little car to Ullswater. If she did not go in the little car someone else would. . . .

'Please, Miss Brown, go to-morrow. . . . The situation will be no worse. . . .'

'It may be. She's desperate. . . .'

Then she hesitated. I saw the temptation rise in all its grand strength like Satan himself, dark and splendid, with the hills for a cloak.

'Don't go, Miss Brown. Oh, *please* don't go!'

She hesitated. She looked the dark Conqueror in the face. He wrapped the hills about him like a cloak and was gone.

'Good-bye, Mr. Westcott. I shall be back to-morrow or the day after.'

There was only one thing left for me to do. I must not let Humphrey out of my sight. I did not. I insisted that I should accompany the expedition to Ullswater. They did not want me. I think that for an hour or two Rose Violet hated me. Not for more than that. Prolonged hatred, or indeed emotion of any kind, was bad for the complexion. I went with them to Ullswater, I walked with them, talked with them, had tea with them, and, as I have noticed on other such occasions, Rose Violet was able to throw around herself a sort of additional beauty, an added glow, an extra loveliness. Humphrey walked, talked, drank his tea like a man bemused. Mrs. Potter used all her arts to conduct me on a little walk *à deux*. She failed.

Back in the hotel again, I played ping-pong with Humphrey, I dined with him, I drank with him. Into the garden after dinner he went with mother and daughter. I accompanied them. The September night was cold. We returned into the sitting-room and sat, all four of us together, near old Miss Mathias, who was wrinkling her brow over Demon patience.

The clock struck eleven. I thought that we were saved, for I was sure, yes, positive, that Lucy would by to-morrow afternoon be with us again. Then for the second time on that day Satan, who knows no weariness nor turning, threw his splendid shadow over the flowery wallpaper, the water-colours of Buttermere and the Pikes, the coffee-cups and the bridge table. Old Miss Mathias gave a little cry like a wounded sparrow and fainted. She was an old lady of an indomitable courage but a weak heart. Her Demon had excited her; her heart failed to respond. . . .

I was sitting next to her, but there were others who might have gone to her rescue. But I was a gentleman, an English gentleman, the child of English gentlemen. Satan drew near. His sad and gracious smile hovered over me. But what can Satan do against an English gentleman? I carried Miss Mathias (she was as light as a feather) from the room, I found water, I bathed her old cheeks, I laid her on her bed, I rubbed her old hands, I whispered, I conjured, I even swore. . . . The lady of the hotel came at last. Miss Mathias opened her eyes and smiled.

Downstairs I rushed. I was too late. Humphrey and the Potter family were nowhere to be seen.

Twenty minutes later Mrs. Potter, her crooked eyebrows all aglee, told me that Miss Rose Violet Potter had promised to become, after a decent interval, Mrs. Humphrey Smith.

On the following afternoon Lucy Brown returned. I saw her congratulate Miss Potter.

'No,' she told me, 'there was nothing much the matter with the poor child. It was hysteria a good deal, I think. Of course, the man has behaved shockingly. Men *are* odd, don't you think?'

That evening Rose Violet said to me: 'I do like Miss Brown. Think how kind she is! She has already given me a wedding present.'

She showed me a box of blue and white enamel.

'Isn't it pretty? Smell, Mr. Westcott. It has the sweetest scent. Like honeysuckle.'

I smelt.

'Charming, isn't it?' she said. 'And isn't it quaint, the words on the lid?'

I read: 'Unto the End I Love my Friend.'

'Fancy,' she said, 'anyone putting *that* on a box nowadays.'

'Yes,' I said. 'It smells just like honey.'

THE FEAR OF DEATH

I WILL ACKNOWLEDGE that I was disgusted when I heard that William Rollin was in the hotel. That seemed to me, at the moment, the very worst piece of bad luck. I had come to Sark to escape from everyone, to have a real holiday, and here in this same small hotel, on this same small island, was one of the human beings whom I deeply, with all my soul, disliked. One dislikes, I fancy, very few people with one's soul. Only once or twice in a lifetime does one encounter a man who affects one so strongly on a very slight acquaintance.

I had met Rollin once or twice, in London, and a good many years ago. He was a man of very considerable reputation, and all of that reputation bad. The human race, I have found, is almost universally fond of gossip and at the same time charitable. When one or two are gathered together they will tear anyone you please to shreds, but in all kindness of heart, simply because they want to pass a pleasant hour and be thought, by their fellows, amusing, interesting and broad-minded. Once and again, however, someone appears whom society agrees to consider dangerous and beyond the pale. This dislike (which is also fear) does not come, especially in these days, from any horror at act or even crime. I have known men and women whose lives were publicly notorious, but there has been about them some quality of kindness or stupidity that has, on the whole, exonerated them. Rollin's moral reputation was bad, but no moral reputation worries anyone any more, unless it is emphasised by the newspapers. No, it was the man himself, an atmosphere that accompanied him, that people could not endure. He had, of course, his own cronies, and the man was so intelligent that he was often excellent company, but he was an animal whose brilliance was dangerous. He was, for no very clear reason, an enemy to society, always involved in squabbles, disputes . . . and yet there was also something pathetic about him. He was of the jungle, but always alone there—and he knew it.

There was no reason, except his intelligence, for his position of importance (for he had undoubtedly a *kind* of importance). He was ugly, a bounder, a sycophant, a snob, a bully. His financial affairs were always on the edge of desperation. He had for many years been in and out of the hands of money-lenders; he had debts everywhere, and it was one of his specially charming characteristics that he never either attempted to repay, nor did he forgive anyone who was fool enough to lend him money.

Nevertheless, his intelligence was remarkable. Had his character and personality not betrayed him, he could have done anything. He was many-sided, cared about games and played them well, was an excellent linguist, read voluminously, had an interest in everything except, oddly, horses. He used to say that he had never been to a race-meeting in his life. I say 'oddly' because to look at him you would think that he had spent his life in and around stables.

His supreme passion was for pictures. Had he had money he would have been one of the finest collectors of our time; having less than none he yet managed to pick up, for almost nothing, some lovely things. He possessed a beautiful little Canaletto, a lovely Renoir still-life, a Matisse that he had bought for nothing at all in his younger days in Paris, and an Italian Primitive which in its freshness of colour and sincerity of feeling was one of the most enchanting things I have ever seen. His knowledge of and taste for pictures was extremely catholic, his judgment superb, and when he talked of them a different soul seemed to peep out from his mean little eyes. . . .

His one genius, however, did not cover the unpleasantness of the rest of him, and it may be imagined with what disgust I saw him, when on the day after arrival I went into breakfast, seated at a table near me with a woman who was, I knew, his second wife. There was no avoiding him. I stood at his table for a moment and he introduced me to his wife. He always met one like an animal on the defensive, as though he expected an attack. An uglier man I have seldom encountered. He was short, thick-set, and wore, generally, clothes of a light colour, rather 'horsy.' He was almost bald, had small, suspicious eyes and a cruel and greedy mouth, but it was his complexion which was his real trouble. He drank a good deal, I imagine, but he had not exactly the colour of a drunkard. He was like a piece of undercooked beef, white and red and streaky. His hand was flabby to the touch, and he always withdrew it quickly as though he were afraid that you would hold it firmly and lead him off to gaol. I know that I seem here to be describing a real Surrey-side villain. But Rollin was not a villain. He was simply a bad, nasty man, one bad man in a million kindly, weak and well-intentioned ones. Bad men are extremely rare. I have known, in fact, only two others beside Rollin.

The really curious thing was that before two days were passed I felt so strongly the pathos of the man that I almost liked him. I have always been greatly touched by men victims to the two powers of Fear and Jealousy. I have known them so well in my own nature and the misery and loneliness that these possessive demons inflict on their victims; indeed, with regard to the second of them there is no profession so harried and riven by it as that of Letters. . . .

I very soon discovered that these two held Rollin in thrall. His jealousy was of a peculiar kind. Once he was assured that my attitude to him was friendly, words poured from him, all in that sharp, ugly assertive voice of his. Assertive he was, but never with convincing authority except in the matter of pictures. There he allowed no personal fears or jealousies to influence him, and had his worst enemy (and, by Jupiter, he had a few!) painted a good picture, he would have said that it was a good picture.

But with regard to every other occupation possible to mankind, jealousy raged in him. It did not matter in the least—politics, the Arts, the Services, religion, Society, whosoever it might be, anyone of prominence was damned, accused of dreadful offences against Society and the State, dismissed to perdition. 'Mind you, Westcott,' he said with that faint touch of Midland accent that he so greatly disliked in himself, 'I'm not jealous. Last thing I am is jealous. Nobody could call me that. Only it makes me sick to see men like Webster getting away with it. Why, do you know. . . .'

By the second day I was both sorry for him and tired of him, so I tried to break away.

'Look here, Rollin,' I said. 'People aren't as bad as you say. We all have our little weaknesses, you know. We all live in glass houses. Why throw stones?'

Then I saw fear in his eyes, the fear that after this conversation never again, I think, left him.

'What do you mean, Westcott? I hate this hinting. . . .'

'I don't mean anything except that we *are* all in the same boat, and abusing one another seems a futile business. I came up to London about nineteen-hundred. I'm getting on for sixty. I've been writing and publishing novels for more than thirty years. During that time I've been abused times without number, and very often with reason, but in all that time I've experienced only one piece of real dirty meanness.'

'Oh, well. . . .' He looked at me with patronage. He would have liked to say something rude: I could hear him back in

London: 'Oh yes, we went to Sark for our holiday. Peter Westcott, the novelist, was there, all geniality and speaking well of his fellows. Finds it pays. . . .'

But he was afraid. He broke abruptly into another topic:

'Well, that's as may be. But, look here! Have you ever thought about death?'

'Death?' I asked lazily. We were lying on Dixcart beach, stretched out full-length watching the blue-green breakers, shining in the sunlight, break into foam on the pebbles. 'Of course I have. Everyone has.'

'Doesn't it seem awful to you that one's got to die? The inevitability of it——'

'No, I can't say that it does. If I'm depressed it seems a dreary business like everything else. But in general, no. In the war death became so ordinary, part of the day's work. . . .'

'Oh yes, I know.' His hand touched my arm. 'But if one only knew the way it was going to be. God, to die in one's bed like Armstrong the other day! What luck! Not to realise that it's coming! It's that moment of realisation that's so awful to me, Westcott. The moment when you say to yourself: "My God! I'm going to die! It's coming! It's nearly here!" '

His hand shook on my arm.

'Life's merciful,' I answered. 'Most sick people pass into some kind of coma long before they die. And, anyway, haven't you often had nightmares when you have that moment of realisation? You must have died in your dreams a thousand times over. Actual death is no worse than that.'

'I should think I have,' he said, shuddering. 'There's a dream I have——'

Just then his wife joined us.

She was a small, compact, pretty woman with unusually light-blue eyes. I had seen little of her as yet, but she struck me as one of the quietest women I had ever encountered. It was not only that she said very little, but her whole personality struck me as a waiting, listening, determining one. I had heard in London that Rollin behaved to her abominably, that she had once run away from him, but had returned and had told a friend that she had come back because she had to. She couldn't help herself. But now, as she came towards us, neat, square-shouldered, walking with quiet resolution as though she knew precisely what she intended to do and that nothing would stop her, I couldn't exactly see her committing any act 'because she couldn't help herself.' She was as controlled, as superior to fears, superstitions, gusts of temper and violence as he was inferior.

He did not want her just then, and showed it. I disliked his manner to her so much that soon I got up and left him. I might be sorry for him, but indeed and indeed he was a nasty specimen!

The little hotel where we were was a very primitive and simple place. You had to fuss for a day if you wanted a hot bath, the sanitation was more than primitive, and there was no electric light. All the same, I liked it. The proprietor, the servants, were kind and obliging. Everyone was friendly. But Rollin, of course, had soon a thousand complaints. The food, he said, was scanty and monotonous, the lack of water a disgrace, the beds hard, and so on. He complained to everyone, and everyone disliked him as much as they liked his wife. This, I should imagine, was a common experience wherever they went, and it did not make him love his wife any the better.

Sark is the ideal island for anyone who wants absolute seclusion: indeed, in these harried and public days I should think there is no island in the world quite so secluded. The South Seas are, I understand, as crowded as Piccadilly! It is not an easy island to escape from. If you wish to pay a visit to Jersey you must go for a night at least, and even the trip to Guernsey must be taken in so small a boat that the mildest of rough seas can be alarming. Moreover, the island itself likes to make you feel that it is difficult. There are few beaches and the paths to them are precipitous and unruly. The island is so small that you are always finding yourself unexpectedly at the end of it. It has no middle, so to speak—only ends!

This difficulty and apartness can be either enchanting or exasperating. The place has undoubtedly a magic; in the spring and summer it is covered with flowers, threaded with leafy lanes, and the rocky coast is superb. The air, on the warm days, seems scented with honey, and on the wild ones, is splendidly vigorous. There is still the mantle of old history hanging over it, and the old Norman dialect is stronger and more vigorous among the people than English. No motor vehicles are allowed there. There are more dogs and cats, happily domesticated, than in any place that I know. All these things give it uniqueness, and when you have been there for a day or two, you will, if you have any imagination, begin to fancy things. I am not here speaking of the supernatural, although I believe that dead pirates are as ordinary as blackberries, and smugglers, a hundred years in their graves, common company along the lanes of an evening. But that is the kind of imagination stirred by a hundred places. Where Sark is unique is that, being shut in, imprisoned if you like, you very quickly begin to have odd fancies about your fellow-captives.

I should, in any event, have been greatly interested in Rollin and his wife. Bad men, as I have already said, are rare birds, and are food for the novelist when he encounters one. Rollin, for instance—I could speculate about him endlessly. Were his cruelties, greedinesses, fears, private nastinesses the result simply of the lack of a gland or the pressure of bone on the brain? Could a little simple operation transform him into an angel? If so, why did he not have one? Was any of it his own fault? Could he help himself or did he, indeed, want to help himself? I decided very soon that he did not. He thought himself, I very soon saw, an excellent fellow: amusing, good company, vastly more brilliant than most men, broad-minded and enterprising. He had, of course, been unjustly treated, he carried a thousand grudges about with him, and his criticism of everyone was continual. But one thing he could not deny—his fear. Many men had the advantage of him there. He could not understand their serenity, and hated them for it.

Very quickly, however, Mrs. Rollin became to me more interesting than her husband. I would not say that she liked me. She appeared to have learnt, through stress of circumstances, to guard herself against any conceivable emotion. Her restraint was almost terrifying—the restraint and watchfulness of someone on a tight-rope to whom one false step meant death. Not that she was afraid of death. She was afraid, I am convinced, of nothing, having been through all the worst experiences that life has to offer. This restraint of hers soon became to me obsessing, but the odd fact was that she was the one thing in the world of which Rollin appeared to have no fear at all. He was proud of her in a kind of contemptuous fashion—proud of her looks, her composure (out of which no taunts of his ever seemed to drive her), her *savoir-faire*. But while he was proud of her she exasperated him. She had beaten him in their relationship. She despised him from the bottom of her heart.

Why, feeling about him as she did, she had not long ago left him was one thing that puzzled me. One day, when we were alone, we had a queer little conversation.

'You don't like my husband very much, do you, Mr. Westcott?' she asked me. We were sitting on a spur of Little Sark just above the Coupée and the sea heaved below us, a moving floor of green and purple silk.

'No,' I said, 'I don't.'

'He's not really very likeable,' she went on calmly. 'I know him very well, and the only decent emotion anyone could ever have for him is a kind of pity. He's a very lonely man.'

'Yes,' I said, 'I suppose he is.'

'And I've lost even that emotion about him now. I've had some bad times with him, you know.' She looked at me very quietly out of her pale-blue eyes. 'It isn't decent to talk about one's husband to a stranger—not that you are altogether a stranger. I don't talk about him, you know. . . .'

'As you're frank, I'll be frank too,' I said. 'I wonder that you haven't left him years ago.'

'Do you? I did once. But I came back. I was still in love with him, I think. For a long time he had a physical fascination for me. Now I hate him to touch me—or should if I hated anything. . . . All the same, I think I've had about enough of it at last—at last!' she repeated, looking out to sea.

'I'm years older than you are, Mrs. Rollin,' I said after a long pause. 'It isn't very wise of me to give advice—always a silly thing to do. But leave him. You are young, strong, attractive—if you won't think me impertinent. You have plenty of time to make a new life and a fine one.'

'Yes, I think you're right,' she said, getting up and brushing the grass off her dress.

And it was then, at that moment, that I had for a moment a sense of apprehension. Had Rollin been with us I could almost have called: 'Look out!'

Mrs. Rollin was *very* calm and resolute!

The next thing that occurred was that Rollin developed an almost passionate liking for me. He was a neurotic, and, like all neurotics, saw himself as the centre of a shaking, quivering world and its only nerve-centre himself! This perpetual apprehension meant that he must have perpetual reassurance, whether he found it in whisky, women, or in a character or two safer than himself. It was his sense of my safeness, I think, that made him cling to me.

'Poor old Westcott,' I could hear him saying to himself. 'He's one of those commonplace fellows too ordinary for fate to bother to attack.'

I was like a tree under whose branches he might shelter until the storm was over, but a tree forgotten the moment that the sun was out again. He had also something extremely feminine in his personality. That was one reason why he was not at all to be trusted. Men with feminine souls are often kind, generous, self-sacrificing and even noble—but trustworthy, never!

I cannot say how greatly I disliked this sudden affection of Rollin's. Like Mrs. Rollin, I hated him to touch me, and he began to develop a habit of laying his hand on my arm and pressing into the flesh. At the first excuse I would move, and at the first move I would see that startled look of suspicion flash into his eye.

It was the Misses Mailley who advanced all unwittingly our relationship a little further. The Misses Mailley were bright, bony and athletic. They swam, they played tennis, wore the minimum of clothing, talked incessantly and laughed a great deal. They were frightened of Rollin and so, when he was there, they talked and laughed the more.

One morning, after breakfast, we were all of us—the Rollins, the Mailleys and myself—sitting on the veranda looking down the grassy slope towards a magnificent copper beech, under which an old white horse was whisking his ear at the flies and watching out of one eye for a possible lump of sugar.

'The Silver Mines,' said one of the Miss Mailleys. 'That's the place!'

'The place for what?' asked Mrs. Rollin.

'Oh, for an easy murder! Gladys has been reading some silly book in which a man was murdered and buried in a haystack—a ridiculous place! But the Silver Mines—they're grand! No one would ever discover it.'

Rollin's hand touched my shoulder.

'The Silver Mines?' he asked.

'Yes. They're down towards the sea—near Venus' Bath. You ought to go and see them. They haven't been worked, of course, for ages, but there they are, quite unprotected, not a fence or anything! All you have to do is to take your beloved for a walk, push him down, and then, next morning, say he's left by the early boat. No one would know.'

'No. But you'd be haunted,' said the younger Miss Mailley. 'It wouldn't be worth it.'

'It might be,' said Mrs. Rollin. 'No ghost is so bad as some living people. One could deal with a ghost.'

That evening Rollin said to me:

'Stroll out to the Point, Westcott? It's a lovely evening.'

I did not want to go, but I went. We walked across the field, down the little path, climbed the hill and looked down at the sea.

'Awful girls those Mailleys,' he said. 'I can't stand them.'

'They're all right.'

'Oh, you like everyone! It's a type I hate, all cheerful and bony. Do them good to be pushed down that mine they were joking about.' He pressed his hand into my arm. 'Why have you never married, Westcott?'

'I'm a widower,' I said shortly. I had no desire to discuss my private affairs with Rollin.

'Oh, sorry. I didn't know.'

'That's all right. I was very happy.'

'Oh, marriage is all right.' He stood closer to me as though for protection. 'I've been married twice, you know. Grace' —his present lady—'has learnt my ways by this time. She took a bit of teaching, though. She's devoted to me, and to tell you the truth, Westcott, it makes a man feel safe to have someone he can trust around. I can depend on her absolutely.'

'Yes,' I said.

He came still closer, pressing his body up against mine. 'I haven't been well lately. Get all sorts of ideas in my head. Afraid of my own shadow. Upon my soul, I believe my wife's the one person in the world I'm *not* afraid of! It's nerves, of course. I'm highly-strung and not so young as I was. I don't sleep very well, and I'm a bit of a crank about my health. After all, you catch a cold and before you know where you are it's pneumonia and in a day or two you're gone.' He shivered. 'It's getting cold. Let's turn back.'

Before we reached the hotel he said:

'Thanks for the walk. I think I shall sleep now.'

Next day we went, the three of us, to the pool in the rocks known as Venus' Bath, and had our tea there. Mrs. Rollin and I bathed off the rocks. She was a magnificent swimmer, the day was a glorious one, and just as we reached the rocks Mrs. Rollin said to me:

'I'm glad you were staying here, Mr. Westcott. It's made a difference.'

'Thanks,' I said. 'I'm glad too.'

'Oh, are you? You can't be. We're not an attractive pair.'

On the way back we passed the Silver Mines. There was a ruined tower about whose base flowers—crimson, yellow and blue—clustered. There was the black mouth of a shaft.

'I wonder how deep that is,' Mrs. Rollin said.

'Deep as hell,' Rollin answered.

There comes for me now, as I approach the crisis of my relationship with these two, the difficulty of truth—truth in my story. I mean the truth of facts, as well as the truth of imagination. How soon in this affair did I begin myself to feel an apprehension that, after a time, began to obsess me, so that I was constantly aware of it, constantly shadowed by a sense of my own responsibility? Looking back now, I ask myself what I ought to have done: for it is one of my humiliations to remember that from beginning to end I did exactly nothing. *Could* I have done anything? Should I have tried to persuade Rollin to leave the island by the next morning's boat? Should I have frankly asked Mrs. Rollin certain questions? But, indeed, how could I ask her anything unless she gave me her confidence? That, she never gave me. Or did she? And did she invite me to take a step, or to force her to take a step, that would have saved both herself and him? Would it have been better if such a step had been taken? I don't know. I shall never know. I give you the facts as honestly as I can remember them.

A day or two after our visit to Venus' Bath the weather

broke and rain swept the island. Standing, one afternoon, in my room wondering whether I should read, write, play bridge with the Mailley girls, or sleep till dinner, I heard my door open and, looking up, saw Mrs. Rollin standing there. She was as composed, as quiet, as assured as she ever was. She came in, closing the door behind her.

'I'm not going to stop,' she said. 'If I did the scandal would be, I suppose, terrific. But the trouble of this place is that you can't be alone. I want to ask your advice, Mr. Westcott.'

She sat down in a chair near the bed.

'Tell me——' She looked up at me, smiling. 'How far is anyone justified in breaking a natural law?'

'What do you mean by a natural law?' I asked her.

'Well . . . after thousands of years of living together men have decided that certain laws must be obeyed if society is to keep sane. On the whole the decisions they've come to have been wise ones. But once and again it is better that a law should be broken rather than kept.'

'Yes,' I said, feeling stupid under her quiet gaze.

'Perhaps I am myself insane,' she went on. 'I don't think so—but oneself one can never tell. I feel it right to take action in a certain direction—action that you, everyone, would absolutely condemn. I want, in fact, to take the law in my own hands. Is one ever justified in doing that?'

'Yes,' I answered. 'If you are ready to face the consequences.'

'For myself you mean?'

'Yes.'

'Oh, the consequences for myself—they're nothing. I don't care in the least what happens to *me*. I died long ago. But my ghost—or the ghost of my ghost—has a fragment of hesitation. An odd remnant of religious superstition, I suppose. I don't mind breaking men's laws, you know, but is there another law, something deeper, more permanent?'

I thought then, looking at her, that she *was* insane. Her composure, the thin shadow that lurked in her pale-blue eyes, something marked her for me as a woman who had ceased to reason, because she had been driven beyond the bounds of reasoning.

She got up as abruptly as she entered.

'I wanted to ask you,' she said. 'Do you believe in God?'

'Yes,' I answered. 'I believe in a spiritual world.'

'So do I.' She nodded her head as though pursuing her own thoughts. 'But not in eternal punishment, you know. That's altogether too crude. Never mind—I'll take what comes.' And she went out.

I have said already that Sark is dangerous for the imaginative. One sees so much more than is really there. Every rock in Sark has a double meaning, and even the flowers know too well what they are about. The weather was bad and we were shut in upon ourselves. Rollin would not leave me alone. He cursed everything, the island, the hotel, the visitors, the natives and, behind my back, I do not doubt, myself.

'Well, why don't you go?' I asked him. 'There are two boats a day.'

'I can't make up my mind,' he said. He looked ill. He said that he wasn't sleeping. 'I keep seeing things in this beastly place. It's as though someone was always following one.' He broke down all his reticences. He told me that he hated his wife, but that she was the only person in the world he could trust. 'When I'm with her I'm safe,' he said. 'She's like a wall at my back.'

I think it was true that he hated her, and he became quite intolerable in her company. He bullied her, snapped at her, ordered her about like a servant, was insufferably rude to her. Once, when he had been especially intolerable, I left him. He came after me to my room.

'What did you go for?' he asked. 'You said you were coming for a walk.'

So, given the opportunity, I told him what I thought of him.

But he scarcely listened. 'Oh, you don't know,' he said. 'You've no idea how aggravating she can be. This weather gets on my nerves. I've got an idea I'm never going to leave this damned island. I shall die here, rot to pieces all amongst the ferns and stones.'

That same night I woke with a sudden start to be aware that someone was in the room. I struck a match, lit a candle (there was no electric light in the hotel), and woke up to find Rollin standing by my bed in his pyjamas, shaking from crown to heel. He sat down on the edge of the bed and caught my arm.

'What's up?' I asked.

'Let me stay here five minutes. I've had a fright.'

How I hated his pressure on my arm, his whole physical self with his pyjama-jacket open, his mottled complexion, the very colour of his red bedroom-slippers! And yet, even as I hated him, I was sorry for him. How could I be otherwise? He was a haunted man. He told me an incoherent story. He couldn't sleep, then he dropped into deep slumber and dreamt—a horrible dream in which he was lying at the bottom of a deep, black pit in a pool of sluggish water. Scaly fishes swam across his eyeballs. His body was broken and his arms waggled in the water.

'You've been eating something,' I said.

'I was dead—I was alive—I suffered. Good God, Westcott, what I suffered! But the worst moment was before I fell. I knew I was going to fall and I cried out to you, Westcott, to save me! I knew I was going to die—then—then—that moment!'

He lay down beside me on the outside of the bed. I said what I could, told him he'd been drinking too much (which he had).

'I know you think I'm a fool,' I said. 'But I'll give you some good advice. Go back to London. Try to take a decent view of things. Don't curse everybody, and behave better to your wife.'

'Oh, it's all very well for you to talk, Westcott. You're one of those damned optimists and well you may be. Everything's always gone well with you.'

'Well, it hasn't,' I answered shortly. 'When I was a boy in Cornwall, there was an old fisherman had a motto—a sloppy, sentimental motto that men like you would laugh yourselves sick over. "It isn't life that matters, but the courage you bring to it." That will be a sort of maiden's prayer to you,' I added, yawning (for I was extremely sleepy), 'but it meets your case all the same. You're a coward, Rollin, frightened of your own shadow.'

He thought the motto very comic, and that did him good.

'You ought to take Sunday-school class, Westcott. Was your father a clergyman?'

'My father,' I answered, 'was the rottenest, most drunken old swine ever a son had. That's why I found that motto useful.'

He was calmer, and at last, thank God, he left me.

But that night was enough for him. He told me, next morning, that they were leaving for London on the following day.

What a morning that was! Shall I ever forget it? The whole island was veiled in a wet, creeping mist. You couldn't see a yard in front of you, and a tree jumped out at you as though it were an American gangster bidding you hold your hands up. I'm not a nervous man—or no more than most—but I woke in a state of fear and consternation. Those are the only words that I can use. I must do something—but what? I couldn't leave Rollin out of my sight. All afternoon I played bridge with him and the Mailley girls.

'What a day for a murder,' one of them said brightly. 'Three hearts . . .'

I looked up and saw Mrs. Rollin standing at the window watching the wet mist as it coiled like a snake against the pane. I was dummy, and I got up and went over to her.

'You're leaving to-morrow, I hear,' I said.

'Yes,' she said, turning round and smiling at me.

She stood there, motionless, scarcely breathing, but her eyes stared into mine. It was as though she said: 'Well—what are you going to do about it?'

Then she did an odd thing. She pushed with her bare palms at the window-pane as though she would break it. I was sure then that she was not sane. . . .

At about half-past six that evening I came on to the veranda and saw the two Rollins in mackintoshes.

'Hallo!' I cried. 'Where are you two off to?' It was odd, but it was as though I had known that they would be there.

'We are going for a walk,' said Mrs. Rollin.

'A walk—in this weather?'

'Yes. It's been so stuffy all day. We want a little exercise, don't we, Will?'

'I'll come, too,' I said.

'No. Don't,' she answered. 'You'd hate it.'

Rollin said not a word.

'Where are you going?' I asked.

'Oh, I don't know. Over the Coupée to Little Sark. Down by Venus' Bath, perhaps.'

'Don't fall into the Silver Mines,' I said.

She did not answer. We none of us spoke. I shall never forget Rollin. He was like a hypnotised man, like a man in a dream. Her eyes never left his face.

I longed to cry out: 'Rollin, don't go! Don't go!' But it was as though I were hypnotised, too. I only stood and stared at them. They moved off into the mist, he following her like a dog.

They were not in their places at dinner. I watched and watched the door to see them enter. At about nine o'clock I thought I heard Rollin's voice calling just outside the window: 'Westcott! Westcott!' I ran out, but the wet mist was so thick that I could see nothing. I ran a little way down the road calling: 'Rollin! Rollin!'

But, of course, there was no answer, only the distant murmur of the sea. I slept brokenly, waking again and again. . . .

And at breakfast Mrs. Rollin was there, eating very quietly her bacon and eggs.

I went over to her.

'Good-morning,' I said. 'I'm afraid you must have got very wet last night.'

'Yes, we did.'

'Where's Rollin?' I asked.

'Oh, he went by the seven-thirty boat. He had some business in Guernsey. I'm following by the ten o'clock.' Then she held out her hand, smiling. 'Goodbye,' she said.

'Goodbye,' I answered.

FIELD WITH FIVE TREES

I WAS ASKED not long ago, at one of those dinner-parties where people ask such questions, to describe for my fellow-guests the oddest and queerest experience of my life. When one looks back, one discovers so many queer experiences, and then at the same time one realises that most of them refuse not only description but analysis—so I suppose with this one that I am about to relate.

I went to keep an appointment—five trees barred the way, and that was all there was to it. You can believe it or not, as you please.

It happened years and years ago before the war. I am now between sixty and seventy years of age, a widower with two grown-up children, on the whole content, although I have achieved so little—on the whole tranquil, even in this frantically disturbed world. It wasn't so disturbed then.

I had been married for five years. I had no children. I was a writer of sorts, and lived in a little stone cottage half way up the hill from the village of Grange on Derwentwater in Cumberland, where I still live.

One of the important elements of this story, if it is to be true at all, is that I shall be frank about Mary Ellen, my wife. Poor Mary! She has been dead for fifteen years, but still keeps me company, as those one has truly loved always do, however long their bodies have been dust.

I think if Mary were to appear here now and give you an account of herself as she saw herself, she would agree very much with my estimate of her, except that she never knew as I did, how grandly unselfish, how sweetly forgiving, how beautifully maternal she was. She was above all things else, long before she had any children of her own, a mother. She mothered me, who badly needed it, with a goodness, a sense of humour, and a tolerance that I've never known any other human being to equal. I loved her and she loved me. But there came a time, as there comes in every marriage, when we were dissatisfied, fools that we were. Yet she loved me dearly—especially the companionship that we had. She was a wonderful companion. She had a grand, even a splendid sense of enjoyment. She loved little things. She was perfectly content on our small income—perfectly happy to be there in the country alone with me from one end of the year to the other. The only thing that she wanted that she hadn't got was children.

It was just a year after this strange adventure that we had our first child. We had been married, as I've said, five years—and suddenly everything went wrong. That is the queerest thing about any relationship between two human beings, that for no reason at all, everything suddenly moves out of perspective. Little personal tricks that have meant nothing for years are in a moment exasperating.

Mary had, I remember, a habit of leaving the room without shutting the door. And contrariwise, she would enter a room with a rush, banging the door behind her. Often she would look untidy; her soft, brown hair, which I had once thought the most beautiful thing in the world, would tumble about her forehead. She was not very clever about her clothes. She was strong, robust, rosy-faced, bright-eyed, clean like an apple. Sometimes, when she was happy, she would talk very loudly and with great excitement.

I, on the other hand, in those days took myself rather grimly. I was determined to become a great writer, a thing,

God forgive me, that I have never managed to be. I was earning a fair income at that time with my novels and stories, but I thought that I had real genius and that one day all the world would know it. Mary, I can now see on looking back, knew very well that genius I had not and would never have. Perhaps I detected, beneath her laughing praise and encouragement, this sense of disappointment. I was at that time meticulous in my habits. I liked everything to be very neat and careful about me. In fact, I took myself altogether with an absurd seriousness. I was immature for my years and she knew it. I was always a boy to her, to the very end. Perhaps that also, without my knowing it, irritated me.

We had, however, many things in common. We were, on the whole, amazingly happy. One joy that we deeply shared was our love for this especial country. I have no wish to employ pages of description in the manner of Mr. Fitz, the famous novelist, or Mrs. Grundy, the writer about gardens, but it is important to my little story that I should make it clear why Mary and I were happier here on this exact spot of ground than anywhere else in the world.

It wasn't that I didn't know other places. I've experienced the long, purple nights of Arizona—the lovely, benignant glow of the Russian white night—the tawny, boastful pride of the Pyrenees—the lakes and blossoms of Japan—the flowered valleys of Cashmere.

I know that this small square of Cumbrian and Westmoreland ground can seem like a mud patch on a wet day, like a garish coloured picture postcard on a sunny afternoon in August, can shrivel up and disappear and disappoint—do all the things that its detractors charge against it. But its beauty, when it chooses to be beautiful, no other place in the world can boast of.

This country was, in effect, the one thing that at this time Mary and I shared best with one another. Everything else began to have an edge—an edge of suspicion, mistrust and danger. But at no time from the first to last did we lose our companionship in this country—and I had almost forgotten to mention the sign and seal of the whole affair, namely, the field with the five trees.

I can see it now as I look from my library window, although it is closest and best visible from the windows of the bedroom Mary and I shared for so many years, and that I still inhabit. It is a field above Lodore on the way to Watendlath, formed like a half-moon. Its grass is, under sunlight, of the intensest green. The five trees that edge the ground are so alike that they resemble the brother Volsungs in Morris's *Sigurd*, except that they are not so tall as those splendid heroes were.

I remember saying to Mary when we first came to the cottage, that this field had eyes—or rather it was she, I think, who said that to me. 'We will never,' she said, 'be able to do anything that we are ashamed of, because that field will always know it. It is, I am sure, looking after us.' In any case, it became one of the great joys of our daily life, to awaken in the morning and see first thing that field and those trees, so beautiful, quiet, permanent and strong. We, both of us, clung to it the more when our troubles began.

These troubles were at first all on my side. Which of us does not know the times when we are irritable without reason—when shame at ourselves makes us yet more irritable—and when we strike at the persons we love most because, I suppose, they will endure our tempers the most patiently? At first I thought I was ill—that it was my liver or indigestion. Then I thought it was because my work was going badly, and here I began to complain bitterly of Mary. Whatever she said about it, my work was wrong.

Then examining myself and at heart bitterly ashamed of my unreason, I decided that I was still a young man—and was I, because I had married a good English woman, to spend the rest of my days as a kind of hermit? And one dreadful evening I broke out with all this, saying so much more than I really meant, reproaching her most unfairly for things that she had never done, accusing her of being what she was not. That evening I desperately hurt her pride. She was so seldom angry, never sulky, and very, very hard to offend. But that evening I offended her. She said very little—only at the end, quietly, 'I'm sorry. I see that you should have married someone quite different. But I can't change, however much you might wish it. I'm myself.' And she went out of the room.

It was after this that Mary made her great mistake. She invited her mother to stay with us. I don't know—I shall never know—whether she did this in a spirit of feminine revenge or whether it was simply that she thought the old lady would give her some companionship at a time when she must have been desperately lonely. Indeed, as I learned afterward, she was far more lonely and unhappy than I knew. I would say in passing that we never allow sufficiently for the loneliness of those near to us. We are aware often enough of our own loneliness and cry out bitterly against it, but we think that we are exceptional creatures in this.

Mary knew well enough that I detested her mother, Mrs. Millicent. She knew, too, that Mrs. Millicent cordially disliked me.

Physically she was unpleasant to me because she had bobbed her hair, painted her cheeks, wore dresses too young for her, and was altogether, I thought, a silly, tiresome, scandal-mongering old horror. And I did her a great injustice, as one always does when one dislikes people too much. She was courageous, had fine qualities of independence, adored Mary, and made a brave show of what life remained to her.

She thought me idle, lazy, spoiled, and altogether unworthy of her daughter. Her hatred of Cumberland was almost fanatical.

She was a sharp old lady and very soon discovered something was wrong between us.

When mothers discover that their beloved daughters are

unhappy and that sons-in-law whom they greatly dislike are responsible, they have only one ambition in life—to punish the sons-in-law! And my mother-in-law wished not only to punish me, but also Cumberland, the English countryside, and everything rustic. She made, at once, my field with the five trees a symbol of her attack.

'I really believe, Walter,' she would say, 'that you could gladly sit all day and gaze at that silly field. Why don't you buy it if you are so fond of it?'

I have no doubt but that she also attacked Mary and tried to drag her secret from her. But there was no secret. We were moving in the dark—away, away, and knew no reason why.

One night I caught her to me and said to her, 'Mary, Mary, what is it?'

'I don't know—I don't know,' she sobbed. 'You don't love me any more.'

'I do—I do,' I answered her. But as I said it I thought that I did not. I lay there, listening to the rain, and longed to escape, not only from Mary, perhaps, indeed not from Mary at all, but chiefly from myself. I think that this was the first time in my life when, poor defenceless egoist that I was, I began to wonder whether I was worth anyone's bother. But at least it was a step in the right direction! Love acts always independently of lovers. Sometimes it moves with them. Then, with a shrug of its beautiful shoulders, it moves away. 'Catch me if you can,' Love cries, and there is no way to recapture its company save to wait and be patient. But what lover ever was patient?

And then the country deserted us. After all, if you worship a place, it demands, I suppose, on your part, a certain fineness of conduct.

But we did not love the rain at that particular crisis in our lives, and oh! how old Mrs. Millicent hated it! I am sure that she thought it of my providing.

Then, as is always the way when the circumstances are

ready for it, a quarrel emphasised the breach and made it appear intolerable.

Breakfast is a dangerous meal, as many writers before me have observed. It was especially dangerous for Mrs. Millicent, for she was an old lady who should never meet her fellows before midday. But there she was, as fresh as her paint and powder could make her, drinking her coffee, and thinking of her enforced, unhappy rusticity. For many a day, Mary and I each read our paper at breakfast and threw to one another little excitements from China or the latest gossip from London. Mrs. Millicent did not read a paper and, therefore, quite naturally hated that others should do so. On this especial morning I glanced at the pictures of my newspaper and then stared across at my beloved field, just now almost fraudulently green, with the five trees guarding it.

'Well,' said Mrs. Millicent, 'I've always hated that field—but at least I owe it something. It's made Walter polite at breakfast.'

And then I lost my temper. All the misery of the last weeks came out in that moment. I told the old lady all that I thought of her, all that I had ever thought of her. I blamed her for all the trouble between Mary and me. I said that I could not work while she was in the house. I said—oh, what matters now, after all these years, the things that I said!

Mrs. Millicent rose from her seat and said, 'Enough! Mary, I leave this house.' And Mary, rising also, said, 'Mother, if you go I go, too.'

And the field looked across at me and veiled its green with shadow and once again the rain began to fall. Of course, the trouble was for the moment calmed. Later in the day I apologised.

That night Mary said, 'Walter, what has come to you? What is it? Tell me and I will help. I must help or we're lost—both of us.' Which sounds melodramatic for Mary, but the word 'lost' was true. We were, indeed, close to some fatal and irreparable separation.

On the following day, so pat that it seemed as though fate were taking a maliciously personal interest in my small affairs, I met a lady. Here, even after all these years, I write with hesitation. Pearl Richardson is dead. I've not seen her for many, many years. I feel now that I never knew her, never had any real contact with her, that she was a shadow from a world filled with shadows, and yet at this moment as I sit here, she is more vivid and actual to me than men who have been my friends for a lifetime—more vivid to me than any woman I've ever known, except Mary.

I was in Keswick, miserable, without plan or purpose. It had been a wet morning, but the sun had come out and the hills, as they so often are after rain, were sharp and brilliant as though they had received an extra coat of paint. All the little town was gleaming and glittering. In the market square where I was standing, the light was almost blinding. Into this light stepped a young woman.

I'd been wondering what I would do. While I was hesitating the girl passed me. She was wearing, as I so vividly remember, a dress of bright green which ill suited her pale face with the light, fair eyebrows. Just after she passed me she turned and looked at me. It was a look of quiet and considering investigation. She stood there looking at me and then came toward me smiling.

'Could you tell me,' she asked, 'where I can find the Keswick Art Shop?'

'Oh, yes,' I answered. 'It's straight along in front of you—over the little bridge and you'll find it on the left.' And as I spoke, it seemed to me that thereafter I would move like a man in a dream. I put it in that way, because I was still pausing on the border of that dangerous country. A moment's chance remained to me of turning around and walking away, and I knew with absolute certainty that if I did not walk away, I would be a free agent no longer. I've never felt that with any other man or woman before or since. But

I suppose on that particular day I was acutely unhappy, very lonely, with that kind of hurt pride and selfish resentment that comes from not getting one's own way.

She was, and it seems very odd to me now looking back, the exact opposite of Mary physically. She was pale, with rather weak grey eyes, with no cheerfulness, no sense of well-being about her at all. But my heart was thumping and I even stammered a little as I said, 'If you will allow me, I'm going that way and I'll show you where it is.'

'Thank you very much,' she said, and she spoke as though it were no new thing for her to be escorted by a stranger.

As we walked along we said very little to each other, but by the time that we had reached the bridge we had come to that sort of mutual agreement which strangers, who both want the same thing and want it badly, generally discover. We stood on the bridge before moving on, looking down at the little stream sparkling in the sunlight. She told me something about herself. She said that she was staying at the Station Hotel with a girl friend—that she'd never been in Cumberland before—that it had rained ever since their arrival, and that this was the first bit of sunshine that she had had—and as she said that, she looked at me.

'You are so bored, I suppose,' I said, 'that you'll be leaving early to-morrow.'

'Oh, no, I'm not,' she answered. 'Gracie, my friend is. She can't stand the place, but I like it. It's grand when it rains.'

'Oh, then,' I said, 'this is the country for you.'

'Yes, it is,' she said. 'I don't know why I never came here before.' Then she looked at me and said abruptly, 'You live here? Are you married?'

I said that I did live here and that I was married.

'That's a pity,' she said, 'your being married, I mean.'

'Why?' I asked her.

'Oh, because we could have seen a bit of each other if you hadn't been,' she answered.

'We can, anyway,' I replied.

I remember that little conversation as though the words are being spoken now in this room in front of me by two complete strangers whom I am coldly observing. I remember that I thought that I didn't like her, and that I should like her less the more I saw of her. I remember, too, a funny fancy that I had that her green dress was like the green of my field in the sun. Yes, I remember that I didn't like her, and that I wanted there and then to take her in my arms and cover her face with kisses. She was so different from anything that I'd known for so long that she seemed to me exactly what I desperately needed. And I suppose, too, in the low, dark cellars of my mind, there was the thought that I would teach Mary a lesson, and above all, show that nasty old woman, her mother, that there were other things in the world. I was certainly not the first man, nor the last, whom Miss Pearl Richardson tried to devour. In any case, whatever her purpose was, we succeeded in those few minutes in establishing a relationship. Before I left her I had promised to give her dinner in Keswick the following evening.

I was no less unhappy when I went back that afternoon, but I was almost wildly excited. Why? I'm afraid I cannot say. I've always thought that love, in spite of modern cynicism, is the finest thing in the world. Besides, at this particular moment, although I did not then know it, I loved Mary more deeply than I had ever loved her.

Within a very few hours, Mary discovered that I had changed, and then, as she told me afterward, she began to be very frightened.

'It was that afternoon,' she said many months later, 'that I thought for the first time that I might really be going to lose you. Up to then I'd known something was very wrong, but I'd been sure that nothing could truly separate us. But as soon as you came in that day, and with a kind of forced geniality greeted us and talked with an empty friendliness about anything or nothing so that I knew that your mind was elsewhere, I was terrified. I knew that there was someone somewhere that I must fight, but I was fighting in the dark. I hadn't an idea what to do.'

I was to learn one more curious thing. Next morning, when I awoke and looked across at the field, I had a strange impression that it was nearer to me than it had ever been before. I could see every detail of it. It was almost as though I could count the blades of grass. I'd always had the absurd notion that the five trees were active—that they could move—and sometimes I would look expecting to find only three there, or two.

I lived, I suppose, although my memory of that is very faint, in a kind of armed truce with Mary during these weeks. Everything was unreal to me except Pearl. I remember that I hated her name. I thought it foolish and affected, and her first occasion for rapping me over the knuckles was my saying so. She was deeply offended. I was detached enough about her to realise that her vanity was excessive and that everything that belonged to her—the especial kind of rouge that she used, the flower that she wore on her dress, relations of hers (although she didn't like them), even places where she had been—were sanctified and important because she had had some connection with them. Even I took on a kind of importance because she thought that I was in love with her.

I'm quite sure that she was never in love with me—that she had from the very first a vindictiveness towards Mary, whom, of course, she had never seen—because if Mary had not been there, she could have swallowed me up more quickly. She was irritated, too, and the more determined because I would not make love to her as other men had done. She said I behaved like a hero in one of the old story-books, by which she meant, I suppose, that I did nothing more than kiss her. The odd thing was that she represented to me, and this I find the hardest of all to understand, adventure and romance.

And yet I knew that she was common, with no interest in

anything except herself and men, that she never would be different from this. I think for these very reasons she became pathetic to me—someone whom I wished to protect, educate as though she were a poor, strayed child come to me for help. Of all the sentimental nonsense! She was anything but a poor, strayed child.

Women, I venture to think, are of two kinds. Either they must look up to the man they love or they must protect him. Sometimes they must do both. With some women the worse a man is, the more they must protect him. But with many women, as with Mary, if they despise, they cannot love. If I did this she would despise me for ever. And how fantastic it is, upon looking back, that I could seriously contemplate this flight with someone whom I neither admired nor loved, throwing everything away for nothing at all. And yet this is what men so often do.

I was afraid lest people should talk, and Pearl therefore went to stay, of all places in the world, in the lonely hamlet of Watendlath. That, now I think of it, was her principal virtue. She really did love this country. She would meet me in a little valley between Watendlath and Lodore, or I would come up to the farm for tea, or she would be at the bottom of the hill in Rosthwaite.

The day came when I agreed to go with her for a fortnight to Scarborough. I went back to my home that night after it was settled, knowing quite well that I was, as Mary had said, a lost man. As I sat by myself that evening, looking across at my field which now to my excited fancy seemed to be so close that it was almost staring in at my window, I felt the same excitement that I'd known at the very first moment when I met the girl. It was a hot, feverish excitement, and when Mary came into the room and told me supper was ready, it was as though she were removed from me by a whole life of experience.

I only wanted to sit beside the girl and look at her. When I was with her I felt a sort of weariness, as though I'd had no sleep for weeks. But when I was away from her, I ached to be with her again. I had no satisfaction, no calm, no peace, whether with her or away from her. We made our arrangements. There was to be a trap waiting at Rosthwaite. I was to walk over, meet her at the farm, take her down to the trap, and then we would drive away. A man from Keswick drove the trap with our bags out to Rosthwaite and left it there, and early on a dark afternoon, I started to walk up from the lake road. Dusk came very early at that time of the year and I knew that we should have a dark walk down to Rosthwaite, but the path was easy to follow and I wanted nobody to see us.

I left my house that morning to drive into Keswick. Mary and I had a few last words.

'You will be back for supper?' she asked me.

'Yes,' I said, 'about seven.' And that was really the first lie that I had ever told her. She said nothing, gave me one look, and then I left her.

Now this is the strange part of my little story. I can hardly expect you to believe me . . . I don't know that I even want you to . . . I only know that every word I say is true.

I walked up the path, across the bridge above the tumbling stream, and then stood looking back at what is one of the loveliest views in the world—across Lodore to the lake.

I passed the line of bungalows on my right and came to my beloved field. As I reached its edge darkness began to gather. It was too early for dusk and yet the field was obscure, as though curtained by some thin mist. I was really out of breath and I leaned against a little stone wall, wondering what was the matter with me. As I stayed there some thorn from a bush close by pricked my hand. I looked, but there was no bush near enough, I thought, to have touched me. The feeling of hostility greatly increased and I wondered what was the matter with my nerves.

I came away from the little wall and started to walk. The mist gathered more thickly and I found myself wondering, of all things in the world, whether I would find my way. Find my way—when I knew this field and the path that ran beside it utterly by heart. But I suddenly thought—no, I will cross the wall and go up the other side away from the field. But when I turned to find the wall, I found that I was slipping down a bank into the stream that ran under the wall. I caught at the turf with my hand, it broke away, and before I could stop myself, I was down in the stream. I stumbled about among the stones, the water soaking into my shoes, and clambered up again. Then, as I reached the top, I felt exactly as though someone had struck me in the face. I had a momentary impulse to call out abusively, as though it had been a living person, and then I realised my folly. How strong the wind was, and yet it seemed nothing compared with so many other times I'd known. I couldn't find the stone wall again, so I turned and began to climb the field which runs on a gentle slope to the fell. The dusky light showed me quite clearly the separate forms of five trees. As I moved up the open ground they were well away from me. Yet, very soon it was as though the wind was beating me toward the left, and although I moved forward, I seemed to make no real progress. It is a very small field and can be crossed in two minutes. But now, as the rain began to fall, striking my face, I felt as though I were blinded. I put my hand before my eyes and then stumbled and fell on to my knees, and now I began to feel quite unreasoning terror.

The rain was falling fast and the mist was thick. But through the mist I seemed to see trees marching. I could see against the skyline the faint shape of the fell which seemed an infinite distance away. I began to draw my breath with difficulty. It came in gasps and my heart was hammering unsteadily. One knows that in nightmare dreams, and sometimes in actual fact, one moves round and round a very small space, losing altogether one's sense of direction. Now when I moved forward, I could no longer see the line of the fell or the stone wall. But quite clearly outlined against the mist were five trees, forming, as it seemed to me (and this was, of course, a hallucination), a complete circle around me. So strong was this impression, however, (and after all what is reality except what one's fancy makes it?) that I saw what I thought was a gap between two of the trees and made desperately for it. And then the two trees seemed to close together and advance toward me. Panic seized me. I put my hands before my face and ran stumbling forward. Once again, this time more severely, I dashed against what seemed to be now a wall of rough and hostile bark. I even called out, 'Let me go! Let me go!'

Then I fell on my knees. The air about me seemed to grow suffocatingly close, just as though the walls of a room were closing in upon me. I could smell the wet bark, the thin timber essence of branches. I put up my hand, touched a branch, which broke, and then I felt tendrils about my legs. I began to beat with my hands, scraping the skin against the bark. The sense of suffocation grew more appalling with each instant, and the bitter scent of wet wood filled my nostrils. I rose to my feet and looked. I could see with absolute distinctness the five trees close ringed about me. They seemed to be of great thickness and intolerable height. It was as though they whispered to me an order. I obeyed it and turned and climbed out with little frightened gasps. Down the hill toward Lodore I ran, as though dreadful destruction pursued me. I remember stumbling and falling—getting up again, going on past the bungalows, over the bridge, down the road to the lake, and then somehow I found my way home.

Mary has told me since how I arrived at the house that night. My hat was gone; my face, covered with scratches, was bleeding; my clothes were torn, my knees soaked with mud. She was sitting reading. When I appeared at the door, she stood up. I cried, 'Mary! Mary!' and ran to her. Kneeling down before her and straining upward, I laid my bleeding face against her breast.

That is all. I did not see or hear of Miss Pearl Richardson again until five years later. There was a paragraph in the paper saying that in a lodging-house in Sheffield a woman named Pearl Richardson had killed herself by gas poisoning.

This is the queerest experience of my life.

A year after this, as I have said, our first child was born, and until Mary's death there were not, I am sure, two happier married people anywhere in England. And the field with the five trees looks across at me now benevolently as I write. God allows us more protection from our follies than we know.

HAVING NO HEARTS

Mr. and Mrs. William Thrush owned a very sweet little house in Benedict Canyon, Los Angeles. That is, the postal address was Los Angeles, but Benedict Canyon is a Hollywood district if ever there was one. The Thrushes liked it for that reason, among others, and it gave William Thrush a very real pleasure when he heard the big motor wagons, between seven and eight in the morning, thundering down the Canyon on their way to location. This was about as near as he ever got to Pictures. He didn't wish to get any nearer, because he had a certain pride; not very much, but enough to make him desire to live in a society where he would be valued. Every morning he read the columns of film-making gossip in his daily paper, and always remarked to Isabelle: 'Goodness! If they don't have a time!' Then they both felt happy and a little superior too.

Isabelle Thrush had more pride than William. In fact, she had a great deal, and she spent most of her time in feeding it or inducing other people to do so. Would you say they were a happy pair? If you didn't know all about them, certainly yes. If you did know all about them, you would probably be doubtful, as William often was. There was something wrong between Isabelle and himself, although they'd been married for ten years and very seldom squabbled about anything. They didn't quarrel, because William refused to. Isabelle had undoubtedly a shrill temper, especially when she didn't get what she wanted. Of course, she couldn't get all the things that she wanted because William, who was a clerk in one of the leading banks in Los Angeles, had but a moderate salary. It happened, however, that a wealthy aunt of his had died some three or four years before and left him a pretty little sum. He invested this wisely, so that even through the depression it remained. But Isabelle had all of it and then a little more.

He asked himself sometimes, in the privacy of the night, whether she were greedy. He couldn't be sure, because he often read in American magazines about the tyranny of the American wife and how she eagerly bled her husband. Well, Isabelle wasn't as bad as that. Gosh! He'd see to it if she tried anything like that on him. And so, he decided comfortably, she was better than most American wives. Isabelle considered herself a really magnificent creature, filled with all the virtues—courage, wisdom, self-sacrifice, love and endurance. She thought that William was extremely lucky to be married to her. And this thought produced in her a kindly, motherly air when he was around, as though she were saying: 'Little man, I'll look after you. Don't be afraid.' And then: 'How lucky really you are!'

The Thrushes had no children. That was Isabelle's wish, because she said it was wicked to bring a child into the world when you weren't going to give it everything of the best. William, once when he was feeling peevish because of his indigestion, remarked to her that his aunt's money would look after the child all right. But Isabelle was indignant, indeed, and said that there was a cruel strain in his nature which he would have to watch or he'd be a real sadist.

Having no children, Isabelle thought that it would be pleasant to have a dog. Many of her lady friends had them. There were, in fact, far more hospitals for dogs in Beverly and Hollywood than for human beings. And everybody said that the dog hospitals were so perfectly run that it was worth having a dog just for that reason alone. Isabelle wanted a dog, but there were problems to be settled. She understood that unless you had it as a puppy, it never became really fond of you. On the other hand puppies had to be trained, and one's beautiful rugs and carpets suffered in the process. Then, what kind of dog should she have? There were the darling Cockers, the adorable Scotch Terriers, the amusing Dachshunds and the great big splendid Setters and Airedales. Some very lonely women had Pekingese, and then there were French Bulldogs. She couldn't make up her mind and used to ask William which sort he preferred. And William, while he was trying to guess what she wanted him to say, would look at her with that slow, puzzling stare, which Isabelle always interpreted as a tribute of gratified recognition of her brilliance and beauty. In reality, what he was saying was: 'What is the matter with Isabelle? She has gone somewhere and I don't know quite where.'

They lived the social life of ladies and gentlemen of moderate means in Hollywood. That is, they went to previews of celebrated pictures; in the summer they sat in the Bowl and wiped the damp off their fingers as they listened confusedly to symphonies by Brahms and Beethoven; they occasionally, with great daring, went with a friend or two to a Burlesque in Los Angeles; they played bridge quite badly and gave little dinner-parties at which the coloured maid was never quite satisfactory. On the whole, it was a happy life.

Then one day, William, sitting alone and doing a crossword puzzle in the patio of his little Spanish house, had a visitor. Isabelle was out playing bridge with some friends and he was enjoying the lovely tranquil sunset, which lay like a golden sheet let down from heaven protectingly over the Canyon. In another half-hour the light would be gone, the air would be chill and sharp and he would go indoors and read his evening newspaper, turn on the heat, and wonder why he wasn't as happy as he ought to be. Then he saw enter his little garden, through a hole in the hedge, a French bulldog.

This dog sniffed around, looked at him from a distance with a very nervous expression, and then slowly advanced towards him, twisting and bending his thick body as though it were made of some elastic substance. William Thrush looked at the dog and disliked it exceedingly. He'd never had a great passion for dogs, ever since, years and years ago, his mother in a real temper had shaken him and told him he was as silly as a terrier puppy. So he'd grown up disliking dogs. And being himself a short little man, with large glasses and rather bowed legs, short dogs were especially unpleasant to him.

In any case, this dog seemed to him the ugliest ever. The dog seemed to him to be so very ugly that he felt a sort of nausea. He said, 'Shoo! Go away!' But the dog was evidently accustomed to being disliked. On looking back over this first meeting, William reflected on the fact that the dog resembled himself, in that if anyone disliked him some kind of paralysis seized him and he simply stayed and stayed, although he knew that he ought to go away. So did the dog now. He didn't come up to William, but lay at full length on the grass at a short distance and looked at him with his bulging, ugly, and in some unpleasant way, very human eyes.

William went up to him that he might frighten him out of the garden. But instead of that, the dog lay over on his back, wriggling his stomach and waving his legs feebly in the air. 'You're horrible!' William said aloud. 'I don't like dogs and never have. For God's sake get out of here!' and then had a dreadful sense of speaking to himself—telling himself to get out of the house and garden and go somewhere. The dog turned over, sat up, gave him a beseeching but intimate look, as though he said: 'I know you much better than you think I do. Nothing could destroy our intimacy,' and then went quietly out of the garden.

His wife returned later, vexed because she had lost at bridge. 'Such cards, my dear, you would have thought there was a spell on me. I don't know what to do about it. The cards I've been having lately!' He told her about the dog, but she wasn't in the very least interested, and after her absent-minded 'Really? How revolting!' went on with a long story about a shop in Los Angeles, where you could get a mink coat, or if it wasn't mink it looked very like it, by paying so small a sum weekly that you really didn't know you were paying it.

'No, you wouldn't,' said William, who was most unexpectedly cross, 'because I should be paying it.'

This upset her very much indeed. She detested mean people, and suddenly, standing there in the garden, which the sun had left so that it was cold and dead, she realised that William *was* mean, and that she had been living with a mean man for years and years, and it was quite wonderful for her to endure it. William on his part felt, oddly enough, that she had behaved to him just as he had behaved to the dog. 'Damn that dog!' he thought to himself. 'I can't get it out of my mind.'

Next morning, however, Isabelle was in excellent temper again, and for this reason: Helena Peters rang her up on the telephone and informed her that she had the most enchanting Cocker puppy. In fact she had two, a male and a female. Which of them would Isabelle prefer? It seems that the breed was perfect and its price in any kind of market would be fifty dollars apiece, but Helena was giving this dog to Isabelle and it was an act of friendship, because she loved Isabelle so dearly.

'I don't know why she's doing it,' Isabelle said to William. 'She wants something or other. Helena never gives anything for nothing—but it sounds a perfect puppy. I'll go around for it myself this morning.'

William very feebly suggested the disadvantages of having puppies—the wear and tear, the unpleasant hidden smells, the certainty that the dog would have distemper and die and so on. Isabelle waved all these objections aside. She had cherished them herself until William mentioned them. But, as was so often the case, her brain, so superior to William's, insisted that anything that he said must be foolish. So she went around and fetched the puppy.

Standing in the doorway at lunch-time, her face rosy with pleasure, the puppy lying in her arms against her dark green dress, its large amber eyes turned up to hers, its tongue suddenly licking her cheek, its soft brown body, its long silken ears, there was a picture so lovely that William, with a pang at his heart, wondered why it was that he didn't love her more dearly.

The puppy slowly turned its head towards William and looked at him. Was there in its eyes, even from the very first moment, a certain contempt? Had it hoped, young as it was, to find William someone quite different? Did its gaze wander to the incipient paunch, the bowed legs, and rise again to the round, rather pathetic face in which the eyes, William's best feature, were hidden behind the dull, gleaming glasses?

As they stood together in the cosy living-room, while the puppy wandered cautiously from table to chair, from chair to sofa, he was sure that Isabelle was above the puppy's social line, and that he, alas! was below it. The puppy sat down. 'Look out!' William cried. 'He had better be put in the garden.' Isabelle regarded him scornfully.

'*This* puppy is intelligent. Helena tells the most amazing stories about it. It isn't, technically, house-trained, of course, but it is wonderfully mature for a puppy. Helena says it avoids all the really valuable rugs.'

And the puppy did seem to be wonderfully sophisticated. Not that it wasn't a real puppy. It rushed about madly, it bit everything and everybody within sight, played with a string as though it had discovered the secret of perpetual motion at last, it went suddenly to sleep in your arms in the most adorable manner. It had everything that a puppy ought to have. The trouble was that it knew all about its charm. It was perfectly aware that when it lay on its side and grinned at you over its silken ear, it was entirely bewitching. And when it pretended to be angry, growling, showing its white little teeth and flashing its amber eyes, no one in the world could resist it.

Isabelle insisted that it should be called Roosevelt.

'Why?' asked William.

'Well, I think he's the most wonderful man in the world, and now, when people are turning against him and saying horrid things about the New Deal and that he's a Socialist and everything of that sort, one has to stand up for him and come right out into the open.'

'I don't see,' said William, 'that calling the puppy Roosevelt is coming out into the open.'

'It's a kind of demonstration. After all, isn't the puppy the sweetest thing in the world?'

'I don't think,' said William, sulkily, 'that Roosevelt would like anyone to call him the sweetest thing in the world. He isn't at all that kind of man.'

She looked at him reflectively. What had happened to him? Was it, perhaps, that she was only now really beginning to discover him? And if she discovered him a little further, how would it be then? Would she be able to endure it?

There is no doubt that after the arrival of the puppy, they bickered a good deal. A happy marriage between two persons depends altogether on mutual charity, unless one of the two is so absolutely a sheep that he doesn't mind what is done to him. Isabelle was a woman who had charity for everyone and everybody, but it was charity of a kind. It never worked unless Isabelle's pride was properly fed first. William, unfortunately, continued increasingly to look at her with that puzzled bewildered expression that is so justly irritating to wives.

And then the puppy confirmed her in her growing sense of injustice. People love dogs because they are so flattering. If you are unjust to your friend and feel a certain shame, your dog swiftly restores your self-confidence. It never knows that you have been mean or jealous or grasping. It encourages you to be kindly to itself, and when you respond, it loves you.

The puppy, Roosevelt, must have been born a courtier; its tact was perfectly astonishing. For instance, when it arrived in the bedroom in the morning and greeted the twin beds with little yelps of ecstatic pleasure, it almost at once discriminated between Isabelle's bed and William's. It went to William first so that Isabelle, looking enchanting in her early-morning sleepy bewilderment, was given the opportunity to say: 'Isn't he coming to Mummy then?' and Isabelle's little smile of gratified pleasure when it rushed over to her, as though William never existed, was something delightful to witness.

When guests were present, as they often were, how Roosevelt was adored! And how then he made it appear that it was really because of Isabelle that he seemed so charming. He bit delicately at a lady's dress, or chewed playfully at the corner of a handsome purse with a side glance at Isabelle, as though he were saying to the ladies: 'It is because I love her so. It is because she is such a perfect darling. It is because I'm so wonderfully happy with her that I'm behaving like this.' William had never greatly cared for Isabelle's lady friends and generally avoided occasions when they would be present. That was one of Isabelle's complaints. But now he simply could not bear to be there. Isabelle's patronage of him was one thing, but Isabelle and Roosevelt together were more than any man could endure. And so they had a quarrel.

'You're behaving ridiculously about that dog.'

'Ridiculously?' That was something that Isabelle never would forgive. 'You've hated it,' she asserted, her eyes flashing, 'ever since its arrival. And why? Why? Shall I tell you?'

'Please do,' said William, stony-faced.

'Because it prefers me to you, because it always has.'

'Oh, damn the dog!' said William.

Meanwhile, the French bulldog made frequent appearances, but never when Isabelle was about. Greatly though William disliked it, he began, very reluctantly, to be interested in its personality. It wanted so terribly to be loved, and it was a certainty nobody loved it. Building was in process near by. And William, after he shaved in the morning, looking out of the window, would watch its approach to the different workmen, wiggling its body and leaping heavily up and down, and all the workmen repulsed it. They were good, kindly men, no doubt, as most American workmen are, but they felt about it as William did, that it was too ugly to be born. He christened it Ugly, and as soon as he had given it a name, it seemed to have at once a closer relationship with him.

'Get away, Ugly, you beastly dog!' he would say. And the dog would be apparently in an ecstasy of enjoyment at being called anything at all. Once in a fit of abstraction, sitting there wondering why it was that he was so lonely, wondering why everything was going wrong with Isabelle and what it was that she really lacked, Ugly came close to him, and not knowing what he did, he stroked its back and tickled it behind the ear. He was aware then of a wave of affection that was almost terrifying.

As soon as William realised what he had done, he moved away with an irritated murmur. The dog did not follow him, but stayed there stretched out looking at him. How unpleasant is this naked sentimentality in this modern realistic world! How we run from sentiment and how right it is that we should do so! And yet William was sentimental too. Someone loved him, and although he detested the dog, he was not quite as lonely as he'd been before.

It happened, of course, that Roosevelt and Ugly had various encounters. Ugly would come across the path into the garden, and finding Roosevelt there, hoped that they might have a game. But Roosevelt, young as he was, played only with his social equals. He did not snarl at Ugly. He did nothing mean nor common. He allowed Ugly supplicatingly to sniff him, to walk around him, even to cavort and prance a little, and then very quietly he strolled indoors. And then Isabelle realised that Ugly existed.

'William, do look at that hideous dog! What's it doing here? Shoo! Shoo! Get away, you horrible animal!' and Ugly went. William found himself, to his own surprise, defending Ugly.

'He isn't so bad,' he said. 'Not much to look at, of course, but friendly, obedient, rather a decent dog.'

'Oh, you would!' said Isabelle. 'It only needs the most hideous animal I've seen in my life to come your way for you to praise it. Really, William, I don't know what's happening to you.'

William smiled at her and said very gently: 'I don't know what's happening, either.' He made then, almost as though it were under Ugly's instructions, a serious attempt to persuade Isabelle to love him again. He was very patient, thoughtful, generous. A few people in the world knew that William Thrush had an extraordinary amount of charm—even a kind of penetrating wit when he liked. But William's charm was unconscious. It failed him when he tried to summon it. And now the more he tried, the more irritating to her he became.

The breach grew wider and Isabelle confessed to her closer friends that she didn't know whether she could stand it much longer. Then, as nothing ever stays where it is but always advances to its appointed climax, the catastrophe occurred.

One of the troubles between William and Isabelle had always been that William liked to read and Isabelle did not. William liked long, long novels, preferably about family life. Novels that went on and on for ever and ever, in which you could be completely lost. Novels that deceived you with so friendly and profuse a carelessness that it was like a personal compliment to yourself. Isabelle, on the other hand, could not bear to read. She looked at the social column of the daily paper and sometimes a film magazine or a fashion monthly. But for the most part, as she said, she adored to read, but 'just didn't have the time to open a book.'

This had once been very sad to William, who in his young glowing days had imagined sitting on one side of the fire reading aloud to his dear little wife, who was sewing things for the baby, but nevertheless able to take it all in and speculate about the characters. Well, on this particular day, he was deep in a novel by one of those English novelists who have so many characters in their family that they have to have a genealogical table at the end of the book. To this same table he would often refer with a pleasing sense that he was staying in the most delightful house with an enormous family of cousins. He read cosily and comfortably. The door leading on to the porch was open and the afternoon sun poured bountifully in. He was aware then that something had occurred. There had been no sound, no movement, but looking up, he beheld a very horrible sight.

Ugly was advancing towards him, and one of his eyes, a blood-red ball, was nearly torn from his head. The dog made no sound whatever. He simply came towards William, only once and again lifting a paw feebly, as though he were absurdly puzzled as to what had happened to him. When he got near to William, he crouched down, and still without a sound, looked up into his face.

William's first feeling was of nausea. He hated the sight of blood. His sensitive soul was intensely distressed by any kind of physical suffering. This seemed to him quite horrible. Then almost at once he was overwhelmed with pity. He'd never in his life before been so sorry for anything. Something in the distressed trusting patience of the dog won his heart completely and for ever. That the animal should be so silent, making no complaint, seemed to him himself as he ought to be. That was how he'd wish to behave had such a terrible thing happened to him. How, he was sure, he would *not* behave.

He said nothing, but arose from his chair, was about to take the dog in his arms and hasten at once with it to the nearest dog hospital, when Isabelle entered and Roosevelt scampered out from a room near by. She was smiling and happy. She greeted the cocker puppy with little cries of baby joy. 'Oh, the darling! The ickle, ickle darling! Wasn't he an angel to come and see his mummy?' And then she saw the other dog. Ugly had turned his head and was looking at her. She screamed. She put her hands in front of her face.

'Oh, William, how horrible! How frightful! It must be killed at once!'

William got up, took the heavy, bleeding dog in his arms, and without a word, passed her and went out.

He went into the garage, laid the dog on the old rug, got out his car, picked up the dog again, got into the car with him and drove off to the dog hospital. Here he talked to a very kindly plump little man and discussed whether Ugly should be destroyed or not. When the little man took Ugly in his arms to examine him, the dog very slowly turned his head, and, with his one eye, looked at William as much as to say: 'If you think this is the right thing for me to do, I'll suffer it.' William even nodded his head to the dog and a silent understanding seemed to pass between them.

'It seems to have no damage anywhere else,' the doctor said. 'It was done, of course, by another dog. They do that. They just take hold of one place and don't let go again. Poor old fellow!' The dog doctor caressed him. 'Not very handsome, anyway, is he?'

'Oh, I don't know,' said William; 'he's got a kind of character about him, I think.'

'Is he your dog?' asked the doctor.

'No. I don't think he belongs to anybody, but he comes to our garden sometimes. I've grown interested in him.'

'Well, I can tell you this,' the doctor said, 'I guess he'll be all right. We can sew it up so you'll hardly notice it. He won't exactly be a beauty, you know.'

'Yes, I know,' said William, who wasn't a beauty, either. He went home.

For some reason or another, Isabelle had been greatly excited by the incident. She sat there and gave William a terrific lecture, the total of which was that for ever so long now he'd been letting himself go. He was becoming soppy, almost a sissy, in fact.

'A sissy?' said William, indignantly.

'Oh, well, you know what I mean. You're getting dreadfully sentimental. You always had a tendency that way, but lately it's been terrible. All my friends notice it.'

I don't know why it is, but there is almost nothing so irritating in the world as to be told by someone that one's friends have been silently, mysteriously, observing one to one's disadvantage. William, for the first time in their married life, lost all control of himself. He stood up and raved. He said that it didn't matter whether he was getting sentimental or not, but anyway, perhaps sentiment wasn't a bad thing. What really mattered was that Isabelle was selfish, cold and unkind! That she hadn't any idea of the horrible woman she was becoming. Isabelle suitably replied. In fact, they both thoroughly lost their tempers. And while this was going on, Roosevelt sat in Isabelle's lap making little playful bites at Isabelle's dress and beautiful fingers. While he sat there, he looked at William with a really terrible sarcasm in his soft, amber eyes—sarcasm and scorn.

'I tell you what,' William cried in a last frenzy, 'I hate that dog! Puppies ought to be nice, gentle, loving creatures. Look at him! He's hard as iron and the most horrid snob.'

So then Isabelle burst into tears, went to her room and locked her door. There followed days of constrained silence, and after that William went down to the dog hospital.

'He's a patient dog, I must say,' the doctor remarked. 'Never a whine. Seems fond of you too.'

William was surprised at the pleasure that he felt at the tribute. The day came when Ugly's eye was gone, the empty space sewed up, and his whole air rather that of a drunken soldier who had been in the wars. What was to be done with him? William, realising that the crisis of his life was upon him, decided that if Isabelle had her Roosevelt, he should have his Ugly. He went home and told her so. This was at breakfast. She said no word and he left for his work in the city.

When he returned in the late afternoon there was a strange silence about the house. He had been thinking and had decided that in some way or another this awful trouble with Isabelle must be stopped. After all, surely he loved her. Or if he didn't, they were at least man and wife. How miserable, how lost, he would be without her! Would he? At that appalling wonder, his whole soul shook. So he returned home with every intention of making everything all right again, although how he was to do that he didn't in the least know.

Ugly greeted him, coming in from the garden, rolling his body about, baring his teeth, showing an ecstasy of pleasure. But Isabelle was not there, nor Roosevelt. On his writing-table lay the note so essential to all dramatists and novelists who have learnt their job. What it said was that Isabelle had gone to her mother in Santa Barbara and would remain there. She wished that William would give her a divorce. She had been seeing for a long time how impossible things were. She had taken Roosevelt with her.

William read the note and felt a dreadful shame and despair. His impulse was to depart at once for Santa Barbara. And so he would have done if it had not been for Ugly. But he could not leave him just then. The dog was new to the house and the servants had no especial affection for him. In a day or two he would go. But he did not. The days passed and he did not.

A quite terrible thing happened to him. He found that he liked the house better without Isabelle than with her. He found that he adored his freedom. That he could now have liberty of action and thought, that showed him what all these years he'd been missing. He discovered a number of other things. He took long walks up the Canyon with Ugly. He talked to the dog and it seemed to him that the dog answered him. Strangest of all, he was less lonely than he had been when Isabelle was there. It was as though for years there had been a padlock on his mind. Someone, something, had all the time inhibited his thought.

A letter came from Isabelle and he made his discovery. In her letter she said she was now ready to return. Santa Barbara wasn't half the place it had once been, and her mother was in many ways unsympathetic, and he would be glad to hear, she missed her dear old William. As he wrote his reply to her letter, he solved his problem. This was the letter he wrote.

Dear Isabelle,

I don't want you to come back. This sounds very unkind and rude on my part, but I've done a lot of thinking in the last few weeks and I know that I must be honest. For a long while I've been wondering what it was that was wrong between us. I admire you so much. You are far finer than I. You have been so good and so kind for so long, that it seems absurd to say that you are lacking in anything. But you are. You have no heart. That sounds like a thing you read in a novel, but I mean it just like that. I don't think you're any the worse for not having one—it is only that I have suddenly discovered while I've been alone here that that is the one real difference between human beings. Either you have a heart, or you haven't one. What I mean is, either the heart is the part of your body that functions more than any other or not. This is the one insuperable difference between people. Not whether you're a Fascist or Communist, American or French, teetotaller or a drunkard, clever or stupid. All those things can be got over quite easily. I'm not saying either that the people with hearts are preferable to those without. I think it is possibly just the opposite. The people with hearts are nearly always too sentimental, too emotional, prevent the work of the world being done, get in the way of the real thinkers. The people without hearts are, as the world is now going, the ones we really want. But the difference is there. I can't help feeling emotionally about things. You can't help the opposite. But we mustn't live together any more. This is a difference that nothing can get over.

Yours sincerely,
WILLIAM

P.S.—There is the same difference between Roosevelt and Ugly.

When he had posted the letter and was walking in a last cool flash of sunshine up the Canyon, Ugly ambling along beside him, he thought that possibly no one had ever written so silly a letter. And yet, he had this sense that he had made this marvellous discovery. He looked at all his friends, male and female, and saw the dividing line with absolute clearness. He looked beyond the other great figures in the world. Einstein had a heart—Hitler, even. On the other hand, Mussolini possibly not. And Simon Callahan, the manager of his bank in Los Angeles, most certainly not! Ugly, whose vision of course was now sadly dimmed, saw a golden leaf, one of the first signs of autumn, twirling through the air. He leapt rather foolishly, ran a little way and looked back at William. William smiled encouragement. Then he turned back home, Ugly delightedly following.

THE CONJURER

EVERYONE who looks back to childhood must be aware of the strange confusion of fact and fairy-story that those early memories arouse. Here there is detail so sharp and clear that its truth cannot be questioned—the screen with the pictures from the Christmas numbers, the green china saucer in which the mustard and cress was sown, the oak guarding the lawn hung with festoons of crystal snow, the murmur of the pigeons above the rose-coloured garden wall, and, with these, the oddest figures—fairies, leprechauns, wizards—and scenes of fantasy when the cuckoo flew out of the clock, the Chinese mandarin from the drawing-room mantelpiece wiped his long moustaches with a cambric handkerchief, and the spotted rocking-horse without a tail bumped down the flight of stairs from the schoolroom to the hall-door. What is reality? Where do dreams begin? What is Truth? asked jesting Pilate.

With wonder such as this I look back to an adventure of my childhood never narrated by me before because, perhaps, I have been afraid of my neighbour's incredulity. It may be that at last I perceive that the whole of life is nothing but a succession of wonders and one adventure in it no more unreal than another. Or it may be that I am old enough now not to fear my neighbour's mocking laughter. He has laughed at me too often, and, like the bluebottle in the fairy-tale, 'I have grown accustomed to my cousin bluebottle's impertinent buzzing.' In any case, however that may be, for the first time I relate this remarkable story, giving you the details exactly as I remember them.

I must have been at the time aged thirteen or so. I was a shy, nervous and self-conscious boy—the more so that my elder brother and sister had not a doubt about anything and laughed at me, when they thought of me, for my paltry spirit.

It was, I am afraid, true. I *had* a paltry spirit. It seemed to me that so very easily, with a word or a look, with the closing of a door or the opening of a window, things might go so very wrong. The day—every day—was packed with danger, whether at school or at home. I loved my father and mother, but, at that time, also feared them. I hated to see that look in my mother's eyes as though, in spite of her love for me, the thought would come to her: 'Is this child never going to have any sense? What are we to do with him?'

Sarah, my elder sister, a boisterous, happy and extremely popular child, would look at me and say, laughing: 'Well, you *are* a little fool!'—which I was, I have no doubt. But it would have been better had she not laughed. She was (as I have since told her) in those years so carelessly contemptuous of me.

However, I am not here attempting to blame anybody. That I deserved all I got I don't for a moment doubt. I was a shy, awkward, unattractive child—which only makes this adventure the more remarkable. For several years of my childhood my father, who was a doctor, had a practice in the village of Gosforth in Cumberland. Gosforth was three miles from the sea, and some six miles from Wastwater lake. The village consisted of a long, straggling street. It was famous principally for its church, and the church was famous because of the remarkable cross in the graveyard. This cross was one of the most ancient—if not *the* most ancient—in the whole of Great Britain, and was the more remarkable because it was carved with certain pagan figures. Antiquarians in large numbers used to visit the cross, and still do, I don't doubt.

Altogether, with the sea so near, with the lake (the darkest, most mysterious of all the lakes) only a bicycle-ride away, the strange cross, the beautiful outline of Black Combe on the horizon, Gosforth was the very place to nurture the illogical fancies of a romantic child.

We lived in an old rambling house, half a mile from the village. This house had a wild, unkempt garden, a thick tangled wood ran at the back of it, and for birds, for singing, chattering, gossipy, happy birds, I have never known a place to equal it! Neither my father nor mother, nor Sarah and Fred—my sister and brother—lived very much in the world of the imagination. During the holidays—I went at this time to Sedbergh School—every minute was filled with practical doings. My father's belief was that it was bad for children to be idle, and so from morning to night we were busily employed. We were encouraged to play games, and it was one of my troubles that at any and every game I was a duffer. Not so Sarah and Fred, who simply rejoiced in them and gathered other children to share in them from near and far. Children were not in those days hard to find. It was before the times of constant universal motoring, and, therefore, also before the times of a passionate and perpetually disappointed restlessness. We took our pleasures eagerly, but had that best of all the fairy's gifts—a conscious and excited enjoyment of little things. Almost nothing was too slight for our amusement.

It happened that, although in my childish, lonely soul I was thirsting for affection, none of the children who came to our house found me attractive. There were the Bellishaws of Uffdale, the Croxtons from Moor Park, the Adderleys from Gosforth village. The Adderleys are important in my story and so I must say a word about them—without prejudice, I hope, although even at this great distance of time I can't pretend that I love them!

The Rector of Gosforth was a bachelor, and lived in rooms at the Wastwater end of the village. The Rectory was a big rambling old house, and expensive to run, so he let it to Sir John and Lady Adderley, and lived with perfect content in a frowsty study and a small stuffy bedroom. (I can see him now, following the stream beyond the village, his black clerical hat on one side of his head, a huge pipe in his mouth, and the gleam of delighted anticipation in his eye!)

So the Adderleys took the Rectory for a year and made a considerable splash in the neighbourhood. They were, as a family, designed for a splash; noisy, happy, confident, most exceedingly self-assured. Lady Adderley, I remember, was a large, broad woman with a big, red, freckled face, and I see her always in a vast floppy hat and gardening gloves, and carrying an enormous pair of scissors. But the three children were the important thing—Ambrose, Grace and Samuel. They were, I suppose, very 'bossy' children. At any rate, as I look back upon them they always ran everything, and that instantly. I can hear Ambrose's commanding voice now as he arrived at our door—'I say! Look here, we're going to play croquet, and bags I the red ball!'

Of course, they despised me thoroughly. They teased me, mocked me, derided me, all most good-naturedly, of course. They were bursting with rude health, and had to give freedom to some of their energy. And there I was, hopeless at games and easily stirred into a temper that was an amusing game for all of them. 'Let's make Humphrey waxy,' was their jolly cry—and waxy I was very easily made!

It happened, therefore, that when the Adderley children appeared I, whenever possible, slipped away. I hid in the wood or I slunk up the road, and then, safe for the time being from persecution, allowed my imagination its freedom, telling myself stories, or, more often, inventing wonderful crises when I played the hero—fires when I saved my sister and the Adderley girl, expeditions when we would be lost in the hills and I only discover the way out, or accidents at sea when I would swim through monstrous waves to secure assistance.

It was on one of these lonely walks that I first saw Mr. Claribel.

I have already said that, as I look back, I cannot be sure of what was real and what unreal. I know for certain that it was a cold winter's day, with a little, whining, lonely wind that blew a few last shrunken leaves twistedly in the air before they fell. Above the far turn of the road the hump of Black Combe—black against the grey-white chilly sky—looked frowning upon me. And down the road came Mr. Claribel. It has always been my constant belief that he was *dancing* down the road. That, too, may be fancy, but in my memory's eye I see him, oh, so clearly! with his round black hat, his umbrella ill folded, dancing along while the cold thin air trembled through the branches.

When we met he stopped. I had never seen him before (although he had been living in the village for some considerable time) and I must have stared in a very rude way. He was odd at first sight, with his little, meagre body, his brown face, his bright blue eyes, and his long, black coat-tails flapping behind him.

Our conversation (the first of many) was something like this:

'Well, little boy, what are you doing here?'

'Walking, sir.'

'What—all alone? Haven't you anyone to walk with?'

'I like to be alone, sir.' (I was at times a priggish little boy.)

'Like to be alone? Tut! Tut! That's wrong at your age! How old are you?'

'Thirteen and three months.'

'Thirteen and three months—and all by yourself. Where's your father and mother?'

'At Grange Hall, sir. My father's the doctor.'

'Your father's the doctor? And have you no brother and sister?'

'Yes, sir. One brother and one sister.'

'And what are *they* doing?'

'Playing.'

'And so ought you to be.' It must have been about now that he came very close to me, peering into my face. 'You haven't seen a little dog anywhere?'

'No, sir.'

'It's a small brown dog, and answers to the name of Napoleon. He's disappeared. He's always disappearing. But then so's everything else.'

I remember quite clearly that he asked me then: 'Do you know what's the secret of a happy life?'

'No, sir.'

'Never to be astonished at anything. Take it all as it comes. It's no use your being astonished, because IT doesn't care if you are. IT doesn't care what you feel.'

He said IT with terrific emphasis.

'Dear, dear,' he said. 'It's very cold talking here. Have you had your tea?'

'No, sir.'

'Well, come and have it with me.'

We started along together, he walking at a great pace, sometimes muttering to himself, sometimes dropping his umbrella, which I picked up for him, and, once and again, calling out in a high, shrill treble: 'Napoleon! Napoleon!'

Then, when we were very near to the village, a little brown dog appeared from nowhere. Really from nowhere at all. It was most uncanny. There it was, in the middle of the road, a very nice little dog, with curly brown hair, wagging its tail and looking most friendly.

'Where have you been?' Mr. Claribel said severely. But the little dog didn't mind, only chased a leaf that the wind was playing with, and ran in front of us as though it hadn't a care in the world.

I remember that I wondered whether it was right to go to tea with a complete stranger. I had always been warned that

I must never speak to strangers or take anything from them, but I didn't see what harm this gentleman could do me, and I fancy that I was pleased at the thought of disobeying my family for once. Little they cared, I thought, what I did!

We arrived at the little house, with a bare little garden in front of it. This garden was remarkable to me for a large, round silver ball (like a witch-ball) that was posed on a stone pedestal in the very middle of the garden bed. There was also what should have been a small fountain (although no water was playing) and a child's railway train lying dejectedly on its side in the gravel path. I remember all the details of this house as though I were walking in at the front door this very minute.

Mr. Claribel and Napoleon led the way. He helped me off with my coat and muffler, patting me on the shoulder as he did so. Then I followed him into the very queerest room I had ever seen. It was a small room, with a bright, prattling little fire, a pot of Christmas roses in the window, and a small table laid for tea. The queer thing about it was that it was crammed with the most incongruous things. There were, I remember, two sets of chessmen, a sailing ship modelled in silver with a glass bowl covering it, a large, speckled fish stretched out against the wall, a doll's house with very bright-looking miniature furniture, one of those large glass balls containing a house painted blue which you turn upside-down and it snows (I know because I tried), a crimson drum with the gilt arms of some regiment on the crimson, an ivory elephant, a musical box painted with little country scenes (I know it was a musical box because afterwards I played it), and many, many things more, although these are the only ones that I definitely remember. I never saw a room so crowded, and yet, in some quite happy way, we fitted in exactly, I sitting on one side of the fire, and he on the other, with Napoleon stretched out at his feet.

Soon an old lady arrived with the tea, and we turned to the table.

'I always sit up to the table at tea,' he remarked (and I observed that he took his napkin and tucked it in under his sharp, little brown chin). 'One eats so much more. Don't you think so?'

We certainly ate a great deal that evening! We had thick, rich blackberry jam; thick, rich gingerbread cake, black as thunder, sweet as heaven, damp in the middle; scones and buns and sandwiches and hot buttered toast; tea out of a magnificent old teapot with patterns of leaves and roses in silver as thick as your thumb. I remember that, while I gorged, I asked myself the question: Does he have tea all by himself to this extent every day? Could he have been expecting someone? But how could he have known that he would meet me?

And then, as he so often did, he read my thoughts.

'I knew you were coming to tea,' he said. 'There were tea-leaves in my cup at breakfast this morning.' But he didn't mean that. He had had some way of knowing. I was sure of it. But how could he . . . when I wasn't sure of it myself!

Before I left him that afternoon he asked me every sort of question, and some of them very unusual. I may, in fact, be inventing here. Isn't it incredible, for instance, that he should have asked me whether I collected acorns? I said, of course, that I did not. He shook his head and said that was a pity. He asked me whether the big toe of my left foot ever ached, and I said that, as a matter of fact, it sometimes did. He smiled, and said that that was an excellent sign, and that he was glad to hear it. He asked me whether I liked to read, and I said I did. What books did I like best? I said Stevenson, Rider Haggard and Stanley Weyman.

He said that he had a book to give me, and out of a drawer near the fireplace he produced a thin, flat book with faded red covers. Inside there were coloured pictures, pictures of remarkable animals, animals with two heads and long swords coming out of their foreheads. There were also maps of the planetary system, and there were ladies with crowns on their heads, and one picture of a large green tree crowded with birds. There were many pages covered entirely with numbers and letters of the alphabet.

'Now, if you could learn what all that means, Humphrey,' he said, 'you could turn yourself into anything you liked any time you liked.'

'Could I really?' I asked, quite fascinated.

'Indeed you could.'

'And can you turn yourself into anything you like?' I enquired.

'Ah,' he answered, smiling. 'That's asking. But Napoleon can.'

After that I went home, swollen with food and clutching the red book under my arm. I was greatly excited. I had made a friend. I knew someone that my family didn't know. After this, in the next few weeks, I saw him frequently. I had tea with him on several occasions. Very soon I loved him dearly, for I was a sentimental little boy, longing for affection. No one had ever been so kind to me. He made me, too, begin to have some belief in myself. I brushed my hair and put on a clean collar, and really began to have some opinions of my own and assert them.

Then, of course, my new friendship was discovered. I was seen walking down the street with Mr. Claribel. It was not directly disapproved of, but I was terribly teased about it. I found that Mr. Claribel was considered in the village as someone altogether off his head. No one could charge him with any crime; on the contrary, he was a kind, crazy, old man who gave sweets to the children, visited old Mrs. Mumble when she was in bed with a bad leg, and helped Mr. Somerthwaite when his cow died. But he was *queer*, and that is enough in this world to divide a man from his fellows. As though we are not, all of us, queer as queer! If we are not queer in one way, we are certainly queer in another!

The Adderley children were especially amused at my friendship.

'Let's do Mr. Claribel asking Humphrey to tea!' Ambrose would cry, and he would present an absurd imitation of Mr. Claribel with his coat-tails and badly-folded umbrella. More than that, this new interest of mine seemed to separate me from the others more than ever. Mr. Claribel was mad, and I liked him, so I must be mad too. And then I had something that *they* hadn't got. Children are cruel not because they want to be, but because they are not yet civilised. I was like a sick or injured member of the herd, and the healthy ones must make a protest.

A strange thing was that Mr. Claribel knew exactly what they were doing. I didn't have to tell him a thing. 'If they don't look out,' he said one day, 'I'll give those children the fright of their lives,' and for a moment, as he said it, he appeared quite dangerous! But no one could have been kinder to me than he was. The stories he told me, the presents he made me (I have the round ball with the snow inside it to this day!), the affection he showed me!

So we moved on towards Christmas. A week before Christmas the snow came. It snowed steadily for three days—real hard snow that covered the ground and stayed there. This is unusual for Cumberland, for snow rarely lies on the lower ground. After the snowfall we had one brilliant blue sky after another. We woke to glittering, sparkling mornings and looked out of the window to a lawn so thick with diamonds that it hurt the eye to gaze on it, and its virgin whiteness was unbroken save for the tiny imprints of the birds. Over everything there was a marvellous hush. You could hear voices calling or dogs barking from great distances, and the shadows cast on the snow by the fir-trees were a deep and tender purple. The oak-tree on the lawn was so heavy with snow that it seemed that, strong though it was, it must bend with its burden.

Inside the house, what excitement! In those days Christmas was an event of mystery, of almost passionate anticipation, of blissful realisation! We had no outside aids. There were one or two parties, a Christmas tree for the village children, but all the realities we must spin, like silkworms, out of ourselves!

It was a fine year, I remember, for holly—the berries were thick—and soon the house was decorated from kitchen to attic. But the principal enterprise was the inventing of presents. These were secrets evolved behind locked doors, wrapped away in paper and hidden in drawers. We children had little money, and the only place for purchases was the village shop. I had, in all, about six shillings of my own, and four people must have major presents, and by major I meant something of real importance, something original, something startling. Never mind now what my presents were. I have, in fact, altogether forgotten.

But what I do remember is that, as Christmas Day approached, I began to be overwhelmed with a sense of coming failure. I wanted this time to assert myself, to show them all that I *did* matter! My presents were to be so unusual that they would be compelled to consider me. But, of course, they were not. And, as the others grew ever more busy and important and excited, I, as I always did when the whole family was excited, became less and less of anything. When they needed a messenger or a scapegoat or an 'odd boy' they made use of me—and with good-humoured contempt. So at least I thought. I have no doubt that I imagined all this, and that they were too busy, too jolly, too happy to think of me at all, or, if they did, fancied that I was jolly and happy too. But because, perhaps, my new friendship with Mr. Claribel had given me new hopes I felt all the more deeply that I was a wretched failure, and of no use to anyone.

And the worst thing of all was the Adderleys' party. This was to be on Christmas Eve—a grand affair at the Rectory; children from all the neighbourhood, supper and games and a Christmas tree. I never suffered anywhere as I did at the

Adderley parties, for it was there that I was most completely disregarded. Nobody's fault but my own. I was tongue-tied in a large company, or, if I did speak, made a remark at which everyone laughed. I *wanted* to be gay, but happiness on these occasions seemed to be always just out of my reach.

As the hours passed the thought of the Adderley festivity clouded my eyes. I saw myself, in my sensitive, excited imagination, mocked and derided, the more bitterly a failure in that I could picture to myself so easily how wonderful it would be were I a success. I could see myself applauded, could hear the comments—'What a remarkable boy! A most unusual child!' Not that I thought myself remarkable or unusual, but for once how splendid it would be if I appeared so!

My unhappiness reached a climax on the morning of Christmas Eve. I was carrying something for my mother and dropped it; I could not find something for my brother; my father said 'Come, come, Humphrey—where are your wits?' In the middle of the morning—a lovely crystal-clear day it was—I slipped away and took Mr. Claribel my present. After much thought and balancing of possibilities, I had decided that I would give him a penknife. An absurd present, perhaps, but among all his possessions I had never seen a penknife, and, as it was a thing that I needed at the time very badly myself, it was obvious that other people must need one, too.

The one that I bought at the village shop (with, I am afraid, quite half my available riches) was made of tortoise-shell. (Imitation? I fear so. I didn't know it then.) It had only one blade, but it *looked* bright, and it *could* cut, because I tested it. Indeed, I remember that I liked it so much that I had a moment's awful temptation to keep it for myself. I didn't know then what I know now—that when one keeps for oneself a present that one has bought for someone else it turns, inevitably, to dust and ashes. No, I loved Mr. Claribel, and by the time that I had reached his house I was delighted at the thought of his pleasure. And he *was* pleased! He kissed me very ceremoniously on the forehead. I detested to be kissed, but on this occasion it warmed my heart, made me think suddenly of the Adderley party, created in some way a sharp picture of my clumsiness and isolation there—and I burst into tears!

The little man made all sorts of sounds of distress, brought out the black gingerbread cake, sat with his arm on my shoulder while I ate it, then gave me *his* present, which was none other than the beautiful musical box with the pictures. I was so terribly pleased about this that I threw my arms round his neck and kissed him in my turn.

He asked me then why I was unhappy, and I told him. It was the Adderley party. I didn't like the Adderleys, and their parties were *awful*. I knew that I should make a fool of myself, that I should disgrace my father and mother, that I should come home from it so miserable that Christmas would be altogether spoilt. He nodded his head a number of times. Then he said:

'Now, don't you worry. I promise that you shall enjoy the party.'

I shook my head dismally.

'Just you wait. I've never promised anything yet that I haven't brought off. Just you wait.'

In some mysterious way relieved, I ran home, clutching my musical box.

At the appointed hour, muffled up to our noses, our hands in thick woollen gloves, my father carrying a lantern, we set out for the Rectory.

Here it may be that, because of after events, my imagination once more leads me astray, but, looking back, I seem now to recover a kind of magic in the air that night. The sky crackled with stars, our breath drove in front of the lantern in cloudy bursts, illuminated by that fitful gleam. The star-shimmering light was brilliant enough to haze the air with a kind of silver twilight, and within this the trees and hedges seemed to sail in shapes of white marble across the fields. The frost was heavy, and the snow crunched and protested under our boots. There would be a little shiver in the air, and a dust of snow would scatter over our shoulders. There was every witness to Christmas Eve. At old Miss Mark's house down the road a little group were singing carols, and their lantern seemed to greet ours in a roguish fashion, as much as to say: 'What are *you* doing leading those ridiculous mortals along the road? Why not drop them into a pond?'

All in a quite friendly way, of course!

Across the fields came the tumbling, tangled melody of the church bells. They were practising for to-morrow, and I could see Joe Churcher, who was rather a friend of mine and a very fat man, straining at the rope, and little Harry Bone, who was so short and thin, standing on tip-toe. In any case, there they were, those rich, rollicking, impetuous chimes rolling over the white, frosted fields as though they were so wildly excited by good news that they were tumbling over themselves to tell it.

As we approached the Rectory, I was moved, I remember, by two very opposite impulses. One was to run away and hide. I tramped along in the rear of our family procession with all the certainty of being forgotten and neglected that I had all day long been expecting. The family had, up to this evening, the most curious fashion of behaving as though I didn't exist; *after* this evening they were never unconscious of me again! I felt miserable, and socially a pariah, but at the same time I was excited with expectation. I was quite certain that Mr. Claribel would keep his promise.

How he would do it I did not of course know, but something would happen, something that would astonish everybody!

Inside the house we were borne along on the general stream. Our wraps were taken from us, we patted our hair, straightened our waistcoats, tried to look as grown-up as possible. I remember, that, in a rather miserable, doomed kind of way, watching my sister Sarah, I decided that she looked too silly for anything. She was *not* a beauty (none of us, I fear, was that), her figure was lumpy, and her stockings *would* go crooked and her nose shiny! (Dear Sarah! how I learnt to love you afterwards! What I would give to have you sitting beside me now!) I was a caustic little critic in those days, but a critic (like so many critics) who could be changed, by a kind personal word, into an appreciator.

There were, however, for me no kind words during the first part of that evening. Everything went as wrong as it could possibly go! We all tumbled into the drawing-room and stood about, looking, most of us, angry and shy.

Lady Adderley, red in the face and fastened into a too-tight costume of light blue silk, sailed into the midst of us, shouting out cheerful remarks to break the ice. The room was very gay, with its blaze of lights and holly over all the pictures, a thick clump of mistletoe, burdened with berries, hanging from the centre illumination that shivered with a thousand silver pennies as we moved about under it.

The ice must be broken, so we started with musical chairs, and then, at the very beginning of the evening, I disgraced myself. For a long, thin lady with a tiresome train was skirting the chairs just in front of me. She was one of those middle-aged ladies who, at a children's party, are 'younger than the youngest', for she passed along, clutching at the back of every chair, and uttering shrill cries of pleasure and excitement. I was just behind her and trod on her train. There was a rent and a cry. The lady turned, and, for a moment, I thought that she would slap me, she looked so vexed. But she pulled herself together, smiled a bitter smile, said that it didn't matter in the least, and retired to have something done to it.

Of course, everyone had seen that I was responsible. 'Just like Humphrey,' I heard someone say. I was now in that parlous state, known to all of us in nightmares, when every step is perilous. Move where I would, I should assist some catastrophe. Oddly enough, I believe that everyone else felt something of the same discomfort. It promised to be one of those parties upon which unhappy hostesses look back, with dismay, for the rest of their lives. At the end of that very first game there was trouble because a fat little boy, clinging to the seat of the last chair, protested that *he* had won and not the thin boy with the rabbit teeth who was sitting on the chair-edge as though he were Casabianca. Other people took sides. A little girl said it was a 'shame.' We then played Blind Man's Buff, a dangerous game, because it degenerates so readily into horse-play. It did so now, and a big boy pushed a little girl over, and she started loudly to cry.

Yes, things were very wrong, and I saw Lady Adderley consulting with her husband. She was asking him, I expect, whether it would not be wise to hurry things forward. I was myself so completely neglected that I might have been a little lonely ghost, invisible to all the world. I spoke to no one. No one spoke to me. There are no miseries in after life to compare with these miseries of childhood.

Then the door opened. A maid stood there and I heard her say quite clearly:

'My lady—the conjurer . . .'

It happened that I was standing near to Lady Adderley, and I could mark very easily her expression. Startled it was! Plainly she had invited no conjurer, nor, had she had one up her sleeve, would it have been such a man as now stood waiting in the doorway. He was tall and thin, with a long pale face, a very pronounced hooked nose, and black hair that stood up stiffly on end. He was dressed entirely in black, and over his shoulders there hung a short black cape. In one hand he carried a black soft hat with a high crown, and in the other a square red leather box which he held by a bright brass handle. He stood there, very quietly, his long legs close together, not moving at all, as thin and straight and still as a mast waiting for its flag.

Lady Adderley had invited no conjurer—that was plain. She was astonished as though she had seen a witch with a broomstick. She intended, I've no doubt, to protest, to ask who it was had come thus uninvited. She took a step forward, then she stopped. Was it something in the conjurer's eyes, politely bent upon hers, his still, assured attitude, his black cloak, even his red leather box?

Or was it simply that she felt that her party was threatened with failure, that something must be done to save it? Or was it just that she could not help herself?

In any case, she suddenly turned to her husband and I heard her say: 'This is the surprise I had for you, dear.' Then she went up to the conjurer and invited him to come forward.

I cannot be sure, but I fancy that from the moment of the conjurer's entrance the spirit of the party changed. It may have been that we were all delighted to have a surprise—a conjurer was the very last thing that we had expected! It may have been that we ourselves were beginning to be frightened at the spirit of discontent and bad temper that was springing up among us.

In any case, everybody, laughing, chattering, in the very best of tempers, settled down, forming a big circle, the older people on chairs and most of the children cross-legged on the floor.

The conjurer, who seemed to be a solemn man, for he did not smile, walked forward and took his place on a long, thick, purple rug in front of the windows. Lady Adderley placed a table in front of him, and on this he laid his red leather box. Then—so suddenly as to make everyone jump—from somewhere within his cloak, it seemed, he produced a long wand, coloured crimson with a silver tip at the end of it. Then he spoke to us, and his voice was soft, and every word as clear as a bell.

He told us not to be astonished at anything that we saw, that there were a great many things more wonderful in this world than we would ever suppose, that we must never say that anything wasn't possible. For, he said, smiling for the first time (I, staring at him, felt as though I had seen that smile before), things became impossible to us as we grew older only because we closed our minds up as tight as his red leather box. Of course, if we *would* shut ourselves up inside a red leather box, that was our own fault—but he hoped that *we'd* be wiser than that. We all laughed at that, and thought within ourselves that of course we would be!

Then he waved his wand and began his tricks. At first they were quite ordinary. He brought rolls of coloured paper from his black hat, a flower in a pot from under a table, an egg out of his left ear; and a pack of cards disappeared into thin air. I heard Ambrose, who was sitting near to me, murmur: 'He's only an ordinary conjurer, after all.' Then he paused, came forward nearer to us, and looked at us all with his piercing black eyes.

'You've seen those things before, haven't you?' he said. 'Well, now you're going to see something new.'

A little shiver of excitement ran through all of us.

'But first,' he said, 'I must have a boy to help me.'

Several boys sprang up—the kind of boys who, all their lives afterwards, would be springing forward on just such occasions.

But he shook his head.

'No,' he said. 'I want the *right* kind of boy.' He looked round, searching through the company. '*That's* the boy I want!' he said, and he nodded his head in my direction.

Even then I didn't think that it was myself he wanted! I was packed away behind a fat boy and between two fat girls. The fat boy thought that it was he! With puffs of pleasure he rose to his feet.

'No,' said the conjurer. 'That's the boy I'm going to have'—and with his red wand he pointed directly at me.

How astonished everybody was! That was the first triumph of my young life. Humphrey Porter, whom no one considered anything at all; Humphrey Porter, who was quite certain to make a mess of it! Poor conjurer! He would soon see how grave his mistake! But here was a curious thing. I, who was terrified of doing anything before others, on this occasion knew no fear. I can see myself now, climbing through the other children, and then, before their mocking derisive eyes, taking my place quietly beside the little table, waiting for my orders.

'Thank you!' said the conjurer gravely. 'That will do very nicely.'

Then for the first time he opened the red box and took from it a number of things. There were some small china saucers, a number of little coloured boxes, a tiny pistol, some children's bricks, three small coloured flags, red, white and blue, a mouse-trap, a silver bell, a toy trumpet. Over all these things he spread a very large white handkerchief. The ground of this handkerchief was white, but I saw that it was covered with pictures of little blue ships all in full sail.

'Now,' he said. 'I want you all to understand that this is a very exceptional boy. An ordinary boy wouldn't do in the least. I'm very lucky to have found such a boy.'

(At this point I should have hung my head. But I didn't. I stared in front of me and smiled at my mother, who smiled back at me.)

'What is your name, boy?' he asked me.

'Humphrey,' I answered, and for some reason or other was quite sure that he knew without my telling him.

'Now show all your friends what you can do!' he said.

And what didn't I do in the next half-hour? I was handed the toy trumpet and, quite confidently, played beautiful tunes upon it—I who had never played a tune in my life! At his command I whistled like a bird, nay, like a whole forest of birds. 'That's a thrush,' he said, nodding his head contentedly. 'Now a blackbird. And now—what about the nightingale?' I pursed my lips together and the room was filled with the song of the nightingale.

'Now take these little boxes, Humphrey,' he said, 'and throw them into the air.'

I threw them into the air, and behold, there they stayed, suspended, shining in all their colours under the glittering silver lights. ('I know how you did *that*,' Ambrose said confidently afterwards. 'There were invisible wires coming out of the red box.' Well, if *he* knew, it was more than I did.)

I took up, under his instructions, the little silver bell and it rang a perfect carillon of chimes. I took the mouse-trap and, walking backwards and forwards, holding it in front of the audience, drew out of it one small white mouse after another. They ran up my sleeve, over my shoulders, then disappeared into the mouse-trap again. I waved the coloured flags and they grew larger and larger until they seemed to reach to the ceiling.

'Now, Humphrey,' he said, putting his hand on my shoulder (why was that touch so very familiar?), 'tell that lady over there what she has in her little white bag.'

'That lady,' I said, without hesitation, 'has in her bag a small white handkerchief, a little looking-glass with a blue border, a pink needle-case, and a small bottle of smelling-salts with a crystal stopper.'

How everyone gasped, as well they might! The lady was asked to open her bag, and there were the articles I had named. (I need scarcely say that I was as greatly astonished as any one!)

'And that boy,' he said, pointing to Ambrose, who was standing up with his mouth wide open. 'What has *he* got in his trouser-pocket? You may as well tell us in French,' he added casually.

So, in perfect French, I told Ambrose that he was carrying in his pocket a lump of toffee, a knife with a broken blade, three coppers and a half-crown, and a catapult. (Strange things to carry in your Eton suit, but then Ambrose was very acquisitive, and I didn't know until later that Ambrose had stolen the knife from his brother and had been forbidden by